PRAISE FOR THE NOVELS OF
CONNIE JOHNSON HAMBLEY

THE TROUBLES

"*The Troubles* is a sweeping narrative that travels across generations and continents to paint a richly textured, historically accurate picture of a troubled country fighting to find its soul amid clashing loyalties and political chaos. Hambley skillfully unfolds several urgent mysteries at once, while giving us complex characters, gorgeous settings, and a prose that sings with the cadences of Ireland. (As a bonus, *The Troubles* also boasts the best descriptions of horse races you'll find anywhere.)"

–ELISABETH ELO, AUTHOR OF *NORTH OF BOSTON*

"Seeking to escape her troubled and violent past, Jessica Wyeth journeys to a land where she is instead surrounded by powerful enemies. With danger on all sides, she struggles for the truth and wonders who to trust, as agents of a multi-generational terrorist conspiracy close in. Fast-paced action in this follow-up to *The Charity* that blends a love of horses, Ireland, and mystery. Highly recommended."

–DALE T. PHILLIPS, DERRINGER AWARD NOMINEE
AND AUTHOR OF THE *ZACK TAYLOR* MYSTERY SERIES

THE CHARITY

THE
TROUBLES

THE TROUBLES

A STORY OF TERRORISM AND IDENTITY FOUND

BY CONNIE JOHNSON HAMBLEY

Published 2015 by Charylar Press in the United States of America

Copyright 2015 by Connie Johnson Hambley

Library of Congress Cataloging-in-Publication Data

2015905812

Hambley, Connie Johnson

The Troubles/Connie Johnson Hambley

p. cm.

PB ISBN: 978-0692417928

Epub ISBN: 978-1310494765

1. Family Secrets—Fiction 2. Adoption—fiction 3. Northern
Ireland—Fiction

4. Irish Republican Army—Terrorism—Fiction 5. Horse Training—
Fiction I. Title.

Charylar Press

To Scott,
Thirty years. Time flies.

AUTHOR'S NOTE

ON JUNE 15, 1996, a red and white box truck parked in front of the Marks & Spencer store in the Arndale shopping district of Manchester, England. Phone calls made to news organizations and police ensured no bystanders remained in the area when the truck exploded at 11:17 a.m. The Irish Republican Army claimed responsibility.

Nearly twenty years later, the crime remains unsolved.

Saturday, June 15, 1996
Manchester, England
United Kingdom

THE ARNDALE SHOPPING district of Manchester, England thrummed with activity. The next day's Euro 96 football championship match between Russia and Germany promised to be a corker, and families rushed to get their shopping done before the anticipated Father's Day visiting and game watching. Hot summer temperatures encouraged people to shed their jackets and walk rather than ride the Metrolink. Young and old filled the streets and shops.

Paddy and Tik ignored the crowds as they parked their red and white cargo truck in front of the Marks and Spencer store on Corporation Street. They didn't need to speak or check to see what the other was doing. A quick glance at the dashboard clock was the only excess movement as Tik maneuvered the truck curbside, disregarding the double yellow lines. They pulled their hoodies over their heads and got out. Paddy walked down the street and around the corner. Tik turned a slow circle checking for surveillance cameras. Satisfied, he strode off in the opposite direction.

Tik rounded the corner of Cannon street and used a second set of keys to drive off in a waiting car. It took exactly ten minutes for him to pull into the underground car park of the Glenhoe Apartments and another six minutes to switch cars and drive the four blocks west to the Tavendish flat. Within twenty-two minutes, he had his hand on the phone and looked again at his watch. The second hand swept up and touched "XII." He made his first call.

Paddy took twelve minutes to get to a phone, recite the carefully constructed sentences and precise words, and begin his escape from Manchester. Each man knew only enough about the other's movements to understand why they had to carry out each step exactly right. Tik was to wait before he began his trek south.

He flipped on the telly and checked his watch again. It took only six minutes from his first call and sixteen minutes from Paddy's for each channel to carry the same information—that police and news stations had received word that a truck carrying a large amount of explosives was parked near the Arndale shopping district and would explode in less than one hour. The newsreaders emphasized that the warning was immediately authenticated, as the callers, both male with Irish accents, used unique phrasing and a designated code word of the Irish Republican Army. The authorities urged people not to second-guess the warning in whatever complacency that may have grown over the past months during the IRA's ceasefire. The code word and abandoned truck were all the anti-terrorist units needed to swing into high gear.

The Special Bulletins carried the same information. Civilians needed to evacuate the surrounding areas immediately. News commentators estimated that over seven thousand people were scrambling for cover. Their reports showed live images of mothers dragging crying children behind them and police with loudhailers pushing people away from the truck in bigger and bigger circles. The images on the screen blended with the sounds of sirens on the street below, skewing Tik's sense of reality.

He expected to feel something. He did, sort of, but excitement wasn't it. Neither was bloodlust. Tik leaned forward and methodically viewed each channel's coverage, assessing the evacuation efforts. Images of people scurrying in fear gripped him.

"C'mon man! Move! Move!" he implored the figures on the screen, marveling at their stupidity. "Don't stop there, woman! Grab yer kid and run, damn it!" He clicked around the stations in a twitch, never settling in to watch one for more than a few seconds.

A throng of screaming people flickered on the screen. Some clutched their handbags, others their children. The crowd ran up a street and parted as it passed an old man and woman. The elderly couple shuffled along, struggling to go faster. The man supported his wife at her elbow, urging her on, encouraging her progress, only to be jostled and ignored by the fleeing masses.

Tik froze and stared at the telly, confused by what he saw. He expected people would help one another, wouldn't leave anyone in peril. "Can't you bloody well see they need help?" he screamed at the running crowd. They weren't doing what they were supposed to do, what he had been told they would do. "What's wrong with you people?" He pressed his face to the TV screen, craning his neck as if he could see around the corners of the building. "Feckin' stupid idiots," he said. Then the image changed, and Tik rhythmically clicked more stations to find another that showed the old couple.

Unsuccessful, he fidgeted in the cheap plastic chair until he could sit no longer. He jumped up and paced in a circle, never allowing his eyes to leave the television. Glancing at his watch, he counted down the minutes. The TV continued its live coverage, showing a robotic drone rolling its way around the truck. An odd telescoping neck held the single eye of a camera lens. Tik watched the robot jerk and whirl around the pocked pavement as the British tried to get as much film evidence as possible of the truck before the whole damn thing evaporated in the blast.

He looked at his watch, 11:15 a.m. He waited. Another minute ticked by. The only movement was a trickle of sweat that rolled down his temple. His mouth went dry.

At 11:17 a.m., the force of the blast raced down the street. Bits of glass and paper flittered by the window, pushed by a torrent of air. The building ticked and shifted as the shockwave hit.

He watched in mild fascination as a web of silver cracks streaked across the pane of glass while a mushroom cloud of dirt and masonry rose in the not-so-distant sky.

~ SIX WEEKS EARLIER ~

WEDNESDAY, MAY 8, 1996
ANTRIM, NORTHERN IRELAND
UNITED KINGDOM

MICHAEL CONANT LOOKED across the conference table at a man he had hoped to trust. They could not have been more different. Where Michael wore crisp khakis and couldn't remember the last time he wore a tie, Aidan McGurnaghan, headmaster of Saint Mark's School for the Disadvantaged, wore musty tweeds and shirts with soiled collars. Aidan relied upon his past to entitle him to his standing. Michael strove for his future by being rooted in the present. The fissures formed from the clash of a traditional, class-oriented culture and brash American one threatened to crack open.

Aidan stared at a spot on the table as he spoke. "Now then, tell me again how you view my role here."

Portraits of past headmasters hung in neat rows on both sides of a dark, wood-paneled room. Engraved plaques displayed the names of Riobeard O'Shaughnessy, Daibheid Ui Neill, Padraig McGurnaghan. Tenures dated back over a century. Michael mused silently that the once lofty gene pool had run its course.

Michael was in no mood to babysit Aidan's ego, but his instincts told him to stroke and warm the relationship as much as his gut revolted against it. Today's meeting with the directors had to affirm a new direction for the school, and he desperately wanted it to go smoothly. He modulated his voice, determined not to be dismissed as too young or inexperienced.

"You take care of the day-to-day operations and make sure things run smoothly. You're my eyes and ears here." Michael nodded at the other men seated at the table to emphasize his compliment, hoping it did not sound gratuitous. "You're an indispensible ally."

Aidan sniffed, but allowed himself to be cajoled. "You're making decisions that impact the running of the school. The financials are already under your control and you want *more*?"

"We need to stay focused on our objectives. As Headmaster, your actions clearly set a fine example for the staff during this admittedly difficult transition. It's more than simply adding 'for the Disadvantaged' to the school's name. We will redirect the school and those it touches. It takes time for these changes to take effect and for benefits to be noticed." He studiously made eye contact with each director as he spoke, implicitly engendering their agreement.

Aidan cleared his throat and raised his narrow chin in an effort to express his indignation. "I've heard that you've kept me on as a point of continuity for the community, not as a vote for my competency. You've said I should feel secure in my job and that I have the support and confidence of the other directors here." He swept his gaze over the men seated at the table. "Perhaps I should be clear on how I see your role, then," he lowered his tinny voice for emphasis, "You might be able to pour money into our coffers, but you will never buy our history. You'll have to stand on your own legs to build your legitimacy and reputation, and I daresay there's not enough money in the world to do that." Leaning back, he gave a hearty laugh, encouraging others to join in. Nervous laughter rippled around the table.

Aidan's words signaled open mutiny to Michael's new leadership. Their private talking, cajoling, negotiating, pleading, and, often, threatening, had boiled down into a thick sludge of distrust. Their feigned smiles and firm handshakes would no longer fool others. Business and fate threw them together. Not working together wasn't an option.

Slowly, he willed his shoulders to relax, but the smile that grew on his face did not reach his eyes. Their visible feud undermined his authority. "That's just your opinion, Aidan. I've kept my promises and I've kept this school from decay. We are continuing to be successful. I will not alter our course now."

The tension between the two men escalated to a near boiling point when a figure at the far end of the table raised himself halfway out of his chair in a formal request to be acknowledged. The old man's shock of white hair stood out in the darkened room. The intensity of his blue stare was matched only by Michael's. Michael nodded permission to his uncle to speak.

Liam Connaught cleared his throat. "You two have framed your differences and solutions in more than one meeting, so there's nothing new here. Aidan, you're as pigheaded as your father and as bright as your mother. You need to stop thinking of ways to stop progress here and start thinking of ways to work with us."

"Your nephew has spent millions on the campus. I want more to show for it than manicured lawns," complained Aidan, failing to conceal his petulance.

"We do," said Liam.

"What about our students?"

"What about them?"

"By allowing the right students to come to Saint Mark's we carve out our future," Aidan whined. "When I say *right*, I speak of the sons of fathers who have walked these halls and lead lives of success for which we educated them. Focusing on lesser families is not what the school is about."

Liam sat back and looked at the headmaster, letting his shoulders slump as he shook his head back and forth. "We've been over this and will not start again. At this point you'll need to question whether you can continue here or if you would be happier elsewhere." He addressed the other men in the room. "I suggest you all do the same."

Liam walked to the door, opening it with one hand and using the other in a graceful sweep of invitation. "All of you are invited to leave. For those of you who understand and accept our mission, you are invited back here tomorrow afternoon at two o'clock. Goodbye."

The startled silence remained until the men slowly rose from their chairs and walked out the door. Some gave Liam and Michael a hearty handshake and assurances that they would indeed be seeing them tomorrow. Others left with heads down and faces set in expressions of deep thought. They shook hands with a stiffened formality that evidenced their inner turmoil.

After the last footstep faded, only Michael and Liam remained. "Tomorrow will be an interesting day indeed." Liam poured himself a Scotch, neat, from the decanter set in the middle of the conference table. One by one, he dropped ice cubes into another glass, added Scotch, and pushed it across the table.

Michael positioned himself at the window. The sun still high, he could see the departing directors walk down the brick path to their waiting cars. The waters of Lough Neagh shimmered just beyond the green sweep of the quad. "My estimate is half will come back," Liam began, almost reading Michael's thoughts, "and some of those will be for curiosity only."

Michael picked up the glass and sat down heavily next to Liam. "I memorized the bios you sent me on each director. Your insights were dead-on, as usual. I don't know how I could do this without your help. I'm barely grasping the structure, and you're finessing the right team members. The invitation to rejoin us tomorrow was the perfect test of loyalty. I wish I had thought of it." He raised his glass in a silent toast. "Thank you for coming."

"It's me who should be thanking you. My brother stepped up to fill our father's shoes as you are stepping up to fill his. Now that he's has gone to his maker, it's your turn."

"His maker? I doubt even the devil wants him back."

Liam chuckled. "He went astray, I'm afraid."

"And what about you? Shouldn't you be stepping into your brother's role? To them, I'm the American. An outsider. You saw them today. They'll never accept my leadership."

"It's not about them accepting you as leader, Michael. It's about you accepting the responsibilities of leadership and all that goes with it. Magnus knew this."

"My father's ways will never be mine, and you know it. He was a butcher and a thief."

"And if you believe the stories about me, I'm an old drunkard and a half-crazy obstructionist who cares more about his homes and mistresses than for any cause." He paused, using the moment to heave a resigned sigh. "They'll have an even harder time accepting me as their leader, Michael. I represent the past, what could have been, with all of the regrets of paths not taken. The Charity needs you. Without you clearly staking your claim to your father's mission, there will be more blood spilled. To shrink away and hide would be cowardly at best and murderous at worse."

Liam left the truth unspoken. Faith in Michael's leadership of the school and his father's organization was in jeopardy. The Charity was something Michael did not want to acknowledge, let alone be a part of. That multi-tentacle behemoth he feared only feigned slumber. He raked his fingers through his hair, his desperation clear. "I don't want to walk in my father's footsteps. You know the organization and the people. You should lead. I . . . I'd support you. I'd help you."

Liam interrupted, "Spare me the high-minded drivel. You're a smart man. The Charity's network of corporations and charities feed and support one another, with legitimate businesses laundering money for the illegitimate ones. Your father anticipated this day and created an entire business mechanism that would function with or without him but only temporarily. He handpicked his soldiers for their discretion and ruthless-ness. But he's been dead a few weeks, and without a clear message from you his authority will fade. He wanted you to work by his side. He created this for you—for your future."

"Bullshit. He never once thought of me." Michael paced the room in an effort to control himself. "He destroyed good people by draining their businesses of hard-earned cash and killing or maiming their loved ones to ensure their loyalty. I want the school to undo some of his harm. If he ever thought of me, it was only in how to control me."

"You could have refused to take his place and continued to hide behind the life you created in the States." Liam raised his eyebrows and shook his head in disbelief at the thought. "But you chose to be here. You left the U.S. and brought that girl with you."

"Jessica. Her name is Jessica."

Liam grew impatient. "You knew damned well what you were getting into." He raised his voice to stop any more conversation. "I have neither the talent nor the inclination to assume leadership here. It's done. You are the head of the Magnus Connaught's Charity. You have to start acting like it."

Michael downed his Scotch and rattled the ice in the empty glass, deep in thought. He felt Liam's eyes join with the cracked and oily stares of past headmasters as the grandfather clock's pendulum ticked away the minutes. He retrieved a file from his briefcase and tossed it on the table in front of them. "I had no idea how big the Charity had become. I thought his illegal operations were limited to some extortion and money laundering operations in the States to supply his pet organizations. I've been looking at the accounts—Bahrain, Venezuela, Spain, and Italy. I can see the money running through the corporations like a rat eaten by a snake—one huge bulge twisting through until it's spit out the other end."

"In a manner of speaking."

"But there's more I'm not seeing."

"Magnus was a brilliant man. He used charitable organizations as fronts for the other businesses he ran. You're using the school the same way. Students don't have to roam these hallways for the school to meet its obligations."

Michael pushed away the papers with barely contained anger. "My management of the school is completely different. I don't have to tell you that."

"Aidan seems to think otherwise." Liam's eyes rounded in a studied expression of innocence. "From his perspective, following you or Magnus looks exactly the same."

"Fuck Aidan."

"You don't want more blood on your hands," he said, absently inspecting his own. He cleared his throat and stared at his nephew. The soft folds of his lids draped his eyes, keeping his expression neutral. His shoulders, once square with intimidating strength, were rounded and soft under his tweed jacket. "Magnus didn't start off as a violent man. When we were boys together, he was always the first to share his lunch with a hungry man. I'm not sure when it crystallized, but he used money like a drug dealer would. He gave only enough to get people hooked and used his charitable donations strategically. Once he saw how the politicians swarmed, he began to look at other ways to wield power."

"Since his death, the money has started to flow to Belfast again." Michael scanned the columns of numbers on the spreadsheets, scrutinizing the red and black ink as if all would suddenly make sense. He ran his index finger down the rows to bring certain transactions to his uncle's attention. "If I can't see the final disbursements and payments out, how can I tell who is getting the money?"

"Time will tell."

"How?" Michael pressed.

Liam looked at his nephew with a mixture of impatience and sadness. "You'll know. The numbers will tell you only what you want to see. You have to understand the people in order to know the whole story. I've set meetings up for you."

Giving up, he gathered the spreadsheets and shoved them back into his briefcase. He respected his uncle and knew he held the key to bridging the gap between the growing factions inside the Charity. Keeping his uncle happy was essential. He could take his time to run the numbers to fully grasp the intricacies. "I want to get away for a few days."

"You've barely gotten your feet wet. If you're going to see that girl instead of tending to business, what message does that send," Liam quipped, more a statement than a question.

"Her name is *Jessica*," he reminded his uncle again. "I won't be gone long."

"Is that wise? You've not hidden your concern for her, and there's agitation in the ranks. Without a strong presence, people will sniff out and prey upon a weakness. Anyone that wants to make a point with you might use her as leverage."

Michael nodded in agreement. "That's no secret. I've stayed away from her as much as I can. My contacts in the States helped me find her a short training gig over the border in the Republic of Ireland, not here in Northern Ireland."

"I'm not stupid."

"She couldn't go back to the States. You know that."

"Do I? You brought her here for you or for her?"

"For her . . . her own protection."

10

Liam put down his glass and turned to his nephew, his eyes bloodshot with age and fatigue. "It's bad enough that you want me to believe that—I'm sad for her that you do."

Michael shook his head. "She was exposed in the States. There had been attempts to kill her. Hell, they nearly succeeded." He could feel himself grow tense at the memory. He took a steadying breath. "It . . . it wasn't safe."

"Wasn't it? She was one of the most recognized faces in the U.S. The only people hunting her were scoop-hungry reporters. Yes, she would have been badgered for a few weeks, but the attention of the American public would have flitted on to the next scandal soon enough."

Michael angered at being forced through this exercise. "She exposed my father and his dealings."

"Don't fool yourself. The people who wanted her dead for the damage she did to the Charity don't pay attention to international borders. You said it yourself. People kill for revenge, too."

"Damn it, Liam! I need your help in knowing who to trust. The only way I can protect her is in Ireland with your handpicked Charity members keeping a watchful eye on her."

Liam walked over to Michael, grabbed his upper arms, and gave him a little shake. "Listen to yourself. You've brought a kitten into a lion's den. Send her home with the same setup you gave her at the cottage. Give her a body guard or two and a stable full of horses, but send her home."

"She," he stammered, "she could be useful here."

"Don't be daft." Liam released Michael's shoulders with a shove. "She'll never want to be one of us. Send her back to the States, Michael. If not the States, then anywhere. Tell her to hide again."

"I can't ask her to do that. She spent years under assumed names. She's done with that."

Fatigue deepened the lines on Liam's face. "I'm an old man, Michael. I'm doing what I can to prevent an all out mutiny. I'll keep Aidan in line so no more directors will support his insurrection, but my days of endless number crunching, phone calls, meetings, and schmoozing are over. I envy your youth and energy. You're a quick study of the numbers, but of people? You're thickheaded. I'm afraid you still don't grasp just how much of an outsider you really are."

Raphoe, Ireland

JESSICA WYETH NEEDED to cool and blanket her horse before he chilled. A heavy mist fell, coating her hands and face in beads of moisture. She ran her hands down the big gray's legs checking for soreness that would tell if their ride along in the dips and dells of the countryside was too taxing. The wisps of steam rose from Planxty's back and chest.

As they walked in small circles, she took in the details of her temporary home. A barn and cottage sat on top of a gentle rise. They overlooked fields that held a training ring and jump course. Thickets of trees broke the expanse of hills in the distance. The buildings' windows, framed in weathered wood, dotted their whitewashed sides. A stone-enclosed courtyard hugged the cottage, and a wooden fence separated it from the barn. The barn was rustic but suited her needs. Eight stalls lined a cobbled corridor, and an annex held a tack room, office, and ladder to the hayloft.

Sensing she wasn't alone, she peered into the shadows and sifted through the sounds gripped by the ever-present wind. Only a church bell and the bleating of sheep were carried by it. The birdsong sounded more ragged than melodic, and the earth smelled more of decay than spring. Her surroundings were so different she wondered if it was worth the investment of time to become familiar with them.

Jessica patted Planxty's neck and shook her head free of longings. A chorus of throaty nickers and hooves kicking stall doors greeted her—all welcomed sounds of horses impatient for attention. She was relieved to see a swept corridor and fresh shavings in each of the eight stalls. A full hay bin and feed bucket waited in the empty one. She jotted her observations of the day's ride in the folder for the local trainer hired to help her. Cryptic notes back and forth did not provide enough insight for effective training. She wrote yet another request to speak with him directly.

Walls made from thousands of dark gray stones no larger than footballs and overgrown with wild roses flanked the paddocks. She gingerly picked a fistful of soft pink blooms and headed back to the cottage. Inside a single bedroom off the living room provided enough living area to be comfortable. A wooden bench and a hand-hewn pegboard holding an oiled canvas barn coat and anorak graced the spare stucco hall. Tall black leather field boots and a pair of drab green rubber Wellies sat on a woven rug. She slipped off her wet fleece and boots and headed to the kitchen to hunt for a vase.

A stout, middle-aged woman didn't startle when Jessica burst in to the rustic kitchen. Jessica gave a bemused smile at the man-tailored pants, tattered sweater, and crisply starched white apron. As much as Jessica wanted to have a friend in Ireland, Nan O'Reilly would not be the one. The cottage belonged to Nan, housekeeper and main conduit to the outside world.

"Oh, hi Nan," Jessica said as she picked a thorn out of her thumb. "Do you have anything I can put these in?"

"I do at that." Nan produced a Mason jar from one of the cabinets and set it on a long, rough-hewn wooden table beside a basket made of black, thorny wood. "Beautiful blooms, these roses. Makes the whole place glow in pink."

"I could pick armloads of them." Jessica watched Nan fuss with the flowers with efficient motions. "I wasn't expecting to see you today."

"Fair enough, but you should hear that folks are talkin' about someone riding crazy over the hills." She wiped her hands on her apron. "The county is filled with tales of one form of spirit or another makin' an appearance. I don't listen to such talk, but you should be aware of it."

"Thanks, but that was hardly worth you making a special trip out here to tell me that."

Nan lifted her chin. "We don't get many visitors in these parts, and there's nothing like a new face to get people talkin'. You must take better care not to be seen. The last thing you need is for people to start thinking they've got the "Murdering Heiress" in their backyards."

Leaving that nickname behind and all that came with it were the reasons she agreed to Michael's idea of a training job in Ireland. Hearing it again bothered her. "How?" she stumbled, searching for words. "My rides have been away from any homes. You're the only person I've spoken with."

"I'm just being cautious. You got your share of attention in the papers here as well. You've only been resurrected for a few months and we have those here who question how innocent you really are." Nan's voice betrayed neither empathy nor disgust.

Jessica flushed. Resurrection was a fitting term, but the cloud around her innocence hurt. Nan's concerns drove home the point that it will take more than dropping out of sight for a few months to be reborn and live freely. Michael had taken great care to make sure she remained safe, and he trusted Nan to be discrete. She could stop and catch her breath. Michael gave her that hope, and she wasn't about to let it go easily.

"I don't think you respect the amount of work that's gone on to protect you." Nan's brows formed a straight bar across her forehead. Her expression mixed resentment and stubbornness.

"Of course I do. I answer your questions and follow every rule you give me."

"That's not good enough. Havin' this handy means you might be thinkin' about touring the sights." She fanned herself with a blue book with gold lettering.

Seeing her passport stunned her. She thought she had tucked it away. Snapping it out of Nan's hands, she said, "I don't see how my past trips are your concern. Besides, how anyone could blame me for wanting to travel after what I've been through."

Nan scoffed. "You became my responsibility before you left Gibraltar. You didn't bother to stay away from public beaches so anyone could have recognized you then and followed you. The only full-witted act you did was keep to yourself after Michael left. Rumors stirring make me fret I've overlooked something." She reached into her bag and flopped a file on the table. "Michael wasn't sure I should give you this, but you need to appreciate what I'm up against."

Jessica leafed through pages enough to realize the folder bulging with clippings from *The Boston Globe*, *The New York Times*, *The Washington Post*, *Los Angeles Times*, *Chicago Tribune*. All carried feature articles and photos of her. *The Sun* and *Guardian* of the United Kingdom, *The Irish Times* out of Dublin and *Le Monde* of France could not resist the story of an heiress who faked her death to avoid a murder charge.

For twenty-eight years, Jessica knew herself as Jessica Bridget Wyeth, daughter of Margaret and Jim Wyeth of Hamilton, Massachusetts. For seven of those, the rest of the world knew her by a number of names, "Murdering Heiress" being the most well known. She paid the price of her freedom by enduring the startled reactions of people who recognized her and the ever-present threat of being chased down by a reporter looking for a follow-up story. Michael knew she hated the papers and the people who read them thinking every lie was true. She hated the way strangers looked at her, either shrinking away in fear or challenging her with questions they had no business asking. For someone who had spent the better part of her adult years hiding, the glare of attention withered. The other reasons he wanted her at the cottage remained unspoken.

Jessica didn't fight for freedom only to be locked away in a thatched-roof prison. "Okay. I get it. I'm famous, and you have a harder job because of it. That's no reason to search through my belongings or lurk about in shadows." She wasn't just irritated with Nan, she was irritated with knowing her life had evolved to needing dossiers and bodyguards. The confines Nan wanted to impose chaffed. "How about a telephone?"

"No." Nan kept her voice upbeat as she resumed putting food away. "Strict orders from Michael 'imself. He said you agreed to that."

"I didn't realize how isolated I would be."

"Maybe he doesn't trust you enough. You've known each other, what now? Barely a year? Moreover, how many names have you had? It's hopes and promises that keep many a girl thinking she's in love only to find out her man is gallivanting about. Think of it. You're here waiting. He's off tending to better things." Nan's eyes glittered with unkind thoughts.

Any hope she had of having a warm relationship with Nan faded in that moment. "I didn't ask your opinion." When Michael suggested living in a rocky corner of Ireland with a barn filled with horses, surrounded by fields and in a cottage staffed by his personally chosen people, the idea sounded idyllic. Doubt began to creep around her decision.

"I've done nothing but train these past weeks. Is that all I'm allowed to do every day?"

"You've a job to do, and I'm surprised to hear you complain about it. Those horses need more than a bit of schooling. They're some of Ireland's best. Michael and that woman in Kentucky did a good amount of cajoling before the owners here would let some green trainer like you get a hold of them."

"I know, and I'm not complaining," she quipped. Jessica determined to bend the rules in her favor. "I only have the notes on each horse, and I'd really like to talk to someone about them. There's more to the behaviors I'm seeing than simply poor conditioning or past injuries."

"Are you sayin' the animals are second rate?" Nan needled.

"No. Not at all." Jessica kept her voice even, covering her desire to snarl. "In fact, they are some of the best horses I've ever worked with. Who helped him choose them?"

Nan ignored Jessica's conciliatory manner and returned her focus to rearranging the roses in the jar. "Aye. They need a special hand, and Michael's word is you have it. He said he only wanted the animals that could win."

Jessica was in no mood to be played with. "That doesn't answer my question."

"One of his men picked them."

"The one I've seen here?"

Nan screwed up her face and nodded.

"Then I have to meet him. It's maddening that I haven't spoken with him."

"His job is to work with the horses. Not to talk to you."

"That's ridiculous!" She drummed her fingers on the table, rankled that Nan turned resisting a simple request to meet someone into sport. "He picked them for a reason, and I have to speak with him. I'm tired of him avoiding me."

Nan began to wipe down the already spotless counters, adjusting the canisters of sugar and tea to perfect angles. "How important is it? You've got your notes."

"Look. I have to get these horses ready for a major event in a few weeks. The timing is tight, and the pressure on. I need to be efficient. This guy is good. Really good. But we only have one chance to get the training right, and I need to talk with him." She stood and positioned her body directly in front of Nan, ensuring the housekeeper's full attention. She bent her neck slightly to look directly into Nan's face. "What did you say the man's name was?"

"I didn't."

She took the cloth from Nan's hand and waited.

Finally, Nan responded. "Tim."

"Tim . . .?" She let her voice trail off, asking for more. Getting nothing, her mouth firmed to a straight line. "He chose all of the horses, right? There's no one else I'd need to speak with, right?"

The older woman's eyes narrowed slightly. "Yes."

Jessica considered how to phrase her next question. "How long has Tim worked for Michael?"

"For as long as I can remember."

"But Michael's only been in Ireland a few weeks."

Nan stared at Jessica then shrugged. Without speaking, she gathered up her bags and left.

Jessica was holed up in a safe house, enveloped in an artificial world created for her privacy, with her main contact feeling more like an adversary than an ally. Nan's hint of Michael having a past in Ireland or friends for years only served as a painful reminder of how brutally separated from the world she remained. Isolation is perfect if you wanted to be alone. It becomes a problem when you feel alone.

She realized her hands were shaking from wounds reopened and raw. Ruefully, Jessica acknowledged that she didn't restore her name or her freedom. In some kind of cruel joke, just as she began to reclaim her life, she found out it wasn't hers to begin with.

Jessica felt too heavy to move and too muddled to make sense of the lengthy dawn. Emotional fatigue from the questions unearthed in her conversation with Nan pulled down her. Discordant details continued to impede her rest and, once again, sleep was light and brief with her habit of vigilance unbroken. The unnaturally short night did nothing to help her nerves.

She gave up on sleep and changed into fresh jeans and a light fleece as the sky slowly shifted hues. Hugging herself against the morning air, she headed to the comforting smells and warmth of the barn.

Before the sun peeked from the horizon, the bright morning moon colored the countryside a luminous blue. Stone walls and hedgerows heavy with wild roses crisscrossed patchwork fields. The drizzle of the past day had given way to mist that blurred nature's green, pink, and blue hues. Low-lying clouds clung to the grassy knolls, waiting to be warmed and lifted.

Planxty picked his way up the path, still mellow enough from yesterday's training to be ridden bareback. Jessica used his senses to tell her they were alone and safe. He hung his head on a loose rein, his ears forward as he examined the trail. The loudest sounds were the steady breathing of the horse and his heavy thudding hooves.

Lulled by the sensations of the horse's movements, the hollow hurt of being shunned and cast away diminished. She wanted to ground herself to *this* time and *this* place. Everything that had gone before her existed as no more than a thought. In this moment she simply was. The gray of the horse, her pale skin, and wisp of blonde hair made her feel more a part of the mist than the earth. Whatever painful emotions or memories crept in she willed away before they hardened.

Jessica and Planxty wandered along a countryside suspended in the moment between sleep and wakefulness. She let her horse do most of the thinking as she felt some primal part of her being drawn farther along the ancient trails. The terse interchange with Nan still rang through her head, so she steered away from paths she had ridden before. Maybe she could find the peace she yearned a little farther down the trail.

Only once did Planxty balk at Jessica's choice as he tried to overrule her final turn that took them both to the top of a rounded hill. Roused by the horse's refusal, she listened for any indication that they were not alone. Satisfied, she encouraged the reluctant animal forward and was surprised again when the animal skittered at sounds she could not hear. Habit made her skin prickle from nerves.

When they finally entered the clearing, Jessica caught her breath. The random scattering of rock debris she thought she saw turned out to be a perfectly formed circle of ancient boulders—Stonehenge on a smaller scale. The tall grass on the hilltop bent from its own weight, unkempt and untouched, perfectly bowed as if smoothed by hand. Grass inside the circle was lumpy, having grown over rocks deposited there centuries ago. Boulders varied in size from being somewhat square in shape and about three feet wide to the largest close to eight feet tall and rectangular. Two boulders, that once stood upright and leaned with age, were capped with a slab that threatened to topple off. Their gray and lichen covered sides glowed in the growing light, matched in color only by the mists that were finally warming to life. The scene had an expectant quality, as if waiting for her.

The sun finally conquered the horizon, and she watched in fascination as the white-gold crescent rose, perfectly framed by the three huge stones. Long shadows crept toward her and she turned to see what they marked. A sudden flash made her heart stop. She instinctively ducked, listening for a sound that never came. Raising her head, she was rattled when she saw her own shadow cast upon a church steeple down in the valley. The illusion happened only for an instant and disappeared before a gasp escaped her lips. Planxty stood rooted on stiffened legs with muscles tense and ready.

Even if Jessica wanted to run, she couldn't. Time lengthened, and she became aware of a deep and seductive pull at some unknown part of her. An ache of sorrow grew unchecked. For a moment, the stone circle wasn't foreign or separate, but was as much a part of her as it was to Ireland. The encrusted boulders surrounded her with centuries of myths and history. She could feel the imminent arrival of something. A presence? Mesmerized, she shaded her eyes with a raised arm and watched as films of mist began to glow with the same white gold of the rising sun. The vapor expanded upward in a single layer from the ground and then settled back again—a deep sigh of the earth. The focused heat of the sun warmed one wisp enough for it to separate and become independent. The cloud hovered before it slowly drifted into two. Suspended by an unseen power, the two parts intertwined then parted, each trailing a reluctant finger of vapor behind it.

A cool breath of air teased at the nape of Jessica's neck, and she shrugged her shoulders to usher the feeling away. She listened to the mist's whisperings as it lifted around her, seeming to carry her emptiness with it.

Jessica!

She cocked her head to listen. The line between real and fable dissolved as she let herself be drawn toward whatever wanted her. For a moment, she felt loved, teased with warmth and comfort on the wings of the angelic mists. Sleep-starved and half dreaming, she resisted the beckoning Trojan as too powerful, too familiar. Its proprietary grip lured her senses to believe the impossible. Jessica breathed deeply, teetering between worlds. Then she bore down, forcing out what had so cunningly tried to seduce her. The fight for what she thought was real left her uncertain and uncentered.

Jessica!

The wind carried a whispered word, chilling her. She strained to hear what her eyes didn't see. Was it a bleating sheep or something else? A plaintive, pleading sound rose and fell as if depleted and renewed with giant breaths. Jessica couldn't be sure if the distant wail was human or even real. Her heart stilled as the keening became clearer. No sooner had she determined its direction, the cry was lost again in the morning wind.

Jessica stared at the stone circle, a place now sharpened by a force she couldn't identify. Ancient and timeless, its existence had seeped into her, somehow changing how past and present fit together. A connection to this place existed whether she liked it or not and she stifled a cry, rubbing away the goose bumps that rose on the back of her neck.

The sun rested on the capped headstone of the cairn, forcing shadows to reach across the undulating ground. An energy threatened to pull horse and rider deep within the circle. Rejecting its gravity, Jessica slapped Planxty's rump so hard her hand stung.

She hadn't planned to ride hard on a horse and terrain she barely knew, but as soon as they had turned to the barns with the stone circle at their backs, Planxty fought for his head. He was as spooked as she was, so she didn't question his urgency. If she had not been so muddle-headed, she may have been able to listen more clearly to the message her horse sent— the first in a long line of messages she didn't hear.

Planxty ignored the paths and took the straightest line home. Without the benefit of a saddle, Jessica gripped with her legs and felt the powerful muscles of the horse propel them over walls and streams. Across open fields, the soft sod swallowed up any sound of hooves. The hillside rose and dipped and Jessica barely corrected their course as they barreled through pastures and backyards. Time stopped, and her world narrowed once again to the familiar feelings of flight and relief.

They barreled into the paddock and skidded to a stop. She chastened herself for her lack of judgment in riding like such an idiot, but the pit in her stomach and the knot in her shoulder muscles were gone and the longed for release finally came. She remained content while she cooled Planxty, but her relaxed mood dissolved when she discovered the horses had been tended and, once again, Tim had managed to avoid her.

She entered the cottage to see a large cardboard box sitting on the kitchen table. Battered and bruised, the box had been roughly shuttled from place to place in search of a recipient. Its brown and slightly pinkish sides were plastered with forwarding labels. Postmarks chronicled when and where the package continued its course—no doubt frustrating the obedient civil servants who instinctively knew by looking at the patch-work of addresses that the simplest measure would have been to stamp it "return to sender" and put the box out of its meandering misery. But with every kind of address slapped on it except a return one, a weary bit of obligatory action sent it on its way again.

The addresses read like chapters of her life. Hamilton, Massachusetts. Saddle String, Wyoming. Perc, Kentucky. Boston, Massachusetts. Other places were sprinkled in for good measure but obscured by layered labels. Despite her best efforts to prevent being followed anywhere by anyone, this box had done just that. Its dingy sides smirked at her through its dents and creases, finally victorious. Jessica grabbed a knife and stabbed it open, looking for a note from Michael.

Papers and journals filled the box. Their sudden presence in her life trig-gered only mild amusement—as if someone had dialed a wrong number and yapped on mindlessly before realizing the error. The top layer meant nothing to her. They were old, yellowed notebooks covered in frayed and fading canvas. Abuse from neglect and wear tattered their covers and ruined their pages. The surviving entries were written in the rounded swirls of a young girl's hand. As the journals progressed, the handwriting became smaller and more controlled. The mid layers included scrapbooks of a more recent vintage, holding a variety of clippings and photographs. As she examined each more carefully, her amusement turned to curiosity. Most of the photos were from her childhood. Her excavation stopped as she sank into a chair, stunned. She thought the only thing she possessed of her old life was her name. The box transformed into an unexpected treasure. It made her happy to think Michael took the time to locate them and send them on.

Jessica looked at herself as a young girl in the pictures and felt she was seeing her for the first time. The blue eyes that looked back at her showed only comfort and security. Her face was remarkable only in its complete lack of guile. Framed in long, straight hair alternately pulled back in a skewed ponytail or hung in smoothed and gleaming strands, her expres-sion in each photo showed the open and pure trust of a child loved and protected from the world, free to explore and bloom.

In one picture a young Jessica, about five years old, sat in front of a Christmas tree with her new baby sister, Erin. The tree dripped with tinsel and red and gold ornaments. Frosted glass lights, round and in a variety of colors, covered the tree, and lit the surrounding living room. Beneath the tree sat a trove of carefully wrapped presents. The wooden mantel over the fireplace, painted white in the typical New England fashion, held—as it always did for the holidays—the carved animals and figures of the crèche. Mary and Joseph looked on adoringly as sheep, cows and angels reveled in the presence of the new baby Jesus. The swaddled baby held His arms in a gesture of love and welcome. Young Jessica's expression was one of love, wonder and the barely hidden excitement of knowing Santa had indeed delivered. She cradled her own baby sister with both arms, handling Erin like a china doll.

Sorting through the stack of photos slowly, Jessica paused on another image. In front of the same fireplace adorned with the same decorations, sat a six-year-old Jessica and her year-old sister, both smiling as she helped Erin raise her arms in a gesture meant to imitate the baby Jesus. Even then, the evidence of Erin's brain injury was obvious. The young Jessica didn't have a way to keep Erin's head from lolling to one side.

Pictures from different Christmases brought back a flood of memories. One picture was sent as their Christmas card that year. It showed the traditional holiday tableaux of smiling mother, proud father, with their children as enacted by Margaret cradling Erin and Jim standing behind Jessica with his hand on her shoulder. Their carefully choreographed pose exuded the pinnacle of the happy nuclear family. Pictures chronicled Easters and Halloweens, school parties and country club events at Myopia Hunt Club. All of them showed Margaret and Jim as the proud parents of two beautiful girls. None of them showed the truth.

The smile of nostalgia that crept to her lips soon faded as harder memories came forth. Jessica closed her eyes to the strangers she saw. When she opened them, she dove into the photographs with renewed vigor. This time, instead of letting the memories come to her, she dug through them to see if they could have told her the truth if she had known where to look. A few pictures showed Margaret and Margaret's sister, Bridget. These were of particular interest.

Jessica stared at one particular image for what may have been a half hour, not moving, letting it absorb into her. A nine-year-old Jessica and four-year-old Erin were in the foreground with Jessica holding the halter and lead line of a shaggy pony. Erin smiled her beautiful lopsided grin as a mischievous Jessica drew a carrot up Erin's chin, causing the pony to nibble at the carrot, but only succeeding in lipping Erin's face, tickling her. Erin's shoulders were hitched up to her ears, body twisting, face alight with delight. Jessica cupped her sister's elbow in a protective grip, steadying and ready. Giggles and pure happiness consumed both girls. The scene should have brought an instant smile to the face of any onlooker. Instead, in the background, Margaret and Bridget stood, stiff, arms at their sides with expressions of abject sadness.

Jessica got up and retrieved one of the few items she carried with her on her recent journeys. It was a large, silver-framed portrait of Erin in Jessica's arms. Jessica gathered herself before prying off the back and sliding out a yellowed sheet. The paper told her the pictures documented a lie and were part of a well-constructed veil of deceit.

Her birth certificate showed that her mother was not Margaret Wyeth. For reasons Jessica struggled to understand, Bridget and Margaret lied, hiding the fact that Bridget was Jessica's mother. A palpable sadness inhabited the bodies of the women in the picture. One mother watched her child struggle with a brain injury that no amount of maternal fury or love could rescue her. The other mother held fast to the lie she created when she gave her child to her sister to raise.

A bolt of nervous energy shot through her, and she could no longer sit still. She paced around the room with her hands gripping her upper arms, pausing occasionally to stare at the box and wonder what other stories it might hold if she knew how to see them. The uninvited guest sat expectantly, wanting to belong and claim its place at the head table, but knowing it was an illegitimate friend. Jessica couldn't accept the box's presence. She was irritated that it existed. The presumptive way with which it demanded attention riled her. Her fingertips ran over the seams and sides of the box, feeling the raised edges of the tape and labels. The crushed corners and dented sides tried to telegraph their meaning to her like the raised bits of Braille would talk to the blind. She couldn't begin to comprehend the answers or the questions it presented. The gatecrasher needed to be treated accordingly.

She hastily gathered up papers and photos, unwilling and unready for their revelations. Weaving the flaps together, the box felt resistant as if it had a life of its own, and pretending to know her secrets. It unsettled her. Willing herself not to set the whole damned thing on fire, she compromised by hiding it inside her empty suitcase, which she stuffed as far back into the closet crawlspace as it would go.

Jessica pulled the door tight, checking it twice to make sure a sturdy barrier remained between her and whatever that box truly meant.

A thick veil of fatigue wrapped around her shoulders. The morning's ride sapped her energy. The additional hours of sunlight, bombardment of adjustments she had to accept, and the reality of her situation closed in on her. Constant movement and a refusal to dwell on past traumas had worked for years. Focusing on things outside of herself, like her horses, succeeded in getting her out of bed every day, but the cost of her uprooted life was evident.

Exhausted and fragile, she used the last of her strength to curl herself in the overstuffed armchair. She stared out the window, wishing for coffee, longing for something else.

Nan might not have had a choice to deliver the box, instead she chose to actively avoid Jessica. Standing under the eaves of the cottage, she pushed herself back into its shadow. In the ring below, Jessica rode a chestnut horse, its coat flashing burnished red in the morning light. Clots of earth flew off its hooves as Jessica guided the animal over a series of increasingly larger jumps. Nan liked the girl's grit, but her job was going to be harder because of it. In an unconscious habit Nan performed whenever she felt unsettled, she ran her fingers over a barely visible marking on the door-jamb. Paint flecked off the carving of a circle inside an open-bottomed square, with what looked like a cross on top. She dusted her fingers off on her apron and made her way out to the barn with a resolute stride. Through the open door to the hayloft, she could see shadows moving around.

"Good morning," she said in greeting. The shadows stopped moving, and she could hear footsteps padding down the steps. A man emerged wiping bits of hay off his sweater.

"*Dea-maidin*," he returned.

Nan surveyed Tim carefully. He had piercing green eyes that never seemed to rest. Tall and well built, he had a lanky way of moving many women thought sexy but had little effect on her. Copper colored high-lights peppered his head when the sun hit his sandy hair. He kept his eyes downcast as he talked. If it weren't for the fact that they were alone, she would have thought him distracted by someone else. He appeared to talk more to himself than to her.

She began, "We have a few minutes here. The girl is still wrestling with the Doherty's snotty beast down in the far ring." She pulled a large brown file out from behind her apron. "These are the papers I told you about."

Tim looked at the file with surprise. "What's this?"

"It's more information on her."

"Why are you showing me this now?"

She needed to progress carefully, and adjusted her manner and approach to project calm. "Michael made it clear that he wanted to be . . . ah, how did he say it . . . I know. He wanted to be 'transparent' in his dealings with her and wanted to make sure you knew everything about his girl."

"He does? He said that?"

"Aye. He does. It's coming time for you to meet her."

He shuffled his weight back and forth on his feet. "You said I should stay away from her."

"Things have changed. That's why I want you to read these."

Tim looked at a point somewhere over her shoulder then carefully reviewed each page. He spent the most time on the newspaper clippings. "These aren't about her training."

"Some are," Nan said as she guided him to a clipped section of stories. "But most are about other matters. I scan the news daily. There aren't as many stories in recent weeks as there were, but any time there's a snippet of new information, the stories feed on one another."

"She's beautiful. Can I have these?"

Nan watched Tim's expression carefully, and seized her opportunity when he took an interest in the articles. "She likes our protection and only wants certain people around her. She's been asking to meet you."

"She does? When did she say that?"

"As soon as she heard you were Michael's friend. Liam chose you because of your connection to Michael, and rightly so. The girl appreciates that connection."

"Okay. Okay. Okay. Let me think about that. What else?"

Nan leaned out of the door and peered down to the ring to make sure they were still alone. "She's a nervous wreck, jumping at every squeak and shadow. She leaves all the lights on in the cottage and even hauls a chair over to block the door at night."

"She's afraid?"

"Hmm. That's my thought. 'Tis a pity. She's here all by herself. I don't think she likes that," she cooed. "You'd be wise to keep a closer eye on her."

Tim continued nodding. "What about her days?"

"It's never any different than what you've seen with the training notes."

He watched Jessica school the horse through a series of complex passes. Dark swatches of sweat slicked the horse's bright penny sides. "The horses listen to her."

"In the same way they listen to you. You'd make a good partner with her. She spends hours with the horses, and when she's done she spends hours more makin' notes. There's not been a peep out o' her, but she's getting lonely."

"Has she asked about him? About Michael?"

"A bit. She's love struck for certain." She looked at Tim with intensity, but kept her voice velvety. "You should see the look she gets in her eyes when she talks of him. He can do no wrong in her opinion. I'll bet she'll do anything for him." A slight smile crept up on her lips as Tim's eyes darted back and forth from the newspaper pictures to the figure in the ring. Nan sorted through the file and gave a handful of clippings to Tim. She tucked rest into her trousers' waistband under her apron, then grunted. "I guess she figures he'll show up when he shows up. Poor thing just needs a friend," she added, enough under her breath to not require a response. Remembering herself, she straightened up. "Enough about her. What about you? What are you needing?"

Tim bent over slightly, bracing his arms on his legs, as if the weight of the question was too great. "What's news on the talks?"

"Stalled. No one's makin' a move. All of the positions are out front and parties have dug in their heels."

"I don't understand," he mumbled. "How can all of the positions be out front when all the voices aren't bein' heard? Are you keeping your ears to the signs? Are they still refusing' us a seat at the table?"

"Aye. The loyalists have blocked Gerry Adams and Sinn Fein from being heard. They're simply repeating the rubbish that the IRA is a bunch of criminals, and that Sinn Fein is merely its mouthpiece. Word is they're still refusing to call our men in prison political prisoners and persist in calling them criminals. They refuse to talk about everything including getting their British butts out of our country."

"No. No. No." Tim became agitated, working his fingers on his thighs as if he were playing a piano. "It won't be long. Not long at all. We're ready."

She gently reached out and placed her hands on his arms. "What have I told you? Calm yourself. Remember our lessons. What are you doing right now?"

Tim stopped, shoved his hands in his pockets, and looked at her apologetically. "You said it. You said it was a logjam."

"Well," Nan nodded her approval, "you know what they do for logjams, don't you? A little stick of dynamite works wonders. I got the word, Tim. It's on to bigger and better things."

Tim gave a smile that only touched one corner of his mouth. Looking over his shoulder, he saw Jessica dismount and begin walking a very tired horse around the ring. He raised an eyebrow at Nan asking permission to introduce himself. He straightened his shoulders and turned to go out to meet her but was pulled back into the shadow of the barn.

"Patience, my boy. You've more to learn yet. All in good time."

The wind whipped her hair around her face as Jessica led the exhausted horse back to the barn. She was in a foul mood and wanted to avoid the other trainer who waited for her at the top of the hill. She had asked Nan over a week ago to speak with him, and of all the days he would pick to finally meet, it had to be the one time when she wanted to be left alone in her misery. Planxty favored its right hind leg, no doubt a result of her misjudging his training schedule. It would heal without lingering effects, but the additional time would prolong his training. She worried if the delay would cost her the confidence of his owners. She had no one else to blame but herself and the last thing she wanted to be was civil.

"Well, mornin'! Mornin'! It's good to see you out and about on a lovely day as this."

Jessica looked at the outstretched hand and followed it up the arm. A pair of startling green eyes surrounded by a shock of unruly hair stared at her. Seeing him at a distance gave no hint he was this handsome. The revelation came upon her suddenly, and unprepared, a flush crept into her cheeks. Catching herself, she shook his hand. "I'm Jessica."

He held her hand as if disbelieving his sense of touch, staring, and holding on to it for longer than necessary. "I know that. I'm Tim. Nan told you about me."

Jessica gently pulled her hand away, noticing how warm his hands were. "Oh! Yes," she stammered, flustered that her usual self-control failed her. Embarrassed, she cleared her throat and tried to redirect her attention. "I've been hoping to meet you. You're never here when I am. Perfect timing always." She watched to see if he would flinch at being caught in his obvious avoidance of her.

Nothing flickered over his face. "Nan said that you liked your privacy. I'm here to help with the horses." His eyes swept over her and settled on the horse. "Here now. I haven't seen Planxty in quite a while. Favoring his back leg? Did you push him too hard?"

She winced at the reprimand and noted how easily her miscalculation was uncovered. "I'm afraid I misjudged his conditioning. Daily logging just isn't clear enough. Your notes are good, but cryptic. It's exactly why I wanted to talk with you. You have a lot of insight into the horses." She wanted a good rapport with him but was already off on the wrong foot.

"He can't compete injured." A line of color crept up his neck. He took the reins from her hand and loosened the saddle's girth. "Let me walk this beast and cool him down a bit. You've others to tend today?"

"I do, thanks." Jessica appreciated the added help, but couldn't be sure if his curt manner meant he was angry or uncomfortable. He had the information she needed, which gave her enough motivation to get along. She infused her manner with warmth, hoping being outgoing would help build their relationship. "Walking him out would be perfect. You just gave me an extra hour. Since you're here, I wanted to talk to you about my training strategy and goals."

"Yes. Yes. Yes. That's what I'm here for. I'm here to talk to you." He gave an imperceptible bow.

His manner varied from friendly to irritated, confusing her and making her feel that he might be more irritated at Planxty's lameness than he let on. She kept the topic on what she needed to know. "What do the owners want?"

"Ever hear of Tully Farm?

"Tully Farm? Yes. They are one of the finest breeding farms in the world."

"They're part of the syndicate that owns the horses under your care. They want to get them ready for competition. You might have heard about their most recent champion, Bealltainn?" He waited until she shook her head. "All of their horses are the product of the most advanced breeding and training programs in the world. Some consider their stable more valuable than gold. Bealltainn's stud fees alone were worth a king's ransom. His last stand at stud cost the mare's farm one hundred thousand U.S. dollars." He spoke each word slowly, enunciating each syllable and inflecting his voice carefully. A rehearsed speech delivered. The actions hinted that he worked at being outgoing.

Jessica's eyes rounded. "I knew these horses were great, but I had no idea they were that valuable."

"Bealltainn's not under your care, but he and the others have been written off as worthless." Tim smiled at eliciting a gasp from Jessica. "Even that chestnut you're training."

"Kilkea? Worthless? Impossible. He's a tough one to figure out but he's coming along."

"He won the Grand National and used to be Ireland's national hunt champion."

"If that's the case, then why do the owners disregard him so much?"

"He beat himself, they say. After he earned the title, he had a crash that cost his rider's life and his own nerve."

"What happened?"

"His rider misjudged the dirty tricks other jockeys do during a race. They got cut off and had to shorten an approach to a large jump. The botched flight sent them crashing through the hedgerow. Other horses in the pack were not able to pull up in time and crushed their riders into the turf. If his rider's broken neck didn't kill him, a hoof to the noggin did the deed. Two horses were euthanized on the spot."

"The notes talked about a crash, but I had no idea it was that terrible! It explains a few things. He loves to open up," she said, referring to a horse's desire to run as fast as it is physically able, "but he's skittish to jump over anything he hasn't seen. Can you tell me more?"

"He lost his nerve a cutthroat claiming race. It seemed he knew if he lost the race, he would be claimed by a crappy farm and never see his rider or trainer again. He was lucky Tully Farm decided to take him in, but I swear Kilkea feels the guilt of the loss." Tim rubbed his forehead. "He lost his heart after that, just like a person would."

"Why race a horse like that in a claiming race? Usually those are for horses that haven't lived up to expectations or are past their prime. Or damaged. With the reputation of Tully Farm behind them, the owners could have put any price on him and gotten it. Why gamble like that?"

"Because when the owners are so rich, the only things they have to play with are futures." Tim shifted his weight from foot to foot. "He's raced a bit since then, but he never qualified for the Nationals again. You've a head case to fix."

"I can't 'fix' him. A memory like that scars the best of riders, and horses are not immune from trauma. Thank you for letting me know, but I doubt he'll ever compete again."

Tim stopped shuffling his feet and looked down at the ground. His voice was a mixture of iron and anger. His tone changed abruptly. "Are you saying you're not up to the task of training him?"

"It's not about *me* being up to the task," Jessica snapped back. "It's about whether the *animal* is."

Tim's mouth curled in a sly smile. "He's hoped to compete in a private steeplechase."

"Private? I don't follow you."

"You're familiar enough with the Grand National?" Jessica gave a non-committal shrug in response, admitting she was a bit out of her depth. He paused in thought for a moment. "I don't have to tell you about the wager between two Irish Earls to see who could race from one town center to another the fastest, do I? They used the churches to mark the route because their steeples could be seen for miles and were used to help the riders navigate through the unknown countryside."

Jessica interrupted him by touching his arm. "My family raised and trained thoroughbreds for the flat track back in the States. So, if you're going to tell me about steeplechases, I may know a thing or two about them." She wanted to put him at ease with humor. "They're like a hunter pace on steroids."

He fingered his shirt where she touched him and gave an easy natural laugh that stopped as quickly as it started. "Forgive me. I forgot who I was talking to for a minute! We call flat races without jumps 'bumpers' and consider them for babies. You Americans think steeplechases are some bonny tyker race, but here they're serious business. The U.K.'s Aintree and Cheltenham tracks in England are the world's toughest chase courses." His words boomed out like an announcement.

"I've heard of them. Pretty fancy stuff."

"The public races that you've heard of are often the appetizer for the real events that happen post season. In private races, owners get together and wager their best horses. It's a way for them to win back their investments and have some fun. Ever hear of 'betting the farm?' Well, some do that, too. It's where the super-rich strut their manhood."

"And?"

"The owner wants them ready for Aintree. It's a winner-takes-all."

"They can't be serious."

"They are. Get Kilkea ready for a less important race held before the main event. He'll be able to go at his own pace. He's been bred for this kind of thing. It's in his blood. Not givin' him a chance to do what he loves would be cruel."

"I'm not sure what I can do in a month's time."

"The horses go to Aintree with or without your approval."

The stark truth of his message landed with a thud. The owners saw her as merely a hired hand whose opinion meant nothing. "This is exactly the information I've needed for effective training. If they put them in a race too early, it's their fault if they ruin their investment, but they'll blame defeat on me. I'll have no part in it."

Tim stiffened and looked up in surprise at her harsh tone. "You can't quit. You have to stay." He started to sway slightly and his eyes darted to the side, slightly narrowed, as if he was trying to remember something. His face reddened and he tripped over some words, then stopped. Almost mechanically, he leaned closer to her, lowered his voice, and spoke slowly. "You've already done more with these horses than I thought could be done. They need you here. I need . . ." He stopped and rubbed his mouth with his hand. "Y-you're needed here." A beseeching tone crept into his words.

His overly smooth and borderline inappropriate tone jarred her. She stepped back, giving him a sidelong glance and repressed an urge to leave him standing there, alone and acutely aware that she would not be played. Reluctantly, she admitted her own manner may have been off, too. Maybe he detected a flicker of attraction had lit up inside of her. Besides, he was right. Her temporary role in these horses' lives gave her no control. She didn't have a say in the horses' futures. Her only concern, both personally and professionally, had to be for their safety and health, not how the owners maximized or ruined their investment. She dismissed his behavior as a misstep and returned her focus to the horses.

He placed Planxty into crossties and ran his hands over the horse, starting at the neck and working his way down the haunches and legs, keeping up a steady stream of banter as he moved. He lingered over the area causing the horse's stiffness and rhythmically worked his fingers until the horse's muscles softened and he hung his head. He spoke over his shoulder to her. "I'll wash him down with some liniment and walk him out later to keep him loose. If that doesn't work, I'll give him some LPS."

Jessica stopped in her tracks. LPS stood for the injectable drug lipo-polysaccharide, a powerful anti-inflammatory. The thought of using drugs on the horse angered her. Worldwind Farm's reputation toppled because of unscrupulous doping. "These horses have to be able to race clean. I'm not going to prop them up with drugs and I'm not going to risk any drugs being detected on race day. Let's keep the therapies external."

"The drugs help the horses feel good."

"We'll do that without drugs. We've got to understand what we're dealing with and won't have any injuries masked by a painkiller." She went into the storage room and came back rolling a cart. On top sat two metal boxes with dials and something that looked like microphones with a long cord. "Michael had these shipped here last week. We'll use the ultra-sound machine if we're dealing with a serious injury and the other for sound wave therapy. Have you used these?" Tim nodded, and they worked in silence. His entire focus went to the animal and all awkwardness evaporated. He was skilled, and Planxty relaxed under his care. She tried another attempt at conversation. "There is a lot to get used to here."

Tim looked up, cocking his head to one side in thought. "Not so much. Good countryside for riding though."

"I wondered about that. I've been out a few times and am never sure what's public or when I cross onto someone else's land. Would the neighbors have a problem with someone trespassing?"

He laughed, pulling his lips back to show even, white teeth. She noticed how his weathered skin folded back in creases, accentuating his smile. "Nobody knows who owns what around here. That's why the sheep have spray painted marks on them so the farmers can keep track of flocks even if they can't keep track of their lands. Keep the gates as you found them and they won't turn a rifle on you." Any hint of warmth cooled. Agitation replaced his even demeanor. "You're supposed to leave things as they were," he sputtered. "Don't go changing things or goin' into places you're not wanted. If they don't want you there, the owners will put a sign up that says 'Keep Out.' That's the rule. Learn what's expected. Do what you've learned. Follow the rules, and you'll be fine."

His response held more than awkward phrasing. Tim could change from shy to antagonistic and back without warning. Jessica found it hard to establish her footing with him. She ventured another topic. "Have you seen the stone circle? It's on the other side of the farm, up the eastern trails. Can you tell me anything about it?"

He looked out over the hills. "That's Beltany Circle." His upper body rocked a few times, then he stood completely still and spoke as if reciting a page from an encyclopedia. "It's pronounced *BAL-tin-neh.* Ireland is dotted with them. The one you saw is said to be the worship site for Mother Earth and fertility. The locals don't go there."

"Why?"

"We Irish don't question that there is more to our world than what we see."

She didn't need to hear more to decide never to go back there.

He grabbed a brush and began grooming the horse. With each short, quick stroke, he flicked the brush upward and released a tiny cloud of dirt and horsehair. He moved around the horse in tiny steps, keeping up the rhythmic brushing, slowly working his way closer to her.

Hot, then cold. She'd never met anyone like him. Without Nan to talk to, she had no one to connect with. She had to keep trying. "The horses were chosen well," she said, keeping her voice steady. "Michael must have known you had an eye for horses."

"He did."

"How long have you known him?"

"I've known him all my life."

"Oh? You've been to the States?"

His voice lowered, masking whatever it was he felt about his childhood friend. "Never. I've lived in the Irelands all my life."

The prospect of learning more was tantalizing. Michael was born and raised in the U.S. He was as American as she was, yet here was this dyed-in-the-wool Irishman who claimed they were boyhood friends. "How did you know one another?"

"Our fathers were . . ." he worked his mouth to find the right word, "colleagues."

A flatness in his voice wasn't the only indication that made Jessica instinctively want to stay away, but the mention of Magnus, the man responsible for turning her life upside down. As helpful as Tim was, she didn't wholeheartedly welcome his presence. They stopped talking as they put one horse away and prepared another. This time they readied a small bay, its black mane and tail set off by a blaze of white on its face matched with a cap of white on its dock. She needed to break away. "Leg up?"

Tim gave Jessica the requested boost into the saddle and watched as she began an easy trot to the ring. He ran through the pair's physical language, losing himself in the unspoken signals. The horse was easy. Expectant. A rapport had already formed between animal and human. The horse's head hung down, accepting the loose rein without taking advantage of it. Animals don't lie. Their eyes don't shift to the side and fake being nice if they don't like something. Tim craved that honesty, and the world of horses is where he found it. The urge to walk in rapid circles vanished. He wasn't a good poker player because of the quirky and unconscious things he did. He had to learn how to lie by keeping the muscles in his face relaxed or not jamming his hands in his pockets. More important than teaching his body to obey, he learned to spot a lie in someone else.

He saw how the reference to Michael's father stunned Jessica. He watched as she worked her mouth as it went dry and her eyes widened, unblinking, with pupils constricting to tiny dots. It confirmed what he had learned about her—she hid things. Even with the overt threat Magnus held over her, she did not gasp or blink or try to divert attention. Her eyes did not widen in fear, but narrowed in disgust. That told Tim she was gutsy, didn't run from fear, and would be unmanageable if she felt threatened. She was the most exquisite person he had ever met. He wanted to spend hours watching her.

Tim looked back at the cottage. Nan stood in the shadows of the doorway, arms crossed, and the corners of her mouth turned downward. She looked in the direction of the horse and rider then gave a quick nod. He walked back into the barn.

A few minutes later, a van pulled up. Another man emerged and helped carry several large wooden boxes into the barn, keeping a nervous look over his shoulders as he worked.

Tim opened one box and peered down inside. A series of wooden shelves divided the stacked layers. The top layer contained an assortment of horse poultices, wraps, and splint boots that were part of the essential gear of high-end horse care. Lifting this shelf out, he retrieved a plastic bag that held a large coil of wire and several rectangular blocks of a gray, putty-like material. He tossed this bag to his companion, who quickly placed it back into the van.

Tim nodded his satisfaction. They hoisted the boxes up into the loft and hid them behind a carefully stacked wall of hay bales. The day proved warmer than he expected and in the rapid pace of work he broke into a sweat. He gave Nan another quick look. She remained standing with her back to them facing the ring where Jessica rode. Nan's arms were still crossed to signal no one was coming. He rolled up his shirt-sleeves, exposing the pale skin of his forearms to the summer sun. Even a dark tan would not have hidden his tattoo.

A three-leaf shamrock shaded in the colors of Ireland—green, white, and orange—was nearly sliced in two by a long dagger. An intertwining Celtic design decorated the dagger's handle up to the quillion. The black outline of three tears dripped from the blade's edge. He caught the driver of the van stealing a quick look at it and smiled when the younger man seemed to put more effort into his task. Tim's army didn't have fancy uniforms with badges and stripes of rank. The tattoo showed his commitment to the cause and that he had risen to its highest levels. He only needed to add blood red to the tears for the symbol of his ascension to be complete.

What she learned from Tim gnawed at her. She knew so little of Michael but could hardly be angry with him for her ignorance. Michael had a childhood friend whose fathers were colleagues of some sort. Regardless of what she thought of Magnus, it stung that she had scant knowledge on her own roots—her real ones. Resolved, she hastily rummaged around the crawlspace and pulled out a handful of papers from the box. Spreading them across the planks of the kitchen table, she began the process of making sense of the pieces of her life.

She would start with her biological mother. Jessica smoothed the yellowed paper onto the table, settling it for inspection. She stared at her mother's name.

Bridget Heinchon Harvey.

Jessica closed her eyes and drew on every memory she had of Bridget. For years, Jessica rejected the awkward love of a sickly aunt and wondered how their relationship would have been different if she knew her mother *was* with her when she needed one the most during her rebellious teen years. She felt stupid and barren for not realizing it. Stupid, because she thought people just *knew* this stuff, like who their mother really was. Barren because she ached to change how she treated Bridget and to fill up on the warmth of a mother's love.

Margaret was considered a dark Irish—black hair with gray eyes and a crackling wit that her private nature showed only to her closest family. Bridget's gentle manner of speaking only hinted at an Irish brogue. Her alabaster skin was lightly flecked with pale brown freckles. Her hair, gray by the time they lived together, hinted at being blonde flecked with faded strawberry, suggesting her Irish lineage. How could Jessica not have been fully aware that Bridget and Margaret were true Irish—not simply by ancestry but by where they were born? They never spoke of their roots, but Jessica shook her head at being so blind to what should have been obvious, including the physical similarities she shared with Bridget, not Margaret.

Frustrated, she went back to examine her birth certificate. Long versions, like this one, typically provided both the names of the parents and where they were born. The entire document would have been rolled into the carriage of an old typewriter and the information entered, metal keys hitting an inked ribbon, imprinting one perfectly formed letter at a time. Her fingers felt the slight bumps behind each letter where the paper had been struck. At the bottom of the page, she looked for the information she craved but thought she would never see. Beside Bridget's name was a blank place where the mother's place of birth would have gone. She assumed the next line down held a space for the father's name. Jessica had looked at this form before and always thought that this space was blank. Looking more carefully, she noticed the bottom of the document did not have a crisp edge. Instead, the old parchment-like paper was faintly frayed. The thinnest of fibers clung to the slightly fuzzed edge, clearly showing that it had been carefully ripped or cut many years before.

Jessica held the paper up to the kitchen light and studied it for a very long time. The information typed onto the old form did not follow a perfectly straight line. The paper had been loaded into the typewriter at an angle and adjusted clumsily to complete each space. It had been torn through the very information she craved. In the space marked "Next of Kin," the bottom half of the typed letters had been severed. She could tell a rounded capital letter started the first name and a pointed capital started the last name. It fit the convention for "Gus Adams," but the thought pained her. If Jessica could find the bottom half of the certificate, maybe she could learn who her father was and why Bridget gave her away and kept her secret even in death.

This mystery had roiled inside her head ever since the certificate's discovery only a few months before. From that moment, unthinkable possibilities ran through her thoughts every second of every day. The shock she had when she learned the truth had not faded. The fear she had at knowing more grew.

Jessica was given away at birth, but she felt far less a precious gift bestowed upon Margaret than an abandoned, unwanted nuisance. Bridget gave her baby girl to her sister and never broke the secret even after Margaret's tragic death in the automobile accident that also claimed the lives of Erin and Jim. The anger and bewilderment about being lied to in the years Bridget lived in the Wyeth home to care for Jessica threatened to consume her. All of those Sunday night dinners where Jessica sat at one end of the huge dining room table and Bridget sat at the other came rushing back. Nothing but the uncomfortable stirrings in their chairs filled the silence. Jessica believed life could have been different if they *both* knew they were mother and daughter. Instead, they sat in silence as a sickly aunt played guardian to an estranged teenaged niece.

Jessica fingered the yellowed parchment form as if some remnant of memory could seep up through her fingertips and provide the answer. Bridget was born on December 27, 1933 and was thirty-three years old when she had Jessica. It wasn't a lot. But it was a start.

Father Mervyn Archdall smoothed the front of his black cassock over his prominent belly and straightened his slumped shoulders. His skin felt like static electricity raced over it, a physical sign of his intuition. He was determined to project calm and confidence to his flock during today's mass and wait to see what unfolded which would require his attention. As was his habit, he had risen before dawn, bathed, ate a sparse breakfast of brown bread and tea, and slipped out of the rectory without waking his housekeeper and resident deacon.

He walked briskly, hoping to get to his office before anyone else arrived. The Bishop's Cathedral stood a navigation point in the remote countryside. The massive stone structure sat upon the crest of a hill, maximizing the cathedral's impact when approached from the main street. Its stumped steeple did not thwart the illusion that the cathedral was bigger than it really was. Rather than taper to a point, the steeple was either lopped off or never completed, leaving a squared and blunted limb. The walled churchyard enclosed decaying crypts and headstones but no bishop lay buried there. The cathedral earned its name from the clergyman who took refuge within its walls. Legend told of a bishop who dared to question how the Catholic Church raised its money and distributed power. Such questions made him wildly popular with the people, but his superiors held a different opinion. Whispers about a labyrinth of tunnels began when the bishop mysteriously disappeared without a trace after a mass. Rumors persist about subterranean passages under the town and throughout the countryside. Father Archdall would *hrmpf* anyone into silence who suggested their existence.

Once inside, he wandered the hallways of the cathedral—pacing, restless, caged. He tried to channel his nervous energy by performing odd tasks—stacking missiles neatly in pew corners or running a damp cloth over smoothed marbled floors. He dusted the sloped sills of the narrow windows—filled with stained glass interpretations of Jesus' life—and replenished the ancient carved stone bowl at the entrance of the church. Another slight blessing of the holy water to boost its potency completed his tasks.

He considered the cathedral his home more than the rectory. He knew every square inch of the huge stone structure even better than he knew his own body. He unlocked the huge wooden doors and pushed them wide in welcoming. An overturned bucket sat on the steps. He pulled the doors shut and locked them.

His heart pounded. The timing was all wrong. Things were happening much faster than he expected. He felt the generations of priests before him place their hands on his shoulders in support. He played a part in something larger than himself, far larger than all of Donegal parish. He knew his words today would set actions into motion. Sometimes, exact words were provided to him. Other times, a passage of scripture encompassed the reference. He hurried down the hallway to receive the message.

"Morning, *Sagart* Archdall," Mrs. McDonnaugh, the church's treasurer and town registrar chirped her greeting through the cracked opening of her office door, using his Irish title. "Looking for inspiration for another sermon?"

He hid his surprise and pretended to pause his pacing long enough to reply, "Yes. It's coming along well enough." He looked at his watch. "You're here early."

"I had an hour's work to do before mass. The supper last night was well attended. Lots of folks contributed." She shook a zippered money pouch for emphasis. "People showed a good deal of curiosity about that young American girl. We don't often get visitors like her around here."

His raised eyebrows did little to soften his expression. "Oh?"

"I've had a few people come in looking up old deeds or some other such record with an excuse for idle chat. Pickin' my brains for crumbs, they were."

"What did you tell them?" he said with more force.

"I told 'em the truth. She's not come to me to with any questions. Mute as a mouse and gets hustled out as soon as the service is over. She's keepin' to herself, and I'd nothing to tell them."

"Hrmpf," he exclaimed, considerably more relaxed.

"No news will be coming from me, so they can stop their pryin.'"

He was careful not to nod his approval with force enough to set his jowls in motion. "Well done. We don't need to be the source of gossip."

"Right you are, Father. Will you be needing anything more before mass? I wouldn't miss the sermon you're cooking up in that head of yours. It must be a good one. You're wearing out a track in the stone with your pacing." She pulled the door to her office shut.

Father Archdall let his shoulders droop and leaned against the cold stone wall. He had thought he was alone. With renewed energy, he started at the top of the cathedral and worked his way down, checking every hidden corner and shadow for a second and third time. How could he have been so careless as to not realize she was there? He blessed himself, gripped his rosary in his hand, and said a chaplet.

Events were in motion. What they were, he had no idea, but he knew he wouldn't be the one to make a mistake. It took him another twenty minutes to comb the cathedral again. The altar servers would be arriving soon, but he knew he had time. He locked the vestry door behind him. He didn't need light as he made his way down the cellar stairs, for they were as familiar to him as the back of his own hand.

His trips down this darkened passage were more frequent the past weeks, so no cobwebs clung to his face and no grit crushed on the stairs to give away his progress. A growing smile on his face threatened to reveal a hint of self-satisfaction, but he refused to be prideful. He devoted his service to God and man. To those ends, he was fulfilled.

He wound his way to the far most corner of the cellar, entered a small room, pulled boxes away from the hole in the wall, and waited.

Patience in these moments was something he knew well. Rosary laced in his fingers, he sat with his head bowed, listening more than praying. A faint scraping followed by rhythmic thudding grew louder. Peering into the absolute blackness he waited until the something began to shift and take shape. The faintest of light, almost red, appeared at a distant point. He flicked his pen light three times. Stopped. Then four. The red grew to orange, then yellow. Then into a man.

He stepped back as the figure emerged and held out his arm for support. A muscular brute in his early thirties groaned quietly as he stood upright and stretched for the first time in what had been many hours. Once the man steadied himself, he enveloped Father Archdall in a warm embrace. The tunnels and catacombs must have been hell on his back.

"You're safe," was all he needed to say.

Even in the darkened room, he clearly knew the man's emotions. "Thank you," the man said, his voice soft but strong.

"Is it soon?" he asked.

"There's nothing anyone can do to stop it. I'm to give you this." The man pressed a paper into Father Archdall's hand.

"Things are happening quickly."

"I can't say more. Just being careful."

Father Archdall nodded, "And you?"

"The RUC was close on my heels. I never would have gotten over the border without your help."

"Will there be more?"

The man paused before he spoke. "Time will tell."

Father Archdall motioned to a cubby of blankets and food. "You can sleep here for a few hours before your next escort comes. Mass starts soon, but you'll be safe."

He handed the man a thick envelope of papers he knew contained all of the pieces needed for a new life in a new country. Passport, visa, perhaps a summary of a new identity, money, and note with the time and public place to meet the next escort. Never any names. Never any addresses. This packet was a bit thicker than some of the others suggesting this man had a family he was trying to smuggle out as well. The thought gave him a momentary stab of pain, but he had done his part.

The man surprised him when he refused the envelope. Father Archdall tried again to put it into the man's hands.

"Save it for the next one. It belongs to him. I'm using this route only to deliver the message. I won't be back or be needin' more."

Father Archdall had never been refused. The system—or he—never tested or broken. "You're safe?"

"I am."

He thought he heard an unsettling emphasis on "*I*." The man's voice was calm and he had brought a backpack of some sort. Heavy.

An awkward silence hung between them. Gradually it occurred to Father Archdall that his presence was no longer needed or wanted. He turned and made his way slowly up the stairs, saying goodbye as he did so.

"Everything you need is here. I wish you God's speed."

"I'd like you to leave the keys and the Land Rover at the cottage from now on. I really don't' want to bother you each time I go to town," Jessica said, extending her hand for the keys. She stood in the courtyard of the cottage meeting Nan at its entrance. A defensive approach wasn't going to get her the space and autonomy she needed. She tried to be pleasant.

Nan straightened her back. "You're thinkin' of going into town alone?"

"I've been with you enough times on Sundays. I know my way around." Addressing Nan's unspoken concerns she added, "and I know how to take care of myself."

Nan drew her chin down to her chest and steadied herself with an inhale. "And you're thinking of driving these roads by yourself?"

"Of course. I want to get out on my own and explore on something more than horseback."

"Exploring on your own is out of the question. You ever drive in Ireland before?"

"No, but—"

Nan held up her hand and assumed her most affable demeanor, smiling and exaggerating her singsong words. "You'd be takin' your life and the life of a few good people in your hands to drive these roads here."

"Really there's no need to inconvenience you," Jessica said, refusing to be cajoled, "I just want to run an errand in town and—"

Nan cut her off. Pale gray eyes, unblinking and penetrating, looked through her. "Truly," Nan said, "there's no problem to keepin' things as they are. It's worked out well for me to be your guide, and I be goin' into town again anyway. What is it you'd be lookin' for?"

Jessica stumbled over her response. The underlying chill wrapped in feigned warmth irked her. "I, er, I needed to get some wraps for the horses and maybe something for myself."

"Oh, now, deary, that'd be fine. Did you have a store in mind?"

"Well, no. I thought I'd poke around."

Nan hesitated for a moment, looking at Jessica if she was truly stupid. "No," she said in a tone that ended the discussion.

With no alternative, Jessica reluctantly agreed and climbed into the passenger seat of the Land Rover. As usual, Nan's booted foot seemed a bit too heavy on the accelerator and the two women bumped and swerved their way into town in the ancient vehicle. At the beginning of her stay, Jessica would use the drive for small talk, asking about Michael or more about Nan's work. Inevitably, she ended up disappointed. Nan told her nothing more than broad details Jessica already knew and remained tight-lipped saying Michael that should be the one to give her specifics. Frustrated and tired of being rebuffed, Jessica contented herself by looking at the passing countryside.

A few scattered farms dotted the fields. Clusters of homes became more frequent as they neared town which itself consisted of one main street with a handful of roads peeling away from the center. Rows of gaily painted buildings in different states of repair flanked the main street. Dating back over a century, each store seemed to represent a boom or bust time in Ireland's history. The more substantial stone buildings showed years of relative comfort and wealth. Other wooden buildings, like the families who owned them, barely held on.

On each trip to town, Nan insisted on Jessica wearing some type of hat and glasses. Today was no different. Nan handed her a black baseball cap. It was one of Jessica's favorites from her years at Bowdoin with a white silhouette of a polar bear on the forehead. She took it but was surprised she had left it out at the cottage. Had she hung it on the pegboard? She couldn't remember and looked at it and the pair of aviator style sunglasses offered to her.

Jessica bristled. "I'm not hiding from anyone anymore."

"Of course not," Nan clipped. "But you're not waving a red flag under a bull's nose either."

"I'm tired of this," she said, placing the items in her lap.

"As long as you're under my care, you'll do what I ask." The engine whirred as Nan downshifted.

It was clear she was going to head back to the cottage unless Jessica complied. Reluctantly, she put them on.

Nan pulled the Land Rover in front of one of the wooden buildings. Its faded blue sides with white trim were in dire need of a new paint job, but it put on a brave face to be cheery. The store bore the sign "Dillon's General Store." Nan stood on the sidewalk for a moment and looked up and down the street. She then motioned for Jessica to join her.

Wherever Jessica lived, the hardware store would become her favorite spot. She could relax and get lost in there, generally getting the feel for her new home. The store reflected the people and the needs of the surrounding community, and the merchandise was as interesting as the people who shopped there. Inside, the variety of goods made her feel she had stepped back in time. Dillon's was a general store in the truest sense. It had something for every person and every need. Parts for farm machinery, painting supplies, livestock feeds and buckets, pots and pans, and a multitude of odd tools lined the wooden and metal shelves. Rubber balls and dusty wooden toys sat in a corner. The store evidenced a self-sufficient, practical, and hardworking community.

Jessica could feel Nan's eyes on her and took great care to look in every aisle. The store smelled of old cotton, mineral spirits, household cleaners, oil, and dust. The wood floors creaked as she made her way into different sections, which shelved the perfect item for every need created for running a home or farm. She hoped that if she chewed up enough time dragging out her errands, maybe Nan would get sick of babysitting her and relinquish the keys. She wasn't sure how long she browsed, but when she stole a look at Nan, it surprised her to see Nan leaning against the shelves with an odd expression on her face. Jessica didn't feel watched as much as she felt examined, every move observed and catalogued.

Eventually, Jessica wound her way up the creaking stairs and ended up in the corner of the store dedicated to clothing for men, women, and children. Along one wall were blue jeans and work clothes. To Jessica's ongoing amazement, the other wall held sweaters, pants and a display case of very sensible cotton underwear of all shapes and sizes. As she turned to leave, another woman appeared out of nowhere and guided her over to a rack of dresses. Her ample bosom made her look like she was leaning a bit forward. She handed her a dress of a deep lilac color. "Dillon's just got these in. I'll bet it'll be perfect for you."

Jessica looked at the dress made from the softest and most finely woven wool that she had ever handled. The deep purple wrap would be forgiving on any body type but on Jessica it would be stunning.

"Oh!" Jessica couldn't hide her surprise. "It's beautiful."

"Aye. 'Tis at that," the woman continued and stared intently into Jessica's face as she spoke. "The owner's granddaughter, Eilis, weaves and sews up a storm. Considered the best in all of Ireland. All the young ladies love what her dresses do for their curves. With the shape you've got, you'll be the envy of them."

Jessica fingered the fine wool. "It's incredibly soft. Thank you. I'll go try it on."

Nan came around the corner of a display and placed herself between them. "Good idea. Dressing rooms are over there." She nodded toward the back of the store.

Nan waited outside the dressing room. A few people milled about the store and none seemed to pay any more attention to Jessica. She tried on several outfits, half listening as Nan expertly deflected any curiosity about her by talking about the local events that were bringing tourists in. Shoving her hair back under her cap, Jessica finished shopping and chose a long skirt, several sweaters and the dress the woman picked out. She started to pay for the items but Nan stopped her and produced a wad of bills. Jessica protested, and Nan raised her hand. "No questions," was all she said.

They walked slowly up the main street. Nan nodded and chatted with people she met with obvious familiarity but made no attempt to make introductions even when they showed interest in Jessica. Nan smoothed the rebuffs with exaggerated warmth and always left them chuckling.

Looking at Nan's ease with the townspeople and listening to her share a pleasantry and a joke sent a different kind of pang through Jessica. She had been so close to putting down roots and being a part of a community in Kentucky. Circumstances forced her to lead a nomadic life, not because she wanted to. Even Nan, with her professional personality, at least had the appearance of ties to people. Jessica yearned for that kind of connection. The friendships she had begun in Kentucky were as important to her as anything. Electra Lavielle was Jessica's best friend there. Like Nan, Electra was older and very connected. Unlike Nan, Electra tried to integrate Jessica into the community. The contrast between the two women sharpened Jessica's feelings of detachment, and she felt the isolation as a stigma.

"Looking for your roots, are ya?"

"Excuse me?" Jessica pulled herself out of her thoughts and recognized the woman from Dillon's.

"Your roots? We have Americans come here looking for pieces of their family tree. I thought you might be one of them."

Nan wedged her shoulder between them and looked her in the face. "This lady is looking for peace and quiet."

The woman would not be deterred and extended her hand to Jessica. She stood a head shorter than Nan and wore a buttoned shirt, open sweater and a pleated skirt that reached almost to her ankles. Thick support stockings and sensible shoes completed her look. "I'm Mrs. McDonnaugh, the town magistrate. I have Americans coming here all the time looking for any information on their family tree or ancestral lands. I've hoped I might be seeing you soon at the records office. That's where the other American's end up."

Jessica raised her eyebrows. "That's good to know."

Mrs. McDonnaugh gave Jessica an appraising look, trying to peer around the sunglass and cap. "You seem to have a bit of the Isle in your veins. Where's your family from?"

"Um, Massachusetts."

Mrs. McDonnaugh laughed. "No. I mean where did they start from before they ended up on the shores of Massachusetts?"

Before Jessica could answer, Nan led her away. "She's not one you should be talkin' to," she said, firmly leading Jessica by her elbow.

Jessica allowed herself to be escorted around the corner. When they were no longer at risk of being observed, she shook her arm free and rooted her feet into the ground. "What *was* that? What are you doing?" Her words edged with disbelief and hurt.

"I'm respecting your privacy."

"Look, I appreciate your help, but I'd like to feel comfortable here. Blocking everyone from me doesn't feel helpful."

"It's for your own good. I don't need to remind you about the press and nosey ones every time you're recognized."

"In a small town like this, I would suspect walling me off and sending a signal that I'm untouchable would create even more curiosity."

"You need to rely on my judgment."

"I don't get it," Jessica continued, ignoring Nan's growing impatience. "I can't talk to anyone?"

"It's not that."

"Then what exactly is it?"

Nan's distain was evident. Red climbed up her scalp, and her features hardened to stone. She brought her face as close to Jessica's as her height would allow. Lowering her voice, her words bore into Jessica like a laser.

"I will say this to you only once, then I will deny ever having said it. You do not belong here. You are not of us and never will be. You are not welcome here, and your presence is a thorn in our sides. Train those horses and get out of town. I do for you what I have been asked to do. Do. Not. Question. Me."

Jessica stepped back as if bitten by a viper. She could feel herself grow icy cold with panic. "I . . . I don't understand."

Nan turned her back, and took a deep measured breath while rolling her shoulders and neck in circles. Her body softened and color retreated. Finally composed, she faced Jessica, her manner completely changed. "Well now, deary. Enough of that talk."

The cathedral's bells chimed five times, and Nan looked up and down the empty streets. "You said you wanted a chance to wander the town. Now's as good a time as any. Let's go walk it off." She turned and walked down a side street.

Jessica watched the retreating figure in disbelief. What had just happened? Loneliness enveloped her. The hollowness she had long felt began to fill with an unwelcomed awareness. No past grounded her with memories, nor did an identity define her. Combined with a present that was surreal at best, she felt more abandoned and confused than ever before. She blinked and surveyed the cobbled street, forgetting why she was there.

"Well, come on now. Get a move on!"

Nan beckoned her to follow. Having no other place to go and no means to get there, Jessica put one foot in front of the other and followed.

She didn't know how far she had walked or even what direction she took, but eventually a new wariness set in. Nan adopted her best tour guide tone and kept up a light banter of tidbits meant to entertain but not really inform. Occasionally they would pass a local on their way home, and Nan's commentary was perfectly constructed to deflect them to a discussion of local charms and away from Jessica. They rounded a corner and the back of the cathedral came into view.

"The original building dating back to the medieval period was rebuilt several times. The last major structural revision took place around about 1870. The cathedral's distinctive square tower and the lower entrance were added by Bishop Forster in 1768 and were . . ." Nan stopped, midsentence.

Jessica recognized the bespectacled old man wearing a black cassock as Father Archdall. He seemed smaller than he appeared on the altar, shrunk down as if the sunlight dried him out. The skin of his face, having lost all battles with gravity, sagged in long jowls, his expression forever one of disapproval and reproach. His eyes blinked rapidly as they adjusted to the light.

A feeling passed between them and Nan, but Jessica, still reeling from being chastised, couldn't pinpoint it. Deep down, she sensed her presence caused some sort of tension but couldn't think beyond that. Her feet slowed as a flash of intuition grabbed her. What made her think anything more? She raised her head to observe more carefully.

Nan nodded an aloof greeting. Then she placed her hand in the center of Jessica's back and shoved her in the other direction, her motion uncaring and abrupt. Still reeling from Nan's rebuff, Jessica walked on, mute and bewildered. They continued their hurried pace and were about to return to the Land Rover when Nan stepped quickly to the side, nearly causing Jessica to collide into two large shaggy dogs. Jostled off balance, Jessica felt a strong arm wrap around her waist. The grip remained even after she steadied.

"Well now. Careful there." Two green eyes danced in merriment. Tim gave Jessica an extra wide smile. "These guys have a nose for a beautiful woman and look who they've found."

Jessica exhaled in relief, thankful for a friendly connection. She recovered enough to return a smile that said his flattery would only get him so far. He was strong and held her against him. For a fraction of a second, she let her body yield. Not to him, exactly, but to the illusion of safety he gave her. Tim's masculine strength made her think of Michael, how long it had been since they were together, and how much she missed him. She quickly remembered herself. Gently maneuvering some distance, she leaned down and gave the dogs> ears a good rub in greeting. "These guys are sweethearts, and they're huge!"

"Wolfhounds. Never a wee one in the bunch."

"They seem young."

"Yeah, they are at that. Barely over a year old but as tall as they're goin' to get. All that dog and so little brain."

Jessica laughed, happy to have a reason.

Tim was taller than she first thought and she had to shield her eyes from the afternoon sun to look at him. The disjointed quality she usually observed in talking with him wasn't there. Today his full attention had a sharpness she found intriguing. She tried to take a step back, wanting to stay out of his reach, but as he talked the leashed dogs wound themselves around their legs, forcing them even closer. Tim returned his arm around her, and when she looked up she could feel his breath on her face. The sensation of being held so closely sent another ripple through her gut. For a split moment, she let her guard down as she became wholly aware of him. His strength. His scent. She closed her eyes and let her mind drift to Michael.

His arms tightened long enough to telegraph that he felt an opening in her manner and wouldn't be the one to stop. She put her head down and wriggled free of his arms and dogs, willfully trying to lower the color that crept into her cheeks.

In the awkward moment that followed, Jessica looked around the street to see who may have witnessed the brief encounter. Nan stood in the nook of a doorway. She said nothing as she got into the Land Rover and glared at Jessica over the steering wheel. And waited.

Jessica looked at Nan and back at Tim. The impact of being plunked down in the middle of a strange country and cut off from her own means became very clear. She didn't like it.

"Give me a lift back?"

Tim's eyes gave a flicker of surprise, then his grin widened. He made a sweeping gesture with his arm and bowed low. "I'd be most honored to give me lady a ride. But only if the boss herself agrees," he said, looking over at Nan.

Nan answered by wheeling the Land Rover away, engine racing.

"Whew," Jessica said, watching the retreating vehicle. She searched for the right words. "Nan's pretty intense. What's her story?"

"Intense?" Tim opened up the tailgate to his pickup and helped the two dogs jump in. Jessica got in the other side and he drove off a side street as he talked. "She's not one for the titters and smiles. One thing I'll say, you'll always be clear on where you stand with her."

Jessica gave a dry laugh. "Yeah. I got that impression already. Seriously though, tell me about her.

"There's nothing to say about Nan. You need something done, she'll do it."

"She's lived here long?"

Tim made a face, as if the question struck him as odd. "She can trace her roots back through eight generations of potato and sheep farmers and can count most of the citizens of County Donegal as one kind of distant relative or another."

"She seems to know everything about everyone in the town."

"Aye. She does at that but is beholden to none. She's not one to tamper with tradition. She sees the past as something to be cherished, but she's not much for socializin.'"

"No? Why not?"

"She goes about her business as she pleases. As much as she charts her own course, she'll scrap with anyone who threatens family or tradition. I'll say this for her, she loves her home. The land the cottage sits on has been in her family for centuries. Look at it," he said as they drove. "This land has barely changed."

Jessica looked out her window. Stone ruins of homesteads abandoned from either feuds or famine dotted the countryside. Gently rolling green and yellow hills made a patchwork when crisscrossed with walls and hedgerows. On a distant knoll sat the hulking stone ruin of a castle.

Tim continued. "Some of those ruins Nan can point to as homes of her grandfathers passed. Being in the northwest corner of the Republic of Ireland means this area is sandwiched between ocean cliffs to the west and the border to Northern Ireland to the east."

Her interest perked up. "I've been so focused on my job, I didn't really give a lot of thought to what was around me. How close are we to the border?"

"Only a few kilometers at best. It's another reason few people make this forsaken corner their home and even fewer come to visit," he said, looking at Jessica from the corner of his eye. "You being here is a bit out of the ordinary. I'm sure people will be askin' about you around town if they haven't already."

"That's why Nan keeps people away?"

"She's just doin' her job."

"Michael trusts her?"

Tim looked at Jessica with an expression that made her feel embarrassed and vulnerable. She didn't like those feelings at all. "Aye," he said. "He does at that."

"And, um, your fathers were, um, friends?"

"*Colleagues.*"

"So, how—?"

Tim slowed the truck and looked at her. "You need to get used to things here. The whole island is like one small town, and most of us don't pay attention to borders. We all know one another. We're all connected. You can't cry on a stranger's shoulder in a pub on Saturday without hearing about it from your Great Aunt Bessie at church on Sunday. Michael's father was a powerful man who fought hard for all the people of Ireland, and he was loved by many. My father worshipped him and gave his life for him."

Jessica sat, stunned. "And you and Michael were friends?"

"My father worked for his father. I was born into his service, and there is no greater honor. There's hardly a person in Ireland who doesn't recognize your face or what you did to destroy Magnus."

She drew in her breath in shock and fear. "I . . . I didn't destroy him. H-he was—"

"You asked me a question, and I answered it. People here believe Magnus took the fall for the murder you were framed for."

"He was an influential man with powerful friends. That's why I ran."

He put his hand up as if on cue to stop her explanations. "Your story is famous enough, but people loved him and were shocked when he was undone by you. Maybe you can understand why you're holed away in that cottage." Tim was different. More assured. His movements and words were more fluid. It was as if he stepped into a role to play. She wasn't sure if she liked it.

She let the silence speak for her as they bounced over the roads, occasionally uttering squeaks of fright at moments when they rounded corners at speeds she felt excessive for the narrow lanes. Tim merely smiled at her reaction. Each blind corner held its own kind of challenge, and she gripped the door with her left hand and placed her right on the dashboard. Everything was opposite where it should have been. Reluctantly, she admitted to herself that Nan was right. She would need more than a bit of practice to be not a hazard to everyone else on the road.

A metal gate blocked the road. He stopped the truck, clamored out, opened the gate, got back in the truck, drove it through, climbed back out of the truck, closed the gate, and finally settled back in the truck to continue their drive. "It's not really a shortcut, but it's a pretty drive."

Jessica chuckled and welcomed a change in conversation. "What about them?" she asked, pointing to two black and white border collies herding sheep from one pasture to the next in front of them. A rolling sea of white woolly backs with sprayed dots of pink approached the gate.

Tim waved at a farmer wearing oversized green and mud-caked Wellies. He leaned on a walking staff with one arm and cradled a rifle in the other. "That's just sheep and old man O'Malley. Sheep are stupid and will blindly follow whatever stubbed tail is in front of their noses. That's why it's so easy for the collies to herd them. The dogs target the leader. Once the leaders are in check, the rest follow."

Jessica heard three short, shrill whistles. The dogs took off at a run so fast their bodies looked like flattened dashes streaking across the field. Two more whistles and the dogs abruptly turned left, separated, and then began to run an invisible course back and forth, funneling the sheep through the gate.

She smiled. "Pretty impressive. Can your dogs do that?"

"Wolfhounds are different. They ache to obey, but they're not born with smarts like a border collie. They're not quick to the mark, but none could ask more of their loyalty."

One long whistle and the dogs returned to the farmer's side. She nodded in his direction. "What about him? Why the rifle?"

"He knows better than anyone that all manner of spirit can come and go as they please."

She eyed the gun, a stark contrast to the image of a welcoming farmer. "Really? Doesn't look it."

"He's just protecting his sheep from hungry wolves."

"Wolves? In Ireland?"

He looked at the sun hitting her blonde hair with an expression of mild fascination. "There are all manner of wolves and spirits in Ireland. I'm surprised you haven't heard. In fact, I've been hearin' from the locals that a *banshee* is back."

"Banshee? I used to have a pony by that name. I hear the word's Irish for ghost."

"A little pony named Banshee?" In a perfectly choreographed move, Tim slapped his knee with laughter as they resumed their ride down the rutted road, unexpectedly causing the truck to veer off the track. The unthinking reflex that would have corrected the minor error evaded him. For a flash of a second too long, he froze, looking at some undefined point in front of them. Not a muscle moved. Then his head gave a slight jerk, and his eyes refocused.

He gripped the steering wheel with two hands and worked it back and forth, trying to right their course. His face moved in a series of subtle flickers, cheeks hitching up to his eyes on some, mouth drooping on others. Once they were back on course, he continued as if nothing happened. "That's fitting! The word is from the Gaelic *bean sidhe* meaning 'fairy woman.' The locals are swearin' one is back and haunting the hills."

"Oh?" she said, trying to sound indifferent. Tim projected neither embarrassment nor concern at his near accident, seamlessly resuming their conversation like a needle skipping across a record. She watched him with more interest.

He continued talking, slipping back into the comfortable topic. "Aye, indeed. We Irish believe that this fairy woman begins to wail when someone is about to die. She's a messenger of death, that one, and your neighbors are none too pleased that she's dashing about the hedgerows in the early mornings."

Jessica cocked her head, intrigued. "What exactly did you hear?"

"Well, now," he declaimed, relishing the tale. "About a week or so ago, not long after sunrise, old man O'Malley heard the most mournful wail. When he went outside, he saw the mists spill down from the top of the hill, then float across the fields, gathering speed. He was lookin' into the sun, but O'Malley swears he saw a woman riding on a ghost horse, floating through the hedgerows as if they weren't even there. Scared the bits right out of the good man."

The corners of her mouth tucked in as she tried not to smile. "Is a banshee ever associated with a living person?"

"What's that you say? You mean does she attach herself to a person instead of a place?"

"Something like that, yes."

"Well now, come to think of it, she does. The spirit follows the person who's to die or their loved ones as a warning."

"And if someone knew a banshee was about, would they stay away?"

"No question about it. Old man O'Malley would have sprinted to Bishop's Cathedral quicker than scat if he wasn't sportin' just boxers." The pitch-perfect laugh landed on cue. "For all the living that man has done, it was the first time he swears he saw her."

"Do you believe he saw something?"

Tim's eyes unfocused as he thought. "I've no reason to question the man. If he was in his cups the night before, he'd be howling at the moon and not seeing banshees about."

"Are you so sure about that? Maybe he got confused. Nan said the locals were talking about seeing me in town."

"I'll bet she said that to keep you under her thumb. She doesn't like it when she can't control someone."

She shrugged. "She wants people to keep away from me. Maybe I can help her by scaring them away."

Tim's face widened with unchecked glee. "They shouldn't be waggin' on about an American. She should skitter them away with tales of a ghost."

Jessica finally let her smile pull free. "That's right! Then you tell your old man O'Malley and anyone else who will listen that I saw and heard a banshee, too, over on that hill over there, by the stone circle," she said, pointing.

He slowed to a stop and looked to where she was pointing. His head cocked to one side. "What's that you say now? Are you foolin' with me or did something happen?"

"I was out riding Planxty early one morning. Something startled us, and I couldn't get back to the barn fast enough. I rode the fastest, most direct line and must have passed within a few yards of him."

Tim straightened up in his seat and listened with greater attention. Every bit of his body seemed to be dedicated to listening and understanding each word she spoke. The muscles of his cheek fluttered just beneath the surface of his skin. Seconds went by before he said, "I'm familiar with that land. If you're telling me that you're the banshee O'Malley saw, then you rode over country that would've mucked all but the best horse and rider." He spoke slowly, measuring out each word. In an older person, Tim's actions would have been evidence of an aged brain no longer able to process information at lightning speed.

The pause between new information in and response out was longer than typically needed for easy conversation, but Tim was in the prime of his life. The gaps filled with twitches were disconcerting. The bouts of silence even more so. Some episodes lasted a mere flash of a moment. Others longer. His expression was blank as the gears in his brain ground into place. The time to process was how Erin's injured brain lagged between input and reaction, sometimes producing storms of involuntary movements. Jessica wondered if they shared a cause.

He had stopped the truck in a dell surrounded by hills. Wind through the open windows had blown Jessica's hair out of its loose ponytail. Loose strands fell across her face. A movement in his eyes was the first indication that he was back in the present moment with her. His pupils enlarged as they looked at a point just over her head. A nervous smile touched the corners of his mouth as he reached up. He stopped himself before pulling at a strand of her hair.

The bawls of the sheep and blasts from the whistle faded. His body made a barely perceptible move toward her. She pulled her head away and angled her body to look out the window. Her body language was clear. Don't touch.

His mouth stretched back, flashing his white even teeth, and his tongue curled around his lips like a hungry man when presented with a meal. Calculations mulled behind his eyes. "When Kilkea's owner agreed to try you out as its trainer, it was to see whether the horse could ever compete again. I assured him Kilkea would." He leaned closer to her in the seat. "You said it yourself. The horse will fly when it trusts its pilot. You should ride Kilkea in the race. That way you're assured of his safety."

Tim's ambition didn't sway her. "No. I'm not qualified to ride a race like that, and he's not ready."

"I've seen you ride, and Kilkea is in better condition than he has ever been."

"He might not be able to move beyond his trauma."

"And how are you supposed to know that?" Tim asked in a tone dangerously close to mocking. "Do you have the horse lay upon a wee little couch to hear him say, 'Okay, Doctor Jessica, I've put the trauma in perspective. I'm ready to jump again.'?"

His brazen disrespect made her laugh. He grinned back, happy she enjoyed his humor. He used the moment to lean closer. She pressed herself against the truck door. "After what you've said about his past, a rider can never really be sure the horse can ever perform without fear. When I say he'll never compete at an international level again, I mean that a rider will never be sure how far to push him or what his breaking point would be. Every horse has its button that can't be pushed. It would be different if he were in the ring by himself competing over fences, like in a Grand Prix, but he's too hot-wired for a civilized show circuit. In a steeplechase, he's in the middle of a mad crush of horses and riders. He knows what will happen because it happened before. A stumble by him could be the first domino in a fatal series of falls for horse and rider. He's experienced that hell. With that memory it's doubtful I could ever clear him for that level of competition."

"I saw you with him myself. He's jumping bigger and better than he ever has, and I told his owner so."

"I just told you!" A crisp edge to her voice ensured she'd be understood. "Performing solo on a course is vastly different than riding in a pack. Just because he's jumping big does not mean he's fit."

"He's fit enough for his owner."

"This is crazy. He would be a hazard to himself and others on the course. He needs time to put it behind him and to develop trust in his rider again."

"How much time does he need?"

Jessica could not believe what she was hearing. "Time? It could be weeks. Months," she said with emphasis. "It could be never."

"What can you do in a month?"

"I can recondition his muscles, not his attitude."

Tim put his hand on her thigh and gave it a squeeze. The hunger returned to his eyes. "You just confirmed everything I've ever heard about you." He moved his hand slightly upward. "Kilkea has his heart in it. You can feel it. You're incredible with animals. The way they respond to you. The way they know what you want. You know you want this." He began to pull himself toward her.

She saw the tattoo as she pushed his hand off her thigh. The meaning too frightening to mistake. The first time she saw the symbol of the Charity was on the arm of the man who murdered Gus Adams. Her life came to a sudden and severe halt that night. She remembered the cold-blooded assassin as he sliced open Gus' belly with a blade sharper than any she had ever seen. Magnus was there, watching the killing with detached interest, like a manager would watch workers load freight at a dock. Seeing the tattoo triggered something inside of her and panic rose. The Charity was something she had learned to fear and detest, but now it surrounded her in a cloak of protection. She didn't have time to think. If this was protection, she wanted no part of it.

She pushed her arms against his chest.

Instead of backing off, he bent forward, pressing his hand down on her leg. It was hot, and she felt his breath on her skin. He moved his body to close the gap between them. Her thoughts raced. Was he serious? Did he actually believe he could make a move on her and think she would accept it? Her heart beat harder in her chest. She turned her head and was surprised to see him looking directly into her eyes—not off to the side or out the window as he usually did—but directly at her. They didn't carry a question of more, only the certainty this was what he wanted. In the green shimmered something unreadable, sending a shiver of warning down her spine. He pulled her mouth to his, trying to claim her. He kissed her mouth, her face and moved down her neck.

"Tim. Don't." She was breathless, shocked at his advance. She tried to squirm away.

His hands moved over her, gripping her. Running over her jeans. Smoothing over her shirt. Feeling her. Letting himself build.

"Please. Stop." His mouth was over hers. Stopping her from talking. His tongue tried to work through her clenched teeth and ran over her lips. She gasped again, hardly able to breathe. He seemed emboldened by it. She took both her arms and pushed him away as hard as she could. He wouldn't be denied and reached for her again.

"Stop it!" she screamed and slapped him as hard as she could, but the door hindered her movement. She tried to scream again, but he had his mouth on hers, stopping any sound from escaping. He was all power. No hint remained of the contrite and awkward man of a few days ago. He took her hands and tried to pin them against the seat, all the while his mouth was kissing. Exploring. She twisted her body away from him, freeing one hand. Finally, she fumbled with the door handle. The door flew open, and she tumbled out of the truck.

"STOP IT," she yelled.

Tim jumped out and stood in front of her, the expression on his face unchanged, eyes clouded and assessing. His heavy breathing steadied as he stood stock still. Slowly, his hands wrung together, and his face seemed to melt as his emotions surfaced. "Ah! Jesus!" he cried. "What have I done? I'm so sorry." His distress built by the moment. "I . . . I thought you wanted that. Well, you were supposed to—"

"No." Jessica wiped her mouth against her shoulder, not taking her eyes off him.

Tim changed. The practiced and calculated actions dissolved. It was as if she was seeing a raw version of the rehearsed man. He shook his head from side to side. "I'm so, so sorry. It was all my mistake," he said, alternating wringing his hands then flapping them as if he was shaking them dry. His voice increased its crescendo, matching the distraught motions. He shuffled his weight from foot to foot, upper body rocking slightly as he tapped. The confident man completely dissolved. It was a perfectly orchestrated counterpoint. "Please don't tell anyone. It won't ever happen again."

The dogs took the opportunity to jump out of the truck and sniff about the field. Tim made a slight ticking sound with his tongue accompanied by a flicked hand gesture. They returned to his side and sat down, eyes on his face, tongues hanging from their mouths, waiting for the next command.

Jessica scanned the hillsides and got her bearings. Old man O'Malley walked slowly up a distant hill, oblivious to them but within earshot if she screamed. She hoped the gun was loaded with buckshot.

"I'm going to walk the rest of the way. Let me be clear, I don't want you around me. Ever. Keep away from me."

She turned on her heel and strode up the hill. At the top, she saw the cottage barely half a mile away and heard Tim's truck bouncing its way out of the field and back to the road. The short walk gave her time to cool her fury and collect her thoughts. Something was definitely off with Tim, but that was no excuse. It was easy to be angry with him, but she was even more so at herself. She questioned her every move and what she was doing or not doing to keep herself safe and decided she was doing a terrible job at it.

Once back inside, she pressed her back against the door and heard the satisfying click as the lock secured into place. She paced back and forth in the kitchen, rubbing her hands up and down her arms. Needing something to do, she searched the cupboards for coffee and reluctantly put the kettle on for tea, happy that it would at least be hot and caffeinated. Out the window, she saw an empty space on the far side of the barn where Tim usually parked his truck.

"Asshole," she muttered.

The shrill whistle of the kettle made her jump. A mug of tea was not going to soothe her. She looked for something—*anything*—to take her mind off Tim. Injury or nature made him unreadable and impeded his abilities to read people, but the balance was he was almost telepathic with animals, a sign of a truly skilled trainer.

Something about how he acted was reminiscent of Erin, but he was in his own league. Whatever his deficit was, he still had the motor and mental abilities to overcome what he could and mask the rest. She doubted it was from an injury, but some sort of mental challenge inhibited him. Stories occasionally filled the news of children harmed by vaccines or of a diagnosis of a spectrum disorder as an adult, but she had no way of knowing what was off with Tim, only that something was. As with Erin, she suspected the more Tim rehearsed and practiced an action, the more fluid the responses or words became.

A soft breath of air, like someone gently exhaling, drifted against the back of her neck. She brought her hand up and rubbed the feeling away, giving her shoulders an extra shake for insurance.

"I'm *alone* here!" she said aloud, needing, more than believing, it to be true.

Craving activity and something to keep her imagination in check, Jessica retrieved the box from the crawlspace, not caring or noticing the shambles she created in her rush. She unfolded the top flaps, closed her eyes and plunged her hand deep inside, like a child at a birthday party, searching for the best treat in a grab bag. Feeling around for the most satisfying find, she settled on a thick book. Hastily, she refolded the flaps over one another, and placed the box back under the eaves.

From the kitchen she grabbed a notepad and pencil and looked at the journal with a mix of curiosity and dread, not sure if she wanted the knowledge it contained.

Settled in the chair, her legs draped over one arm and back propped against the other. She centered herself in preparation for whatever she may learn by closing her eyes and letting memories wash over her. The hair on the back of her arms stood up as she traced the contours of Bridget's face, sharper than in any image. Bridget's body was so thin it seemed to cave in on itself. Her shoulders rounded from protecting her chest from the constant painful spasms of her coughs. Her skin seemed painfully thin, too white and papery not to tear with every movement. Jessica drew in a breath and shifted deeper into the cushions. The mug of tea and biscuit sat on the floor next to her, unwanted and untouched. A cup of coffee and a bagel would have been so much more satisfying.

A faded blue canvas cloth bound the inexpensive but sturdy book, and frayed threads wisped along the edges. The words *Diary 1950* were stamped deeply into the cover, the letters only slightly visible against the wear of hands and soil. No gold leaf ever graced the cover or pages. Happy with her diversion, Jessica opened it and stared at the words on the first page. Absently, she reached down, brought the mug of tea to her lips, sipped, and returned the mug to the floor all without moving her eyes.

The paper was unlined, but lines were hardly necessary, for the keeper of the journal had perfect handwriting. Some pages had been ripped out, their jagged remains a feathery reminder that a person's past is no more real than the memories they leave behind. The surviving pages were filled with impeccably formed script in neat, clean lines that did not gradually drift upward. A light, almost powdery scent mixed with the smells of old paper, dust, and ink. "This Journal Belongs to:" was printed in black ink from the printer's press, the only machine made letters in the entire book. Below it in the space provided, written in the faded and hued blue of a fountain pen, were painstakingly formed letters that created the words, *Bridget Heinchon.* Below that, large block numbers announced *1950.* One blue line crossed out the zero and the number five written in its place.

Slowly, Jessica turned the page and began to read.

25 July '55
6 eggs
Inniu thug mé míle maith agat.
One more day to Gean Cánach! It was miserable hot today. You could have boiled water on the tabletop in our little house if you'd had a mind for it. M, D, P and me finished up our chores for Ma and we gathered up the kids and dashed on down to the lough. They all scurried about with their cups and spoons and set about digging and making mud pies. M peeled her shoes off and hitched her skirt up to her knees. I thought I saw steam come off her legs! D ran in the water straightaway with a great splash that nearly toppled her over. Of course he told me that a proper girl did what M does—just dab herself with water. A proper lady would never JUMP IN! Then he proceeded to show me how to dab myself with water, as if I was taking lessons from him! That cheeky lad. It was worth my Ma's wrath just to see the look on his face when I walked, all nicely slow and ladylike, right into the water. I thought he and M were out to catch flies their mouths were open so wide. I was right about Ma. I got back home looking like a drowned sheep and she made me sweep out the missus' rooms, too.

Jessica hunted through other entries and decided that "M" was shorthand for "Meggie," "P" for Patrick, and "D" was for Daniel. She sat quietly and mulled over what she was learning. In 1955, Bridget would have been twenty-two years old and Margaret—who Jessica assumed was "Meggie"—would have been about twelve. Neither of them ever mentioned Patrick or Dan that Jessica could recall, and they hardly, if ever, spoke of their mother. Keeping track of eggs and knowing Gaelic were a surprise, too. Jessica began to feel as if her arms were missing and no one bothered to tell her until now. She kept reading.

26 July '55
7 eggs
Mé riamh ag iarraidh saoire seo go deireadh.
I'm up much too late but I can't sleep. Gean Cánach arrives in the morning! It was another miserable hot day. Ma was feeling well enough to sit with us by the lough, with the wee ones of some of the other ladies by her feet. We were all in good spirits and laughed at ourselves wondering what the little people were doing on a day like this! I kept Ma happy and only waded up to my shins, but I could see her look at me in her way. M and D walked along the edge and even from where I stood I could see the blush in her cheeks as she pretended not to look at the other lads. Ma would look at them and back at me, barely hearing what the missus was chattering on about. Ma knows. But she's waiting for the missus to say something first.
After supper we sat on the lawn for hours and waited until the sun went down. I listened to Ma and the missus sing some songs they knew from their men. I was so happy not to be back in our flat in the city as the heat was taking a terrible toll on Ma. The missus is an angel from Heaven to bring Ma here. Mr. Taggart heard that GC was due to arrive and delivered a basket of bread and a half leg of mutton! Imagine that!

27 July '55
8 eggs
An bhfuil sé indéanta go breá níos mó?
Gean Cánach is here! Blessed Jesus he is safe. I felt Ma's eyes on me all morning as I tidied up the camp. She knows, but I was trying to hide my excitement from her. As soon as he arrived and he did his greetings, we went to the lough along the wood path. He was as desperate to see me as I him and we made care to stand a distance apart even on the path. Ah! The sight and the smell of him made my knees weak. Once he stood so close to me that our hands touched and I watched his eyes close at the feel of it. He was right about Ma needing time away from the flats to get her color back and now he has a few days that he's to spend with his Ma and P and D. He told me all

about his work and the meetings I've missed. People are suffering something terrible. He told me about the eviction notices landed two days ago and the lines around the block at the community office inquiring for more flats and I told him I wanted to get back to Belfast today! Blessed GC, he told me that nothing is going to change overnight, that there'll be time enough for my help, but for these next few days he was here and he wanted to see me smiling. I was smiling enough when GC and the boys did their greetings. Our Mas were all about fixing a dinner for a king and laid it out by the lough. GC and D and P fit us with tears and our cheeks hurt from smiling when telling us how they would sneak out under their Ma's nose for a midnight dip. Blessed that my brothers are here and not stirring up trouble for themselves in the city. Both our Mas had their weights lifted. I was with my GC. M, D, P. All were happy with food and folly. Aye. Life was fine today.

As Jessica read, a new picture emerged of her mother. Bridget was well into the age when most women married, but it sounded like she was almost too busy with her own home life, caring for the details because her own mother could not. Jessica's grandma did not sound well. Other entries mentioned Ballymurphy and Belfast, names she had never associated with her mother or aunt and had no idea what the meetings were that seemed so important. Bridget was more than a little in love with *Gean Cánach*, 'GC', whoever that was. Jessica got an insight into the answers as she continued to read the diary. Interspersed with talks of egg counts and lazy summer days at the lake, Jessica read other passages to piece together why a beautiful young woman would not be married to the man of her dreams when they were obviously crazy about one another.

Flipping through the pages, she discovered the journal had a shallow pocket built into the back cover. Looking more carefully, this pocket hid its contents from the eyes of any casual onlooker. The glue, yellow and brittle, caused a fissure to open by the spine. Jessica gently felt around the flap and pulled out several neatly folded letters. The handwriting did not match Bridget's. It was a man's writing, larger and bolder. The paper felt as thin as tissue paper but was stronger somehow. Not even the handwriting had ripped it.

She opened each one. Each had the same writing. Each looked as if it had been opened and read many times before, refolded with great care, and replaced in its secret spot. She was dismayed to read the Gaelic words and she admit couldn't understand one.

What was the most intriguing and gave her heart a quick zap was that each was signed, *"Gach mo ghrá go deo."* The name beneath always smudged into oblivion.

AUGUST 1957
LOUGH NEAGH
AGHALEE, NORTHERN IRELAND

STRAY BARS OF music floated up from the cottages along the shore and mixed with late afternoon laughter from musicians and workers, mothers and fathers, children and grandparents who could not resist its pull. The ale had already begun to flow. Soon, a steady stream of dancers would gather for the reel, thumping to tempos set by the fiddles and fifes. No one ever cared a fig if they could keep perfect time. Tonight, as in countless celebrations, men would drink and girls would blush at words spoken on the torrent of it.

The night promised to be clear.

After weeks of rain, the gathering had no cause for celebration other than a release from the damp, dark weather they had endured for weeks. Most of the men had come up to the lough to escape the crowded, dirty conditions of their flats in Belfast. Everyone brought what they could, knowing that a loaf of bread, jug of hard cider, or growler of ale would be joined by other offerings to create a small feast.

The revelry started midday. Men sauntered to the cluster of cottages, rolled up their sleeves in the hot summer sun, and claimed a stump by the fire that would inevitably burn until the next day. Women only let go of their children's hands once they turned up the long dirt drive. The hedges would keep most wee lads and lasses from wandering too far, and the men would keep the rest in line. Women smiled and greeted one another with kisses and squeals, hitching their skirts above their knees for freedom from heat and movement, securing them in lopsided bustles with apron strings and twine.

Bridget Heinchon ran up to one woman who struggled with a heavy pottery jug of cider and large basket of food. The summer sun had bleached the color from Bridget's thick hair, leaving a straw-hued rope secured in an easy braid at the nape of her neck. Loose strands were absently swept behind her ear. Cotton pant legs rolled to mid-calf, and her blouse cinched with a knot at her waist. The day's heat and excitement of the growing gathering brought a flush to her cheeks. She hoisted the jug onto her hip with one arm and embraced her dearest friend with the other. "Mary! I've not seen you in ages! Here, let me help you with that," she said, settling the jug on her side.

Mary Breen kissed her friend and exhaled with relief from a burden that once again Bridget would help bear. "I've been here, working in the laundry, love! I've not been flittin' back and forth to the big city like yourself."

"How is Crissy? And Davies?" Bridget asked, breathless and impatient to catch up, "You have to tell me all."

Mary stretched her back, caught the eye of another friend and waved, answering Bridget in the shorthand reserved for the closest of friends. "Crissy's yearning for a man would make a whore blush, and Davies' no wiser for his time at Maghaberry. Dreadful place, that is. He's soon to be out. A sane person would never risk it twice, but he'll be back in soon enough. His ma's been asking me for grandchildren. Now, how can I do that with her son sleeping in a cell's bunk instead of his wife's bed?" Mary shook her head and pursed her lips in disbelief. "Count my blessings, I should. I don't see how other wives manage their broods without the help of their husbands. I couldn't. I just couldn't."

Bridget laughed and put her arm around Mary's shoulder, giving her a kiss and trying to lighten her mood. "What are we to do with our men? They take too much time to train and then they either get themselves locked back up or taken away by the cause, just in time to miss changin' the nappies!"

Mary shared her friend's laugher, but her eyes betrayed their pain.

Bridget continued, "Lots of folks are coming by the church for help. We try to find them steady jobs, but the only hiring is for day jobbers. It's hard to feed a family when the money comes in spits and spurts. We give to all who ask, but it's never enough to cure their hunger."

"Are you dealing with the men, too?"

"I find my sympathies run with the women. They hide their frustration by keeping their homes and their children in order as best they can. The men handle it with anger and by making plans for revenge. If that doesn't work, they drink. I keep hoping for a miracle."

"I heard your brother Patrick was almost nicked by the RUC again," Mary said as she scanned the growing gathering. "He went to get his old job back at Geary's Grocery. Ol' man Taggart wouldn't even look at 'im. Said Patrick let Geary's down by getting 'imself locked up the first time.

Imagine that! He went so far to say that Patrick brought disruption and despair to Geary's by bringing his papist friends around."

Bridget shook her head, trying to keep her anger in check. "Old man Taggart needs to get his brain out of his arse. Patrick's been helping at Geary's since he was a wee tot, sweeping around the store and lugging anything that needed lugging. He kept that store afloat. Now Taggart won't talk to him? That's nothing to do with where he bends his knees to pray, that's got to do with the damned English tryin' to get us 'papists' to move out of town and havin' the RUC do their biddin'," she said, nearly spitting the words from of her mouth.

Mary barely raised an eyebrow at Bridget's colorful tirade. Instead, she gave a discrete nod in the direction of a group of men piling logs and bits of odd lumber for the night's bonfire. She smiled. "I suggest you unscrew your face and put a smile on. Gus Adams and Kavan Hughes are here and looking in this direction."

A slight flush crept up Bridget's cheeks. She tried hard not to look toward the men. "Stop it, now. I've lots of friends."

"You do at that, but none make you blush like a rose. They're as busy lookin' for you as you're busy trying not to look." Mary grabbed a basket of crisps and held it out to Bridget. "Here. Those men look hungry. And I'd bet they'd like some food, too."

"Och! Shame on you!" Bridget smoothed another wayward strand behind her ear and lowered her chin. "Well, it wouldn't be right not to give them a greeting." She gave her own cheeks a quick pinch for extra color and looked at her friend with a question. "Ready?"

"You're as ready as ever, Miss Heinchon. Now go over and score yourself a man. Most women hardly find one, and you've got two to choose from." Mary leaned over and gave Bridget one last spit and polish, brushing a few stray crumbs off Bridget's blouse. "I'd say the deacon doesn't stand a fightin' chance."

Bridget scoffed. "I'm too old for all your nonsense. If Deacon Kavan Hughes was going to succumb to any woman's charms, he would have done so before he became an ordinand. Besides, I'm suspecting ol' man Taggart might be giving me the gleam nowadays."

"You're wrong. Kavan's always pined for you, just never could find the nerve to ask you."

"And you want me to flirt with the devil as well?"

"He's not ordained yet, and he's a man."

"Never," Bridget said forcefully. "He's begun his vows. He's a man, certainly, but a man of his word. He's made his choice—and it's not me."

Mary gave her friend a quick hug and kiss on the cheek. "Oh, Bridgie. Don't despair."

"I'm not despairin', Mary. I know what a love for others feels like. I understand him."

"Besides, he's not the only man there hoping to see you."

Bridget looked over at the group of men and caught the motion of one head darting down. "You mean Gus?"

Mary gave Bridget a crooked smile. "The same."

Bridget steadied herself on Mary's arm while she gave a forced laugh. "Gus Adams? He and his brothers have been a pestering thorn in my side since our mams placed us in nappies! Gus is more fly paper on my shoe than a skitter to my heart."

"Bridgie! Stop your lies! He's kind and steadfast. You and he have spent many summer nights by the lough. Don't look so surprised!" She wagged a disapproving finger in Bridget's face. "The two of you have long been sweet on one another."

"Aye," Bridget said, voice trailing off as she got lost in her memories. "We have at that."

"He's never let you down. Anyone can see he's been waiting for you."

"Gus. Sweet Gussie Adams," she said, color deepening in her cheeks.

"I've heard he's got a good job as a barn manager and head trainer at a thoroughbred farm in County Fermanagh. He's ready and waiting for you."

"He's been a brother and a father to me. But anything more than that?" she questioned, giving an exaggerated shudder. "It feels wrong somehow. Just too close."

Mary narrowed her eyes. "You're not foolin' me, Miss Heinchon."

"Gus and Kavan are best friends. What would either of them do if I let it be known I chose one over the other?"

"You think too much. Stop thinking and start living. Give 'em some crisps and a smile. I'm bettin' you'll have a great evening."

"You think crisps will do the trick, do you?"

"Bridget Elizabeth Heinchon," Mary said in mocked reprimand. "You've got to let yourself have a life. Your brothers are off on their own gettin' into God knows what mischief. Your sister is nearly fifteen and a young woman for sure. Your mother and father, God rest their souls, have gone to their maker. You've been a good daughter and done what you should by raising your mother's brood as your own. It's your time now, my lovely friend. It's time you begin to live a life for yourself. Get married. Have a family."

"*Married!*" Bridget spat out the word. "I've told you I'll never marry and I meant it. Look at what my ma went through. She never would have had the brood she did if she could have rid herself of my pa. He was a drunk and a louse, but my ma did what she thought a good girl did and married the first man who asked. She married into a living hell."

"Not every man is bad."

"Still, I'm not the marryin' type. I don't want to give up my life for someone else."

"*Give up* your life? You're too busy with your organizin' and your meetin's and all for the benefit of people you hardly know. Findin' housing and food and jobs for anyone who asks. Start living your life for *you* and not others. You're entitled."

"How can I stop living my life for others? Yes, I've helped my ma, but that hasn't stopped me from living my life. I can't stop what I'm doing when people are hungry around me. You've helped. You've seen the look in their eyes when we've found flats in Ballymurphy and a job or two for desperate folks."

Mary wrinkled her face in disgust. "The loyalists're so bloody scared that we're goin' to take a job or use our holy water to drown them all."

"It's not their jobs they're afraid of. Those idiots are sayin' they want to forge a 'national identity' of one people in Northern Ireland. You know, when they plowed down the row of estates and built us those concrete blocks of buildings, they said they were doin' us a favor. Mark my words, Mary, that place is like a boilin' pot with the lid on too tight. You can't have people livin' on top o' one another like that without jobs or hopes and expect things to end well."

"They believe puttin' us in concrete flats like sardines is going to make us feel like this is our country, too?"

Bridget shook her head, feeling energized by the conversation. She lowered her voice and brought her mouth closer to Mary's ear. "I was at a meetin' last week. There's a strong river of courage running through our people. There's folks, the nationalists, who are finding those who want a unified Ireland, one nation. They're building strength to get the British out of our knickers."

"Folks? You mean Gus and his brothers."

"Yes. Gus," she said, eyes darting to the side, "and the others."

Mary tried to hide her concern as she looked around to see who could be listening. "Shhh. As soon as your ma's brood was out of nappies you started with the meetings. No self-respecting girl would go to the organizer meetin's, but you did. Leave the organizing to Kavan and the details to Gus. Kavan can do even more when he gets behind the altar, and Gus has access to the means to get the things done. You've done an amazing job, now enough's enough!"

"The cause is more important to me than runnin' after babes or waitin' at home for something to happen. I can't stop now." Bridget lowered her voice. "Your sweet Davies got his arse locked up for organizing a march down Shankill road to keep the St. John's parish school open and teaching Gaelic. You said it yourself. It's only a matter of time before he risks his freedom again for us."

"Bridgie," Mary said with her voice wavering, "I . . . I don't think I could last a minute more if anything happened to him. If . . . if he had to spend more time in Maghaberry. If. . ."

Bridget rested her hand against Mary's cheek. "Ah, my friend. You'll soon be done with your time as a prison widow, and you'll have those children you yearn for."

"Och, I can only hope."

"It will happen. I pray to our Virgin Mother herself. Have faith."

Mary swallowed away the growing lump in her throat. She forced a smile onto her face. With one eyebrow cocked, she poked Bridget in the arm. "At least I've a husband and tasted the sweets of marriage."

"You don't need the confines of marriage to taste its sweets."

"Bridgie!" Mary's cheeks flushed scarlet. She quickly touched the sign of the cross over her body for protection. "I'm worn to the nib prayin' for my country and husband. Now I have to add your virtue to my list. You will not inch one more year closer to spinsterhood. Go on. Get a move on."

Bridget lifted her chin in defiance of her friend's words and gave her a kiss on the forehead. "I'd say my virtue was past the point of prayer." She grabbed the basket and sauntered through the crowd.

The clearing was crowded with men, women, and children. Clusters of children scampered up the rocky shore and jumped off into the cold waters of the lake. The most daring of them challenged the older boys to swim out to the oddly-shaped, but not too distant, rocky island and back. Older women sat around husking corn and peeling potatoes, the youngest children sat at their knees playing happily with flat sticks, a rusty tin cup, and a bent stub of a spoon. Younger mothers idly chatted while they helped adorn lopsided mounds of sand with bits of moss and leaves, lifting their faces to catch the lengthening rays of the day's sun. Blue sky and rounded green hills reflected off the still, deep waters. Teenage boys strung a long rope over a leaning tree and swung each other ever higher over the water, mugging fright and bravery as they plunged into the lake, daring the girls to try but happy they would watch.

By the time Bridget made her way closer to the men, a few notes from fiddles and guitars floated as instruments were tuned and readied. Her basket of crisps was almost emptied, but she had schemed to have a few left to make a polite offer when she reached them. The men wore variations of the same theme: loosely woven cotton or linen shirts, light wool trousers. Some wore belts and others suspenders, but all had their shirtsleeves rolled up, exposing pale and freckled forearms. Bridget kept her eyes down as she waited.

Finally, she recognized the well-muscled forearm reach into the basket. "Miss Heinchon's crisps. None finer in all of Belfast and Lough Neagh."

Bridget willed the color not to rise in her cheeks. "Father Hughes. The fuss you make over a few thin-sliced potatoes and salt. One would think you're daft."

A flash of perfect teeth and a gaze from pale blue eyes that gave her goose flesh met her remark. "I'm not 'Father' yet, Miss Heinchon. And it's not the crisps that make me daft."

Deep color rushed to her cheeks, and she noticed the other men tightening their circle, forcing Bridget to stand even closer. "Careful there, Father, or even the Pope himself will not be able to wash away your sins during your next confession."

The men roared with laughter, and Gus stepped up and ushered Bridget to the side, handing her an apple with a theatrical flourish. His head was a mass of dark curls, and his blue eyes flashed with mischief. "But one has to be able to see the action as wicked before it can be called a sin. Perhaps a bite of this will help you see *Father* Hughes more clearly."

Bridget grabbed the apple, circled its rosy skin with her tongue, and took a noisy bite. Staring Gus directly in the eye, she wiped her mouth with the back of her hand, using the silence of the stunned men to her advantage as she slowly chewed. "I think I have a pretty good view on things, don't you, Mr. Adams?"

"Ah, Ireland's Eve."

"And who'd be the serpent, Mr. Adams?" she asked, looking him up and down.

"I'd like to hear who you believe the serpent is, too, Gus," said Kavan, with a questioning look. "After all, we need to know who to thank when this young woman finally succumbs to temptation."

The two friends burst into laughter. "Oh, to be able to listen in to the confessions on a Monday morning after a weekend such as this! If I give you absolution, will you promise to tell me a few?" Gus asked, throwing his arm around his friend's shoulder. Kavan hooted and roughed up Gus' curly hair, using the motion to put him in a headlock.

In a pantomime acted out hundreds of times in their lives, the two friends mock wrestled, each exaggerating knockouts and recoveries with rolling eyes and daffy expressions. If a real competition existed between them, they hid it with chest thumps and arm flexing. The larger group roared with good-natured laughter, the *craic* of the moment high. Smiles only grew when Gus stumbled over a root and fell backward. Still laughing, he extended a hand up to Kavan for a hoist up. Kavan turned his back and shook his clasped fists over each of his shoulders in feigned victory. A renewed roar of laughter met the motion.

Before anyone could start another conversation, a line of dancers looking for fresh partners entered the group and swept Bridget away. Musicians followed, and they all quickly fell into step. She tried in vain to catch either Kavan's or Gus' eye with hope to pair with one or the other to dance. She caught a glimpse of Gus, standing with his brother. Gus' curly dark hair, rounded cheeks, and stocky frame stood in contrast to his younger brother's lanky build and bearded face. His posture told her they were deep in conversation, and she should wait until he found her for their banter to continue.

The next hours were some of the happiest in Bridget's life. For one night, bellies were full. Love and kindness flowed as freely as the pints of ale hoisted and shared. Music mixed with dance and laughter under the spell of the late summer evening.

Forgotten were the pangs of poverty and hunger. Forgotten were the jobs denied or forced evictions. Forgotten were the tongues silenced for speaking the truth. Young and old were determined to enjoy their summer night. Whatever waited for them when morning returned could wait a little longer.

The sun stayed high well into evening. By the time it set, exhaustion had extinguished the tantrums of little ones enough so that even stomping feet and loud voices could not disturb their peace. Old Lorries and sedans crept up the rutted path. Into their backseats and boots, mothers loaded children—limp and heavy—and baskets, empty for another day's feast.

Long after the faded purples of twilight blended into the night sky, long after the last of the trucks bounced back to the main road, Bridget laid naked and entwined once again in the arms of the only man she would love forever.

RAPHOE, IRELAND

"WELL IT'S ABOUT damned time."

Jessica, startled out of her thoughts, opened her eyes quickly, then squeezed them shut again, not believing what she saw. When she allowed herself another look, a smile grew on her lips.

"You should talk."

Jessica pulled the horse to a stop and swung down into Michael's waiting arms. She could feel his hands tangle in her hair as he kissed her cheeks and lips, arms encircling her, pulling her to him. She reached and ran her hands over his back, his hips. She inhaled his scent and felt his presence fill the tiny fissures that opened whenever they were apart. Neither was in a hurry for conversation. His energy seeped into her, and she could feel herself expand, replenished. Her mind cleared to see if she had imagined anything about him, to see if in their time apart she conjured something that wasn't true, if she created something impossible. He placed a line of kisses down to the hollow of her neck and up behind her ear. She was aware of his every movement and how each cell in her being responded and opened to him. Her response to him was immediate—and very real.

Michael took a step back and returned her smile with a sly grin, showing a southern gentleman's grace that could not quite wipe out his northern edge. He was slightly rumpled from his travels—black hair tousled, casual chinos and shirt no longer crisp, and a day's stubble shadowed his face. Everything about him was orchestrated to appear easy and relaxed, but his eyes gave him away.

"I've missed you," he said as he pressed his lips to the top of her head.

"You too." She buried her face into his shoulder, happy his familiar scent surrounded her. "Finally."

The hours she had spent thinking of him and the time they spent apart evaporated. It didn't matter to her that outsiders would judge their relationship as too new, untried, or ill-fated. With him, she shared the unspoken bond of the other half found. Instinct prevailed over logic. He knew her truths. She knew his lies. At least some of them.

He took the reins from her hand and gave the bay a quick rub on her neck. "She looks good."

"Just goes to show what time and patience will do." She shoved her hand into his back pocket as they walked to the barn. Another world immediately enveloped her and she felt complete with his presence. She picked up where they left off. "Thanks for the box of stuff. It's kept me busy even with you being gone for so long."

He was distracted by thoughts that had not completely arrived with him. "What? Oh, I'm sorry. I wanted to be here sooner, but, other matters—"

Jessica brought her mouth to his to stop him. Somehow, she knew she'd be hearing excuses and didn't want to start then and there. "Forget it. Quiet works for me," she said and continued walking to the barn.

Their shoulders just touched. The sound of the horse's hooves striking the packed earth and its breathing filled the air around them. The sated moments after a long day of training were blissful. Jessica lapsed into a contented quiet, no longer needing a steady stream of conversation. He cleared his throat and started to say something, stopped, and tried again. They had worked enough in the barn together to savor peaceful moments, but today he was agitated.

He broke the silence, speaking more to himself than to her. "There's a lot I need to bring you up to date on."

New details etched into his profile. Creases of worry edged his mouth and brow. His shoulders, broad with strength, rounded as if the world had settled on them. He was having trouble bearing the weight of it.

"Are you okay?"

The slight shift in his appearance could have been due to fatigue more than worry. Like her, he was a chameleon. He picked up cues from his environment and adapted to them without thinking. His colors gradually shifted from distracted to present. His eyes softened as he smoothed her hair behind her ear. "Right now? Yeah. Definitely." His energy made her weak with yearning. "I'm where I want to be."

She blushed slightly, more at her thoughts than his words, and placed the horse into crossties. Brushing out the saddle marks, she focused on what she had to do in that moment, not what she wanted to do.

They moved in an easy ballet of everyday tasks. He handed her an item before she asked. She brushed up against him before he moved toward her. Whether they were aware of this ease or not didn't matter. It just was.

Jessica kept her mind on her work until Michael stepped forward. He ran his hands under her shirt, fingers hot on her skin, and kissed her. The balance tipped and she responded, opening her mouth to his, exploring and tasting, then gently pulling his lower lip with her teeth.

"Oh, Miss Wyeth. The power you have."

Her expression said she would not be patient one minute longer, and she began to untuck his shirt. With one eyebrow cocked up, she dared him to say no and pulled their bodies closer while backing into a stall.

The door to the hayloft swung shut and clicked, and they looked up toward the sound. Michael's smile faded almost as soon as it appeared. Tim stood silhouetted against the light. It was unclear how long he had been standing there.

Jessica straightened her clothes, wary.

Michael helped smooth Jessica back together and took a deep breath, reluctant to have the moment end. "Tim!" he welcomed.

"Michael," Tim responded, in a greeting more formal than necessary for a reunion that had been waiting for years. He did not look at Michael, instead seemed to search for something on the ground.

"My God, man. How long has it been?" Michael asked with genuine enthusiasm.

Tim paused for a moment. "Twelve years, four months and five days." His eyes darted from Jessica to Michael and back to Jessica, lingering longer on her loosely buttoned shirt than necessary.

His response only added to the tension of his sudden appearance. Self-conscious, she fingered the front of her shirt closer to her neck. Michael walked up the barn corridor and grabbed Tim's hand in both of his. He pumped it and slapped Tim on the back, harder than seemed necessary for a greeting between friends.

"The last time I saw you was before I left for college. My uncle's been keeping me up on you."

"Uncle? Your uncle? Liam?" Tim sputtered. His cheeks reddened as he grew more animated. "He's been good to me. Good."

Michael forced a grin. "I'd guess he's been keeping you under his wing. He's told me you're doing well."

Tim's upper body pulsed slightly, in sync with his pounding heart. His eyes continued their constant flitting, from the stalls to the ceiling and to Jessica, never pausing for more than a moment.

She hated being in his presence and needed to leave. "I'll let you two catch up," and moved to go the cottage.

Michael stopped her, wrapping his arm around her waist and smiling at Tim at the same time. The motion instinctively proprietary. "The horses look good."

"Thank you. Thank you. Just like Nan said, she's good. She's good to have on the team here." He tapped his feet, together and apart. He looked everywhere, but his eyes kept falling back to Jessica. She bristled.

"The best," Michael replied, placing another light kiss on her head. He let his lips linger for another moment and looked back at Tim. "We'll talk tomorrow?"

Tim's rocking increased as he wrung his hands together, distressed. "She asked me not to come around the barn. It's the groom's day off. I was only gettin' a few things."

Michael looked at the stricken looks on both of their faces. "Alright then. We'll catch up tomorrow. In town?"

"Tomorrow is fine. I'll bed the animals for the night." He coughed, almost choking on his words and hurried past them.

Michael led Jessica out of the barn and retrieved a leather satchel and backpack from his BMW, the black coupe's gleaming lines and tinted windows out of place in the cottage's gravel drive. He swung his bags up in one easy motion, beeping the car locked as he went. He was silent as he approached the door, and paused long enough to run his fingers over the marking carved into the side of the house. He shrugged and pushed the door open with his back, tossing his bags through to the kitchen floor with an exhausted thump.

Once inside, Jessica followed him with her eyes as the habits of a sheriff kicked in. He walked around checking doors and looking out the windows, testing their sashes for strength. She waited until he was ready to talk. After what seemed to be a very long time, the sound of truck tires on gravel signaled that Tim had finally left.

Michael visibly relaxed and poured them each a glass of wine.

Jessica noticed the change. "Tim picked some great horses."

Michael shifted uncomfortably and handed her a glass. "I'm glad you feel that way. My uncle said he was one of the best."

"Hmm. He knows his stuff, but he's an asshole."

He suppressed a chuckle. "It's good you can keep your opinions to yourself. But, what was all that tension I felt from you in the barn?"

She recalled too vividly Tim's hands on her, how forceful he was, how his strength crumbled into unabashed tears. Tim's unreadable manner unnerved her, and she scoured her memories for anything she did that he may have misinterpreted as her attraction to him. His relationship with Michael was unknown territory. They were boyhood friends, and causing a rift between them was not something she wanted. His distraught apology seemed genuine, and she was confident she could handle the situation. Telling Michael would only complicate things. "He's full of himself," was all she said, but a distinctive edge creased her voice, and she couldn't hide the look of disgust as it rippled over her.

"I know you too well to accept that. It's not like you to dislike someone outright. What's up?"

Tim's behavior was unacceptable, but she had something more important to discuss. "I saw the tattoo." Her voice was flat, but her eyes rose to gauge his reaction.

Michael took their wine glasses and set them on the table. Leaning against it, he drew her to him, folding her arms up between them. "I should have said something. I'm sorry. It must have terrified you."

"I, um, I just wasn't prepared for it. It's a symbol I learned to hate. Having it around me and pretending everything is A-OK is confusing."

"He's trusted or he wouldn't be here."

Jessica rested her cheek on his chest, only slightly soothed by his words. "I have a job to do and not a lot of time to do it. I need his help but only want him here when someone else is around."

He looked puzzled. "I'm staying for a while, but is there something I'm missing?"

She weighed how much to say. How much mucking about did she want to risk? "He said your fathers were friends and that he's known you since you were boys. You know, buddies."

"I wouldn't call him a 'buddy' as much as a convenient playmate. His father was one of my father's men. On trips to Ireland, Tim and I would be thrust together while they conducted business. It's been years since I've seen him." When she remained quiet, he continued. "You're safe here. We've all taken great care to make sure it stays that way."

She nodded weakly. "Well, Nan's been tough to figure out, and that tattoo definitely threw me off. I guess I'd feel better about being surrounded by the Charity if I knew your uncle better." She hesitated. "How close was he to your father?"

"Liam was the only connection to family I had after my mother died, and I refused to communicate with my father. I'm closer to him than anyone."

Keeping a connection with family was something she understood and envied. Family helped shape and define you, even if estranged. In many ways, Michael was as adrift as she was. Becoming more familiar with Liam would give her insight into Michael. "Why doesn't he run the Charity? He's much more familiar with it than you are."

"I've asked him that. He flat out refuses. He says saying he's too old to take on an enterprise as sprawling as it's become. I have to agree with him. It's more than anything I imagined. Even Liam's been surprised at its breadth. He said he never worked intimately with Magnus because he never wanted to support violent groups. He didn't grasp how to stop it. A complete change in leadership makes sense.

With Magnus dead, the fissures in the organization are surfacing. Liam knows the players well enough to keep things together for a while. As for the money side, people who knew my father," his voice trailed off in search of the right words, "expect me to be like him. And what's worse is they expect me to know everything he knew. They want a seamless transition, but I just can't give them that. Magnus was old school. He kept everything in his head. When he died, the knowledge died with him."

"You're expected to be in control."

"Yes."

"And Liam expects you to lead like Magnus."

"I won't lead as ruthlessly as Magnus, that's for sure. But, yes, Liam expects me to take hold of an organization I barely know filled with people who are strangers to me. This transition would be hard even if I had been at my father's knee all these years—and I wasn't. I'm just as unknown to them as they are to me." He stopped talking and rummaged through the cupboards. Eventually he returned to the table with a plate filled with food left by Nan earlier in the day.

"The more I dig into the business, the more I find that it's a self-sustaining machine. All the pieces interconnect. I don't want to tip over one domino until I understand how it impacts the whole. I thought it would be easier."

"And now you're stuck."

"No. Not stuck. I feel like a lab rat thrown into the middle of a maze," he said, grimacing at the thought. He moved to look out the window. "Lots of turns but only one clear path."

Returning to the table, he stood while he took a sip of wine. Then he placed a slice of cheese and cold lamb on a crust of bread, using the actions to indicate he no longer wanted to talk about himself. He handed the food to her, then made another for himself. "I needed some time away. This is the perfect place to unplug."

"So I noticed. No phone. No newspapers. No computer."

"Computer?" he said with a small laugh. "I doubt they have Internet access this far into the country anyway. Ireland is coming along, but it lags behind the U.S."

The issue of being unreachable was different. She used the moment to ask something that had been bothering her. "Nan said you gave strict orders that I was not to have any outside communication. Is that true?"

He held a chair, motioned for her to sit, and sat down opposite her. "Not exactly. What I told her was to make sure no one came around the farm. I didn't want to take the chance that someone would recognize you and then run off to tell the whole town that they have a famous American in their midst. Besides, while I'm here, her responsibilities are less. She won't be around as much."

"I won't say I'm sad to hear that. It's worked out well enough. Without any distractions, I took some time to learn about my mother."

"I don't understand."

"I mean, what kid would question whether her parents really were her parents? All that stuff about where they were born and who they were never got answered for me. Any time I asked any questions they would wall over," she said, moving the palm of her hand across her expressionless face, "and I gave up trying after a while."

"So, now you're interested in learning about Bridget?"

"I sure as hell am," she said jabbing a knife into the hunk of cheese. "Both Margaret and Bridget were born in Ireland. They never talked about it, and I never asked. I was a typical kid thinking that her here-and-now was way more important than her that-was-then."

"What do you mean?"

"Margaret worked hard at being the perfect American suburban mom including losing the brogue and cultivating a Bostonian accent. She volunteered in my elementary school, worked on all of the right volunteer committees, and joined the right clubs. She was very private and seemed quite happy. She loved me with a fierceness that I marvel at when I look back."

"What's not to love?" he asked, trying to lighten her mood.

She softened. "I was a wild child from the start. I wasn't a good country club brat. I loved the barns over the clubhouse, ignoring the rules Margaret and Jim tried to have me live by. Pretty typical for a fledgling rebel. Up until the accident, Bridget had only visited once in a while and was completely unprepared to manage an unmanageable kid. She finally had to send me to private school and a couple of wilderness camps. I was really focused on what *I* wanted and what *I* needed. I could have given a hoot about a sick old widowed aunt."

"And that was Bridget?"

"She never told me she was my *mother*." The anger and confusion Jessica felt rose to the surface. Hunks of cheese littered the platter as she continued to stab away at them. "I can't even begin to wrap my head around why. She gave me away to be raised by her sister. I lived with Bridget for *ten years* after they were killed. She kept her mouth so tightly shut I never even questioned the crap story I was being fed."

"What did you think happened?"

Jessica gulped her wine and gathered her thoughts. "I had a sister named Erin, who was born with special needs, but she turned out to be my cousin that one of your father's goons hurt as an infant in order to keep everyone afraid and in line. I was so clueless I even thought the car accident was just an accident."

Michael stiffened into stone. Had Jessica been looking at him, she may have quelled. Instead, she stared at the growing pile of cheese and listened to his smooth tone. "It's hard, Jessica. I'm sorry. Just so damned sorry."

She shook her head in amazement. "I've been in a bubble here these past few of weeks, riding and thinking. I'm trying to settle into being the new me but I don't have all of the pieces to my puzzle yet."

"Then you're saying that I was right to leave you here alone while I tended to business?"

"For the most part," she answered playfully, evading bringing up Nan or Tim. "You were definitely smart to have me engrossed with horses and the papers. My mind has been off my troubles."

They turned the conversation to other topics and slipped into the uncomplicated ease of simply being with one another. The edges of the world blurred leaving only each other in focus. Learning that Michael had spent much of his childhood in Northern Ireland opened up a trove of hysterical stories about being a New England Yankee trying to figure out the culture and customs of the Irish. Then he stumbled through the culture shock of being a Yankee in Kentucky as he tried to conduct business on behalf of the schools he chartered. Laughter melded them together as one.

At nearly ten o'clock, the sun began to set behind the rolling hills. Jessica noticed the lines on Michael's face had sunk deeper with fatigue.

"You must be exhausted. It's later than I thought."

"It's nice now, but when you only have seven hours of daylight in the winter, you feel that these evenings are well earned."

"Still, there's something special about the night," she said. They cleared the dinner dishes and Michael came up behind her, brushed her hair aside and kissed her where her neck and shoulder curved together. He moved his hands down her shoulders and up under her shirt.

She let the plates clatter into the sink and turned to him.

The next morning Jessica woke to the sound of a heavy wind-driven rain pelting against the roof. Grateful for an excuse not to jump out of bed and rush to the barn, she pulled the comforter up over her shoulders and spooned her body closer to Michael's. Her skin warmed against his. She kissed his neck and face and ran her hands down his body. His breathing, deep and steady, didn't change. The lines on his face seemed less than last night. She decided not to wake him.

She padded into the kitchen, craving a strong cup of black coffee. Knowing none was available, she made a cup of tea and grabbed her notepad, filled with pages of handwritten notes. Every spare moment was spent culling over photographs and journals for solid facts---people, places and dates. At first, she settled into her chair, hugging a journal with anticipation of more stories of idyllic summers and first loves, but soon discovered stories that were at times surprising and other times simply heart wrenching.

Bridget Heinchon was the oldest sister of Patrick, Daniel, Eileen, and Margaret. Her father died when her mother was pregnant with Margaret. Bridget was nine years old. Very few journal pages survived from Bridget's early years. What remained told the story of a girl thrust into the role of mother when her own mother was not able to cope with the loss of her husband. 'Ma' sounded sickly and terrified to have to fend for herself and five children in the slums of Belfast. As soon as Patrick and Daniel were able, they were sent out to the streets to bring home anything they could. They were hungry and often had to be satisfied with a thin broth of cabbage soup. On occasion, the boys brought home a loaf of bread or a chicken, and Bridget knew never to ask where such delights came from.

Eileen was weak from birth and died of 'the failing' by the time she was five. This made her mother cling all that more fiercely to the surviving sisters and ignited in Bridget a fiercely protective urge to do all she could for her brothers and sister. Margaret was not one to be coddled but was afraid to reject any maternal love, regardless of how desperate it was. When she could, Bridget would take Margaret to their church where the discovery of a coin that missed the coffers was a joyous but secret event. Bridget would buy her siblings a sweet and make sure they ate it all before returning home so no trace of it could be detected, for if Ma thought money was close by, she would ransack pockets and scour corners until it was found.

Gradually, Bridget became aware that she was the power and glue behind her family unit. As Bridget became more competent in running the household, Ma grew more disconnected to the outside world and dependent on her daughters. The only allowable excuses Bridget could use to leave their cramped apartment were church and school. When Bridget was fourteen, her formal schooling—and that of all the Heinchon children—stopped abruptly. Not because her mother dictated it, but because the state stopped funding the Irish Catholic school she and her siblings attended. Reassignments of students to all-English secular schools was common, and their school's closure forced them to walk many blocks through Protestant neighborhoods. Stories of harassment and beatings were common. No child in the Heinchon home wanted to take that risk.

Tensions and resentments built. Protestant schools, flush with funding, said they were open to all children, but the Heinchons were not the only family to want an education that was Irish as well as Catholic. Families had difficulty adjusting to targeted restrictions. The school's closure was the catalyst of a major social shift. Churches did what they could to continue education within their parishes, but the city government forbade them from opening regular schools, leaving only Sundays open for formal educational activity. Bridget grabbed the opportunity. Normal school hours could not confine her drive to read, write, and understand the world around her to. As a young teen, Bridget's entries described the class she started in the church basement, teaching anyone who would come to read and write. She felt safe there and never considered what she was doing in any way unusual. When she wanted to do something, she did it. As Bridget matured, the church and the community offered her a refuge that she wrote about often. Surrounded by hardship, she read all she could on the disparate lives of Belfast citizens.

The journal brought to life a strong, vibrant intellectual who felt supremely trapped by her roles and responsibilities. Bridget wrote pages about the lack of a proper future for her brothers and herself. Her brothers scraped by as day jobbers for physical work despite top grades. University was out of the question for them. The best prospect for a Catholic woman in Belfast during the 1950's and 1960's—as domestic help in an upscale house—was hard to find and harder to keep—especially if rumors surfaced that her family's political leanings were not the same as the hiring household. Protestants and English sympathizers had the money, which meant Catholics needed to keep their mouths shut if they wanted to work. Any whiff that politics mattered jeopardized job prospects.

As she read, Jessica could hear Bridget's increasing grievances with a government that, at best, turned a blind eye to the systemic and pervasive shortage of jobs and food and, at worst, was the power behind it.

Most of Bridget's peers became wives and mothers before age twenty, and happiness often remained out of their reach. She wrote fondly of her best friend—referred to with simply the letters MB—and poured out her dissatisfaction for her lot in life and compassion for her. Passages in the journal told of friends, like MB, who battled with drunken husbands or abusive fathers, or coped with their absence due to work or jail. Since Bridget was thrust into the role of mother to her siblings, she always knew that getting married and becoming a housewife would never make her happy. Instead, she became an indispensable friend. As much as she doted on MB's children, she never pined for one of her own.

As far as Jessica could tell, Bridget's moments of joy were rare. Her worries lifted during long walks on the hillsides or when reading books borrowed from libraries or loaned by friends. She especially savored newspapers found discarded on park benches or discover in trash bins in front of the cathedral. The papers wrote obituaries, police reports, or current events. Bridget wrote about deaths of friends from hunger or illness and crimes born from desperation. Street names of Falls Road, Shankill, and Divis peppered the pages and were ones Jessica was familiar with from news reports in the States. She was intrigued that her mother walked those same streets, connecting Bridget to the Troubles in a way Jessica never fathomed.

Freedom was an idea that fascinated Bridget. As the eldest child, she was obliged to fill the voids left by the death of her father and her progressively ailing mother. The burden of keeping her family together and fed fell on her, and she refused to let their education be forfeited luxury. Neighbors in their crowded apartment building expected her to keep two increasingly wild brothers out of harm's way. Bridget did her best to corral them to mass on Sundays even as she railed against many church teachings. Her brothers knew better than to subscribe to biblical hierarchy that elevated the wants and needs of the man as head of the household over all others. Wasn't she the head of their home? What had her father given her mother aside from five children on top of who-knew-how-many other pregnancies? That was enough to be the head of a home? Nonsense. Her brothers yielded to her authority out of obedience and regard. No greater compliment could be given.

Jessica reflected on her growing knowledge with stunned fascination. Bridget's inner life was in turmoil. Outwardly, the girl grew into a young woman who performed her duties perfectly. Even as some looked upon her as a bit of an oddity for not being married, others appreciated her for all she did for her own family and, increasingly, her community. She was respected. She was a pillar of strength. Inwardly, Bridget Heinchon was a hellion.

Margaret was the center of Bridget's world, down to the extra tidbits of food saved for her. Bridget made sure her sister was educated in numbers and words, and Margaret thrived under Bridget's care. Proud note was made of a spelling bee won or a math test aced, though the reality that no more promise existed for Margaret's future than her own, almost brought Bridget to her breaking point.

When Margaret turned fifteen, Bridget took action. Through her church connections, Bridget determined that a governess job in the United States was Margaret's best hope for a future. With utmost secrecy, Bridget set about saving the pennies and pounds needed for passage. It took years; the needs of the family often required her to dip into her private funds. Journal pages were few and far between during this period, but Jessica could gather the threads. Bridget knew sending her sister abroad would destroy her mother, so she began preparations with painstaking stealth. The only person Bridget referred to as being aware of the scheme and supportive of it was *Gean Cánach*. She only brought Margaret into the preparations when they were too far along to be stopped, thwarting any protest that could be launched. Ma's death cleared the way.

Jessica looked through the other odds and ends and discovered a faded pink paper the consistency of an onion's skin. On it was scrawled the words *RMS Presidential* and *Margaret*. Heavy, thick lines underscored each word.

After several hours, Jessica had a list of dates and places but few names and details. She decided to pay Mrs. McDonnaugh a visit, but that would be after she paid Michael one.

She slipped under the covers and curled up close to him, chilled by the morning air. He stirred so she could rest her head on his shoulder. "You've been up?" he asked, not fully awake.

"For a little while. I was reading."

"It's dark."

"No. It's raining."

Michael pulled the covers over them, surrounding them in a cocoon of warmth. "A remote cottage, a rainy day and a beautiful, naked, woman beside me in bed. I'd say my life just got pretty damned good." He ran his fingers lightly along the line of her shoulder. "Perfect way to spend a day."

"Well, maybe the morning anyway." She nestled closer, pressing her forehead to his cheek.

"Are you questioning my endurance, Miss Wyeth?" he chided, pulling her to him.

She gave a light trill of laughter as she could feel his interest grow. "Hardly. It's just that I want to go back into town and start getting some answers on my family. I met a woman who manages the town registry. She gave me the idea to do some digging into my family history." Pressing her body against his, she kissed his neck, loving the feeling of his hands running over her sides and back.

"Not a good idea."

"Oh. Okay. I'll stop," and playfully moved her body away.

"No. This is a very good idea." He hugged her close again, the motion met with another burst of light laughter. "I meant going into town was a bad idea."

"Sure it is," she cooed. Her hand smoothed across his chest. She moved her body closer, letting him feel her warmth. "It's an excellent idea," she said between kisses.

"Being an unknown American tourist in town is one thing. Being Jessica Wyeth looking for her roots is another." He spoke slowly, words stringing out as he lost concentration.

Jessica pulled his hips to hers, keeping a little too far away. Teasing. "C'mon," she said, almost in a whisper. She kissed him with an open mouth, moving her tongue over his lips and scraping her teeth along his jaw. "Let's drive that fancy car of yours—"

Michael groaned softly. "Car? N-no." He spoke with decreasing conviction.

She rolled on top of him, letting him fill her. Grabbing his wrists, she leaned over, pinning his arms above his head. "Say yes." She was breathless, moving.

"How can I say no?"

Researching public records in Ireland required more patience than Jessica had. It wasn't as if she could sit herself down in front of one book and know it would hold the answers she wanted. She barely knew what questions to ask, so even knowing where to look was impossible. Records of births, deaths, marriages, and baptisms were the domain of the church. Efforts to modernize the records into computerized databases had not reached all corners of rural Ireland. Raphoe's public archives were kept in an ancillary wing of the cathedral.

It was still pouring when Jessica and Michael splashed through the doorway.

"Gracious! You gave me a fright," said Mrs. McDonnaugh as she sat bolt upright in her chair. "What brings you two out on a day like this?"

Jessica brought out her notes, sensing they had interrupted the woman's nap. "I thought you could help point me in the right direction to find some information about my mother."

"Och, that's splendid! I was hopin' you'd get the itch. Now, what information are we starting with?"

The stout registrar read Jessica's notes on Bridget's journal entries with interest and confirmed the information Jessica needed in order to determine which public archive held her answers. Town names and certain events gave Mrs. McDonnaugh a good idea where to focus Jessica's search.

Jessica's strategy was to learn as much as she could about her mother's family, then piece together the answers to find out the exact plan that Bridget and Margaret had pulled off so perfectly. Without the name of the town or county where Bridget was born, tracing her full family tree was nearly impossible.

"Young ladies of that time would not have ventured far from their homes. You're right about many of those street names being in Belfast. It sounds like she lived on the Catholic side." She waited for Jessica to nod before she went on. "She was lucky to have friends out of the city.

The towns your mother mentioned, BallyClare and Carrickfergus, were Catholic parishes in County Antrim in Northern Ireland. Aghalee Township is on the shores of Lough Neagh, a large freshwater lake that still is a major attraction, especially for folks summering from Belfast."

Jessica paused. "Antrim and Lough Neagh? I know those names."

Michael stepped forward. "County Antrim is a large county that reaches outside of Belfast up the eastern shore of the lake. The school is there."

"She has other entries in her journal, but she's written them in Gaelic. I need someone to translate them," Jessica said as she searched through the papers. "Here. I took a couple of the pages to show you."

Mrs. McDonnaugh scanned the yellowed paper. "I only speak a bit of old Irish, but it looks like your mother mentions Derry—that's what the locals call Londonderry—and Strabane as places that were important to her. Those are in County Tyrone in Northern Ireland and are easier to get to from here. Derry has a substantial newspaper archive that might have some interesting tidbits surrounding the dates. Strabane has a less extensive archive, and the lad there can translate anything. That might hold some interest for you. Of course, you'll have to cross the border to search church records in either county's seat." She rummaged through her desk and handed Jessica a list of names and addresses.

"Where should I start?" Jessica asked, slightly overwhelmed.

"Well, Strabane's a stone's throw from here. It's only ten kilometers directly east. Since you need some translation, I'd start there to get a better idea on where best to focus your efforts," Mrs. McDonnaugh answered.

Michael stepped forward, reaching for the paper in Jessica's hands. "I'll see what I can find for you there. No need to leave here if I can do some research for you."

Jessica instinctively deflected his reach. "No."

Michael kept his voice low, his words only for her ears. "Now is not the time."

"I'm going."

"It's not like skipping across the border from the U.S. into Canada. It's different, Jessica."

"I want to go. Please don't step in my way."

"Don't be naïve," he said in a hoarse whisper.

An angry flush crept into Jessica's cheeks, but before she could protest, Mrs. McDonnaugh continued talking, unaware of the sudden tension. "I'm familiar with the *RMS Presidential*. It's registered out of Sligo and was operating during the dates you're interested in. Sligo is on the west coast about a two hour drive from here." She raised her voice slightly, intent upon gaining Jessica's full attention. "The public library has a pretty good archive of ship manifests." She looked at the calendar and clock. "In fact, the archives are open late today."

Jessica's heart skipped a beat, happy to have another course of action she could take.

Michael asked, "Couldn't they research it and send you the information?"

"You're best to go to Sligo yourself." Father Archdall walked around the corner from what Jessica assumed was his office.

"Ah! Father!" Mrs. McDonnaugh exclaimed, flustered by his sudden appearance yet happy for support. "This young lady is from the States and is shaking the branches of her family tree."

"Is she now?" He reached out his hand in welcome. "Pleasure to finally meet you. No need to sit in the back of the church and scurry out after communion, you know."

Jessica timidly shook his hand. "I . . . I didn't think anyone would notice."

The priest peered down his nose. "Think again."

"Father," Mrs. McDonnaugh bustled, "you're a learned man. Can you give a go at these papers and tell us what they say?"

He reviewed the pages of Bridget's journal with interest, holding the pages up to the light and running his finger over the words. "It's a treasure to have family papers such as this. You carried them with you from the States?"

Jessica shook her head and smiled at Michael, who was busy studying a map on the wall. "No. They arrived not long after I got here."

The priest put his head down. His jowls masked his expression as he handed the papers back to her. "I'm afraid I can't help you. But I agree with Mrs. McDonnaugh. The manifests at Sligo could be most helpful. Those dolts are always looking to cut corners. They'd tell you they looked everywhere, but they'd only be sitting on their fat arses. No. You'd best go there directly."

"That's just what I was tellin' her!" said Mrs. McDonnaugh, victorious in her opinion.

Jessica turned to Michael. "Sligo?"

"It's a beautiful drive. You'll love it. You've got time for today if you hurry. Get going!"

Mrs. McDonnaugh was too cheery to refuse, and Father Archdall wasn't someone Jessica wanted to spend more time with, so they headed out to the street. Raphoe was decidedly busier than it was during her first visit. Even with the wind and rain, a steady flow of traffic moved along the streets and most parking spaces were full. Michael's sleek coupe stood out against the row of compact cars and Lorries.

Enjoying the fact that she was not under the watchful eye of Nan, Jessica started to shove her baseball cap into her pocket but thought better of it when she saw Michael's disapproving look. Not allowing her mood to be marred, she tucked her hair up under her cap and pulled the hood of her anorak up, hugging Michael's arm as they walked up the street. Convincing him to take her to town was fun enough, and she smiled at what payment he would expect in order to go to Sligo.

She tried to break the silence. "Sligo sounds amazing. Have you been there?"

"Once. It's a gritty port town that has seen its better days. Not my first choice if you want to see the quaint side of Ireland."

"Still, it gets me out to see more of the country."

He smiled and directed her up the street to a cafe. "Fair enough. Hungry? Let's grab some lunch before we go."

She moved toward him and was shocked when a strong shove to her back pushed her to the ground. An unseen hand pulled the hood of her anorak down.

"What the—?" she yelled.

A red-faced and disheveled woman stood over her, slightly swaying and peering into her face. "Faith and b'glory! It's true! Agnes! Agnes!" she called.

Michael flipped up Jessica's hood and put himself between the woman and Jessica. "Are you okay?" he asked, pulling her to her feet.

She was about to respond when she noticed another woman emerge from the pub and stop dead in her tracks, mouth agape from a combination of amazement and ale.

"Damn it," Michael muttered.

"Jaysus, Agnes! It's her! I told you I saw her in church last week!" The first woman, about thirty years old with a head of curly auburn hair, fished in her purse and produced a dog-eared tabloid. She jabbed her finger at the image on the cover. "You're the 'Heiress,' aren't you? The one from the States?"

Jessica kept her expression as neutral as she could. "Excuse me?" she said, feigning confusion. "You're mistaken." She looked at Michael with a combination of concern and amusement.

Agnes chimed in. "Mother-to-be, Helen, You're right! Miss Wyeth! Will you give us an autograph?" She fumbled in her purse and finally extended an envelope and a pen.

Helen had stuck her head back into the pub and called for reinforcements. "Tyler! Chris! It's her! I wasn't foolin'!" Within moments, the patrons of the pub spilled out into the street.

Michael looked back down the street and gave his head a quick nod. Within seconds, Tim appeared leading his two wolfhounds. The dogs' eyes glinted with excitement.

"Well, now! Well, now," Tim exclaimed as his two dogs skipped and jumped around the women. Tim's waving hand movements and commands of "Down boys! Down!" seemed to rile them up even more. His steady stream of "I'm so sorry! They're just puppies," only added to the commotion of women, leashes, purses, and dogs.

In spite of herself, Jessica gave him a look of thanks and kept her head down. Michael's arm around her waist pulled her to her feet. "Get me out of here," her words breathless with shock. This is what Nan had feared and what Jessica hated. It was also what Michael had taken such pains to protect against.

Michael guided her out of the growing crowd, both women shrieking with surprise and laughter. Tyler and Chris, equally sodden, were no help in untangling the mess.

"She's with me." Michael kept walking. He made eye contact with one of the more sober looking men. "I know. All beautiful blonde Americans look alike." He laughed slightly and gave his most disarming smile.

It almost worked until Mrs. McDonnaugh came trotting down the street. "Miss Wyeth! Jessica! You forgot your notes!"

Michael intercepted her before she progressed too far down the street. He grabbed the papers and escorted Jessica to his car with its tinted windows. By the time he pulled away, she could see the group of flustered people and jumping dogs close in around Tim—maybe even a camera or two.

When they were well away from town, her jaw unclenched and she relaxed.

"Tim will handle things there," Michael said. "Nan will tell us when it's safe to go back to the cottage."

"I'm sorry."

"No. I am. I should have known better. Nan has done a great job keeping the lid on your whereabouts and making sure Tim was close by in case we needed him." He glanced in the rearview mirror and gave a nod of satisfaction. "We did. I shouldn't have listened to you, but you can be very persuasive."

Color rose to her cheeks, and she looked back toward the town. "Thank you for . . . for," she faltered, "You're behind all of this and I, well, I've been looking over my shoulder for a long time. It feels really good when I can relax. It's nice to have someone on my side."

"I do it for my own selfish reasons." He accelerated onto the main road, ensuring distance between them and any ambitious followers.

The corners of his mouth turned up slightly. "You're a devilishly difficult person to find once you decide to run, and I've decided I like being with you."

Jessica relaxed, enjoying his lighter mood. "So, now?"

"This is the only time people will be certain they recognized you. Tim will have them chasing in circles and will make sure that other woman—"

"Mrs. McDonnaugh."

"Right. He'll make sure she stays quiet." He checked his mirrors again. "Sligo?"

Jessica raised one eyebrow and gave a half smile as a response knowing he could not say no. She settled back into her seat and watched the countryside zip by.

The weather cleared as they traveled southwest toward the coast, taking the N15 through Ballybofey and Bundoran. The highway was hardly more than a well-kept two-lane road, but the lack of potholes and loose gravel allowed for speed. The route wound through towns with stucco houses and over miles of roads marked by narrow bends with signs that warned *Ná Scoitear* or *No Passing*. Rocky land void of trees rolled over hills. Lush grasses, clinging to thin soil, were grazed to the nub by herds of sheep and cows. They passed bogs swept clean by ceaseless wind and loughs with shores of black rock.

After an hour, Michael detoured west off the main highway toward the coast. He enjoyed the opportunity of driving his BMW 840CI on the winding roads. Jessica was impressed that he adapted his driving style so easily to roads with confusing signs and foreign customs. The vistas sparked a feeling of adventure, and Sligo promised to be another quaint Irish city. Jessica found herself looking forward to an afternoon of exploring. She was surprised to be disappointed when instead of finding cobbled streets and brightly painted buildings, she found a broken down city dominated by creaking and decaying piers. Sligo was a city still pulled down by its past.

The brief walk down Stephen Street to the library archives took them past a monument of bone-thin figures huddled together. A plaque explained that the city was the main departure port in the 1850s, when scores of Irish tried to flee the Great Famine. Ships quickly earned a reputation as coffin ships for the barely survivable conditions on board. Jessica stopped walking and looked at the statue.

"I can't believe a whole country was starving."

Michael looked at the figures and nodded. "Not just Ireland. Europe was suffering, too. Many people claimed ample food was available but accused the British of withholding it."

Jessica gasped. "Genocide?"

"That's what many claimed then, and some historians agree with now. What's not disputed is the fact that British policies about land ownership and taxation placed a disproportionate strain on the Irish. The gulf between the two countries widened."

Jessica turned her attention back to the memorial. Lured by promises of "spacious berths and comforts for the travel at sea," trusting and unsuspecting men, women, and children scraped together passage fares and paid them to unscrupulous ship owners. The hellish ships were overburdened and under-supplied, maximizing money in and expenditures out. By some estimates, over one third of passengers died on the crossing and never saw the golden streets of America themselves.

Jessica shuddered at their experience but knew that Margaret had traveled years after such strife. Still, she wondered she'd find any common threads. As they entered the library, a cheery man greeted her. Half-moon spectacles barely clung to the tip of his nose. He gripped and pumped her extended hand with energy.

"Greetings to you! Father Archdall called ahead. I've gone ahead and pulled some records for you. Only ships that sailed from Sligo to Boston? Most of our voyages terminated in Nova Scotia or Canada, as it shortened the trip. A passage to Boston would have been more expensive, so there were fewer of them. That should make your research easier."

Jessica followed the stooped man down a worn flight of slate stairs into a large room filled with rows of tall bookcases. Over long wooden tables hung humming florescent lights, yellowed with age and dotted with dead flies. Along one wall was a group of college-aged students, each huddled over a machine that looked like a large photocopier. "We're only now getting to puttin' our records in electronic storage. If the images on the old microfiche aren't sharp enough, these interns will help you locate the original." Beside a microfiche reader sat a pile of oversized, leather-bound books.

"Once you identify which ship and voyage you want to look at from the fiche, you can review the passenger lists and other ship information in these volumes here," he said, motioning to the books.

Jessica got to work searching the records while Michael wandered off to review models of old ships that dotted the walls. A young girl with large round glasses and a bouncing walk approached her and offered assistance.

Within an hour, the girl had helped to locate some information.

"Here you go, Miss. This is the list of passengers on the day of sail and what leg of the trip they were on, like whether they were leaving Ireland or simply returning to the States. That would alter the documentation expected from them. You're right. Miss Margaret Heinchon sailed from Sligo to Boston in April 1958."

Jessica's heart skipped a beat. "Does it say anything more?"

"It wouldn't have been typical for a girl of that age to travel by herself and arrive in a strange city without some kind of escort or having a contact at the other end."

"You mean she wouldn't have gone alone? That she had some kind of connection in the States?"

"See here?" the girl pointed to the paper. "She checked the box that said she was emigrating."

"She was intending to leave Ireland for good?"

"Yes. Emigrating to the States also means she would've needed to have a sponsor. Most sponsors were employers of some sort. It was easy to get a visa if you had a job waiting at the other end of your trip."

"Okay, that means I could be looking for both a sponsor and an escort?"

"More than likely. Sometimes sponsors hired an escort for insurance to make sure their new employee got to them, but that was for highly skilled and valuable workers of some sort. For laborers or domestic help, the escort was usually a friend of the family, or they traveled alone. I've seen records of boys as young as eight making this passage alone."

The girl hoisted another thick book from the stack. After a few minutes, she pointed to another form.

"These books are the paperwork filled out by the passengers themselves." She ran her fingers down the page. "Here's something. It says here that she was to be employed on Beacon Hill in Boston, Massachusetts as a governess. Her future employer and sponsor was P.A. Wyeth. Is that a relative?"

"'P.A.'? That must have been Paul Andrew Wyeth. My, er, grandfather," she said in surprise.

Michael walked over when he saw the shocked look on Jessica's face. "What's up?"

Jessica told him her discovery. "Paul's wife had died many years before and left him to raise three children. Jim was the oldest and would have been about seventeen years old when Margaret arrived. Jim and Margaret eventually married." She leaned forward in her chair, stirred by this new information. "I knew they met in Boston, but I never knew she was a governess to Jim's younger brother and sister. Did she travel alone?"

The girl ran her fingers down the columns of names in the registry. "Nothing here . . . but there's one more place I can look." A half hour later, she hauled out another book and placed it on the long wooden table. She scanned more columns of names and figures, running her index finger down each page. She paused at one entry. "These books are the bursar's records. Looks like a Gilchrist Adams paid cash on the balances for two passages the morning of departure. It seems she was escorted by Mr. Adams," she said looking over her eyeglasses. "Does that mean anything to you?"

"*Gilchrist*?" Jessica asked, incredulous. "Could that be Gus?"

"Yes. 'Gus' is the common nickname for 'Gilchrist.'"

"She traveled with *Gus Adams*?"

"Well, it certainly seems so," was the reply.

Michael gave a low whistle. "Wow. I didn't expect that."

"I didn't either."

Jessica was silent for a long time. "Bridget. Margaret. Jim," she said, her voice a monotone. "That I barely understand. But *Gus*? They all knew. They *knew* the truth and never told me. I don't get it."

"Maybe they never found the right time." He tried to soften the edges of a jagged wound.

"Bridget lived with me for ten years after the accident. *Ten years!* Gus was at the farm for as long as I can remember, and you're trying to say they never found the *time*?" She pressed the heels of her hands into her eyes and breathed deeply. "They knew," she repeated, fury fading into sorrow. "They knew."

"Excuse me? Knew what?" the girl asked, interested in the mystery.

"Nothing," Jessica snapped, more discourteously than she intended.

The girl shrank back. "Are you done with these, then?"

Jessica took a quick look at the register and nodded.

Michael could see her confusion and hurt and didn't want to push beyond her limits. "I took a look at the ship's specifications in the archive. The *RMS Presidential* was predominately a goods and livestock cargo ship that had limited passenger accommodations."

"Livestock?"

"Yes. From what I learned, it looks like it was one of the best transports for horses. It made frequent trips back and forth from Boston to Sligo. It was decommissioned in the late '70s when its parent company was sold. Their shipping license is still active."

"Oh? Fine."

Their trip back sunk into silence. Jessica looked out the window and barely acknowledged Michael's presence. Occasionally she would sniffle. Michael was at a loss of what to do.

The silence broke when a phone began ringing. Jessica was startled to see Michael reach into the console and pull out a handset.

"So then it's clear?" he said, irritation in his words. He hung up.

"That was Nan. The curiosity seekers have been mollified. We're safe back at the cottage."

"What? Oh. Okay. Good." Jessica's voice sounded thick.

"You okay?"

She looked at him with red-rimmed eyes. "Bridget raised the money for Margaret's passage and gave it to Gus." She pinched the bridge of her nose as she fought to control the catch in her voice. "They all knew each other. Here. In Ireland. They were all connected somehow. When Bridget needed help, she relied on Gus." A gasp, almost a sob, escaped. "But it was Gus who connected them to the Charity!" The words, nearly screamed, released full cries of anguish and confusion.

Michael pulled the car over on a remote stretch of road. He gathered Jessica in his arms and waited for the sobs to subside.

Jessica's words came out in chokes and sputters. "Gus. . . .Why?"

Michael tried to soothe her. "Gus wanted to protect you."

"He was *killed* for it!" Jessica pushed Michael away and looked at him. "By your father!"

"I know." He was helpless for more words. "I know."

"I thought Gus got into the Wyeth's b-business to find a way to f-funnel money to the Charity. Th-that he was ordered to by your father."

"You've told me enough about Gus for me not to doubt that he loved you."

"I don't want to imagine what that could mean. I never d-dreamed a relationship between the Wyeth's and Gus formed before he went to work for Jim, but now," she rubbed her face with her hands, "The fact that there was a connection between Gus and Bridget before they met at the farm is . . . is . . ." Her voice trailed off as words failed her. As suddenly as the sobs had started, they stopped. Jessica and Michael sat in the quiet of the car, unsure of what to do next.

They didn't talk the rest of the drive back to the cottage. Michael tried, but Jessica kept to herself. Pain and confusion shadowed her face and after a while, he left her to her thoughts. His cell phone rang a couple of times, and he made his apologies to Jessica for needing to speak privately. She merely shrugged her acquiescence, but the truth was she barely noticed. The only thing Jessica wanted to do was to get back to the crawlspace and retrieve more of Bridget's diaries. What she had already learned about her mother's young life in Northern Ireland was compelling enough, but the connection to Gus was astonishing. Learning of this earlier connection unsettled her even more.

Jessica waited until Michael was asleep. Careful not to make any additional sound, she sifted through the contents with greater care, noticing some items for the first time. More journals begged to be read, but an old tin proudly proclaiming it once held *John McCann's Steel Cut Oatmeal since 1876*, got her attention. A faint whiff of vinegar mixed with bath powder filled the air when she pried off the rusting lid. She shook out the tattered black and white photographs, their once shiny surfaces cracked with age.

Jessica spread the old photographs over the kitchen table. She was lucky to find dates on some, and others had a town name or other location written in the faded blues hues of a fountain pen. Although it wasn't surprising, Jessica was a bit disappointed that the majority of the photos were taken when Bridget was on a holiday at the lake and very few showed anyone in Belfast. Having a photograph of a special place or event made sense. The normal day-to-day drudgery of home was to be escaped, not memorialized as a keepsake.

The images were of young boys and shy girls in the back of a wooden wagon stacked high with hay and pulled by donkeys. Others showed men with rolled up sleeves and broad-brimmed hats, smiling with a fiddle on their laps under a shady tree. Each showed Jessica a simple way of life still glimpsed during her rides around Raphoe. Stern faced women, forcing unaccustomed smiles, wore long dresses and equally long aprons. They stood with babies in their arms or freshly scrubbed toddlers at their knees. Children's toes dug into the ground or fingers dallied in their mouths. Occasionally, a tall man dressed in the cassock and white collar of a priest would be in the middle of a smiling and reverent group of adults—mostly men—too honored a guest to be subjected to unruly children. Other pictures showed the happy and pious faces of women, pinched round by the wimples of their habits, and what looked to Jessica like large beaded rosaries hanging from their waists. Sometimes Jessica could pick out the faces of a young Bridget or Margaret and the joy they felt in such company was evident.

Jessica lingered longest over series of photographs taken at a lakeshore. Bridget was in most of the photos and looked to be in her mid-teens to late twenties. Unlike other women who dressed in shin-length skirts or long dresses, Bridget wore trousers and loose-fitting shirts like many of the men, reminiscent of a young Katherine Hepburn, with the same spark of independence and incredible beauty. In a few pictures, Bridget's attention was off to the side of the camera, smiling and angling her glance to look up a tiny bit from under her lashes. In others, her head was tossed back, her smile broad, caught in the midst of a hearty laugh. Bridget's face and smile were as familiar as Jessica's own, but the personality behind them was a stranger. Jessica had never known her mother to be happy, vibrant, or carefree.

The men, barely of an age that one could call them such, stood shoulder to shoulder with arms crossed over their chests or hands thrust on their hips in postures intended to look casual, but came off as stiff and posed beside the young women they so desperately wanted to impress. Some wore suspenders, and others vests as they sweltered on a summer's day. The flushed cheeks of the men and sheen on the women's faces told of nods to formality over comfort. Tweed caps donned at jaunty angles conveyed the right sense of roguish confidence and swagger.

A picture of three people grabbed her attention; all of them looked to be in their mid-twenties. One man, head turned upward as he laughed, was more familiar to her than she wanted to admit. She could almost hear Gus' laughter, and the corners of her mouth tugged at the memory. Bridget stood between Gus and another very handsome young man. Each wore a straw hat and wide grins, with arms flung across one another's shoulders. The joy they felt in that moment softened the edge of the pain that tore through her. It was true. Bridget and Gus knew one another. Here. In Ireland. She didn't feel victorious in her discovery. She felt insignificant. Two of the people in the photograph had tossed her away. Jessica fought against her feelings of abandonment by digging through the photos with greater intensity.

Organizing the photos took more time than she expected, stopping and looking at the inscriptions to see if any of the names or places matched those she had read about in Bridget's journals. She carefully identified the names of Mary, Meggie, Ma, Patrick, and Danny with journal entries containing the same names. Putting faces to names seemed to push breath into Bridget's memories, and the paper almost warmed to life under Jessica's fingers. No photo had the name she was hoping to find. Jessica wanted proof that Bridget's beloved was Gus. It was a rude joke that the only reference to Bridget's important *Gean Cánach* was on a photo of maybe fifteen men. A simple "GC" hand printed on the back. The men stood in front of a huge piece of ancient farm equipment with hands on hips and legs propped up on it like big game hunters showing off the spoils of their hunt. Jessica searched for any familiar face from other photos and did her best to eliminate those she thought could not be him. Still ten men could have been Gus, faces obscured by hats or shadows.

After sorting them into probable dates and places, doing her best to cross-reference them to the journals Jessica had already read, she carefully indexed them by placing each photograph into the pages she thought referenced them. Occasionally she would shake her shoulders at the unexpected chill on the early summer evening, but that was the only distraction from her task. She was about to put the remaining photos back into the tin, when one last photograph fluttered to the floor.

The picture showed Margaret standing in a barren field, with a look of desperation that was timeless in its misery. She appeared to be about fifteen years old, and her face was a study of grief hidden with great effort. Margaret looked directly at the camera, lower lip bitten by even teeth, eyes still moist from recent tears. Beside her were two huge leather suitcases held together by thick straps that buckled at each end. She wore clothes that looked crisp and new, even if they were a bit too large for her. The photo was not dated or marked with a place but had the worn look of something frequently handled, if not kissed, the time and place of its taking forever seared into memory of its viewer.

The pure desolation that leapt off the photo filled Jessica with sadness. She pressed it to her cheek to see if some filament of memory that perhaps still clung to the image could seep into her. What Jessica did not know the picture was taken a few miles from where she sat at the cottage's kitchen table. Days before the fifteen-year-old Margaret departed to the United States, Bridget had met Gus at the Beltany stone circle and gave her precious sister over to his care. It took all of the Heinchon girls' strength not to fall into a heap of despair, each trying to be brave and excited by this adventure but nearly withering at the pain of good-bye. Bridget kissed then blew a soft stream of breath at the nape of Margaret's neck, long a secret symbol of their bond. When Gus finally pulled the women apart, the sisters trailed an arm behind them, keeping contact as long as they could until their fingertips parted.

Jessica looked at the unread journals with renewed interest, but the emotional toll of her long day caught up with her. Rubbing the back of her neck against a persistent chill, she rested her head on her crossed arms and instantly fell asleep.

November 1959
Saint Peter's Cathedral
Belfast, Northern Ireland

BRIDGET SAT IN a wooden pew and allowed herself to grieve, her soft sobs lost in the cavernous enclave. Two small white caskets rested upon catafalques before an ornate altar. Bunches of flowers, held together by bows of recycled ribbons and a wad of dampened cloth around their stems, showed signs of wilt in spite of their care. She was determined to drain herself of sorrow before the funeral so she could be strong for her friend. Her sorrow was for the young lives gone, and for her failures.

"You mustn't be sad for them, Bridgie." Father Storm gave a sad smile and sat down quietly beside her.

Bridget hastily wiped away her tears and searched for a hanky. She accepted the neatly folded and monogrammed rectangle produced from under a cassock.

"I'm sorry. I thought I was alone," she said as she blew her nose. She straightened herself up and looked at the thick gray hair and eyes surrounded by black framed glasses. "And don't give me any of that 'you're never alone here' and 'they've gone to a better place' drivel."

"They were beyond earthly help. It's always the most difficult on those left behind when the ones who go before us are so young. We cannot fight the Lord's ways but find a way to accept His wisdom and continue to live and work in His name."

"No. No! This did not have to be. These children were starving and were living with two other families in a basement flat. They were too weak from the failures of this world, Father. We failed them. Their mother prayed for the Lord to provide, and they died hungry and cold."

"We cannot doubt His way."

"She came to you for help."

"We have to help many and gave her what we could."

Bridget tried to check her building anger and spoke, trying to vent her frustration. "I know that, Father. It's just that it was so little. I tried everything I could think of. I tried community groups but was told she lived in the wrong neighborhood. I went to her neighborhood and was told her children went to the wrong schools. I went to her school but found out it was forced to close by the state. I went to the state, but was told that no family of a criminal convicted for crimes against the state would get aid from them."

Bridget's words echoed then faded into silence. They remained seated, and the shifting light cast the interior in a golden glow. The richness of the colors, carvings, and art did not soothe her pain. Lost in her thoughts, she chuffed at a memory. "So, did you hear what Mary's husband's crime was? He carried the Northern Ireland flag in a march, and the idiots at Stormont saw fit to throw him into jail for three years. This was a good, churchgoing, God-fearing, hardworking man, who carried a flag. That was his state-censured act."

"He had been in jail before that, too. Let's not forget his past."

"You're starting to sound like them idiots in Stormont! You're forgetting the assumption you're considered rehabilitated and are no longer a threat once you serve your time. So, are you implying that his past transgressions forever taint him? Whatever happened to absolution? Redemption?" The stricken look on the priest's face told her she was dangerously close to blasphemy. Even that was a line that the fiery Bridget Heinchon would not taunt.

A soft cry from the back of the church caught their attention. Mary was seated in a long wooden pew, hunched over her damp hanky as if trying to make herself even smaller in the huge space.

Bridget walked up the aisle, genuflecting and blessing herself out of habit when she crossed in front of the crucifix. She sat down as gently as she could, fearing that any sudden movement would fracture her friend into jagged pieces.

"I can't feel the pain any less. These were my children, too."

Mary looked at Bridget with red, swollen eyes. "Aye, Bridgie, they were that. Maeve and Geroid loved you as their own ma, no doubt there." She accepted Bridget's arm around her and placed her head on her friend's shoulder. "They're in a better place now."

Bridget bit down on her inner cheek and gave her friend an extra hug. She glanced up and saw Father Storm looking at her with an expression that said, "Let the woman have her peace." She nodded, and he exited through the vestibule.

Mary's sobs began to strengthen as another wave of grief washed over her. Bridget tried to console her friend as best she could, but Mary would not be stilled. The more her friend sobbed, the more Bridget put aside her own grief to help her friend carry her burden.

The force of Mary's sobs caught her words and drove them from her lips. Guttural wails formed from a source larger than the tiny woman making them. Bridget listened to her friend mourn the loss of her children in the timeless and transcendent sounds of pure grief. She determined to give Mary as much time as she needed to empty herself of the pain.

The strength behind the sobs subsided as fatigue began to numb her. The words that she was fighting to utter finally began to take shape. Bridget listened as a torrent of words rushed out.

"My baby. My baby. Sweet Jesus in heaven. Why? She was so good . . . so . . . so good. You had to take her? She was but a wee little mite. So good. No more mark on her soul than our sweet mother in Heaven. Why did she have to suffer so?" Mary looked at Bridget with haunted eyes and grabbed at her coat sleeve. "She was sufferin' with fever and never a complaint out of her. I was out of my mind with worry for her. You saw her. You saw how weak she was. You were trying to be strong for the both of us. May He bless your soul for the help you tried to give. You saw how sick she was. You felt her body shake with chills even as she raged with fever. You saw her!"

Mary rocked back and forth in her pain, unable to clear her head of memories. "You left us that night to find us more help. You didn't see her turn blue. You didn't see her ribs heave with the effort to breathe. You didn't hear her cry."

"No. I didn't hear her. It is a mother's hardship to be at her child's side in sickness."

"I prayed the hardest I have ever prayed. I . . . I began to question if it was me who had to suffer. That it was His will that I break into pieces for something I've done . . . that I didn't receive forgiveness for. The signs were always around me. M-my miscarriages. The babies I wanted, but died inside of me. As I prayed, I asked Him to tell me what I had done so I could be forgiven by Him," she said as she clutched Bridget's sleeve even tighter. "Bridie . . . Bridie . . . you know that I have tried to be a good wife."

"Aye. You have been a loving and devoted wife even with your husband's troubles."

"And . . . and I have been a good friend to you, haven't I?

"You have been the best friend."

"I stayed by your side even when others stayed away."

"You . . . you're . . . a wonderful woman and mother."

"So . . . why . . . what did I do to make my child suffer?"

"It wasn't your fault. These things happen." Bridget could hear the hollowness of her words and hated their impotence but couldn't offer other words of comfort.

"She . . . she . . . Maeve . . . she . . . d-died in my arms. S-s-she stopped struggling, and for a moment I thought I saw a bloom of color on her cheeks. L-like our Mother's rose, just for a moment and then she . . . she just let go. She. Let. Go. Just like that. She let go . . . let go." Mary's sobs threatened to renew and Bridget stroked her hands to calm her. "She was at peace then. She looked so rested and peaceful." Mary continued to rock back and forth as she stared off at an unseen point beyond the altar. "And that was it."

Mary's barely whispered statement faded into the dark corners of the vast cathedral. The two caskets waited patiently for the venting and reliving of both of Mary's children's death. The pain from the loss of a child is so great that it travels through one person and into another like a static shock, slightly lessened, but no less sharp, and the pain inside Bridget was acute. The loss of one child was unimaginable, but the loss of two incomprehensible. Bridget continued to stroke and hold her friend, trying to take from her what pain she could. She waited patiently for the pouring forth of the remaining grief and let the minutes pass. Mary seemed lost in her grief and too far away, but Bridget sensed that an equal pouring of her sorrow had to spill forth. Gently, she prodded her friend.

"Geroid loved his sister dearly. Maeve was lucky to have a brother like him."

Bridget had braced herself for a renewed wail of grief, but what she received sent shivers over her skin. Mary stopped rocking and gave a throaty laugh.

"I gave him his last wish. I . . . I was a good mother to him to the very end. I gave him his last wish."

Mary's faint voice and flat stare made Bridget flinch. "Of course. Of course. You were a good mother. You were there for him, too. You held him in the end, too," she said, trying to find words that didn't fade into platitudes.

Mary started to breathe rapidly, almost panting, and her torrent of words started up again, stuttering and fading as she talked. "He . . . he . . . he w-w-was holding h-his sister's hand. J-just patting her, tellin' her she'll be alright, that her mama's th-th-there. He said th-that morning will be comin' s-soon and the d-daylight will warm her. He h-had been feelin' better. Color was in his cheeks again. H-h-he was tellin' her how tomorrow was goin' to be better. Th-that there would be s-s-sweets for her. He was tellin' her how everything was going to be shiny and bright." She turned her head to Bridget like a drunken sailor and stared at her. "He was lyin' to her. I couldn't stand it. He was lying to her, telling her everything was going to be dandy when I knew the truth, that I couldn't help Maeve breathe, and I couldn't make the night go away and I couldn't make tomorrow better.

"I knew we were still going to be sharing our flat and be hungry and cold and that their pappy was still going to be in jail and that we were still going to be hated for being Catholic and for bein' Irish and proud of it. I was still going to fail at giving my children food or a roof over their heads because no one wants a filthy papist cleaning their house. He w-was just there, pattin' her hand. Tellin' her he'd always be with her, that he would be the strong one for her. That's why he was gettin' better, so he could be there to help her. H-he was lookin' at me . . . askin' me that we'd always be family. H-he was tellin' me that he'd never leave the family, like his father done, and that he'd always be there for Maeve, that I was never to worry about her. And that's when it dawned on me, that he was right, that he was the right person to always be there for her, and that he had no other worries in his life than to be there for her forever and that he made his wish, the wish that he would always be with her forever. S-so you're r-r-right. I . . . I . . . I held him. I . . . I held him tighter than I had e-ever h-held him. I . . . I . . . I held his face to my chest until he s-stopped his struggle. I . . . I held him until the v-very end." Mary's breathing began to slow. "I held him until the end and gave him his last wish. I was a good mother to him. You know that I was."

Bridget's mouth had gone dry and she sat motionless beside her friend. Mary, exhausted with grief and heavy with truth, rested her head once again on Bridget's shoulder, not realizing that what was once filled with warmth had now grown cold.

No tears streamed down Bridget's cheeks. The two white coffins taunted her as did the shell of a mother she held in her arms. She felt nothing. No sorrow or hatred or love. The faintest of sounds, like a far off splintering of ice on a frozen lake, made Bridget turn her head. Listening, she lowered her head, ashamed at the realization that the source was from deep inside of her.

The light slanted deeper into the sky, and the golden hues of the cathedral shifted to gray and silver, making the statues of Jesus, Joseph, and the Virgin Mary appear stark and white. A few people began to sift in for the service and take their places kneeling in deep prayer. Bridget and Mary were seated in a smaller chapel at the end of the cathedral's transept. The funeral for the two children was the only service to be held that day. Bridget kept Mary in the back row until Father Storm motioned for them to sit in the front pew, the formal place of honor for the families of the dead.

With a ramrod straight spine and shoulders pulled tightly back, Bridget guided her friend to her seat in the front of the cathedral. The pews filled with the few people of the community who knew Mary and her children and a few more who only knew the pain of a mother's loss and came to console. No organ music played or thin soprano voice sang. To have either would have required the expected donation at the end of the service, and no one could pretend to put one forth. The only sounds were hushed whispers of mourners who greeted one another, muted sorrow and sniffles from those who truly grieved.

Father Storm prepared for the service with the help of Father Kavan Hughes. Each priest had changed into the white vestments of mourning to recall the purity of the soul during baptism—not black, which Bridget felt best fit her heart. Father Storm's full head of snow-white hair matched the white linen palls embroidered with gold crosses draped over each coffin. The altar boys wore black cassocks under their white albs, watching for their cues and carefully performing their duties.

Bridget watched Father Hughes move from one side of the altar to the other, her eyes dry, and her mind clear. He was taller than Father Storm, straighter. She thought about their times at the lake, where they all laughed together, she and Mary and Kavan, and the times when she watched him play hurling with Gus, wooden Hurley sticks crashing and sometimes breaking with great effect. He was as competitive then as he was now; making sure his every move was that one bit better than his betters. He was here today as a favor to her, not Mary, and Bridget knew his sermon would be filled with fire at the loss they all suffered today. Kavan would not let the service be only about the loss of two children, but would make sure every person felt the blame.

Bridget wondered if he felt the same guilt she did, for her failings were his, too. They worked side by side, scratching up donations and paying them out as best they could. He worked tirelessly to keep his flock fed and clothed and still found time to focus his energy on change. Did Geroid and Maeve brand his heart as they did Bridget's? She knew they did.

Kavan stood at the center of the altar and looked out over the congregation. When his eyes followed someone in the back, Bridget turned to see but only caught a glimpse of some boys in the shadows. When their eyes met, she saw them change for the split second that was enough. The friendship and connection they shared was acknowledged, and she was careful not to stare at him, dropping her eyes for fear he could see through her. Father Storm motioned for him to join them in walking over to Mary for the ritualistic greeting of the family before the official start of the service. Kavan lowered his head in respect and followed in the older priest's footsteps. When Father Storm clasped both of Bridget's hands in his own, Father Hughes clasped Mary's. When Father Storm clasped Mary's hands, Kavan grasped Bridget's.

A few more people shuffled in, keeping to the back of the cathedral, embarrassed by their late arrival. Bridget watched as Kavan narrowed his eyes ever so slightly, and she followed his gaze. Gus was in the last pew—on the aisle and closest to the door—his customary perch. He half-knelt, half-sat, hands clasped and elbows resting on the back of the pew in front of him. His bowed head supported by thumbs pressed to eye sockets, too heavy with knowledge and grief. He, too, was there out of his love for her. She wanted to run to him, screaming to stop his worship, telling him the truths she knew, but she could not, fearing that the release of truth would weaken her to the point of dissolution and ruin.

The service began. Father Storm commanded the liturgy in Latin, held up the Eucharist, and intoned for their souls. The congregation was stone quiet as the soft chime of the gold thurible, hitting its brass chain, lulled them. Wisps of blue incense floated over the coffins, symbolically cleansing souls that had no opportunity for soil. The pungent aroma slowly crept along each pew. For Bridget, sitting closest, the minutes she sat inside of the cloud were wasted. She let herself breathe deeply, imagining the smoke filling her, swirling inside of her to be expelled along with her sins, but she knew that no amount of rite could absolve her. For those watching, Bridget seemed to touch the grieving mother in the most gentle of way, looking as if she knew that a firm hold could scorch through her friend like a tempered blade. They could not see inside Bridget's heart or deep into her soul, for if they could, soft soughs of sorrow would have grown into searing cries of mercy.

Bridget kept her eyes closed and head down, kneeling and standing by rote. Others looked on as she blessed herself, recited her Our Father's, and received Holy Communion. She was the picture of a perfectly devoted friend.

RAPHOE, IRELAND

AS DAWN STRENGTHENED into day, Jessica's eyes opened. The faint outline of the wooden cabinets and chairs came into focus as she realized with a start that she had fallen asleep sprawled over the kitchen table. Photos and papers littered the surface. Her back screamed for her soft bed, but she could see the slumbering form of Michael under the covers. Having him so near served to deepen her confusion. She wanted to be close but somehow feared that the safety she felt in his arms was an illusion. Opting to curl on the sofa, she yawned and let herself doze, too early to start her day.

Her mind teetered in a state of half sleep, half dream. A watery image of the long, tree-lined drive that swept up to her childhood home drifted into focus. Margaret came onto the porch of their huge white farmhouse carrying Erin, arms and legs too long to be held properly, and placed her on the glider, propping her up with pillows and securing her harness. Bridget stood off to the side, wringing her hands. She looked over her shoulder, fretting about something in the distance, beyond the edge of her dream.

Jerking awake, Jessica laid still and oriented herself in time and place. No sounds filled the cottage. Her back forgave its abuse as she stood and stretched. At some point in the night, Michael had placed a blanket over her but didn't return to bed. Their growing relationship did nothing to lessen her turmoil. She couldn't see how all the pieces fit together and that troubled her. Instead of glowing in the warmth of her reclaimed life, she felt hurt, angry, and isolated. She didn't know if *afraid* should be added to the list.

The grind of a hoof on gravel outside caught her attention. Michael sat astride Planxty and holding the reins of Kilkea. The massive chestnut horse arched his neck and almost danced with excitement.

She dashed outside wearing the same clothes from the day before. A pair of worn jeans ripped at one knee, western style boots, blue oxford style shirt untucked on one side, with one of the thin camisoles she favored underneath. An old stirrup leather from one of her saddles cinched her waist, and a thin scrap of leather secured her hair at the nape of her neck. She rarely put time into her appearance. It hardly mattered. She could feel his eyes follow her legs and hips as she swung into the saddle in one fluid motion.

"Morning," Michael said with a lazy grin, working the southern gentleman's charms as best as he could.

Her stomach fluttered. She tried to ignore it. "Are you sure you know what you're doing up there? I didn't think you could ride."

"You're not the only person who knows how to sit on a horse, pull on its mouth, and make it do what you want it to." He leaned down and handed her Kilkea's reins. "Just take it easy on me."

Jessica started off on a slow walk until she had time to assess Michael's skill. He seemed comfortable enough so she brought him up to a trot and then a slow canter. If he was nervous, he hid it well. They didn't talk much on the ride, and she welcomed the silence.

The morning air was fresh and cool and the only sounds were the scurry of birds in the rose thickets and the rhythmic thod of hooves on soft ground. Worried Michael may be too unskilled to ride a spirited horse, she glanced over at him and saw he was surprisingly comfortable. After a half hour of riding in easy silence, they pulled up into a clearing and dismounted. The one person who could see beyond the defensive wall she had built did exactly what she needed in that moment. He helped her down by holding her hips and guiding her to the ground, then he grabbed the saddlebags and produced a thermos.

Jessica inhaled. "Oh my God, you have coffee! And the foundation on the cathedral didn't crack?"

He smiled at her pleasure. "I had it sent from Boston. Good old New England tendered rocket fuel."

"Seriously. I had given up hope. I asked Nan a few times, but she never seemed to be able to find any." She took a sip, drawing in air to cool the black liquid. "Hmmm. Thanks. I'll be able to lift mountains after this."

Michael dug around the bags and produced some muffins and a long lead line for the horses to graze while they ate. He motioned to a spot on the stone wall where two flat rocks made a decent bench.

Jessica refilled her cup and watched him carefully. "Having my horse ready. Coffee. Working your charms. Not to mention you actually riding yourself." She sipped her coffee and looked at him over the rim of her cup. "Something on your mind?"

"Yeah. A couple of things." He sat down beside her. "First, are you okay? I'm worried about you. You had quite a shock yesterday."

"I have a lot to mull over," she agreed.

"Why don't you start by telling me about Gus and your family."

She drew in a breath and started from the beginning. "Gus worked for my father, um, rather, Jim Wyeth, for as long as I can remember. Gus and Jim made Wyeth's Worldwind Farms the world leader in thoroughbred racing. I never knew their success was because the horses were doped and the races fixed." She tipped her head in thought. "Gus was considered part of the family, but he never acted like it. The most time I spent around him was in the barn. Margaret and Jim would fuss around me, trying to get me to go to events they deemed ladylike and genteel, but I would rip the ribbons out of my hair and dash to the barn as soon as I was free. Gus got a real kick out of that. He was careful not to encourage me, but let me do what I wanted."

They sat in silence as Jessica struggled to reconcile those memories with a different reality.

"What else?" he prodded gently.

"After the accident, Gus stepped up. He traveled back and forth to Ireland a lot, scouting horses and shipping them back to the States. He and Bridget were solidly on deck when it came to running the farm and caring for me. It wasn't until . . ." she swallowed, cleared her throat, and began again. "It wasn't until I told him I wanted to take over the family business that he showed any belligerence toward me." She looked at Michael with a mixture of contempt and grief. "You know the rest."

Michael flinched at her words but kept his tone measured. "Gus tried to keep you out of the Charity, and that's why he was killed."

"I never imagined that Bridget and Margaret shared any history with Gus," she said, shifting to get comfortable. "Bridget kept to herself when she came to live at the farm. They weren't really together, like a couple. At least not that they let me see."

"You said she was sick? Of what?"

"I guess her illness was something she fought for many years. She had trouble breathing and didn't leave the house much. I'm pretty sure she had lung cancer, but she never talked about it with me beyond, 'It's God's will.' She died a few months before I graduated from Bowdoin. I never knew her as being vibrant or robust. Her journals were written by someone I never knew existed."

"Did Bridget ever write about Gus?"

"These were her private writings, and she took precautions from being exposed if anyone spied on her diaries. She seldom referred to people by name. More often she identified them only with one letter or a nickname."

"So, who did she write about?"

"I, um, I think someone named Gene Something. Oh, right! *Gean Cánach*. She was head over heels in love with him."

Michael turned away, making a failed attempt to hide his amusement. "Really? That's who Bridget was in love with?"

She tilted her head, not seeing the humor. "Yeah. She wrote about him a lot. It was a lot more than a schoolgirl crush, Michael."

"According to Irish legends, *Gean Cánach* means 'love talker.' He's a male spirit who seduces human maidens." His smile faded. "GC? Gilchrist? Could that be who your father is?"

Jessica became agitated. "Bridget claimed she was a widow, but she never spoke of a late husband. The only fact I have was that she used 'Harvey' as her last name. I got the feeling that either her marriage was a short-lived mistake or that her husband died shortly after they were married. What if Gus was my father but Mr. Harvey was still alive? Bridget struck me as a very uptight woman who would do nothing as extreme as having an affair that produced an out-of-wedlock child, but after reading her journals . . ." she slipped into thought, "I'm not so sure. It doesn't answer why they never appeared to be more than just friends when they lived on the farm."

Michael stretched his legs out in front of him and motioned for her to sit closer. "It does address the secrecy, the pictures, and the diary entries. You were away at school, and when you were home you barely paid attention to her. It's possible you simply didn't see what they wanted to keep from you."

Desperation and grief seeped into her voice. "If that's true, then I witnessed my father's murder." Her voice was a taught wire. "And then I was framed for it."

So many layers existed, each one more painful and impossible than the next.

She continued, pushing her hands in the air in front of her to shove away the thought. "No. I want to find out more about her husband—this Harvey. I haven't found any reference to his first name. He could be that GC guy she wrote about." Her voice faded and eyes shimmered. "But *why*? If they all knew the truth, why the secrecy from me?"

Michael's voice was gentle. "I want you to try to remember. Maybe there are connections you couldn't see. Whatever Bridget and Gus did, they did for you."

"I don't know that! Damn it!" She gnawed her finger. "How can deception be the same as love?" She swallowed back the urge to scream at him, at Bridget, at Gus. The sorrow that wanted to spill over didn't, but she let herself be embraced, ragdoll limp, and stared over his shoulder.

"I've pushed you too hard. Are you okay?"

"Yeah," she said, voice flat. "I'm always okay." She squirmed to be released, the pressure of her emotions threatened to crack her in two.

"No. You're not. It's got to be confusing for you. I know you hurt. Christ! I would change everything in a heartbeat if I could." Reluctantly, he dropped his arms, using the motion to take her hands. His palms, rough with calluses, pressed on top. "This mess isn't what either one of us wanted. We can't stop moving forward just because we don't like where we came from. We'll figure this out together."

Jessica searched his eyes for deception. "You might be able to live with these truths, but I'm not sure I can. I need to understand." She accepted his kisses, feeling his urgency and need for connection, knowing he wanted her. All of her. It didn't matter to him if she felt incomplete and unwanted. He loved her regardless. Maybe that was a good thing, but she couldn't be whole until she understood not only who she was, but *why*. If Bridget had an affair with Gus, why was her mother ashamed of herself and embarrassed by the child that came from that union? She had grown up thinking she was the product of a loving relationship and a strong marriage. Finding out otherwise threatened to swallow her whole. Finding Bridget's husband might help Jessica move toward feeling wanted.

She pulled away and gathered up their picnic. The combustible mix of shame, hurt, and confusion came dangerously close to exploding. She watched him tuck the food back in the saddlebags through a haze of emotions. The ground under her feet disappeared and a tightness grew in her chest as if her heart were splitting from the effort of its beat. Her ears began to ring. She put the reins over Kilkea's neck and swung up onto his back.

"Let's go."

This time, Jessica showed no mercy. She had ridden both horses before and knew what they could do. Then and there, she couldn't have given a rat's ass if Michael was capable of keeping up with her. She had to ride hard, for *her*. The ringing faded as anger replaced numbness, and all of it channeled into Kilkea. Immediately her horse was on alert. Kilkea's muscles coiled as she wheeled him around. Within three strides, they picked up speed and cleared the first of the hedgerows, increasing their speed as they raced across the field. Jessica ignored the meandering paths they had ridden earlier and chose the most direct route back to the barns. Kilkea jumped ditches and walls, giving a solid clearance revealing the horse had more game than earlier training sessions had uncovered.

Her breathing deepened and head cleared as her tension began to fade. The ground below blurred, and she could see only a few strides ahead for any obvious dangers. A hole. A sharp rock. A sudden dip. Any deviation could mean a broken leg for the horse and a broken neck for her. But her world shrank to the half-ton rocket she sat astride and for this one moment—this insane and perfectly encapsulated moment—she checked her brain at the gate and let hell flow. Opening up was reckless, but she didn't care. She didn't care about the speed or about who her parents were or weren't. She didn't think about Kilkea, and she didn't give a damn about Michael.

Galloping unchecked was as exhilarating as flooring the pedal of a sports car, but instead of being pushed back by the acceleration, Jessica brought herself forward over Kilkea's neck and shoulders. Her arms pumped in rhythm with each stride. Launching over hurdles, she gave encouragement with her legs and brought her body more forward on his neck, allowing extra leeway with the reins so Kilkea could stretch his head out, helping with balance and to see their landing. She started a soft sing-song of words, using her voice as another point of connection.

Jessica's mind began to click through the points of Kilkea's performance when she felt the horse gather up and give an extra burst of speed. Something ignited, and the horse dug down deep. What caused the change? Pounding hooves grew louder. Stealing a glance over her shoulder, she was shocked to see Michael still astride. Not being able to see his face, she couldn't tell if he was enjoying his ride or not.

Kilkea's spark was his true competitiveness, which thrilled Jessica. Kilkea had somehow worked out in his head that Planxty was not going to get the best of him. Humans do crazy stunts because of a sheer desire to win. Many horses are no different.

Jessica refocused on her ride, chastising herself for being reckless but not caring enough to stop or pull up. Kilkea exposed his potential and grew stronger. She turned toward the east end of the field where the hedgerow was lower. Kilkea refused her signal, insisting on going straight. The jump was over five feet, and she pulled hard on the left rein and pushed with her legs to steer to the lower jump. They were moving too fast. Jessica checked her center of balance, body position, and inhaled. She fought the impulse to close her eyes as they approached the last hedge. Kilkea's muscles coiled, then sprang forward. Time and sound stopped. In that moment, her tension broke, and she felt free.

Kilkea's front hooves slipped on the wet turf when they landed. He took a half stride to regain his balance, skid again, then took two complete strides before Jessica brought him to a trot, then to a walk. She barely had time to reach down and rub his neck with praise before Planxty thundered through the hedge—branches and leaves flying—and skidded to a stop.

Michael, nearly unseated at their abrupt halt, held onto Planxty's neck until he could right himself in the saddle. He looked at Jessica, his eyes rounded with amazement.

She sat stunned for a moment herself before laughter overtook her. "I had no idea you could ride like that!" The release of laughter felt good. She let it flow, feeling slightly unhinged as she did so. "I thought for sure you'd be trotting down the lane for another hour before you got here."

"I stayed on . . . barely. I'm not sure I can call that knowing how to ride, can you?"

Her laughter trickled to a chuckle and they stood grinning at each other with the shared adventure. She indicated a need to keep the horses moving until their sides stopped heaving and their bodies cooled. Happy again, they walked side by side, as their horses hung their heads and stole mouthfuls of grass when they could.

"Sweet Jesus! That was amazing."

Jessica turned her head to see Tim striding over. He parked in front of the barn, and the door to his truck hung open. His two dogs sat poised in the truck bed, waiting for his command to join them.

"Jesus, Mary and Joseph," he exclaimed, sounding to Jessica more like "Jaysus, Meerie and Jyoseph." He continued, "I've not seen Kilkea do anything more than a polite canter and low hurdles since he's come under my care, and you have him flying over hedgerows."

"Today was fun. That's all." She took a step backward, ducking behind Michael's shoulder as a shield.

"Fun? Then that means you thought it was easy."

"I guess I do."

"Easy. Easy. Easy," Tim rocked with excitement, eyes darting back and forth to spots on the ground in front of their feet. "The hedgerows. Hedgerows. Hanging back then moving forward. Said it was easy."

Michael waited until Tim had calmed down to hand over Planxty's reins. "Tim?" he asked in a steady voice.

Tim twitched his head and reached for the reins. "That was something. That was something, Michael."

"It was," Michael answered smoothly. He nodded his head in the direction of the driveway. "Who are those people?"

Tim and Jessica looked up to see a boy and a girl, each about fourteen, watching at them. Their two heads dropped in unison when they saw Michael's gaze on them.

"Kids. Just kids. Neighborhood kids. Never seen them about before."

"What do they want?"

Tim glanced quickly at Jessica then back to Michael. He started to say something, but Michael stopped him with a look. Tim nodded and walked down the drive toward the teens. "Hey! There's nothing for you here!" he yelled.

"And so it begins." She turned on her heel and walked back to the barn.

APRIL 1966
LOUGH NEAGH
AGHALEE, NORTHERN IRELAND

BRIDGET POKED THE coals of a fire with a stick. The dried peat filled the air with a pungent and earthy smell, reminiscent of the finer scotches she once sipped. She wrapped the woolen shawl around her shoulders and wished she could to throw another chunk of peat into the grate. She had to conserve what she had until the men came.

The wind rattled the windows of the wooden cottage and the thin curtains covering the windows swayed slightly, betraying the fact that the cottage was not airtight. Once a home of open windows, where on hot days children ran freely in and out, the cottage survived now as a dry husk, grimly holding its place until summer rolled around again.

A ruddy-faced girl with a thick rope of wild red hair that refused to be tamed by a ribbon, walked over to her with a steaming mug of tea.

"I thought you'd need this to warm yourself," the girl said, timid in her approach.

Bridget smiled and thanked the girl. "It's Anna Marie, right?"

The girl's face split into a huge smile, showing a broken front tooth. "Yes, Mrs. Harvey."

"Please call me Bridget."

Anna Marie drew in a short breath, but nodded quickly. "Thank you, Bri-Bridget," she stammered, a bit awestruck at using the first name of someone she revered.

Bridget took a sip of the tea and made a point of showing how much she enjoyed it. Wrapping her hands around the mug, she walked over to the table and began to read some of the papers strewn about, pretending not to notice how the other women at the table looked at one another with a mixture of surprise and pride at being so close to her. She hand picked them based on vision and grit and knew them by name, but they knew her by reputation and tried to hide the fact they were star-struck.

She didn't want her stature to distance her from them. Around the table sat six of the most capable young women Bridget had ever known. Their backgrounds were varied. Some were from wealthy families who had studied in the States and came back filled with passions about protests in the streets and the firsthand witnessing of the grief the American people felt from the loss of their young and dashing Irish President. Others wore the struggle of their parents in guarded eyes that flashed with anger when anyone tried to put them in check. What they had in common was a youthful idealism galvanized by recent events and a newfound strength that they could change the world if they could only harness the people's power. Some were as young as nineteen and the oldest, Anna Marie, was twenty-two. At thirty-four, Bridget wondered if she seemed ancient to them.

How different they were from her when she had been their age. No. Not different. The times they were in began to accept young women with hearts and minds of their own. At least in these times women could be more independent so that being surrounded by their support seemed normal, if not prevalent. Speaking their minds in public made newspaper headlines and crushed the hearts of many parents, but because they had each other they didn't feel like freaks for it. They encouraged one another and knew they were among the catalysts of incredible change. Indira Gandhi was Prime Minister of India, American youth were protesting the Vietnam War almost as much as their parents were fighting against The Pill. The British, flexing their muscle to show they possessed Northern Ireland, closed more Irish language schools, restricted jobs in areas known to be either Catholic or Nationalist, and began a quiet campaign of internment—locking up men they suspected of organizing against them. These campaigns targeted men, but everyone knew the women and children were the ones who suffered. Bridget harnessed their hidden power in ways that supported their men and their cause.

When the British cut funding to any organization that flew the Northern Ireland flag instead of the Union Jack, Bridget led a group of women to respond by organizing the Civil Rights Movement, after the movement black Americans were successfully pursuing. In a few short months, Bridget would also be instrumental in pushing that movement to form NICRA—the Northern Ireland Civil Rights Association. She was incredulous that merely speaking out for equality between Catholics and Protestants, Irish and English, NICRA would become an organization that threatened the British government to its core.

The new Beatles song "We Can Work it Out," played on a phonograph as Anna Marie passed a joint to another woman at the table. The smell of pot mingled with the peat fire. Bridget knew their woolen clothes would reek for hours, if not days. She declined the offer. Instead, she yearned for a glass of fine Scotch. Neat.

Bridget had never felt as comfortable in her own skin as she did now. Her passion and work were paying off with major milestones. Some of the women chided her for not taking credit, knowing that Bridget was the brains behind much of the civil organizing. But Bridget had made peace with her world—a world where she served every man, woman and child as an equal. A world, as she saw it, which was not yet ready to have a woman at the helm. She wanted the men around her succeeded but quickly cut out anyone stupid enough to claim her work as his own. She had no false modesty or subservience in allowing men be seen as the leaders. She needed the safe image of a married woman more than one as a hell raiser. Adopting the name Mrs. Harvey, she cultivated a retiring image and not to be too public in her opinions. She protected herself against the midnight knock and raid that had claimed so many of their men.

The mug cooled in her hands as she stood beside the table. Her body was still lithe and strong. Her once strawberry blonde hair had faded to more straw than berry, and she secured it at the nape of her neck with a piece of a discarded bootlace. She carried herself with a chieftain's confidence. Over the years, her insights into people and politics were the foundation of coalitions. Her assurances won over opposition with unwavering vision and brilliant strategies. No person who knew her was fool enough to question her authority.

Eventually sounds of trucks lumbering along the rutted road grew louder. The women slowly gathered papers, looking at each page and organizing them into piles. Bridget watched each carefully to see which one stole a quick look at their reflection or fussed with a stray strand of hair. If one had betrayed a crush, Bridget would be careful to filter any news or advice from that besotted girl lest she be unknowingly biased. Or, if the flutter seemed too animated, Bridget would sternly ask her to leave. She could afford no mistakes, and mistakes of the heart were the hardest to guard against.

The trucks pulled around to the back of the cottage. Soon the small space filled with men, barking dogs, and laughter. It was Bridget's favorite time of day.

Gus came over to her and wrapped her in a huge hug. She accepted his welcoming kiss eagerly, thankful for his safe return. For a brief moment, they paused, fingers interlaced, forehead to forehead, in a silent prayer of gratitude. He quickly threw a clot of peat in the grate and motioned to another man to put his armful of the dried fuel in the large woven basket waiting, nearly empty, beside the hearth. She turned to greet Dan and Patrick with a peck on their cheeks and a tousle of their hair. She greeted each man in kind and suddenly stopped cold. Kavan stood outside the door, waiting for his invitation to enter. In an unconscious gesture, she smoothed the front of her shirt.

He had thrown back the hood of his oilcloth coat, revealing he was not wearing the black and white starched clerical collar. Rather, he wore clothes he hoped would fade him into the background—white cotton shirt, woolen pants and a thickly knitted sweater—the only clue to his stature being the quality of the fabrics. His effort at blending in didn't work. They lived in a time when the uniform of the rebellious was ripped jeans and band t-shirts, neither of which he could pull off. Even his choice of clothes conspired to expose him—the loose fit serving to accentuate his powerful build, not hide it. Bridget could see the ripple of attention he received from the women at the table. Anna Marie watched his arrival carefully, and Bridget knew her lustful look would crumple into a blush and a quick prayer for the Lord's forgiveness if her admiring the physique of a man of the cloth were discovered. Bridget stared at Anna Marie, ensuring that the young woman felt watched as Kavan made his way into the cottage.

Bridget walked over to take his coat and accepted a light kiss on each cheek. She leaned close to his ear and whispered, "You're taking too big a risk."

Gus came over and slapped Kavan on the back, barely containing his joy at seeing his friend. "Kavan! No one told me you'd be joining us tonight. What brings you here?" The two men brought their clasped fists to their chests in a gesture as close to a hug as real men dared.

Kavan surveyed the room rustling with the activity of people settling in. "We have much to talk about when we can."

Gus and Bridget exchanged a look, their pride in their chosen family evident. "Have you eaten?" Gus asked, addressing Bridget. When she indicated no, he added, "Fine then. Our group is starving. We can talk about the developments better over a meal than we can over our growling stomachs. Kavan? Join us?"

"It'd be my honor," Kavan answered, smoothly scanning the room.

Plates filled with steaming food balanced on knees as men and women sat down to eat. The talk quickly moved from the day's events to the larger movement, voices rising with excitement as the points were plotted.

Bridget walked around the room, eavesdropping on conversations, listening in on updates and strategies, and offering her suggestions and insights to finely tune the planned actions. She did not push, and she did not to betray a larger plan with a poorly executed step. Bridget knew that her efforts identifying skilled organizers and educating them on the new theories of civil disruption were having an impact. She was creating contained, disciplined groups that would focus their efforts on a single goal. She empowered the few with education and knowledge so they would have an impact on the many. Tasks were mapped out and broken down into pieces and groups formed over one task or another. Eventually, the room emptied as people broke off to work.

Gus and Kavan remained seated at the table, which functioned as a conference room, staging area, and kitchen table. Anna Marie sat between them, heads bowed in animated discussion. Dan and Patrick sat on either side of the men, listening intently. Bridget watched, pleased that men and women equally shared the labors of leadership. Gus poured glasses of Scotch so they might toast one another with all the flourish that could roll off their tongues. They felt the *craic* of the moment and savored it. Each would easily give up his or her life for any of the others, and Bridget was struck by how alike their relationships were. Brothers and sisters all, blood not needed. Having received her update and instructions, Anna Marie excused herself to inform the others.

The talk inevitably turned to recent events. "The hole in the British mind where Nelson's Pillar monument stood will begin to fester. They'll be looking for blood," Dan said.

"They've no leads to come back after us and no deaths to investigate. Besides, the pillar was in Dublin, not London, so they won't feel the threat as much," responded Patrick.

Kavan held up his hand. "Don't be so quick to diminish their opinion. Nelson's Pillar may have been built on Irish soil, but it was no less a symbol of British might. Its demolition sent a clear message that was felt through the hearts of the people." He looked around the room, empty except for this core group of friends. Secure, he lowered his voice. "Job well done, boys."

"What brings you here, Kavan?" Gus asked, concern knitting through his brow.

"The wedge the British is wielding is growing in power. You're aware how the voting districts have cut Divis Flats in two?" He waited until he saw all heads nod. "The impact simply dilutes our votes so fewer nationalists are able to get elected. You and Bridget are addressing that with countermeasures. What concerned me is the breach inside the church."

"What's happened?" Bridget asked, leaning forward.

Kavan grimaced as he spoke. "Father Storm refused to christen a baby with an Irish name."

"Then there's no doubt the church is being used to deflect the real reasons for our conflict," Bridget said, eyes downcast.

"Yes," Kavan replied, "and it's only going to get worse. The British have been trying to restrict how and where we can use our language. They've made teaching our history a crime, and they're doing everything they can to stop us from organizing. With Father Storm feeling forced to take this step, I'm afraid our spoken message is too silent."

"People are losing patience. My girls have more than enough followers and have been identifying the best avenues of resistance."

"What solutions have you found for communications and provisioning once the blockades start?" Gus asked.

Bridget gave a Mona Lisa smile. "We're ready. The tinder is set."

Gus looked each person directly in the eye. "Timing is important. The flashpoint has to happen when the population is ready. Too early, and we risk internal divides. Too late, and we risk discovery."

Dan exchanged a look with Patrick and nodded. "The loyalists formed the Ulster Volunteer Force as a counterforce to our Irish Republican Army. They've got more than a lick and a prayer of support from the RUC. Paddy and I, we've been watching them get arms and training and know their routines. We only need the word to take them on."

The room fell silent. Each man and woman traced the paths that brought them to this moment around the table. Each mulled roads not taken and decisions not made. None found a path that led them any differently. Bridget cursed under her breath. She gave her brothers a long embrace, then kissed each on the backs of their necks as their ma had done when she thought they were sleeping. She wondered if Ma's eyes had welled up with tears. Both brothers smiled at the gesture, a code of their common bond. The three siblings huddled together, soaking in the presence of the others, fearful this would be their last gathering, a *fe* sense telling them they would never again share their *craic*.

Knowing this moment was long in coming did not make the final partings any easier. Gus embraced Dan and Patrick as the brothers secured his promise to watch over Bridget. Kavan clasped the brothers' hands in his and bowed his head as he gave his blessing. Eyes glittered with ambition, the brothers murmured, "Thank you, *Sagart*," and they were out the door. Each person knew the less knowledge they had about the mission of the other, the safer they all would be—and that any further direct communication would be lethal. Silence would speak their love and protection.

Gus stood up and walked slowly around the room. Bridget watched him carefully knowing his movement was as much to cover his emotion as to ensure no one eavesdropped on their conversation. When he found his voice he said, "Once they start that campaign, they cannot stop. They'll need resources."

"I'm well aware of that," Kavan replied, showing uncharacteristic impatience. "Bridget and I are already working together on raising money."

Gus did not see the color rise in Bridget's cheeks. "And?" he managed to ask.

"And we need your continued help in getting shipments to and from the States. Your connections with transporting horses have been invaluable. We need to increase the frequency."

Bridget stepped forward. "No. Gus is already at the point where his activities may be spotted. Increasing shipments is too risky. Find another way."

"I have," Gus said, "but I've been waiting for the right time to tell you."

Bridget's stomach knotted, knowing without being told. "Gus, you promised," she whispered.

"Please hear me out. Margaret came to me with the idea of hiding money and weapons in the animals' gear crates. Horses get shipped back and forth regularly for events. Her plan would use equipment already slated for transportation to avoid suspicions. Brilliant."

"And Jim?"

"Jim doesn't know. It will be simple enough to keep him free from details."

Kavan and Gus looked down simultaneously, giving away their partnership. Kavan spoke up. "The church's darker connections have ways of smuggling people and goods across borders and oceans. It's very secure and we can move enough goods to sustain our men."

Bridget pulled her shoulders back and lifted her chin in resolve. "We need more than sustenance. We need to thrive. No more dialog. No more talk."

Kavan used his hands to wrap Bridget's around a glass of Scotch. They stayed like that as he said, "There is always time for talk. There is always hope. Sometimes our voices need help to be heard."

Gus' eyes narrowed slightly, wondering if this was only the beginning of their troubles.

Raphoe, Ireland

JESSICA WAS FINALLY getting the hang of shifting the BMW through its gears without racing the engine or chugging it at lower speeds. As long as she concentrated, driving on the other side of the road was not difficult. She was happy that at least the accelerator and brake were where they should be. The weight of the car, balanced by its powerful engine, felt lighter and tighter to the touch than she expected. She never appreciated what a fuss people made over their performance cars, but driving the coupe along Raphoe's roads was eye opening. She felt a bit conspicuous in the shiny black car, passing the usual array of lorries, dingy Skoda Octavia hatchbacks and dented Ford Escorts. Being wrapped in the car's leather seats helped her forget the disparity. Once the car approached the open road, she found herself relaxing and enjoying the drive even more. Almost.

Lingering in the background was the pesky reality that at any moment Michael might be on her tail, demanding that she return to the cottage before she got herself into more trouble. As usual, she woke before he did and counted on him assuming that she was riding a horse, not driving his car. With her passport in her back pocket, she needed one, maybe two hours at most and planned to be back before Michael noticed she was gone—or at least before he mobilized a posse. Michael's opinion of her destination would be negative at best. He had secluded her away from prying eyes, but his efforts were opaque and maddening. The people he had placed closest to her were making her nervous. Crossing the border presented a unique set of problems but she wasn't a celebrity or a fugitive. She liked the thought of being a tourist.

The border drew her there, pulling her by some invisible cord. Strabane was close enough for a quick trip to narrow her search. She couldn't pass up a chance to have some of Bridget's papers translated, knowing they would direct her future efforts. Thereafter she could take Michael up on his offer to complete the research in County Antrim, but with the caveat that she'd do the research personally. She appreciated his help—loved him for it, really—but was eager to get back to doing things herself. A change of scenery and a plan that showed Michael she wouldn't tolerate being a kept woman would do them both good.

The fast-flowing River Foyle marked the northwest border between Ireland and Northern Ireland. Concrete banks that funneled the water into a narrow channel further enhanced its velocity. The Foyle had earned a local reputation as being the place for suicides. Several bridges spanning the river offered various heights and access points and, once in, the swirling currents would suck the hapless under in a writhing and determined undertow.

Swollen and water-rotted bodies would bob up in Londonderry or make their way to Lough Foyle before finally being dumped as unclaimed cargo into the Atlantic Ocean. Strabane had also earned a reputation of late as being the most murderous city in Northern Ireland, supplementing the River Foyle's duties. Strangulations and gunshots would help the unfortunate meet their demise, and a few of the decomposing sots would rise again with wrists and ankles still bound.

She had very few roads or routes to choose from, so she decided to approach the River Foyle on R264 and then near Lifford, follow the N14 along the river, using the Lifford Bridge to cross into Northern Ireland. Being unfamiliar with the signage, Jessica pulled over twice to review her map. She swore under her breath when the car bucked as she clutched and shifted gears, clumsy and unpracticed in the ways of precision automobiles. The bucolic country roads gave way to broad concrete swaths lined with what looked like streetlights, but closer inspection revealed more apparatus than simply lights atop the poles. The British world-class surveillance measures, and she assumed the additional equipment was used for border security.

The closer she got, the more she sensed subtle shifts of development but not from peaty countryside to gleaming city as she would have expected. Tract houses formed endless squalid lines. Squat cinderblock squares of empty commercial buildings sat on weedy street corners. The development was like rotted teeth—yellow with decay and eaten away by poverty. Her disorientation increased. Cars zipped by her. The directions on the map didn't jibe with what she was seeing.

The road followed the river south for a short distance before it crossed the bridge. Jessica took in the view as much as she dared. She wished for a wider shoulder next to her travel lane because she was closer to the embankment than she felt comfortable. Checking frequently, her mirrors showed a line of traffic snaking behind her. She waived them on and proceeded slowly, loathe to add angry drivers to her experience for the day. Tractors and Jeeps she could manage. High-powered German cars were a mystery. Overconfident, she attempted to change gears by depressing the brake instead of the clutch, pitching herself forward with a squeal from the tires. Horns blared as she brought the car back up to speed, cursing herself for not being more adept.

The car gave a sudden buck, pushing her head back into the headrest. Her eyes darted down to the dashboard, looking at the dizzying array of dials and gauges. No warning lights flashed as the car gave another buck and swerved to the narrow left shoulder. Her driver's side view mirror showed nothing, but when she looked in her rearview mirror her stomach dropped. She could not see road or headlights or safety. She could only see the grill of a very large truck.

Her head snapped back again, this time with greater force as the car was rammed forward. Her instincts to get away were to steer right, where the shoulder of the road should have been. Instead, she pulled out into oncoming traffic.

She was vaguely aware of the how fast the river approached her as the car spun and rolled down the embankment.

"Jessica? Jessica!" Michael's voice sounded far away. "Are you all right?" He guided her to look at him with a hand cupped under her chin.

Michael's face was a mask of anger. She nodded weakly. "Y-yeah. Fine." Her head throbbed. She was huddled on the side of the hill and had no clear idea how long she had been there and only vaguely aware of the people and lights around her.

"The EMTs want to get you checked out at the hospital."

She pulled her head free from his hand. "No," she said. "Please, I'm okay. Just bring me back." Her face was abraded and swollen where the airbags exploded into it, but she felt lucky. The only thing she was sure of was that an engineered mix of seatbelts, airbags, and crumple zones saved her.

Time was disjointed. Michael spoke briefly with the police and ambulance crew. She wasn't sure what he told them, but they clearly didn't win the argument. He helped her to her feet, steadied her, and walked her up the embankment to Tim's truck. She was vaguely aware as he retrieved her papers from his car and threw them inside.

"I . . . I'm sorry about your car." She rubbed her temples with her fingertips to ease the pain.

"What happened?" His kept his eyes on the road. He was no longer mad, but a sheen of sweat beaded on his forehead.

"I wanted to go over to Strabane to get papers translated and to see if their public archives had more information. My mother felt Strabane and Derry were important, and I wanted to see why. It . . .it happened so quickly. The car was too much to handle and I lost control."

"I want the real version, not what you told the authorities." She watched as the muscles in his jawed pumped. He was struggling to project calm.

She should have known better than to assume he would believe her first answer. It would be fruitless to try to dodge him. "Someone wanted the car off the road. It was rammed."

"You were targeted?" His knuckles went white as they gripped the steering wheel.

She had a headache, and her thoughts jumbled. "That's just it. I'm not sure. The way the car was hit, it wouldn't have made a difference who was behind the wheel. Even with an expert driver, the car still would have landed down the embankment."

"Why didn't you say anything to the police about being rammed?"

"They were quick to dismiss me as the stupid tourist who doesn't know how to drive in Ireland. Besides, I was rattled and not thinking straight. Maybe I should have said something," she said testily, "but that car sticks out like a sore thumb. It's impossible to see through the tinted windows so you can't tell who's in it. You'd be the first person assumed to be driving it."

He inhaled as he started to say something then stopped and held his breath. "No" was the only word that came out on a long exhale.

They were silent the rest of the drive and barely spoke at the cottage. Each time she began to speak, he would bring his finger to her lips. They would talk later. The oasis he offered was tempting, even if it was a shimmering mirage. She wanted—no needed—so much more from him.

In bed, the closeness of his body, his warmth, his gentle touch eased her. She brought her face close to his chest, letting his scent fill her. With his hands and mouth, he questioned how much she wanted him, how much she would let him in. With her body she answered, not thinking. Just being. Just for one night. She let them be as she yearned for them to be. United. Whole. Once ignited, she devoured him, pulling to herself every illusion he happily gave her. Together, as one, with nothing unshared between them.

Her body ached when she woke, and she instinctively reached for the warmth of him but found only cold sheets. He was no doubt off to learn whether the BMW was salvageable. She tried going back to sleep, hopeful for his return, but only tossed and turned, badgered by questions. Admitting defeat, she threw back the covers and stood up, slightly wobbling as she took first steps.

Michael's note on the kitchen table admonished her to stay put, which was the last thing she wanted, but she was in no position to differ. She knew nothing about Mr. Harvey, and her search for details on Bridget's life only showed gaps in what she knew about Gus.

She paced in circles, taking an inventory of her aches. Popping a couple of ibuprofens after surveying her scratches in the mirror, she admitted she needed answers to many things. If she couldn't leave the cottage, then at least she could review some of the notes she had made of Bridget's writings. Not seeing them on the table gave her a moment of panic until her still rattled brain remembered they were still in Tim's truck.

Jessica looked down into the ring and saw Tim lunging Planxty on a long line, the horse trotting in large circles. Two other horses stood tethered close-by, waiting for their turn at the morning's exercise. She assessed Tim's manner and skills, watching him for longer than she would have admitted. His ease with the animals was admirable, a natural horseman. The horses had made substantial progress, and Tim's disciplined help was a huge contribution, even if he was a jerk. He was a stickler for routine, arriving and leaving at the same time each day, working the horses on exactly the same schedule, lunging each for thirty minutes. She gave a quick glance at her watch and walked briskly to his truck.

The notes were not on the center console as she thought. Admittedly, she wasn't thinking clearly. She struggled to recall if she or Michael had placed them somewhere. Sliding her hands along the sun visor, under the seat, and into the glove box, she silently cursed herself for her absent mindedness. Nothing remained unsearched as she became increasingly agitated. She wanted those papers and she wanted answers. Now.

Her head throbbed so much her vision blurred, but she forced herself to search the seats again. The white edge of her notes was barely visible. They must have slipped into the crevasse on the bumpy ride back. She ran her hand between the cushions to free them and recoiled with a hot searing pain. Blood dripped from a clean slice along her fingertips. She looked down to see the sharp point and honed edge of a blade lodged between the seat and backrest. Rolling her hand into her shirttail, she reached with her left hand and inched the blade free.

The knife was ten inches long. Its fine blade was more than half its length and etched with an intricate interlocking Celtic design. The blade ended at a quillion, separating the blade from the hilt. A deep relief of a cross and interlocking circles decorated the grip.

Cold panic filled her as her vision narrowed to a pinpoint, threatening to go black completely. Her fingers bled, but the red-hot pain hit her in the side. This wasn't happening, she thought. The searing pain in her ribs couldn't possibly be real. Repressed memories crashed through, disorienting her with their vivid images. For a few harrowing minutes, Jessica was not secured in a safe house in Ireland. She was dying on a frozen mountain in Kentucky with a madman intent on filleting her with a knife. A knife incredibly like Tim's.

Hands shaking, she fished out the notes and hastily wiped the blade clean before shoving it back into its hiding place. Using her elbow, she did her best to rub away any droplets of blood, focusing on her task and not the rising panic within her. The questions, who was Tim and how dangerous was he, alternately burned and scraped, hollowing her. Without answers, the cycle threatened to continue until nothing remained of her but a tempered, hard shell.

She closed the door to the truck, hurried to the cottage unseen, and threw her back against the door until the latches clicked. Her knees buckled. Then her body sank to the ground and shook with soundless sobs as she held her hand to her chest like an injured bird.

Michael would be back soon. She had to pull herself together. Running her hand under the ice cold water from the faucet didn't lessen the throbbing. Examining the cut, only her thumb and index finger were unscathed. The slice was not deep enough to need stitches. The bleeding eventually stopped, but the stains down the front of her shirt and jeans made the injury look far worse than it was. Her head throbbed in time with her fingers, beating out the seconds passing without answers.

She grabbed a drinking glass and dropped it. The wood floor served more as a buffer than she expected, and the glass merely bounced and rolled under the counter. Grabbing it, she pulled her hand up over her head and threw it onto the ground. It rewarded her by splintering into several large shards. She felt marginally safer with an excuse in place, but the panic only served to crystallize what had been creeping up on her for several days.

The safe house, the bodyguards, the secrecy were sold to her as necessary evils to maintain her privacy. The dagger, the engravings, the tattoo, and its owner were reminders of the darker side of the Charity.

She needed to get the hell out of Raphoe. She assessed her options and didn't like any of them.

Michael's hair was disheveled and his collar was askew on a misbuttoned shirt as he walked through the door.

"Jessica! Are you alright?" His stomach dropped as he looked at her bloodstained shirt and dazed expression. Papers scattered from his dropped satchel as he crossed the floor in one stride. He held her by her upper arms and scanned her for more injuries. She stayed there, stiff and distant, refusing to look him in the eye. Satisfied only her hand that was cut, he led her to a chair and gently sat her down. He carefully dressed her hand and cleaned up the rest of the glass. Then he sat with her.

Her eyes followed him. "I'm fine. Just clumsy."

He had seen that look in her eyes before and it always meant trouble. It was the way she followed his every move without moving her head, sitting forward on the edge of her seat, as if ready to make a break for the door the second his back was turned. He knew the way her eyes took inventory of the room when they weren't following him, looking for something to defend herself with. She was going to bolt, and it was only a matter of time before she did.

The past few days he had been intent on simply being together, feeling united in the unspoken ease they shared, but the accident was more than either one could handle, made even more challenging by how hair-trigger sensitive she was. Over the past week, he watched as the emotion behind her eyes changed from trust and hunger to confusion and hurt and, after yesterday, wariness and fear.

"And a bad driver, too," he teased before bringing up what he really wanted to ask. "Yesterday you said the accident wasn't an accident and that either of us could have been the target." He waited to continue until he saw her reluctant shrug of agreement. "I want to stay focused on you."

"No. Not me, Michael. I need answers. I need you to tell me why someone would target either of us." Her lower lip threatened to tremble. She bit it still.

"I shouldn't have waited to talk to you. I'd been so focused on learning the intricacies of the Charity I failed to see the whole picture. Its legacy includes inheriting enemies, but insiders are a threat, too. You're at risk because you exposed the criminal dealings of my father and the Charity. You did that to save your own skin, but some people hate you for it. It's complicated, but exposure threatens the livelihoods of men and women with families."

Jessica nodded. "I know. I can feel that in my relationship with Nan. She tolerates me as a favor to your uncle, not out of loyalty to you. I'd feel better if I thought your uncle viewed me as more than just a distraction or a dalliance."

"Liam, Nan and Magnus were friends when they were young. Nan looks to Liam as Magnus' successor because she doesn't know me. In her eyes, the whole enterprise is at risk because I'm not in full control. She's like all the others who watch my every move to see how I fill the void."

It wasn't just the legacy of the Charity he grappled with, but the violent legacy of his father. Vestiges of Magnus' leadership haunted him as much as any spirit in the hills, and recent events made him question what else Connaught blood carried. His father killed and maimed to wield control and Michael felt baited to do the same. He wanted to go back to the beaches of Gibraltar with Jessica. He wanted the sun to bake his worries into distant thoughts. The days of wishful thinking were behind him as he looked at his reality. Jessica sat by the window, hunched and weary, sunlight hitting the side of her face. He yearned to go back to their carefree days, but the swollen scrape on her cheek where the airbag slammed into her was a clear reminder that he couldn't. He felt trapped and manipulated, pushed into taking actions he hadn't fully thought through. He had no choice. "I want you out of here."

She turned around and faced him. "Where should I go? I have no family, and my story hasn't faded enough for me to go back to Kentucky without more hiding."

He bent down to eye level and brushed a loose strand of hair off her face. "Let me take care of where to go, okay? Don't take off on your own again." He tried to keep his voice and demeanor upbeat, but he knew his words betrayed his concern.

He was reassured when her body lost some of its tension. She offered a weak smile. "Well, you had an easy enough time tracking me around with that box filled with papers. I'd think you'd be an expert by now."

"The papers? In a box?" He sat back on his heels. "I put together newspaper clippings, court transcripts and some documents for Nan a few weeks ago as background, but I don't know anything about a box."

"Not just the newspaper clippings. I'm talking about my mother's pictures and journals."

"Bridget's journals?" he asked carefully, "They weren't something you brought with you from the States?"

"No," she said, her eyes widening. "I thought you were behind getting them here."

Michael returned to his satchel and picked up the strewn papers, giving himself time to think. The discovery of Bridget's journals and papers surprised him, but he didn't give their presence much thought, believing they were some of the few items Jessica carried with her from her past. He wondered if assuming that was a mistake. "I've never seen the box or I would have asked sooner."

"Then who knew how to find me?"

"Only a few people knew you were here initially. Nan. Liam. Tim. Electra helped secure the training job, so someone at Tully Farm could have guessed your identity via the horse world. If the sender knew who and where you were, I wonder if the accident is connected."

She shook her head. "That doesn't make sense. If they knew who I was, they could have made their move here at the cottage without risking an incident out in public."

Both fell silent as they calculated the possibilities.

"What about people in town?" Jessica asked.

"Tim and Nan have been paying attention. Not until our trip to town did anyone discover who you are." He thought for a moment and picked at the stack of papers. "The car accident could have been targeting me or you. If me, I bet it was out of frustration that I'm not doing enough for the Charity. I'm looking into that, but if you were the target, then I need to see if what we learned in Sligo might have anything to do with the crash."

He put typed notes in front of her. "You were upset, so I wanted to find out more about your mother and maybe put the pieces together to find out who your father is. I thought maybe her husband, Mr. Harvey, might still be living in Ireland and could either be your father or connect us with someone who could help us with answers. I had one of my men do a search for all marriages performed in the Republic of Ireland and Northern Ireland for the time period involved."

Jessica's eyes widened. "Do you suspect Harvey is behind the box?"

"No, Jessica. I don't think that." He took a deep breath and avoided her eyes. He wanted to keep her away from pain, but it felt like each time he opened his mouth, that's all he caused.

"What did you learn?"

He reached out and clasped her two hands in his. "Using Bridget's birth date and name, and even changing a few details to widen the search, we came up with nothing. Your mother never married."

Jessica withdrew her hands. He hated to add shame to the potent mix of fear and turmoil. The shock and hurt sat visibly leaden inside her gut. She gasped, as if her body wanted to expel the news, and tried to mask it with a cough and averted face. Michael reached out to comfort her, but she held both hands up, shielding herself from anything more he might say. She walked out of the kitchen, bracing herself with a hand pressed to the wall, stumbling over her own feet.

They spent a quiet evening together, but Michael knew she was cornered, restless, and ready to flee. His stomach tightened at the thought of her running in a country that showed a ruddy and smiling face to the world but had deep-rooted prejudices and fissures. If Jessica thought she had trouble finding helpful support in the States, she was truly ignorant of her chances in Ireland. Finding another safe place for her was his top priority.

The next morning, he woke with her, intent upon just being near. He scrambled into the hayloft for her, tossing bales through the chute. Holding her bandaged hand to her chest, she grabbed the twine with the other and kicked her knee into the bales' centers. The bales split open, and he threw flakes of fragrant hay into each stall. She measured grain. He delivered buckets. Only stomps and throaty whickers of hungry animals broke the morning's silence. He led the horses to the paddocks for their turnouts and returned to muck stalls. She jotted notes while he spread fresh shavings around each stall.

They worked well side by side, and Michael wanted this kind of simplicity for their future. Barn work done, he sat on the spare stool and idly flipped through yellowed catalogues as Jessica checked feed levels and ordered more. She would begin to write something, then frown, and go back to the feed room to measure again forgotten quantities. Her shoulders were pulled up, tense, her mind elsewhere.

He tried to lighten her mood. "I think you cut yourself on a glass as an excuse not to muck stalls," he teased.

She looked at him with dead eyes and pressed lips. He wished he could bite back the words.

They headed back to the cottage, his arm wrapped around her waist, her head on his shoulder. A movement down the drive drew their attention. Two men, heads bowed in deep discussion, walked toward them. A Range Rover was parked by the far paddock. From a distance, the men looked of average build. They wore the same tweed caps that topped the heads of most men in Ireland regardless of the weather. Their type was immediately recognizable. Whether in the VIP stands at the track or the smoky dens of mansions, they were the money people who went to eyeball their investments and hedge their bets. One man held a sheaf of papers, while the other pointed and gestured with emphasis.

Jessica paused and looked expectantly at Michael, his relaxed manner contrasting to the urgency the men betrayed. When they looked up, one man nudged the other and nodded in her direction. They stopped midstride and assessed her from head to toe so rudely she shuddered. The shorter of the two tipped his hat with his fingers. Michael grimaced as he turned to her.

"Up for some introductions?" he said, placing his hand onto the small of her back. He tried to give her a quick kiss to smooth things over, but Jessica put her head down as she looked at the men with a mixture of animosity and dread.

"I'm thinking I don't have a choice." She gave him an unreadable look.

Tim appeared from behind the barn and stopped. Receiving a cue from Michael, he smoothly turned and gave the men a hearty greeting. Hands were clasped and pumped. Shoulders slapped. Teeth flashed. Michael watched as they walked away toward the paddocks.

Jessica raised her eyebrow. "Friends?"

"Mostly." He was distracted. He wanted this to go smoothly, and he didn't know how to start. He took a moment before giving Jessica his full attention. "The taller man is the head trainer from Tully Farm. The other guy is a member of the syndicate who owns the horses."

He was encouraged when he saw a brief flicker of a smile, but he knew her better than to assume she would go along with his plan easily.

"Tell me their presence is a coincidence." Impatience sharpened her voice.

"I can't say that."

"You invited them here?"

He had to be direct but diplomatic and hoped he wouldn't be judged as being manipulative. "Yes . . ." he began. "Tim and I spoke last night. There's a problem and they need your help."

"What kind of help?"

"They want you to ride. At Aintree."

Jessica scowled and waved off the statement. "That's crazy."

"And they want you to ride Bealltainn."

"Bealltainn? Their high-earning stallion? That's more than crazy. What are they doing racing him to begin with?"

He shrugged. She stood in the drive in tall field boots and slim breeches, unaware of the complete hold she had on him. Her trust in him was hard earned, and he hated this moment jeopardized it. "The men who race at Aintree do so for a lot of reasons. They like to play hard and take risks. For them it's fun. The manager of Tully Farm and members of the syndicate heard you were a hotshot trainer from the States but from the look they just gave you, I'm thinking they assumed you were a man. Regardless, they need you."

"What happened?"

"Their jockey had a nasty fall off Bealltainn." He didn't want to say more but knew he had to tell her the full truth. "Some of the other jockeys said Bealltainn tried to kill him, but Tim says that's nonsense."

"Terrific," her voice was devoid of enthusiasm, "They checked me out like I'm part of the livestock. I guess they're assuming I'm their penned bull?" She brought her hands up to her throat and pulled at the collar of her shirt as if she were loosening an invisible noose. "Aintree would get me out of Raphoe."

This was his opening. "To jettison everything that makes you who you are and take on a whole new life isn't right. You will always have some degree of exposure because of it. The amount of protection I would need to give you at the track would be very visible. You've made it clear you hate that kind of attention."

"I don't want it, but that doesn't mean I have to hide from that, too," she bit back. "You can't protect me here."

Her words stung, but she was right. He failed in giving her the kind of protection she needed. Being run off the road was a reminder that people were growing impatient with him. If he couldn't succeed in protecting her, then he would fail in gaining the confidence of those he needed to lead. Time was moving forward. He couldn't afford to waste a minute. "I'd have to put you in the middle of that snake pit and at the same time put a wall of bodyguards around you. The show of power would send a clear message that Jessica Wyeth is untouchable, and we will not be intimidated."

He took Jessica by the shoulders and looked directly in her eyes. "You can't burrow into a hole and rot. You're the only person I know who can ride an event like that. If I thought for one minute you weren't up to the task, I'd never have even considered it."

"I'd be safe?" she asked, unconsciously touching her cheek.

"You'll be as safe as I am."

In spite of everything, they looked at each other and laughed. He wanted to wrap her in his arms and kiss her.

She straightened her shoulders, the action gently shaking Michael's hands free, and took a step back, stopping suddenly as if she had backed into a wall. "Give me the details."

"The events are in less than two weeks, with the major race on Saturday, June 15th."

"No way! I'll never get the horses ready by then."

"You won't need to," answered another voice. Startled, both Jessica and Michael turned to see Tim and the men approach them. Tim had Kilkea on a lead and the taller of the two men continued to speak. The shorter man stood to the side, engrossed in his papers. "Bealltainn is in top condition as is Kilkea, I'm told."

"Kilkea?"

"Yes. We've heard of his progress with you," the man answered, looking at Tim.

Jessica flashed Michael a fierce look. He watched as the man extended his hand to her. "I'm pleased to meet you. My name is Shamus Doherty. I'm sure Michael has had a chance to tell you about me?"

"Not a word, Mr. Doherty." She shook his hand, eyeing him carefully. "I'm Jessica Wyeth."

Her name had no effect on him. "Kilkea," he said nodding as the horse nibbled on Jessica's shoulder, "is one of mine. You've already coaxed additional performance out of him."

Her mouth softened. She reached out and rubbed Kilkea's head. "I can see why he was a champion. He has an additional gear he can hit when motivated. I wasn't surprised at his competitiveness, but I'm not sure how he would be on a crowded track."

Doherty turned to address Michael. "I trust Tim's judgment. If he says my horses will be in good hands, then we can move forward. She's agreed to ride then?"

Jessica started to step forward, but Michael held her back. "She'll ride at Aintree, but I have certain conditions."

"Conditions?" Doherty asked.

"Yes. The horses will be kept in the central barns under 24-hour surveillance. No one touches them or has anything to do with them without Jessica's express approval. No one feeds them as much as a peppermint that she hasn't seen." Michael put his hand on her shoulder. "I'm placing some of my men in the barns to watch over everything. Jessica's wellbeing will be your top concern, not the horses."

Doherty huffed, then addressed Tim. "I guess we'll be seeing a bit more of you in the coming weeks."

"No. You won't," said Jessica.

Tim's face flickered with displeasure then calmed. "Don't be gettin' too high on yourself. I'll keep out of your face well enough. I'm responsible for the horses' transportation and safe arrival. A Pullman's coming in the morning for the horses not racing. Kilkea and Planxty will be loaded up and sent to Aintree today. We've got their flight chartered and waiting. I've already begun their mild tranqs for easing their trip."

"You've *tranquillized* them without asking me?" She looked at Michael with barely contained fury. "When was I going to be told of this?"

"Today," Michael answered without hesitation. "Tim's job has always been to get these horses to the race track in as good condition as possible. Whether you were going or not was undecided." Michael knew he was pushing her, but the deal was beyond the point of pulling back. "Tim assured me that tranquillizing horses is standard procedure for transporting them long distances and that the drugs will be out of their systems by the time any testing at the track would start."

Jessica nodded. "Yes. That's true. I would've liked to have known."

"I'm sorry. It's just for transport and my men will help keep an eye on things at Aintree." He gave a look to Tim that made sure there'd be no further questions about drugging.

"Well done," Doherty said, enjoying the volley. "Miss Wyeth only needs to pack her things." He motioned to his companion, who produced a list. "Review this. Tell us what you need and I'll have my men pack and ship any other needed items."

"Under my supervision," she interjected.

"I've done it. I've packed most of it." Tim stepped forward, nearly knocking Doherty over.

Doherty continued, ignoring the interruption. "As you see fit. Your flight out is at noon tomorrow. Don't be late."

Jessica was about to say more and stopped, no doubt making mental lists of what she needed to do in a very short time. Michael's expression reflected only calm and composure, but the tiny beads of sweat along his upper lip said otherwise. He barely twitched a muscle as he watched her turn on her heel and walk back to the cottage.

Belfast, Northern Ireland

AOIFE O'SHEA HAULED a heavy basket filled with wet clothes outside to hang on the line. Placing it on the picnic table, she paused for a moment to straighten her back and tuck a loose strand of strawberry blonde hair behind her ear. Reaching up, she grabbed the nylon clothesline with her right hand, a handful of wooden pins with her left, and began the mindless task of hanging knickers and shirts. One horizontal line quickly filled with wet items. Within twenty minutes, all of the day's wash was hung, the tiny backyard filled with flapping clothes. The slight breeze prompted her to judge how long the drying might take before the towering wall that butted the end of her yard eclipsed the sun.

"Brilliant spring day, isn't it?"

Aoife turned and saw her neighbor sitting in her backyard. She gave a quick wave and replied, "Aye. 'tis, Mrs. Reynolds. How are the tabbies today?"

"My sweet Mittens caught a mouse, and Bits was beside 'imself with envy," the older and portly woman replied with a hint of pride. "Just look at how he's struttin' about to get your attention." An orange tabby cat rubbed his whiskers against the screen that separated the porches of their flats.

"I'll come 'round on my way back from the cathedral and give 'im a good head rub. You all should enjoy our spot of sunshine while we have it," she said glancing in the direction of the wall. "I'm guessing we have an hour if the clouds don't cover it first."

Mrs. Reynolds assessed the sun moving across the sky and the height of the wall. "I remember when we had sun all the way to the horizon. We could sit out here on the step enjoying it until evening. Now we have the wall and rush about our tasks, dashing outside at the first hint of sunshine."

"You talk as if that was a million years ago. You're only after tellin' me yourself that you couldn't sit out here because you were afraid to and that was only four years ago! You're safe and sound. Top, sides and bottom!" Aoife shoved the wall for emphasis and looked up at the Plexiglas roof.

"It's a wondrous thing. Even keeps Bits out of my garbage and stops her from peeing in my plants. It should be called the Pees Line not the Peace Line!"

The older woman covered her cheeks with her hands in feigned shock. "Aoife!" she said, exaggerating her name to 'EEEE-faw,' "The things you say!"

Aoife enjoyed the distraction. She would never admit it, but she hated the wall. The decision of their civic association to erect a wall in West Belfast was a necessary evil after the last bit of rioting gutted the neighboring flats. They were not the first country or city to erect such a structure or the first to build it in a flash. The speed and efficiency of the project meant that opposition had no time to mobilize. Civic leaders held perfunctory public meetings while quietly meeting with corporate agents who then brought in engineers who hired builders. Within weeks, the wall was up. Done.

The row of flats and townhouses where they lived was designated a hotbed area and, because of that, enjoyed the added feature of a translucent roof. The high-tech sheets of special Plexiglas shielded residents from decidedly low-tech petrol bombs—beer bottles filled with gasoline tossed with lighted rags shoved down the bottles' necks. The crude, incendiary devices were the citizens' army weapon of choice to hurl over squat buildings into the streets. The roof had proven to be a great protection and deterrent. It did not take long to realize that any petrol bomb that didn't make it all the way over would roll back on the thugs who lobbed it up to begin with.

Belfast's wall along the intersection of Bombay Street and Cupar Way was a visible line of an invisible barrier. The peace line protected both Protestants and Catholics from the bottles and rocks that flew from the hands of the other and the rubber bullets and missiles fired by the Royal Ulster Constabulary, the RUC. A marvel of engineering, it stood twenty feet tall and grew up from a foundation of cement which served not only as a solid stand for the long pillars that held multiple sheets of metal and powerful spotlights, but as a barrier for any vehicle that wanted to drive through. A wire coil mesh crowned the top ridge. In different parts of the city, razor wire topped the mesh where simple barbed wire may not have been enough to deter anyone from the crazy thought of scaling it. Countries built walls to protect their borders and national interests—like keeping the Palestinians out of Israel or Mexicans out of the US. In the case of Belfast, the purpose was to keep Protestants from the Catholics and the loyalists from the nationalists.

People understood which side of the peace line you should live on. When you lived in Northern Ireland, either you were loyal to the British Crown or you weren't.

Another puff of breeze patted against the sheet metal walls and enough escaped around it to flutter the laundry. Aoife grabbed her empty basket and headed back inside.

"I'm going up to Taggarts for some bread and milk. Will the kittens be needin' anything?" she yelled over her shoulder.

Mrs. Reynolds appeared at her front door with two mugs of tea in hand. Aoife smoothed her hands over her khaki pants and freshly pressed white shirt. She drew herself up to her full height, aware that time and circumstance worked against her looking more polished. Mrs. Reynolds' eyes narrowed. "Only Taggarts?"

"Oh, stop looking at me that way you meddling old witch," Aoife laughed. "If you're to be watching my every move and logging my comings and goings, then you should be aware I'm stopping at the cathedral, too. I'm getting a few items for Sunday's coffee hour with my shopping and will do a bit of cleaning for the daily service. Then I'm off to do some work at the women's shelter. Does that meet with your approval?"

Mrs. Reynolds wiped her hands on the floral apron protecting her dress. "When you step out for nights on end, I get worried for you," she said with an exasperated sniff. She wagged a finger in disapproval. "I wish you'd find yourself *one* man and get on with your life. Livin' your days cleaning the altar and nights God knows where is no life at all. You're too fine a lass to be humping a pew."

Aoife roared with laughter. "Sounds like I'm getting to be a good influence on your language! The shock of you!"

"From the young ye shall learn."

They smiled the smile of friendship shared through generations. Aoife tossed her head in the direction of her knickers flapping in the breeze. "You'll take 'em in for me when they're dried?"

"I will, but you should be thinking to be back in time for that. You'll be longer?" Worry shadowed her face as she spoke. "The parades are today. Folks have been getting' increasingly tense. It won't take much to set them off."

"Och!" Aoife exclaimed in disgust. "The Orangemen should be as happy as we are that the bombings have stopped. They flaunt the fact they get to parade every Saturday while others are stopped from doing so. No worries. I've planned my errands to be done before then."

"This'ns not for the orange. It's for the hunger strikers. Bobby Sands' family will be at the front and the word is out for supporters to be wearing the black armbands for mourning."

Aoife sucked in her mouth. "I'm surprised they were able to pry a permit free. That took some doing, but just because I won't be wearin' the armband doesn't mean I'll have a target on my back. Those fecking loyalists march their parades with their Union Jacks right down the heart of our Catholic neighborhoods. It's like waving a red cape at a bull. I hope today's parade uses that precious permit well and marches dead center up the loyalists' neighborhoods just to show 'em a thing or two."

Mrs. Reynolds wrung her hands. "Oh, Aoife. You're a moth to the flame. Don't be naïve."

"I'll be safe enough. They'll have more to worry about than a church lady on a shopping mission. Think of it. If the Americans can have their Fourth of July parades without fuss, we get to have ours."

"But you've said so yourself. It's different here. It's not simply bands and banners. They might have stopped hurling bricks and stones, but parades are no less a weapon. Please be careful." She bent down and patted Bits who had followed her into Aoife's flat. The tabby rubbed its cheek along Mrs. Reynolds ample calf.

Aoife gave her neighbor a quick hug and Bits a scratch under its chin. "It's a fine day, and I'll not take the main streets. I won't press my luck. See you back here before the streets get crowded."

Receiving acknowledgment and taking a last mouthful of tea, she handed the mug back to Mrs. Reynolds, gathered her purse, and set off. Aoife didn't want troubled thoughts to cloud her day. She wanted to enjoy it.

Guided by sunshine, she decided to walk up to Lanark Way, then on to West Kirk and Shankill Roads. Usually she avoided what the politicians called the "interface area," but she didn't want to take the long way around. The streets were calm, and the gate between neighborhoods was open, its graffiti-covered panels served to lift her mood even more. She could see moms and children coming out of one area and walking into the other, nodding greetings to the RUC officer posted there as they passed.

Aoife played a game with herself by looking at how they cradled their rifles to see if she was safe to venture to the other side. If they held them loosely in the crook of their elbow using only one arm, then they had no news or warnings of anything coming. If they held the guns with two hands, one on the barrel and one on the stock, then she knew trouble was coming and would cut her shopping and visits short. The young soldier tipped his hat with his right hand while keeping his rifle cradled with his left and continued his leisurely patrol.

A mother emerging from the nationalist side struggled to hold on to her little boy as he strained to rush through the gate to the park beyond.

She gave Aoife a slight smile and said, "I think we're interfacing just fine this lovely mornin', thank you."

Aoife smiled back and nodded to the boy trying to bolt for freedom. "Aye! And even the holes in the peace line are working wonders!" Both women laughed as she continued, "Best give him a good run today before the parades start. He'll work up an appetite for certain!"

The mother's smile faded to an uncertain expression and she hurried her son along to the park.

AINTREE RACECOURSE
LIVERPOOL, ENGLAND

THE SHORT FLIGHT from Galway, Ireland to Manchester, England was uneventful in every way except to signal a significant change in Jessica's life. Rather than hustling through crowded terminals and packing like a sardine in coach class or even luxuriating in first, she was brought to a smaller area of the airport that catered to private aircrafts. Her car pulled up directly to a waiting jet, with gangway steps open for her. The afternoon sun reflected off the white jet painted with a corporate logo MMC, Ltd. As the only passenger, she had more than enough room to stretch her legs. The flight was short. Pressing her face to the oval window nearly the entire trip, Jessica saw the island of Ireland spread out beneath her, every shade of green quilting the ground.

At the Manchester Airport, one of Michael's men greeted her and grabbed for her suitcase as soon as she neared. When she hesitated, he muttered "Phoenix," or, more precisely, "Bloody damned Phoenix." Safeword spoken, he walked ahead of her, bringing her to a limousine with tinted windows. Sliding into the back seat, she tried her best to look like she rode around in limos all the time, faking the ease that came with the trappings. A leather portfolio contained a map of Aintree Racetrack, stables, facilities and a brief overview of her responsibilities and accommodations. No expense was spared on the help she would have or her comfort. The ride to the stables at Aintree took about fifty minutes, and Jessica used the time to acclimate to her new world and gilded cage.

The limo entered the manicured front gate and headed straight for the stables. At full capacity, Aintree holds over one hundred thousand people. Its facilities catered to the masses with open bleachers and the elite with enclosed pavilions named Lord Sefton, Earl of Derby, and the Princess Royal. Her notes stated that only the great windowed gallery of the Queen Mother Stand would be in use as it afforded the best views of the track. Heated box seats protected its occupants from England's frequent showers. Every detail reinforced the fact that these races were attended by a class of people she had only read about.

Jessica recognized Shamus Doherty immediately. He was older, about sixty or sixty-five years old, tall, and carried himself with a certain athleticism that said he must have been quite the player when he was younger. His shirt was unbuttoned to mid-chest, revealing a silver chain with an old Saint Christopher's medal and a Celtic crucifix on tanned skin. His days of carousing may have been over, but his personality hadn't dimmed.

"Hello! Hello! Hello!" he called with his hand outstretched in greeting. "I trust your trip was good?"

"Good enough to get me here," Jessica answered, instantly regretting her icy tone. She needed to be smooth and even with no sharp edges to hint of nerves.

Doherty stood beside her and motioned for someone to bring a horse forward. He interacted with everyone around him like someone accustomed to getting what he wanted. He was direct, roguish, focused on the horses, and exuded charisma. "Kilkea traveled well," he said. "I'm sure you'll want to check on him."

"And Planxty?"

"Sold in a private sale. He would not be fit to race with his injury. You'll ride Kilkea in the hurdles race one week from Friday."

The abrupt sale saddened her. "Planxty's sold? I wish I had known." Her heart wanted to say her goodbyes to him, but logic dictated she was playing on a different stage now. Sentiment would not be tolerated. This was business. She focused instead on Kilkea. "I doubt Kilkea is ready to compete."

"We'll never know unless we get him out there."

"Mr. Doherty, with all due respect, if you put Kilkea in a race too early, you'll ensure his ruin."

"His value to the syndicate was determined after his last race. Nothing will ruin that."

She was frustrated and concerned for Kilkea's health. Doherty's willful ignorance angered her. Frustration creased her voice. "I wasn't referring to his *value* to the *syndicate*. I was talking about him as an *athlete*."

Doherty looked at her as if she was a little girl, sad that she hadn't grown up yet. "The hurdle race is for maiden horses or younger jockeys that don't have the experience running steeplechases. He's already been a national champion. Racing him down a division has already been decided."

"I won't ride him."

He didn't skip a beat. "Kilkea has nothing to prove, but you do. Kilkea's racing with or without you on his back. If I need to, I'll have one of the workout boys ride him. Your name will still be on the jockey registry, but you'll ride Saturday's claiming race without the benefit of real steeple-chase experience."

Jessica refused to be cowed and tried another tact. "How Kilkea will react is a wild card. If he's ridden poorly he'll be a hazard on the course."

Doherty shrugged. "True enough. There are those who say he'll be more of a hazard if ridden by a woman, so suit yourself. I say get the experience together. That would be the best for both of you. Anyway, the important race is Saturday, and I want you to get a feel for the course and the other jockeys before that. Win or lose, riding that event will break you in nicely, too."

She gave him a look that made it clear she hated being spoken to as one of his assets. Being defiant would only prove his point, but winning would put him in his place. She decided not to risk further friction and focus on her surroundings.

"Fair enough. Can you show me around?"

Doherty relaxed and slipped smoothly into the role of host.

"The facilities here are first-rate. All of my horses has a team comprised of grooms, trainers, handlers, and jockeys. Each knows his job. I expect you to keep up with the detailed notes you did at the cottage." He brought her into one of the five barns that surrounded a central paddock area and stopped in front of a stall specially equipped with rubber floor mats and showerheads. "We have far better facilities here for the animals. After every workout, I want the horses cooled, bathed, and massaged."

She hadn't been around a stable as bustling as this one in a long time. Jessica suspected the care given to the horses was as much for their physical benefit as it was for the games of one-upmanship played by their owners. If gold-plated bridles wouldn't have been laughed out of the barns, she suspected she would have seen them dotting the walls, too.

They entered into another barn where a blue and green sign for Tully Farm hung over one end and a bronze and gold sign for Devon-on-Thames hung at the opposite end. "Each barn stables horses from several farms. Don't stray. I suspect you'll be most comfortable in this area." A stable hand wearing dirty jeans, thick rubber boots and a grubby sweatshirt hustled past her and muttered a barely audible "Phoenix" under his breath. The thought that Michael's men could be a bad display of earpieces and ill-fitting suits had worried her. She was grateful to see how they blended in.

Doherty watched her reaction carefully. "The jockey you're replacing was one of the best, so you'll be scrutinized by our people and the other farms. I don't have to tell you that withstanding the psychological games-manship is part of your training. Letting someone get inside your head to the point of unnerving you could mean the difference between having a clean ride or making a judgment error that could cause a crash or cost the race. We don't have a lot of time and I need you to stay focused."

Jessica understood. Her initial chill toward Doherty thawed when she observed his competence in managing people and horses. Being open to his advice would help them work well together. "I will. I already overheard someone calling me 'Michael's woman.'"

He looked down the corridor to a group of stable hands huddled with their heads together. "The resentment of your celebrity and the prospect of Michael buying your way onto the track is palpable. Ignore it. You Americans like to call our steeplechases accidents waiting to happen. Maybe so. There's chaos on the course for certain. Some of those horses will run like the devil if they have a tail in front of them, but to win, the jockeys will thrash a whip on their rump until they pull ahead."

"I prefer not to use a crop."

Doherty gave her another look as if she barely comprehended what he said. "The Devon-on-Thames team?" he said with a nod in their direction, "they'll just as soon use the crop on you as their horse. Watch out for them. If they can spook a horse to get it off stride or cause its jockey to err, they can take that horse plus others it careens into out of the race."

Her stomach sank. She had a lot to learn in the coming days. They stopped walking. Doherty motioned inside a stall. "This is Bealltainn."

A massive horse stood along the back wall. At over seventeen hands tall, his back was six feet off the ground. When Jessica entered his stall, he raised his head in a prideful gesture, making it impossible for her to reach it. He flared his nostrils and looked down on her with a certainty of purpose that made her skin prickle. Energy buzzed through him, slicking down his inky black coat with a glaze of sweat. Even standing still, light seemed to ripple over him. He had a depth in his eyes that made doubting reincarnation unwise. He was an ancient warrior only temporarily at peace.

She reached out to stroke him when Doherty grabbed her arm. "He's terrified of being whipped."

Bealltainn's white-ringed eyes looked at her with calculated suspicion as his body shied from her hand. It was too late to undo the fear. With a gesture as innocent as a pat, the thought that she was just one more human who would beat him was indelibly burned into his head.

"Damn it," she said under her breath. "That was stupid. I shouldn't have rushed. I don't have the time to build his trust in me."

"Bealltainn knows his job and you know yours. Just focus on fine tuning your communication. His conditioning is excellent, and he has the speed and skills to win the race. As a stallion, he views any horse in front of him as competition for a mare. The urge to be first is primal. Just stay on his back and out of his way."

He brought her to the barn's common area furnished with couches and bulletin boards, intended for informal gatherings during brief breaks. It sat empty and unused. Doherty walked up to a large aerial photograph of the course. Surrounding it were smaller images of the individual fences, or flights, named Becher's Brook, Booth, The Chair, Valentine's Brook and the Canal Turn. Some were as famous as the track itself. "Each flight has been designed to bring horse and rider to the brink of failure. That's why winning here creates legends." He paused for a moment as if considering how much to say. "Legends create wealth. I want you to be as familiar with the course as possible. More is at stake in these races than just winning."

Jessica listened intently to Doherty's overview of the course. The course was two and one-quarter miles with sixteen flights ranging from a low of four feet to a high of five and one-half feet. Ditches in front of several flights forced a horse to jump early. If mistimed, the arc of the jump would be too short, causing the horse and rider to crash into the obstacle. Landings were lower than the take-off point on some flights and higher on others, a factor that worked to constantly undermine confidence and speed. A ditch or water feature behind a flight would make a horse feel the landing had been taken away and cause momentary panic. The Canal Turn was a high hedge fence, but immediately after it, the track made a blind, ninety-degree bend to the left. The horses couldn't anticipate this turn and missing meant plunging into the canal. More importantly, when a herd of horses tackled the obstacles at the same time, a sharp turn by one would mean a collision with another. The variables and perils were endless.

"The maiden race is one lap around, but the private is two. I'm most concerned about this one," he said motioning to Becher's Brook. "It looks easy. The takeoff presents as a four foot ten inch hedge, but the landing is a water-filled ditch at six feet nine inches low. Jockeys say it's like jumping off the edge of the world."

Jessica nodded. "I've heard of it, but mostly because that's where most crashes occur."

"That's right. On the second lap, the horses' legs have turned to rubber and buckle with the effort to keep upright. You'll have to keep your center of gravity as far back as possible and shove your feet home," referring to resting the stirrup iron on the instep of her foot. He demonstrated by leaning backward, extending his arms forward and raising one leg to make it look like he would be lying down on the horse's back, not crouched over its neck. "It's a precarious position jockeys must take mid-flight, but it places them at risk. For a crucial moment, they can't see where they're going. You have no choice if you want to keep your horse upright at the speeds you'll be traveling."

Beside a door labeled "Lockers" was an antique red leather chair with a scale built beside the seat. Brass ballasts moved along a metal rod measured the occupant's weight. "This is used as a conversation piece now, but it's a not-so-subtle reminder not only of the generations of history here, but that cheating won't be tolerated." He motioned for her sit down. "Races used to be fixed by playing with the jockey's weight. If you were clever, you'd fix the scales so your competition would be forced to carry more." He put his hand in his pocket and leaned toward the scale. Without touching it, the scale moved. "Pretty easy," he said with a grin. He pulled his hand out of his pocket and produced a magnet. "Cheating detections and weight rules have gotten more sophisticated."

"My family was entrapped in a cheating ring. That's why I demand to race clean," she assured him.

"I'm glad. Me too. But, you'll have other factors to deal with. Even though your weight is the same as most jockeys, you're taller. It will be harder to fold yourself over a horse's neck and be compact. Your balance will be precarious. They'll use that against you on the course."

She got up and started to walk into the locker room. He pulled her back. "There aren't many other female jockeys during regular season and none here now, so don't even bother to look for the ladies lockers."

He continued the tour and steered away from the Devon-on-Thames area, but not before Jessica saw heads raise and shoulders pull back in challenge. The disgust of having a woman invade a singularly male world was palpable. One groom from Tully Farm grabbed a rake, held it like a battering ram, and moved quickly in front of them. It was a ballet of subtle motion with a very clear meaning.

"Got it. I understand," she said, hoping to sound confident.

"You'll have your first breezes this afternoon and will ride the course on one of our other horses to get the feel for it. Be here at six tomorrow morning." He gave her another apprising look. "Any questions?"

She had more questions to know where to begin. If she started with any, she'd be pegged as ignorant and naïve. She shook her head. "I'll know where to find you if I do."

With a salute of appreciation, he strode off.

The earth was damp with morning fog, and the infield glistened with droplets of moisture as horses and workout boys got started on the day's training. Jessica hugged herself against the morning air, noting how England's famed chill reached into her bones. Extra gauze secured with white medical tape protected her cut fingers. She remained stiff from being tossed around from her car accident, and her one ride around the course proved she needed more conditioning than Bealltainn, but the masseuse and the luxurious soak in a hot bath last night had worked out most of her kinks.

Even through the muffled sounds of a world not quite awake, she could hear the whispers about "the American" or "that woman." Worse, conversations among other stable hands would cease completely as she walked near them. Unfamiliar with the grounds without Doherty as her guide, she took care to enter the barn directly into the Tully Farm stalls. A slight, wiry man with shocking red hair and amber eyes greeted her.

"Mornin' Miss!" he greeted loudly. Then more quietly so only she could hear, "Phoenix." He extended his hand. "I'm Jax. Doherty told you about me."

She immediately relaxed and returned his warm smile. She shook his hand. "Jessica. I'm sure Doherty told you about me as well."

"Aye. He did at that. Even if he was a mute I'd 'a known who you were." He gave a wink and tossed his head toward the opposite end of the barn. "They were settin' to give you a maiden's welcome." He held out his hand showing condoms, deflated and tied at one end. He held up another, bulging with water. "Seems they wanted to give you a token christening."

"Water balloons? Seriously?"

"Sure enough. They won't be doin' that again."

She didn't question his methods. The steely way he commanded the other grooms meant the message was clearly and firmly given. She was off-limits.

A stable hand brought Kilkea, fully tacked, to her. The horse pranced with nervous energy. Jessica started their workout slowly, acclimating Kilkea to the hustle and sounds of a new environment. Working him on the flat track before training over flights, she noted several groups of observers. The people and farms attending the upcoming private race marked a profound shift from those typically found at a track. Impeccable hand-tailored suits stood alongside white thawb robes and red and white shemagh headwear of the oil nations. The traditional seats of equine wealth—United States, England, West Germany, Argentina, and Ireland—were joined by the emerging power centers of Dubai and Saudi Arabia. Some call horseracing the "Sport of Kings," and the farms represented proved that to be true. The passion for horses provided a neutral ground for interactions, politics safely, if temporarily, placed aside while the subtle gamesmanship of mega-national corporate competition raged. The wealth on display was staggering, and she wondered how Michael fit into this world.

Kilkea arched his neck and bucked, not settling even after a long work-out. She mentioned her concern to Jax, who nodded slowly before he walked away.

After riding the course, she decided memorizing the distance in strides would be helpful. She stood in front of the large course map in the common area and calculated distances between flights based on the average amount of ground covered with each galloping stride. Kilkea would cover less ground per stride than the large Bealltainn. Concentrating, she closed her eyes to commit map to memory.

A body pressed up against her and a hand cupped her buttock. She whipped around and saw the back of a man looking with interest at the bulletin board on the other wall. All his movements choreographed to create the guise of innocence if accused of touching her.

"Don't touch me," she said, making sure her meaning was clear.

He turned around with the perfect expression of calculated expression of shock and bewilderment on his face. "What'd you say, Miss?"

"You heard me."

The man had a face misshapen by both birth and fights and a body made more for a boxing ring than a horse's back. A group of men ribbed each other and sniggered as Jax stepped beside her.

"You're alright, Miss?" he asked under his breath.

"Yeah, fine," she answered with enough cut to her words to make him step back.

"That one's Freddy. His mates from Devon-on-Thames follow him like pups."

From the look on Freddy's face, it showed he had decided her misery would be his only mission. She committed their faces to memory and vowed to stay away from them.

It was difficult. With the comings and goings in a busy barn, it was impossible not to cross paths with members of the other teams. Freddy was a skilled schoolyard bully, always keeping his actions just under the radar and rarely getting caught. As the de facto leader, he made sure his men kept up their relentless pressure. He had taught them well, and she couldn't ignore the abrupt and purposeful brushing up or knocking against her at every opportunity when passing in the corridor. The actions were both threatening and degrading. The men worked as a team on and off the track, sending the clear message that she was an outsider and needed to remain that way.

Neither born into money nor having a way to keep it from slipping through his fingers when he had it, Freddy, like the other jockeys, knew how to fight to win. He had a spine of tempered steel and an attitude to match. Once a disgruntled jockey had it out for you, neither human nor horse was safe. At most tracks, little comingling happened up or down the ladder. Trainers socialized with trainers. Owners with owners. Jessica was both trainer and jockey, and she had Michael's wealth behind her. Freddy's resentment of her was clear.

Barnyard bullying wasn't the only harassment she experienced. Next came the discovery of empty syringes discarded in Tully Farm's trash. Jax was ready for the ploy and produced surveillance tapes and blood tests to prove their horses were clean.

Next, Freddy tried to inject a potent and long lasting painkiller into Bealltainn when the horse was in a turnout area.

Jax grabbed Freddy's collar and twisted his hand, tightening the hold to a near choke. "I thought I told you crumpet-sucking febs to stay clear." He pulled back his other hand, fist level with Freddy's nose.

Freddy's face reddened. "Get your Fenian frotch hands off of me," he sputtered. "I'm not doin' nuthin to you." A smile grew on his face as other men drew close in a silent summoning.

Jessica watched the confrontation, amazed that Freddy would try something so bold with no effort to conceal his intent. Two men used their bodies to get her to step backward, away from the growing conflict. She was aware of more movement in the barns.

Freddy snapped the syringe in two, dropping the pieces on the ground. The spilled drug created a tiny milky pool in the dirt. "No need to get your plastic Paddy boys involved." He looked around. "Quite a show you got there for the little lady." His tongue rolled against his lower lip as he smirked.

Jax shoved him away, obviously wishing he could throw a punch. He motioned for one man to stand by Bealltainn's paddock and fell into step beside Jessica as they returned to the barns.

"I'm sorry, Miss Jessica. I took his bait."

She was confused. "Sorry?"

"That stunt gave him a very clear idea of the number of men Michael has watching you. He's a clever bloke. If anyone was questioning whether they should band against you, that scene brought him more allies."

"What's a 'plastic Paddy,'" she asked, confused that the phrase seemed to increase Jax's anger even more than the attempt to drug Bealltainn.

It took a few deep breaths before his color returned to normal and he could answer her. "It means I only pretend to be Irish. It's a reference to me growing up in Belfast and thinking of myself as an Irishman instead of someone who grew up in the United Kingdom."

"Oh," she said slowly. "I understand."

He turned and faced her. "Even workin' with the grooms from Dubai, caring for horses is enough to bridge language barriers. See those men over there?" He indicated men from other barns. Some were lean with creamy tans or olive skin while others had jet-black hair and beards. "Last night at the pub you would have thought it was World Peace Day at the United Nations. Don't be fooled. They'd lose their jobs if they defended their beliefs on the sparked flint of inebriated love. So, we all are smart enough to keep away from politics, but tensions are building. It won't take much to get fists to fly."

Her dread increased. She wasn't an impartial observer. Her very existence had once threatened to tip irreparably the balance of their struggle. She was as tied to their conflict as they were. At the track, the visible hatred and distrust was displayed for being a woman in a man's world. She wondered how much of that chauvinism was a cover for other reasons a target branded her back.

Doherty met them at the barn and handed her an eventing vest. "You'll need to wear this during training runs, too."

The vest was an ingenious device considered a jockey's personal airbag. Clipped to the saddle, the snug-fitting garment surrounded the wearer with arm-sized tubes of cushioning air deployed when the ripcord-like tab was pulled during a fall that separated rider from horse. Pressurized air flooded into the multiple tubes and provided lifesaving protection.

She slipped it over her head like a poncho and secured the sides with a combination of zippers and Velcro tabs to test its fit. "Good idea. Helmets and goggles seem silly when a half-ton animal could fall on you."

Doherty didn't exude his usual charm. He was pre-occupied with scanning the Devon-on-Thames team. "I hope you feel ready for your maiden hurdles race. A few people want to meet you before then. There's an owners dinner tonight. Join me?" He flashed a brilliant smile, well rehearsed to get his desired effect from the ladies.

"No, thank you. I've got a routine that's working for me. I'd rather just stay focused on the races and not be gawked at." He nodded in understanding, gracious at her decline. The real reason she wanted to stay in was nerves. Tension increased before any big event, but what she felt among the men was disproportionate. Some kind of disconnect existed, but she couldn't identify the cause. Michael's men did not belie additional strain, but she found herself pressing her ear to her hotel suite's door and only going to bed when she heard the soft shuffle of the guard in the hall.

Michael had called her each night to check on preparations and to make sure she had everything she needed. His uncle kept him occupied with meetings, and she assured him that her schedule was too hectic for him to be with her. Besides, she was too exhausted at the end of the day to be good company. They agreed that his arrival on the fifteenth for the private race would be best.

The day of the maiden hurdle race arrived, and the stables were full of trainers, owners, and jockeys. Jessica rolled her neck and shoulders around in circles, trying to relax. Immaculate white breeches emerged from her tall black and brown boots. Lettering proclaiming MMC, Ltd sponsorship raced up her right thigh. If Michael wanted to make his presence any more known, he could not have found a more clear way than emblazoning her thigh with his initials. The blue and green silks of her jersey matched the tightly fitting cover of her helmet. Doherty gave her an approving look.

A horn called in the distance signaling ten minutes to race time. Doherty signaled the grooms to bring Kilkea out. Today's field would race eighteen horses. Kilkea hadn't raced against that many horses since his accident. Immediately Jessica knew he was off. His eyes were too wide and darted from the track to the stands. His nostrils flared. With each step, she felt time slow, details sharpened into focus.

A second sounding of the horn called the riders to the starting line. The starts of a hurdles race and steeplechase are different than the start of a flat horse race. Rather than being lead into a long line of individual gates that burst open at the sounding of a bell, the steeplechase starts with the riders trotting or cantering slowly as a group to the starting line. All looked very civilized until the tape would drop and all hell broke loose. Jessica followed the others, wondering about the wisdom of the British way to not use the calming presence of a stable pony as in the States. The horses skittered and danced their way along, jockeys gripping bits up tight to keep the high-strung horses from bolting too soon.

The race consisted of sixteen flights, each slightly different. Jessica's strategy was to keep to the outside, open up and pass on the flat and take the jumps cleanly. The first mile and a half's ten fences were challenging, and she positioned Kilkea to be in the top three horses.

Within seconds of the tape dropping, she knew Kilkea was not ready to be tested. Doherty's assumption that Kilkea could cope in a field of beginners and that the other jockeys would sideline advanced strategies for the hurdle race nearly got her killed. At the twelfth fence, the horse in the second position, ridden by a jockey wearing the bronze colors of Devon-on-Thames, cut her off in midair, bumping them off balance. Kilkea panicked, his front legs stiffened in fear, and he slipped on the landing. Momentum rolled them over, and his hooves flailed wildly. She couldn't hold on and careened over his shoulder. Her vest deployed, surrounding her in a ball of air. One hoof caught her in the side and would have splintered her ribs if she had not been wearing her vest.

Jessica instinctively curled up making her as tiny a target as possible as horses crashed and skidded into a pile. Jockeys cursed and horses screamed. She was as helpless in the muck as a clot of turf.

One jockey remained motionless in the mud, his legs at odd angles—face ashen and racing career over. A horse thrashed its body around, trying to regain its footing, and screeching in pain and confusion. An equine ambulance pulled close, and screens were hurriedly set up to keep the hopeless reality of injury away from investors' eyes. Jessica didn't have to look into the faces of the others to know she would bear the blame.

She limped off the track, head down and avoiding eye contact with the other jockeys. Doherty came up to her and assessed her quickly. Deeming her fit for the next day's race, he went on to deal with Kilkea.

Michael's escorts deposited her back to her suite. As she soaked in a hot bath, she noted the usual bustle of the hotel was missing. Everything appeared quiet and calm.

SATURDAY, JUNE 15
MANCHESTER, ENGLAND

DALLY THORPE WAS about to end her double shift at ETV, Manchester's scraggly answer to the BBC, when the news hotline rang at 10:15 a.m. Reflexively, her stomach clenched as she reached for the black phone.

"N-news Desk. What's your s-s-story?"

"There is a truck with two thousand kilograms of explosives parked at the corner of Commercial and Cannon Streets that will blow at 11:15 a.m."

Dally's heart caught in her throat as she listened to the message. She forced her mind to clear as she assessed each clue. Male. Young. Gruff. Irish.

Dammit.

"How can I be s-sure this is for r-r-real? Who are you representing?"

"Carrickmacross"

The IRA codeword was clear. As soundlessly as she could, Dally stood up and looked across the mostly empty desks of the newsroom. She caught the eye of her editor, Don Hume. The expression on her face was the only clue she gave. Don picked up the other line to listen.

"I said fuckin' Carrickmacross."

"Oh. Okay. I g-got it. Truck. Bomb. Two thousand k-kilograms. Corner of Corporation and Can–" The phone clicked off in her ear.

Don was already dialing the police. Within seconds he confirmed the warning was real and made by the Irish Republican Army. The IRA was back in business.

She turned up the volume on the radio scanner. Calling Grandier news must have been an afterthought because other news stations and police were already on their way. Dally noted how smoothly the threat was made and how quickly the news crews and the police were mobilized by the use of the pre-established code word. How bloody accommodating of those shit-eating IRA bastards to plant a bomb and then give enough of a warning to clear the area of people.

"That's less than a block from the Arndale malls," Dally said as she gathered up her recorder and shoved other papers into her satchel.

Don stopped her before she left. "I have some of the guys already on their way."

"This was my phone c-c-call! My s-s-story," she said, cursing her show of nervousness and struggling for composure. Even towering over her boss did not diminish how insignificant she felt in his presence. She peered down at him and pushed her glasses back up the slightly hooked bridge of her nose. Did she look confident and determined? Doubtful. Her scraggly thin brown hair and wardrobe of a pink cardigan and ill-fitting, too-short trousers robbed her of any chance of gaining such an image. She drew her shoulders back and raised her chin.

Don stepped back and she could see his thoughts churning in his head. As a junior reporter, she had not proven herself with detailed investigations, but she had a knack for crafting words that could build a story out of an anthill. Unfortunately for Grandier News, that combination meant her reporting had drawn the attention of barristers and lawsuits. Maybe this time, her lack of polish and guile would help disarm sources and make them talk on the record. She tried to keep the desperation from her face as she silently willed him to give her this scoop.

He glanced quickly at the classic black and white clock with its long hand clicking downward to VI, then back at her.

"Time's a wastin'. Get a move on."

AINTREE RACECOURSE

FRIDAY'S MAIDEN RACE'S preparations were nothing in comparison to what she saw around her now. For each of the thirty-five horses, a team of at least ten people fussed about. In the States, the wagering occurred after the jockeys and horses paraded around an enclosure, but at Aintree, each jockey wore their silks and stood outside their horse's stall, on display to make the wagering and deal making more informed.

Instead of trainers in threadbare tweeds and owners in last year's fashions, the barns were full of scents and trappings of the super rich. If the cut of the suit and the quality of fabric weren't enough to identify the owners and syndicate members, then the finely-attired and bejeweled women attached to their arms were. Without exception, when they approached Bealltainn's stall, they stopped and gaped. Jessica squirmed at their unhidden shock, then recoiled further when their surprised expressions settled into the machinations of wager. The largest concentration of onlookers clustered around Bealltainn's stall, sheiks and businessmen traded insider glances. It didn't take a mind reader to understand what they thought of her presence in a man's game. A festive atmosphere mixed with the faint smell of bloodlust was unlike anything Jessica had ever experienced.

The bustle before her stood in stark contrast to the near-empty grandstands. Only a handful of seats were occupied.

Doherty approached Bealltainn's stall and assessed Jessica more than the horse. Doherty's interest in Jessica would cease as soon as she brought Bealltainn over the finish line. This temporary and tenuous relationship suited Jessica just fine.

"I won't say it again, but you underestimated the jockeys yesterday and they took advantage of you. They screwed the maiden and spent the evening slapping each other's backs over it."

Jessica's mouth twitched at Doherty's choice of words. "Well, then. They know better than anybody that you only get to screw a maiden once. After that, she has nothing left to lose."

Doherty's mouth opened in a wide grin. "You did well enough yesterday until you trusted that bloke wouldn't cut you off midair. Today will be different. You'll face more horses, and the race is twice as long. The jockeys riding for the same farm will use team strategies against you."

"And they didn't yesterday?"

"Hardly. They're not going to show their hands before they have to. Bealltainn's in superior condition. What about you?"

"I'm fine," she said, rubbing her sides. "A bit stiff, but I'm good."

He appraised her appearance in the same way he judged all of his livestock. When he didn't see any hint of injury from yesterday's fall, he moved on. "Did the new vest fit?"

This vest was heavier than the one she wore yesterday. She argued the additional heft would throw off her balance as well as Bealltainn's. Doherty waived off her objections.

The first horn sounded. Bealltainn stood coiled with his head high, ears flattened, and nostrils wide and red. She had to stand on her toes to double check the adjustments of the bridle and saddle, consciously reminding herself that touching him would not lethally complete an electrical circuit. She looked into his eyes and felt his thoughts with a jolt. *Stay out of my way. Let me run my race.* She adjusted her gloves to hide her shaking hands.

Doherty gave Jessica a leg up into the saddle by grabbing her shin and hoisting upward. Riding Bealltainn for a short time was not nearly enough to know all of his issues, but Doherty had provided the solid guidance she needed. He gave her last minute instructions as she positioned her stirrups, taking his advice to bring her feet closer to her hips than she had with Kilkea. She needed the extra leverage to enable her to stand up over Bealltainn's neck to work with his natural motion.

Jessica breathed deeply to calm herself and hoped it had a similar affect on Bealltainn. A groom tightly held the reins to keep the horse steady as Jessica made her final preparations, bringing her goggles down over her eyes, adjusting the chinstrap of her helmet and pulling her gloves on even tighter. She refused a crop but was unsure if Bealltainn trusted her enough to believe she didn't have one. She felt ready. Nervous and scared, too.

When mounted up, the jockeys towered over the owners and trainers who roamed about the paddock. Each team enjoyed the best preparation. The horses gleaming coats showed their powerful bodies to full advantage. The jockeys wore close fitting jerseys and helmets, making them indistinguishable except for the colors and numbers on the horses. She still stood out because of her height and braided bun secured at the nape of her neck.

Jessica stayed focused and didn't make eye contact with anyone. She had entered the period before each race that every jockey refers to as "the zone." The sounds of the track slipped away. She concentrated on her breathing and heart rate, knowing her legs and hands would telegraph anything she felt to her horse. Had she been less inwardly focused, she may have been able to catch the looks exchanged by several of the jockeys, even if she was not able to understand their meaning. She closed her eyes and pulled images from her memory of each turn and flight. The four-mile race today would last a little over ten minutes and leave horses and riders feeling as if they'd been through a meat grinder.

A repeated pat on her thigh brought her out of her thoughts. She glanced down to see Michael. He looked over at the empty grandstand and back at her.

"Jessica. This race today. . . don't let it catch you off guard."

A flash of annoyance creased her face. "I get it. I crashed yesterday because I did exactly that. You're waiting until now to tell me this?" She shook her head in disbelief. He reached up and rubbed her back but she didn't feel it, her jersey and gear serving their purpose. "Sorry," she stammered, "I mean, hi. I'm looking forward to this being over."

Michael flashed a tense smile. "Good luck. It's just a horse race."

The second horn sounded. Bealltainn chewed his bit and flicked an ear back to show he was engaged in listening to his rider while they cantered slowly to the start. Jessica steadied her breath and brought Bealltainn up more in the mouth, sending a signal to him to slow and gather himself. He felt the energy of the field and started to feed on it, wanting to charge forward and get on with it already. Jessica was astride a keg of lit dynamite.

The tape dropped and the officials waved on a fair start. Jessica heard nothing as her concentration blocked out all sounds except for her own breathing.

The first mile and nine flights were not as easy as she had hoped. As soon as the race began, the field divided into two groups. No one had reached top speed. The jockeys focused on conserving their horses' strength and positioning themselves for taking the obstacles cleanly. Jessica calculated how many horses were in front of her or behind, and figured she was in the middle of the second pack. Three jockeys from the Devon-on-Thames team penned her in, making it impossible to keep up with the faster group. She watched as one jockey in burnished silks came up on her left, looked over his shoulder at her, and smiled.

He switched his crop into his right hand as Jessica felt the space between their horses narrow.

Even Bealltainn knew what was coming. He flattened his ears back and fought to free his head from Jessica's grip. The jockey aimed his blow to Bealltainn's neck. Jessica reached forward and the crop crashed down on her arm. The next five hurdles were a blur. Clumps of wet sod flew past her head. Horses began to falter from exhaustion or incompetence and threatened to fall. She kept urging Bealltainn forward, finding the gaps between horses, or forcing herself into the fray, demanding they make room for her.

In front of her was the jump at Canal Turn, where she and Kilkea were cutoff in midair the day before. She took Bealltainn in at a slight angle, cutting off the goon who had cropped her moments before. Out of the corner of her eye, she saw his horse somersault, crash into another, and then skid to a stop in the turf.

As the track before her opened up, she let Bealltainn close the gap, risking expending precious energy. She checked the condition of the other horses. Two were already seriously bobbing their heads up and down. Their gaits looked disorganized, a clear sign of being overridden and approaching exhaustion. She maneuvered Bealltainn to the inside of the track seconds before one of the two horses missed clearing the hurdle, catching the top of the hedge in its chest and bringing it and another horse down on its rider. Jessica heard the jockey's scream cut off mid-breath and knew he was terribly injured, if he was that lucky.

Before the halfway point, Jessica encountered Becher's Brook for the first time. The horse closest to her was more than four lengths away, giving her room to take the jump as she wanted. She started Bealltainn's jump a half stride early and jammed her feet home in the irons as he crested his arc. With her body as ballast, Bealltainn landed with his weight balanced. She could feel a slight buckle of his front legs but recovered, using his hind legs to lunge ahead. He rocketed forward.

Coming from behind the pack was both a blessing and a curse. She wasn't being jostled or cut off by other horses; she chose a line down the track that kept her clear of unexpected moves. Bealltainn lengthened his stride. Jessica had to choose a fine balance between catching the lead pack on the flat by galloping hard or conserving her horse's strength for the final half mile to the finish line.

Jessica knew Bealltainn was much more experienced than she was at this kind of race. The further they went, the more she trusted his judgment, allowing him to decide the length of his stride and the comfortable closeness to another animal.

Being one of the largest horses on the field meant he was carrying more heft than the others were—and could tire more easily. The added weight of that damned vest didn't help either. The motion of her pulsing arms caused the stiff material to rub off patches of skin. If her attention faltered for a second, she would have felt the sticky wounds, raw and close to bleeding. Instead, she focused on her optimal position, crouched, arms forward, and head down. At mile three, Jessica's back, arms, and thighs began to burn with exertion.

Bealltainn's size had another benefit. The horse was an equine catapult for clearing fences. She soon realized that by jumping clean and big, Bealltainn would gain more ground than he could have by merely running. Her heart gave a little skip as she began to cue him to go bigger, to fly. She crossed the line from riding safe to riding fast.

Out of the corner of her eye she saw several jockeys in burnished silks and one with a malformed face approach her. Freddy yelled something to the other riders. They rode up three abreast. She had barely thought the command when she felt a momentary checking of Bealltainn's speed. That fraction of a second caused one horse to miss its takeoff. She watched with satisfaction as they crashed into the hedge, bringing another horse with him.

The field had separated into two packs. The back of the pack, populated by horses and jockeys who would be happy simply to complete the race, did not concern her. The front held six horses. Freddy was closest to her. Jessica positioned Bealltainn along the rail as they approached Becher's Brook for the second time. She quickly reviewed the others and noted which horses were within strides of collapsing with exhaustion and navigated away from them. Bealltainn refused to be checked and fought to go faster. Flecks of foam streamed from his mouth.

She cued an early jump. The milliseconds felt like hours in that slow motion trick the mind plays when things are going catastrophically wrong. Bealltainn's muscles gathered then exploded, launching them into flight. The earth fell away. At the top of the jump, she leaned back. Feet jammed home. Arms stretched in front. Then chest-crushing pain. A baseball bat or something like it slammed against her chest. She looked for the flailing hoof of a fallen horse, but saw nothing. The pain took her breath away. She sensed, more than saw, the edges of her vision curl in.

Bealltainn descended. The earth rushed to them but teased at being further away. She couldn't rely on instinct. Everything was too new. Too foreign. Her body hadn't had enough time to memorize mechanics into reflex. The world lost its color and faded to shades of gray flecked with meteorites of white. She had to correct her position for their landing, but her muscles would not respond. Bealltainn landed hard, slipped, and veered toward the rail. Reins slipped out of Jessica's hands leaving Bealltainn without a pilot. His front legs shook from the effort of keeping them both upright, hitting the rail on his left side and careening back toward the right—directly in the path of an oncoming horse.

Jessica heard the scream of the horse and the curse of the jockey. A blur of red and brown and flying chunks of turf closed in on her. She was aware of her tingling hands fumbling for the reins. Her heart seemed to have been placed in a vise, stopping it from beating. Bealltainn stumbled and sunk to his knees. A flash of hooves whizzed past her cheek, nicking her helmet, and surged ahead. With one final scramble, Bealltainn found his legs again and pushed himself forward. Survival instinct, not skill, kept Jessica gripped on his back.

The pain in her chest grew. They continued racing on an unstable combination of reflex and luck. Bealltainn was no fool. He took the opportunity of a distracted rider to grip the bit in his teeth, diminishing Jessica's ability to control him. He jumped huge and at a barely perceptible angle, cutting one horse off midair and causing it to slip badly on its landing. Bealltainn surged ahead, and it was too late to stop him from closing the gap between him and the remaining horses, the bronze panels of their riders' jerseys distinct.

She looked ahead and saw Freddy looking over his shoulder to see who was challenging him. Goggles and layers of mud hid any surprise that registered on his face. Fumbling with the reins, Jessica tried to saw the bit back and forth in Bealltainn's mouth, struggling to regain control and desperate to take a line away from the Devon-on-Thames team. It was useless. She couldn't move her arm. Bealltainn moved right, they moved right. Then they blocked left. Bealltainn decided to go between them.

Each jockey switched their crops into the hand closest to Bealltainn and began flailing wildly. Jessica tried to stay away from their full reach, watching them waste precious energy and time trying to crease her or her horse. She could feel Bealltainn panic to move away from the thrashing crops, ears flattened against his head. A whip crashed down on his shoulder, rose up, and crashed down again. Blows landed on his neck and her leg. A white-hot welt rose up her thigh. She lost the rhythm of his stride, and Bealltainn faltered. His momentary hesitation broke up his speed enough to create a gap between the two lead horses. She was no longer the pilot, but that did not stop her from encouraging him on. Her whole demeanor said, "Go!" He snaked his neck forward. One horse could not withstand the pace. Its legs buckled as they pulled to the outside of the track. Only two horses remained between her and the finish line.

Freddy checked his horse, blocking Jessica's attempt to pass on the inside. Bealltainn barreled ahead, wedging himself between them and the rail. Freddy's horse was faltering badly, moving its legs as if they were bags of sand. They approached the hurdle side by side, but Freddy greedily pushed his horse to do more than it was able. He beat the exhausted animal again and again with his crop, alternately trying to catch Bealltainn and Jessica with his swings. Bealltainn stiffened in panic.

"C'mon guy. We can do this." The voice she hoped to soothe and steady him was nothing more than a coarse whisper. Her ability to control Bealltainn decreased with each stride.

Bealltainn surged forward in a blind need to end the race. Celebrating freedom from commands, the horse flattened his body out and covered huge distances with each stride. It was the fastest Jessica had ever ridden— beyond reason, beyond safety—and she didn't care. When the final jump appeared, she couldn't cue Bealltainn to jump big. It didn't matter. The huge horse gathered himself and launched skyward. Freddy's horse faltered under the withering pace and threatened to refuse the jump, sliding on stiffened legs as it approached the hedge. She was too focused on staying on to see if they made it over.

She could feel Bealltainn getting sloppy and loose in his gallop, but the end was in sight. She began to rasp a soft singsong of encouragement— more for her benefit than for Bealltainn's.

Bealltainn had nothing more to give. Jessica's vision cleared enough to see the closest horse was barely a length away. She wrapped her fingers in his mane.

"C'mon guy. Stretch it out. C'mon. Just a little more."

With all of the hurdles behind them, the final sprint put Jessica shoulder to shoulder with one last jockey, his silks flecked with mud and soaked with sweat. The jockey swerved into her path and slowed the pace down. Jessica was too new to the harsh strategies of team racing to recognize a setup. The lead jockey slowed their pace to allow his teammate to catch up.

In seconds, Freddy was beside her again, using his horse to press them into the rail. He thrashed his crop, hitting her in the arms and legs. She ducked her head behind her upper arm to protect her face as much as possible. Freddy and the other jockey tried to box her in, trying to her crash into the rail.

With a few more strides they would have succeeded, but Bealltainn panicked. His only instinct was to get away, and the only tool he had to do so was his massive body. He propelled himself forward and to the right, closer to Freddy's horse. Exhaustion and primal fear worked to make Bealltainn's gait a drunken swagger at breakneck speed. If it were not for his forward momentum, he would have fallen over. He swayed into Freddy and his horse, causing them to crash to the turf.

Freddy's teammate used the distraction to take the lead.

Bealltainn fought on. When they passed the finish line, all Jessica was aware of was that they were shoulder to shoulder. She had no idea who finished first. She willed her fingers to unclench his mane, but her movements were sluggish. Her heart and shoulder were on fire. She stood up in the stirrups, wrapped the reins twice around her hands, and sawed the bit as hard as she could. Finally, she was able to bring Bealltainn to a reluctant canter, then trot. The world swirled. She wanted to praise Bealltainn but was afraid leaning over to rub his neck would send her toppling to the ground. Flecks of light played at the edges of her vision.

The track immediately filled with people and eventually a groom came up, clipping a lead onto Bealltainn's bridle. Voices swirled around her.

"Jaysus! A photo finish! Bloody good race, that one!" a thick-necked groom said as he patted Bealltainn's side. "The horses that stayed standing were running in the spot, but at least they finished."

Jessica couldn't find her voice.

"They're still lookin' at the monitors to see who won! I hain't seen anything like it."

Only after she knew the groom was in control of Bealltainn did she uncurl her fingers from the reins to take off her gloves. Her hands were shaking and cold, her fingers white with deep red gullies imprinted from the reins tingled as blood returned. Her breath came in short, panting intervals as she recovered from the pummeling. Her chest and shoulder hurt. Her skin, abraded by the vest, was sticky and sore.

She and Bealltainn were escorted into the winner's paddock. Doherty was there, but she only cared that Michael was. Doherty was the first to congratulate her.

"Well done! By God, you gave that a cracking ride! Hardly touched a twig." His eyes scanned Bealltainn as he ran his hand down the horse's legs, barely giving Jessica a glance.

Bealltainn's sides heaved and strings of sweat and foam dripped off him. Other horses hung their heads in exhaustion, but he skittered aside while the track officials gathered around him. A cup, referred to as a spit bucket, was used to gather up some of his slobber, and one official walked off toward the compact building that housed the track's offices—standard procedure for drug screening. The remaining officials shared looks a mixture of surprise and disgust. They motioned to Doherty and huddled in conversation.

A roar rippled through the crowd as the results were posted. Bealltainn had lost. Members of the Devon-on-Thames team received slapped backs and high fives. Jessica dropped her head to her chest, too exhausted to be angered by the results.

Doherty looked up at her. "Never mind those cretins. Your horse stayed up, and you stayed on. It's more than most of them can say."

"You rode a spectacular race," Michael said as he reached to help her dismount. "You did a great job. Thank you."

Jessica put her hands on his shoulders and jumped down, legs wobbly and hot from exertion. Her arms and legs stung from repeated blows. No doubt her right thigh would have a winner of a welt tomorrow. She moved to unclip her helmet and remove her goggles, but her left arm felt heavy and sodden. Without fuss, she used her right arm to gently bring her left across her body to rest at her waist. Exhausted and aching, she accepted Michael's embrace and kiss. She let her weight fall against him.

Jax extended his hand. "That was a bloody good ride! One of the best I've ever seen. You've got a future on this track if you have a mind for it."

Jessica smiled weakly. "Thank you, but no. That was truly insane."

"Insane? Hardly. That was barely a quarter hour's worth of work, and you've nothin' to do for the rest of the day but be wined and dined. Enjoy yourself for a change." Jax clipped a lead onto Bealltainn's bridle and walked to the barns.

Doherty looked up at the clock. "You've time enough to change before the luncheon. Then there's the dinner tonight. I'm sure many people will want to make your acquaintance."

She barely acknowledged him. "I guess no one will have to worry about a woman in the winner's circle," she said as she scanned at the sea of faces. She couldn't pick out a friendly expression on any of them. "I'm sorry I lost your horse for you. Bealltainn is a rarity. He's going to be a phenomenal champion."

Doherty's mouth firmed. "Betting and losing is all a part of the sport."

The owner of Devon-on-Thames cut into the conversation. His face reddened with ale that had already begun to flow. Betting slips and tout sheets from the day's race stuffed the pockets of his brown plaid jacket. "Bloody brilliant race! Any horse I own just increased in value because of today. Win or lose, today's race put your farm and our syndicate on everyone's lips."

"My farm was *already* on everyone's lips," quipped Doherty. "I hardly needed your help with that."

Jessica continued to lean against Michael, enduring the formalities and wishing this whole day were over. Not having the adrenalin rush of a win to prop her up and carry her through made the beatings she endured much harder. The thought of sitting through celebratory luncheons and receptions made her wilt, so she didn't resist when Michael ignored the final formalities of the day and declined requests for introductions and interviews. The physical and emotional demands set by the frenetic pace of the last two weeks caught up with her and was grateful for Michael's intervention. She felt increasingly defeated when she realized it was not even eleven thirty in the morning.

One of Michael's men approached. She was vaguely aware of how urgently and quietly he spoke into Michael's ear. Michael replied with a few commands and pulled her closer. She flinched with pain. He looked over her head at the crowd and guided her to the exit.

She felt the tension in his body. "What's going on?" she asked, alert to the sudden change.

"We need to get out of here."

With orchestrated efficiency, his security detail surrounded them. No one looked at one another. As a group, they acted as strangers merely moving in the same direction. Casual. Relaxed. Concealing the fact that they were coiled. Ready. They were almost to the doors when the crowd hushed and cell phones chimed and vibrated in unison. Attention shifted away from horses and owners to anyone with a cell phone. After the hush came a flurry of action.

If lavishing money on their horses wasn't enough to prove the wealth of those in attendance, then hiring the best in personal security was. Private security patrols materialized from the shadows of the empty pavilions and rolled up in front of the Queen Mother's Stand. Some wore crisp uniforms, echoing the countries from which they hailed. Others looked woefully underprepared with sagging trousers and blue blazers, but each spoke with hushed commands and hurried to the sides of their employers. Teams fanned out around the building, eyes straining to see anything remotely threatening. Dogs sniffed. People rushed. No one panicked, but all knew the cease-fire was over. Jessica heard them say "explosion" and "crowded mall." She looked at Michael with widened eyes and a silent question.

"I'll learn more soon," was all he said, placing a protective kiss on her forehead.

Thirty minutes later, she was back in her suite drawing a steaming bath. Michael settled her in, making sure she had everything she needed for a few hours. Then, he had made a quick apology and posted two men at her door before he left, cell phone pressed to his ear. Jessica focused more on slipping into a bath than wondering when he would be back. When she finally looked at her reflection, she almost wanted to laugh. A thick film of ash-gray mud covered her from head to toe. Where her goggles were, her eyes stood out as two white patches.

Streaks of mud continued down her neck and her hair held thick clots of gunk. She unbuttoned her jersey and slipped her arms out, noting how terribly compressed her chest felt. The heavy vest felt even heavier and her left shoulder and arm sluggish and sore. She dropped her silks and began to rip off the vest. What she saw did not make sense.

She laid the vest on the vanity and carefully inspected. It didn't look like the other vest used in her fall off Kilkea. This one was made of thick layers of a semi-flexible material covered with a sturdy brushed canvas fabric in a dark gray color. But, instead of it being a patchwork of ingenious airbags, this one was made out of Kevlar—not to protect equestrians but to protect police officers and soldiers.

That was a revelation in itself. Then a flash caught her attention. In the upper left corner, over her heart, where an emblem could have been, she found something quite different.

The bullet had hit the vest with such a velocity that it had smashed and flattened into a size not much larger than a quarter. The Kevlar bulged out in back, making a dent in Jessica's chest centered below her collarbone and above her heart. The protruding knob compressed the nerves that traveled to her left hand and caused painful pressure and tingling.

Using a nail file, Jessica pried the bullet out of its hollow, not believing what she was seeing. Where the bullet would have entered her, the skin above her left breast was darkening into a deep purple color, showing substantial bruising underneath her skin. Whoever aimed at her didn't want to fail.

It took effort to sit calmly in the bath. The hot water stung her raw and abraded skin. She soaked until the water-cooled and the ibuprofen kicked in. Michael sent a masseuse, who worked on the remaining kinks while she mulled the day's events. Slowly the pain subsided, and she curled up on the couch, hugging her terry robe around her as if it could offer her protection. An hour later, a loud knock on the door startled her and she rose slowly to answer it. Michael's face peered back at her through the peephole.

A uniformed waiter rolled a room service cart into the suite and raised his head in question of where to set up the food. The suite was comprised of a bedroom, bath, and large living room that doubled as a conference room. A dining table able to sit four was in front of large French doors that opened to a small balcony. Michael motioned toward the coffee table in the middle of another seating area that held a couch and two large armchairs.

He waited patiently for the table to be set before he ushered the waiter and empty cart out the door, past his two men stationed in the hallway. He closed the door and secured the chain before he enveloped Jessica in his arms. He held her face and kissed her with urgency. Fingers tangled in her hair as he kissed her lips, her cheeks, and down her neck.

"I was worried about you. It looked like you were about to collapse today."

"That was hell," she said, only half joking. She looked at his casual chinos and a light sweater. "No tux? I thought we were committed to that fancy dinner tonight?"

In just a few hours he had aged twenty years. Lines on his ashen face joined crescents of dark blue under his eyes. He motioned to the table, spread with multiple dishes with metal covers, fresh flowers, and champagne. "I thought I'd keep you to myself tonight. I figured I owed you one after that race today."

"This doesn't even come close to making up for what I've been through." She lifted the stainless steel covers from the variety of plates and platters, reviewing the night's offerings. "Hmm. Looks delicious. But why the change in plans?"

"I know you're not disappointed at staying in," he teased, trying to keep his manner light. "Think of it. You don't have to be ogled at by some Saudi prince."

"You've got a point. There's enough food for an army, but that better mean you're staying."

Michael wouldn't look at her. "As long as I can. Treating you too well might backfire on me. After a bath, massage, and good food, I'm afraid you'll sleep for a week. And then what will I do?"

"It looks like you need some rest, too," she said as she brushed her thumb across his lips. "What was the commotion about?"

Before he answered, he walked over to the credenza and poured himself a Scotch, taking time to find decent music on the stereo. He chose a station with some jazz fusion and turned the volume up. His motions were deliberate and calculated to give him time before he brought his mouth close to her ear. "There was an explosion not far from here in Manchester at a shopping mall. The IRA has taken responsibility."

She gasped. "Today? Was anyone hurt?"

"No one was killed. Some minor injuries were reported. It happened as the race was concluding."

Cold started at her scalp and fell through her, cell by cell. "Is the Charity behind it?" She was surprised at how matter-of-fact she sounded.

"I can't answer that . . . yet," he began. "Someone made a call to the police and different news agencies warning that the area should be cleared. No question it was the IRA, but I don't have any proof one way or the other if the Charity was behind it. I need time to trace the money."

Her heart started that little tattoo in her chest that forewarned of a rising swell of panic. She settled onto the couch and winced. Shifting, her robe parted, exposing her thigh. A long red welt traveled its length.

"Jesus, Jessica. What happened out there?" he asked.

"That's nothing. There's something I want you to see. Grab the vest for me?"

He retrieved the vest from the vanity and examined it with interest, tracing the dent with his index finger. He turned it over and pressed on the bulge, feeling its rigidity. Before he could say more, Jessica held up the slug. His features changed into an unreadable mask.

He reached over and smoothed her hair, bringing her face to his. His kiss was gentle and had lost the edge of desperation that had been there only moments before. He rested his forehead against hers, the horror of what didn't happen mixing with the horror of what did. "Thank God you're safe."

"This is a *bulletproof* vest! You *knew* something was going to happen. That's why you had Doherty switch them out."

He hesitated. "He wouldn't have done it if he didn't see the need, too. The vest protects against all types of extreme impacts. A lot of egos were riding on that race. You faced a rough crowd out there. I'd heard rumors that in past races the jockeys can get violent. I wanted to give you as much protection as I could, but I swear to you I did *not* know anything about today's bombing. What did you see in the barns?"

Jessica told Michael the details of the past week. He listened carefully. "Hmm. Jax kept me posted, too, and what you're telling me fits with what he said. I'm most interested in what happened on the course."

"Becher's Brook is the only jump where the rider's chest is exposed enough to get off a clean shot. I had no idea what hit me." She looked directly into Michael's eyes. "Is this something to do with you?"

Michael fingered the slug. "I don't know. Doherty told me about vicious talk from a few of the owners—oil nations mostly. This race attracts people who behave as if rules don't apply to them, but I think we have to assume this bullet is connected to me. I want you out of here." He made a quick call, giving instructions in an uncompromising tone. A few minutes later, he received a call back. He placed the phone to his chest. "You came in via Galway to Manchester. Right?" Jessica nodded. "Manchester airport is locked down, but we'll work on something to get you out as soon as possible." For the next few minutes he was like a lion in a cage, walking back and forth, hitting an invisible wall in each direction. One last call stopped his pacing.

"Okay. The jet will be waiting and we'll determine the best destination for you in the morning. I'll stay with you until the car comes for you tomorrow."

Jessica laughed, happy to see him relax. "That's one hell of a way to invite yourself to spend the night with a woman."

His relief was visible as he refilled her glass. "I'd like to think you've had worse invitations."

"Maybe, but not by much."

Belfast, Northern Ireland

AOIFE RESTED HER head on knees hugged to her chest. She tried to make sense of the past hours.

Saturday had started as another spectacular day. Taking her cue from the cloudless sky, she had decided to get her provisions from Taggart's mart. It was supposed to be a quick walk around the corner and down Shankill Road. The RUC officer at the peace line checkpoint nodded absently at her when she passed through. Even passing the huge murals proclaiming, "You are entering Loyalist Sandy Row, Heartland of East Belfast Ulster Freedom Fighters," and others with images of fully armed and hooded figures—machine guns pointing in all directions—did not faze her. Each time she ventured outside her flat, she passed street paintings covering the sides of buildings and walls with pro-Union and pro-British sentiments. Normally that stretch of Shankill Road would cause her to quicken her step. But the day was a sunny day, and Aoife thought she'd make the most of it.

Taggarts Market always had a TV blaring as Junior never wanted to miss his soaps. The name "Junior" was the only youthful thing about the wizened shopkeeper, but far be it for Aoife to break the news to him that upgrading his name to "Mister" might be more in keeping with his bald-head and missing teeth. She first heard of the bombing as she paid her tab. The news bulletins interrupted his program, and images of the smoke and terrified people filled the screen.

Junior gazed up at the screen and then returned his attention to Aoife, who was looking at the money he had placed in his till. A cold shiver ran up Aoife's spine, wondering if she would be denied the food that she had already paid for.

"You picked a fine day to come around here. Now be gone," said Junior with a toss of his head toward the door.

She nodded at Junior and put on her best face. "You've the best bread around. Well worth the walk."

He grunted. "Not worth dying for."

Aoife hurried out the door, clutching her groceries to her chest. Being in a shop run by Protestants was fool hardy. She had no intention of staying longer and risking Junior changing his mind. Taggarts had been the recipient of more than one bottle of petrol lit with a rag stuffed in its neck, and today's news could mean more such gifts.

Aoife was barely on the street before she heard the first beats of the crowd. Her heart stilled for a moment as she listened with dread. The sound was far off at first, not much more than a rush of wind or waves crashing upon the shore. Each passing moment it grew louder. She looked down at the opening of the alley to the main thoroughfare and saw people rushing out into the street. Shankill Road was coming alive with people. *Och*, Aoife knew all too well what that would mean. The crowd consisted mostly of men, young and old, with shirtsleeves rolled up, and bats and bottles in their hands. Many women joined them, carrying what weapons they could find in their kitchens and making as much noise as they could by beating pots and pans. They all wore resolute expressions that told they walked up the street with full knowledge of what they'd be facing.

The shortest route back to her flat would be the way she came. No way could she return through the peace line before they closed the gates; they would have done that at the first suspicion of trouble. She had to go down Shankill to Northumberland Street and up Divis before she could cut back over to Cupar Way. Hopefully, she would avoid anything else that might stand in her way.

At first it seemed that her strategy worked. She moved eastward on side streets as the crowd moved west along main thoroughfares. Eventually the side streets filled, and she fought against the increasing tide of people with her head down, not looking to either side, afraid that any eye contact—even with a friend—would spark trouble. The tension gave her feet an additional burst of speed when she realized she carried a bag emblazoned with "Taggarts" on it. She was a Catholic who had the nerve to shop at a loyalist shop in a loyalist part of town. The trouble she was in she had asked for. The Catholics would view her as suspect for supporting the economics of the other side, and the Protestants would be affronted at her brazen crossing of the line.

A few blocks into her trek, she stopped to rest on a bench, taking her items out of the bag and turning it inside out, hiding the logo and a potential reason to harm her. Announcements through loudhailers urged people to remain calm and get off the streets. Aoife took her shoes off and rubbed her sore feet, cursing herself for wearing a skirt and low heels instead of pants and more sensible shoes. Then again, she thought she was only going out for a bit, not a hike. Her bench was in a grassy area under a large tree. She rested in the shadow of several murals. One commemorated the

Belfast Dockers and Carters strike of 1907 was painted to look like a series of black and white Polaroid pictures with the slogan, "Not as Catholics or Protestants. Not as Nationalists or Unionists, but as Belfast Workers Standing Together." Aoife thought it was pitiful that the grandsons shown standing shoulder to shoulder in the mural were about to pelt one another with rubber bullets and rocks. She wanted them to settle their differences so she could get Bits and Mittens their kibble.

A low rumble worked its way through the bench into her gut and grew louder with each passing minute. Armored tanks and personnel carriers loaded with machine-carrying soldiers passed only a few blocks away, going up Shankill road to where she had just been.

Others might not have taken time to rest in the middle of a public square, but she knew the chess game of offensive and defensive moves. Her decision to stay put for a few hours kept her from straying into harm's way. Riots were common and most often kept to the main streets, not side alleys like she was in. Besides, she was confident in her ability to protect herself, especially if engaged in a one-on-one tussle. She rubbed her feet and listened to the building riot with passing concern, hoping it would blow itself out before it grew too big. Today seemed different. The energy released felt greater than other riots and the frenzy seemed to grow with each passing hour instead of slowing burning itself out. By the time she decided to move again, the sounds of gunshots, people screaming, and the roar of flames were all around her.

It wouldn't have mattered which way she turned when she left the relative safety of her park bench. Belfast exploded with the rage and frustration that had built up over months of stalled peace talks. Years of denied civil rights and generations of prejudice boiled over. This wasn't the first time her city ignited with anger, and certainly wouldn't be the last, but this time Aoife was caught in the middle. She had miscalculated and tamped down a growing desperation to find a way out.

A tide of people rushed toward her, away from the deep rumble of the tanks. A few people stopped and picked up whatever loose debris they found then kept running. Within seconds, Aoife heard the sharp "*wssss*" of the rubber bullets overhead, but she remained seated, assessing the best route to take, still hedging that the commotion would bypass her square. The "*wssss*" increased in number and closeness, and people began to shout, "It's live bullets!" and, "Bloody Hell! They's real 'munitions!" A few men dragged limp and bloodied bodies along with them as if to prove their point. The RUC turned the corner with their tanks and carriers. Soldiers, fully protected with helmets, visors, and bulletproof vests, carried rifles, belts of ammunition, grenades, and tear gas launchers. Aoife was left with her inside-out Taggarts bag, bread, and milk.

Cursing herself for being so unprepared, Aoife ran—first with the crowd and then away from it—on any street she thought would carry her to safety. She wanted to run to the sanctuary of the cathedral, but she was on the other side of town, and streets were impassible. Hours passed as she moved with the same pattern; she listened to the gunshots and screams, caught her breath, then ran in the opposite direction. She zigzagged around the alleys of West Belfast, hoping against hope a bullet wouldn't claim her. Gasping for a breath of air not tainted with the acrid smell of CS gas, she stopped in the nook of a doorway and pressed her back against a metal door, concealing herself in its shadow.

She nearly lost her balance when the door flew open, and nearly fainted when she saw the long barrel of a gun pointed directly at her nose. She instinctively assessed the angle of the barrel and the fear in the soldier's eyes, determining the best avenue for her defense. She must have not looked like much of a threat, for the men inside gave her a shove and told her to be on her way. When an opportunity presented to save herself, she knew enough to take it and run. She was halfway down the street before her brain began to use some power reclaimed from her fleeing feet. Could she possibly have seen what she did? Stopping midstride, she turned and looked back at the way she had come.

Men poured out of their mustering place and into the street. They wore the cotton shirts, jeans, and trousers of poor men from the slums, but over that they strapped thick vests, munitions belts, and more of the same type of gear Aoife had seen the RUC wear. They had helmets, not exactly the same as the RUC's, but with clear glass-like shields over their faces, all unscratched and very new. A few men worked together carrying a long pipe, about five inches in diameter and eight feet long. Others carried a drab green box filled with oversized bullets more than half the length of a man's forearm, all strapped together on a long belt. The other end of the alley was suddenly blocked off, not by an RUC tank as Aoife feared, but by a short caravan of mismatched trucks and cars, each filled with shining equipment and fearless men.

Aoife knew enough to get out of their way. She backed up between two large trash bins, flattening herself against the brick wall. The small brigade organized and pulled out into the main street. Within seconds, hideous sounds of explosions and gunfire ricocheted off the buildings.

By the time Aoife stopped running and turned onto her street, only the throbbing of her feet seemed real. Orange flames licked the sky and the flashing lights of the fire trucks and Guarda lined her street. What she pieced together from the fragments of conversation that swirled around her was that the RUC had blown a hole in the peace line using military grade ordinance last used against the Germans in defense of London.

They intended to hit an alleged IRA safe house on the first shot, but hit Mrs. Reynolds' flat instead. The RUC kept trying until they got it right, shattering the peace line, and sending its pieces everywhere.

A thick mantle of shock weighed on Aoife. She sunk down on a stoop that only the day before she had sat to sun herself. The tins of cat food for Bits and Mittens promised to Mrs. Reynolds clanked together as she plunked down her bag of groceries. The milk had warmed and soured, and the bread was flattened and squashed to hardly more than bird food. Her eyes burned from smoke and the CS gas that seemed to fill every inch of the city.

Men yelled and pulled hoses around. Women stood in groups of twos or threes, clucking with fear and concern, thankful the destruction skipped their homes. They wondered aloud what the flat occupants had done to earn a bomb dropped through their roofs. Aoife stared blankly at the fire, feeling its heat on her face, and not aware when someone sat beside her. She only came out of her fog when an arm wrapped around her shoulder. Mrs. Reynolds, with soot on her face and a cat under her arm, hugged her. Both women sat silently as the heat from their homes evaporated tears before they could roll down their cheeks.

Wordlessly, Aoife put her head on the older woman's shoulders and kicked a shredded piece of metal. Thinking it may be worth salvaging, she used her thumb to brush the black ash off raised characters exposing the logo for "2100 Ltd." She shrugged and threw it on the rubbish heap.

LIVERPOOL, ENGLAND

MICHAEL RECLINED IN bed with Jessica cradled in the crook of his arm, her head on his shoulder. She was in the deep sleep of the exhausted. He absently twirled a strand of her hair around his fingers and stared at the ceiling. He found it impossible to sleep as the myriad of scenarios shifted shapes and possibilities. Everything pointed to a well-planned and well-coordinated attack.

The IRA didn't need his father's money to pull off a bombing, but the fact that this was more brazen than any attack before worried him. He calmed himself with the breathing trick he learned at the police academy to center himself before firing a weapon and to fight his instinctive revulsion at pulling the trigger. He drew in a deep breath for five counts and exhaled for ten. Eyes closed, he repeated this until his thoughts narrowed to only what he wanted to focus on.

Columns of numbers and companies faded to the names and faces of countless people his uncle introduced him to over the past weeks. Liam had astutely sat Michael beside the most influential people, listening as he navigated the waters of his father. Michael turned each conversation over in his head, trying to remember any ill-turned phrase or sheen of sweat that would have hinted activities connected to the bombing. Even with his uncle's whispered details, he gained marginal insight into the rifts inside the larger world of the Charity and even less on who was behind the Arndale bombing.

The only tangible truth he gained was if he had been in full control of the Charity, no bombing would have occurred.

The light on his cell phone blinked. He grabbed it and looked at the number of calls he missed. Too many. Each would contain questions he had no answers for. He scanned the incoming calls and saw that none were from Liam. He grumbled in disgust. His uncle no doubt preferred to spend the evening entertained by some trollop, rather than be bothered with current events. The clear message Liam sent was that his interests lay outside of the Charity and that this was Michael's concern to deal with.

166

The clock glowed 3:15 a.m. Sixteen hours. Sixteen stinking hours ago. He cursed himself for his stupidity and inability to stop the inevitable. The IRA was active again. What could he have done with more time? Running all scenarios through his head made him sick. Nothing felt like a coincidence. Instead, he felt played. The maddening part was that he didn't know the rules of the game or who the players were. He only knew the clues when they slapped him in the face, and the vest was one of those pieces.

He slipped his arm out from under Jessica and carefully got out of bed. He walked naked into the living room. The vest was on one of the end tables, looking deceivingly innocuous and non-threatening. Smoothing it flat on the couch, he took his time to examine it carefully.

The vest was top-of-the-line protective gear made, not for police officers or soldiers, as one would think, but for VIPs—dignitaries, heads of states or corporations—who were vulnerable to people who did not share their opinions. Although most people were familiar with Kevlar, this material was a quantum leap of innovation. Lighter, thinner, and more resistant to a variety of impacts, it could stop bullets and ice picks as well as deflect the force of baseball bats and explosions, earning the name "Dragon Skin." Most vests were made for and needed by men, but the new material made tailoring one to a woman's body easier. Overcoats and suit jackets made of this high-tech material allowed for protection without being obvious or bulky. He had even seen prototypes of body armor for dogs.

He looked along the vest's seams and eventually found was he was looking for. The label proclaimed "2100 Ltd." Further down was another tag that read, "Made in the U.S.A."

Until he figured out what was going on, that was the last place he wanted to send her.

"I need to get out of England," she had said, blankets pulled around her like a shield. She looked so small.

"The sooner the better, but you're not going anywhere unless I can be certain you're safe."

"I can drop out of sight again. I don't need your men around me."

"You're alive because of what I've done for you."

"I'm alive in spite of it."

The glare in her eyes kicked him in the gut. The moment was the closest they had ever come to having a bitter fight. "Then I guess you'd say that Ballyronan is out of the question. I'm worried how you'd feel about being surrounded by my father's world."

She rested her chin on her knees. "Your home sounds like a fortress."

"Privacy and comfort won't be a problem. It's in Northern Ireland," he hedged, "on a lake."

She sat up. "Which one? Lough Neah?"

"Yeah, but Lough Neagh is huge. Every county except one touches its shoreline. I don't want you to assume you'd be close to where your mother was."

"Okay. I'll go."

He knew better than to press his luck. Putting her in the symbolic heart of the Charity could be a stroke of strategic genius. It if didn't go well, it could be the mark of astonishing stupidity.

Worried and alone, he punched one hand into the other. He had the money and the resources to send them both anywhere in the world, yet he only wanted Ballyronan. Freedom of choice was an odd thing. It provided the illusion that decisions were made with neither constraint nor coercion, but the reality was quite different. He was blocked and cornered in a scientist's maze, pestered and poked to turn this way and that. The forces were camouflaged, but that did not diminish their effectiveness. Ballyronan was the only place he wanted Jessica to be.

Her bags were packed and a car would be there in an hour. They would leave the hotel together, but he people to see and information he needed to gather. He would join her as soon as he could. He sat hunched, holding his head against a thousand thoughts. A soft breath of air brushed against the back of his neck. He turned, ready to envelop Jessica in his arms. He was surprised to see her still curled up in bed.

He gently climbed beside her. She stretched and turned toward him, not waking. Deep in sleep, the fear of the day shed, her arms rested above her head on the pillow. In the half-light, he looked at her body. What stirred inside of him wasn't lustful, but a deep hardening of anger.

A deep purple bruise half the size of his fist sat beneath her collarbone. His index finger traced it the same way he had traced the dent in the vest. He moved his hand gently down over the swell of her breast. His fingertips felt the smooth lines of scars that ran along her side and stopped a few inches above the end of her ribcage. A cruel fate had one long straight scar intersected by a shorter line at one end. The shape was that of a cross, or a dagger.

· He bent his head and kissed her, starting at her shoulder and slowly moving his lips down her side, feeling the ridges of smooth skin with his lips and tongue. He reached around, pulled her close, and felt her arms tighten in an embrace as she sleepily responded. A deep need replaced his anger, and his kisses became more desperate, pushing his drive beyond his control.

Her soft cry of surprise or pain didn't stop him from his steady and relentless desire to consume her.

MANCHESTER, ENGLAND

DALLY SIFTED THROUGH the piles of photographs and notes that landed on her desk during the past few hours. Her half-eaten ham and pickle sandwich and bag of crisps sat beside the day's fat Sunday edition with headlines proclaiming *Ceasefire Ends* and *The Whole City Shook*. Some of her colleagues would say they began to salivate when following a good lead on a story. For Dally, her eyes teared, and if she became excited, her nose would run, too. She took a tissue out, dabbed her eyes, and pressed a corner to her nose. This bombing was making her watery.

Adding to the transcriptions of interviews she conducted with the police, fire, and ambulance personnel as well eyewitnesses, she estimated she had a month's worth of work to do in the next week and working on her days off was a necessity. First, she had a deadline on giving all she knew about the emerging details of yesterday's bombing to Millie Bartholomew, the vacuous yet perky news presenter for ETV, England's underdog news program.

Dally could write far better than Millie could talk, and her strategy was to give the viewers a framework to understand yesterday's attack and to provide a bridge into any other developments that were sure to arise. She had to keep it straightforward and simple for the viewers, something Millie would benefit from as well. Grandier News was a tiny outfit. Once Millie's words were loaded into the teleprompter, Dally could pound out five column inches for the papers.

The Arndale bombing already had a strong connection to past events, so bridging into the story to create a larger context was her first order of business. One thing was quite clear and would be clear to ETV's audience—the ceasefire called by the IRA was over, not that anyone really believed it was going to last long anyway. The minor explosions of last March were just the appetizers to the main news feast that Arndale represented. She chose her words carefully for the broadcast. Crafting copy that Millie could read while simultaneously sounding intelligent was not easy.

No one had to tell her that Sinn Fein would be somewhere in the mix. To Dally, and any thinking loyalist, they were a radical political party run by papists, nutcakes, and ignorant Irish, who were considered to be the political wing of the paramilitary IRA. As much as the leaders of the Sinn Fein political party had tried to distance themselves from the actions of the IRA, no loyal Englishman considered the posture as real.

The goals of one were the same as the goals of the other. Too often their "independent" actions were perfectly orchestrated together. This bombing was no exception. Dally's blood boiled as she sifted through the players. Sinn Fein's leader, the telegenic but lying Gerry Adams, denied his group's operational and financial connections to the IRA. To Dally, they were simply different parts of the same body. Sinn Fein was the mouth. The IRA provided the dirty hands. Nobody fit the bill for having the brains.

Dally didn't have to be told what yesterday's bombing was about. The newsroom buzzed with opinion and fact.

"Are the Scots any less Scottish because they are members of the United Kingdom? Any ongoing agitation in the six counties of Northern Ireland was nothing more than the sour grapes of a disenchanted few."

"The peace talks are a contrivance by the Irish to undo a hard-won union. ETV's viewers and our readers think the same."

"Did you see the reports? I couldn't tear my eyes away. The whole facade of the Marks and Spencer store was sheared off. The guts and skin of the place were scattered all along Corporation Street leaving not but tendons and sinews of pipes and plaster."

"Last count was hundreds hurt from flying glass and chunks of buildings. Guarda reported no deaths!"

"No doubt those feckin' Feinians fancy themselves heroes for makin' the calls and ensuring an evacuation of the area."

"It's panic they wanted! And fear. They planned the attack when shoppers readied for Father's Day and the Euro football championship."

"I heard from Guarda source that a meter man had begun to write up a violation for the illegally parked truck before he noticed the wires running from the battery through the cab and into a hole to the cargo area. Timing of his radio call to his dispatcher was about when the newsdesk phone rang."

A few eyes had shifted to Dally. She straightened her shoulders and chimed in. "The police had only enough time to deploy a camera robot and record a few minutes of additional details before the whole thing blew to smithereens."

The only chance of staying assigned to the story was to hold on tight to the inside track of information she was gathering. She'd spent the better part of last night culling through information, pictures, and videos. She would keep her discoveries to herself and then stun the world with her reporting.

Her first clues came from security cameras that dotted the streets and buildings. Images showed two men park the truck then walk in separate directions. Both wore hoodies pulled up over their heads and sunglasses. From the shadows on their faces, they seemed to be sporting full beards, but Dally figured the beards came from a costume shop. One of the hoodies looked like it had some kind of logo on it, but she couldn't be sure. The pictures were worthless in trying to identify the men, so she spent her time wondering exactly what kind of demented monsters they were. She shook her head free of the thought, dabbed her eyes, blew her nose, and got back to work.

Simple and succinctly written copy was readied. Don would give it a quick review before delivering it to Millie's inbox. Normally Dally would have spent as much time as she could molding and stretching the facts to fit the whims of ETV's viewership. Gluing the viewers to their tellies with scintillating tidbits was just as important—if not more so—than getting them educated on current events. But she couldn't tear her thoughts away from those stinking Irish pigs. The fact they could roam the earth freely and wreak their havoc irked her. She was equally incensed that this bombing story would track the same as many similar stories then fade away when no hard clues are found.

A difference of opinion between loyalists and nationalists, Catholics and Protestants, led the IRA to bomb the hell out of a "legitimate" target—restaurant, post office, hotel, whatever fit their liking—as if naming a target legitimate would validate their cause. Her fists tightened. The bomb that killed her father was intended for Prime Minister Thatcher. No one cared that innocents would be shredded with shrapnel. Her father was collateral damage. No one gave a fig.

All of the news reports would have a pace. The next flurry of articles would contain a statement released by the bombers, who would no doubt say something along the lines of "The English made us do it" and "Get out of our country and we'll all play nicely again." Then the theater would shift to Gerry Adams, who would denounce the violence and the bombings and reiterate that the testy IRA would not be so testy if the English would let everybody sit at the negotiating table, not merely the chosen few.

Dally glanced at the TV monitors showing images of the riots that broke out in Belfast in the hours following the blast. The news story cut to an impromptu press conference where a bearded and grave Mr. Adams blamed the English for a bombing that happened at the hands of the Irish. "I suppose he's blamin' us for the riots, too," she shouted out loud but to no one in particular. The feckin' Irish had targeted the economic heart of England, ensuring that the costs of the bombing campaign steadily rose.

Dally was hard pressed to believe that Sinn Fein was being "denied a seat at the negotiating table" out of a purely capricious attitude. Adams and his horde were terrorists, hiding behind the guise of statesmanship. Sinn Fein claimed to be the one true voice of the Irish people. They wanted an Ireland free from British rule. Dally failed to see why the Irish fussed so much. Sinn Fein was trying to bomb their way to the negotiating table, and she had no patience for them.

She looked at the images of the truck and noted how clean and new it was. Forensic reports had not been completed, but the word she received from some of the Guarda officers on the scene was that this bomb was slightly different than the others. The force of the blast was extraordinary—far stronger than past explosions. The officers she interviewed observed that if the same kind of material was used in yesterday's explosion as in past explosions, then the truck would have needed twice the capacity to hold it all. Preliminary reports of the residue showed chemical traces of a type of nitrocellulose manufactured in the U.S. and restricted to import into the UK. There would have been a lot of it to cause the damage it did. What did the caller say? Right. Two thousand kilos—over one and a half tons—of explosives were involved and that's not easy to sneak into the country.

The outside of the truck was perfectly shiny, its tags were already being traced with Dally's sources promising to call with the first news. That left the inside of the truck the only avenue for her to examine. Pictures taken immediately prior to the blast showed a twisted umbilical of wires running through the cab. A plain white Styrofoam coffee cup lay tipped over on the passenger seat, covering a slip of paper with a brown stain.

Dally took out a magnifying glass from her upper desk drawer for a closer look. She could see a logo and printing of some sort, but details were impossible to make out anything from the grainy images. A couple of geeks upstairs in Images might be able to give her something more crisp on the men and the interior of the truck. They could be helpful in seeing some small detail, well *any* detail.

She rubbed her eyes without removing her glasses and found herself tamping down a growing anger. Those damned Micks had bought a brand new, top-of-the-line truck, filled it with God knows how many explosive their money could buy, and blew the whole thing up. Then they slipped away into the crowds without a trace. She was pissed. They had so much money to blow, she wished they would give it to her to supplement her pittance of a paycheck.

The money. The new truck. The men. Like Don had said, follow the money and the answers will flow. Dally knew a few good blokes in customs and decided to give them a call.

ANTRIM, NORTHERN IRELAND

THE CLOCK SHOWED 10:30 p.m. when Michael finally tossed his briefcase down on the sofa in his office. The prolonged twilight and the light from the nearly full moon illuminated Saint Mark's grounds in shades of blue. Michael poured himself a Scotch and sat in the leather club chair overlooking the quad and the lake. The campus was quiet now, but he knew that in a few hours time board members would fill the school, expressing their fears and demanding answers. He dragged his fingers through his hair and wasn't aware that he shook his head at some unheard question. People looked to him to be in control. He felt anything but.

Yesterday's bombing put all of his plans in the trash. Unable to sit still, he walked over to his desk and turned on the computer, drumming his fingers while it booted up. With a few clicks, he reviewed the accounts and their daily balances. Individual transactions were tracked separately.

The spreadsheet took an end-of-day snapshot of each account and gave him a bird's-eye view of the breadth of the Charity's holdings. International banking had its vagaries with not every country reporting transactions the same day they occurred. Combined with transactions that occurred on a weekend, not all activity posted or settled until close of business Monday. His accounts were significant enough to merit private management, and notifications of any transactions not yet visible on his balance sheet were emailed to him.

If this were a normal Sunday, he never would have been alerted to look deeper into the details. But this was anything but normal.

What should have been stable and untouched balances on Thursday and Friday, were amounts that fluctuated unpredictably among countries and accounts. A large influx of cash shifted on Saturday. A few more clicks showed another account brought down to a few hundred pounds. He scanned his emails and found a large withdrawal from an offshore account. He could only put together the timing one way.

Someone had bet heavily on Jessica losing the race. Indeed, the purse paid to anyone betting on the Devon-on-Thames team was huge. It should have more than covered the money withdrawn. Obviously, someone was looking for a wash of transfers—money coming back in before anyone noticed that money had gone out. Michael had no doubt that the sharp drop in the account was in payment for the team that carried off the Manchester bombing. No one considered that Jessica could ride like the devil himself. One thing was certain, she was not supposed to win that race. A bullet in her heart was to ensure that fact. What caused a glitch in their plans was the spit bucket.

Even in a private race, the owners abided by track rules, as long as those rules suited them. The rules were promoted to keep the riffraff happy, knowing they would be the source of any leaks if discontent festered. But risks were taken. If anyone outside of the inner circle asked, no horse was to race under the influence of steroids, anti-inflammatories, painkillers, or any other performance enhancing drugs. Jessica had watched over Bealltainn like a hawk to make sure that her horse was not going to be propped up and raced on a body that could not withstand the stresses on its own.

The rules dictated that the winner under such circumstances forfeit the race. The prize would go to the next horse over the finish line, provided they were clean, too. If they were both doped, no one would have raised an eyebrow. That was one of the ways the big boys played to win. Bealltainn came up clean. The Devon-on-Thames horse did not. Even the most unscrupulous owner knew better than to protest a result the Everyman would cheer.

The results sent a shockwave through the owners and track officials alike. Everyone from the grooms, suppliers, owners, and jockeys were questioned. Another few hours passed before pathology screened blood and urine samples of both horses, verifying the results. By that time, Jessica was already in Michael's protective cocoon and on her way out of England. She had pulled off the upset win of the decade and wasn't around to celebrate it. Not that she would have been keen on being the center of the party anyway.

Michael stared at the screen and saw what he feared was the footprint of that upset. Banking across international borders gave some allowances for timing transfers and clearing funds. He suspected that the team that pulled off Saturday's Manchester bombing was paid in cash—most likely the day before the attack or at the very latest, that morning. Hundreds of thousands of dollars went missing from the account sometime Friday night. Checks were paid out to the winners on Saturday immediately following the race, and a corresponding deposit was supposed to have covered the withdrawal.

Clearing times on the checks would have put available funds in the account by Monday morning, erasing any fluctuation, but the drug test results came back and the winner was disqualified. Any checks issued to the winners were canceled and stop payment orders put into place. Instead of one constant balance that would not have raised any suspicions, the balances swung wildly, no doubt showing the panic of whoever was involved.

The scheme should have worked, and he wondered if the bullet lodged in Jessica's vest was evidence of insurance that it would. He could see more than enough covers for the motivation behind her murder. Her minor celebrity and notoriety was eclipsed by the egos of many. Being a woman at Aintree was an affront few could tolerate.

Michael looked out his window and surveyed the school's grounds. Only the faint lights of the emergency exits glowed. The hulks of the buildings sat cold, empty, and dark. His mind was busy. He should have been concerned with who tried to put a bullet into Jessica. He also should have been a lot more worried about how he was going to address the board in a few hours time.

Instead, he could only focus on one thing, knowing the answer would lead to the conclusion he dreaded: Someone inside his organization was behind the Manchester bombing. Did they cover their tracks well enough not to lead back to him? Or, did they even care?

MANCHESTER, ENGLAND

DON HUME TOSSED a pile of newspapers in front of Dally. The scowl on his face told her he was not happy.

"What's got your knickers in a t-t-twist," she asked as she put her cup of tea and papers aside. She tried not to show her fluster but failed.

"Rubbish. These stories are absolute bloody rubbish."

Dally leafed through the newspapers and noted that they were from competing news outlets and not from any of the other holdings of their parent corporation, Multi-Media Central.

Don huffed. "I got word that the Arndale bombing would drop from the major headlines to the secondaries. In a few days, any updates will be relegated to page three and beyond."

"What can you expect? It's not like there's some b-b-big m-mystery about who done it and why. The IRA called us, claimed responsibility, told us why and d-disappeared into the night. It's the same old story."

Don continued to fume as he paced the newsroom. "I'm sick of the same old drivel. Those feckin' micks dream up their schemes then come over here and blow us up, and you mean to tell me no one knows anything? That no one saw anything? I can't believe that for a second."

Dally knew enough to steer clear of Don's rages when he was on a roll. She ventured a timid question. "So, what d-do you want me to do about it?"

"Look, it says here they've got the best folks at MI5 workin' on it. Stick close to them. I want you to come up with a fresh story."

"Look, Chief. Are you serious? You want me to saunter over to MI5's offices, sip a c-cup of tea with the bureau head, and sit enraptured while he spills his secrets to me? In case you haven't noticed, I'm not exactly M-Mata Hari."

Don wiped his hand over his smooth head and snorted. "No. No. Of course not. But there's got to be something in this story that's worth reporting more than Sinn Fein's propaganda and the Prime Minister's ire." He looked over at the pile of notes and photographs on Dally's desk. "What's that you've got there?"

She dove into the opening. "I only found one p-piece of information in the reports that's even remotely interesting." She paused for a moment to see if she had captured his attention. He nodded to her to go on. "A large influx of p-private jets and c-cargo arrived at the Manchester Airport the week before the bombing."

"Where did you hear that?"

"My p-private sources, Chief. You should know better than to ask me that." Dally's buddies in customs had come through once again, and she wasn't about to risk them losing their jobs over talking with her. She kept the conversation going so Don would press for more details. "I didn't dismiss the information as a c-coincidence."

Don crossed his arms over his barrel-shaped chest. "You know damned well why I have to ask you about your sources, Magpie. You lied to me once and I nearly got fired for it."

Her neck muscles contracted as she tried to swallow. The nickname stung. She was a new reporter and had been awarded her first tip to follow up, something that was too juicy to let go. Honestly, she told herself, who wouldn't try to catch the Prince in a compromising position? She pecked around that story until the leads were picked clean and then made a nest for herself with every innuendo and half-truth, sticking to her version of the facts no matter what. Magpie was the name the other reporters gave her after the story imploded, taking the fledgling Grandier News and its print and broadcast outlets with it. Every story she touched after that seemed to be tainted with bad leads. Dally knew what she had to prove and Don knew it, too.

She bristled. "I d-didn't lie."

"There's no proof of that without a verifiable source."

"What ever happened to being able to keep your sources confidential?"

"That might work for others, but you've lost that privilege. I want an on-the-record source that the paper can point back to for verification."

"I was lied to. There's a d-difference." She knew that the difference was only a matter of degrees when ambition made her so hungry she went blind. So far, she was doing good work, but Don would keep her on a tight leash.

He absently rolled the thick hair of his right forearm between the fingers of his left hand as he listened. "Keep talking."

Dally nervously inhaled and rattled off the rest of her research. The tension of speaking to her boss should have launched her into a stuttering standstill. Even years of speech therapy—taken with the wild hope of being in front of the camera rather than handing fresh copy in from the wings—did nothing to abate the maddening catches and halts. Then one day she was singing along with Herman's Hermits *I'm Henry the VIII, I Am* and realized that the words slid off her tongue. From that day forward, Don and her coworkers would hear a mash-up of a number of barely recognizable tunes with lyrics stripped from tabloid headlines. As nasally and off-key her tunes were, the lyrics were something to pay attention to.

"Traffic at the Manchester airport follows fairly predictable patterns," she spoke in unrecognizable atonal notes. "If Heathrow was fogged in or closed for a security reason, or if a large event took place in the Manchester area, spikes in both commercial and private traffic can be seen. With the Euro 96 football match on, both the Old Trafford Stadium here in Manchester and the Anfield Stadium in Liverpool are filled to capacity. That would certainly account for more passenger traffic, but the cargo numbers are spiked even taking into consideration vendor needs. Cargo traffic could also really peak during the Grand Nationals."

Don stopped her, as much to get clarification as to get a break from the dissonant dissertation. "The Grand Nationals?"

"Yes! At Aintree," she sang to the tune of *Hallelujah.*

"But that was a month and a half ago. They've all long since gone home."

"You're right. I looked, and no public events took place during that time period last week, so it looked like there was no reason for crates and boxes to ship there. But it bothered me. The private jet origins read like a study of hometowns of *Who's Who* for the rich and famous. Major conglomerates were represented—oil money, manufacturing, media. Anything that happened last weekend at the Aintree Racetrack involved only the world's wealthiest people. But nothing was reported anywhere about a race, so I thought maybe something would be written about the people who were visiting in town and may have attended it. The thing about the world's richest people is that the average bloke on the street would never have heard of them. If word that Sheik Fareil ah-Sahad was in town, few papers would give a column inch to report it." She paused and took a deep breath, her aria not yet complete. "I knew from past Grand Nationals the horses are such finely tuned machines that no variance in their feed—like a change in the types of grasses used for their hay—could be tolerated. The horses arrived on their own private jets, which carried all of the feed and provisions needed for the event. Crates of wrapped hay and special grains made up the bulk of the shipping manifests. Tack, gear, and other items filled out the rest."

"So, what are you saying?"

"I called up the society editor of the *Liverpool Daily News.* After some digging, she told me that a private race of some kind took place at the track. The horses and handlers arrived a couple of weeks ago, but all of the major players and owners landed on Thursday. Just as I suspected, the names were not going to sell papers, so she didn't spend a lot of time on it. Besides, she learned the hard way that they are a rather litigious crew and would rather sue your panties off than get their name in the society pages. Anyway, they partied their way through Saturday's race and into some fancy-pants dinner. Most flew out that night and only a few stayed on through the weekend, mainly to catch the football matches. The editor was able to match names to their pictures. They would mean nothing to most people, but if you have a nose for money, you would have been amazed. The hundred or so people rumored to have attended represented a full ten percent of global wealth."

Don gave out a low whistle, unintentionally harmonizing to a Eurythmics' tune. Dally hoped he would see that the long drip of a reporter standing in front of him was proving to be a damned good investigator. Maybe he would begin to see that Magpie was on to something.

"Keep going," he said.

Dally allowed herself a silent cheer of glee as she continued. "Airport security has gotten much more stringent in recent years. IRA bombings at Heathrow forced strong measures to be taken. New concepts like watch lists for suspect names, body pat downs, and metal detectors became routine. This pissed off a few passengers, but a mere mention of the Lockerbie airliner crash of 1988 took the wind from them when they realized that was only eight years ago. Delays and invasions of privacy were hard to escape." She looked down at her notes. "Private jet use increased four-fold since stringent security measures on commercial flights were implemented. They are exempt from many of the rules and provisions governing passengers and cargo."

"So what you have is an increase in cargo traffic and a private event at Aintree with lots of private jets. So why should I care?"

"Two reasons. The first is that I learned the explosives used at Arndale are restricted in the U.K. No one would have been able to get their hands on enough to inflict the damage seen. So, it must have come from outside the country."

"Okay. Keep talking."

"And also because of this," she said as she handed him an enlargement of the truck's interior provided to her from her friends in Images. "The Styrofoam coffee cup was nothing distinct. Any one of a hundred vendor carts dispensed gallons of coffee each day in the same type of cup. Even if they had been able to retrieve the cup before the truck blew up, the sides were not of a surface that would have yielded a decent fingerprint. But this is interesting," she pointed at the stained paper. "The logo on one of hoodies worn by one of the bombers is from the Aintree Racetrack and appears to be the same one on this paper. I'm pretty sure it's a betting slip."

"But you said the event was private. No public riffraff allowed."

"The privacy of the event meant that regular people could not just swagger up to a bookie's window and place a bet. Admission was by invitation only. Even so, the stable help and grooms that were temporarily hired for the event sometimes brought in a friend or two for the race and had a side business of their own for the wagers."

Don studied the image for a long while. The variables of what the smudged name and numbers could say were endless. "There's no way to know if the slip is from a recent race or not."

"I've already asked for a better image of this paper because something is nagging at me. You said you wanted a fresh angle, something juicy to spice up the news. One report said the point of origin for the explosives was the U.S., and the IRA can just about spit on us from Northern Ireland and Ireland. What if the increased jet and cargo traffic and this private race were somehow connected to the bombing?"

"You're really going for a stretch here. It's no secret the IRA is a shoe-string operation. They don't have enough money to buy a proper bomb so they steal from the RUC and have the balls to use our own bombs to kill us. They burn tires and run cars filled with barrels of petrol through barricades to stop our tanks. They don't have the money, the means, or the connections to hire a private jet and pull anything off like what you're saying."

Dally sputtered a bit at Don's rebuff but continued in a Gregorian chant. "Think of Sunday's riots in Belfast. You saw the video rushes from our reporters there, right?"

"Yes. So what."

"Then you must have seen this," she said as she leaned over a video player and plugged in a tape. Images of the riots jumped across the screen as she fast-forwarded to the section she wanted. The fragment of action lasted only three or four seconds. Dally inched the action forward, frame by frame. "Look at this. Here are the RUC. You can easily pinpoint exactly who they are by their uniforms and how well they're equipped. Now look here," she said, pointing to a group of three men partially hidden behind the trash bins they were using for cover. The loosely fitting cotton shirts and casual trousers and ripped jeans stood in marked contrast to the helmets, flak jackets, and high-powered rifles they carried. "Somebody's rich uncle just died."

"Hmm. Okay. I get it. You told me earlier about the new truck they used to for the bombing."

"Yes."

"So what you're saying is that with the arrival of money came the arrival of explosives."

"Yes."

Don turned his back to her. "I want to caution you. The cargo manifests don't give a great deal of information. Most of the party names listed are corporations. Very few individuals would have a reason to ship a large crate of goods to Manchester. The last thing I want you to do is to go on a wild goose chase of tracking down companies and shipments. Tracking a company can bring you down a lot of blind alleys as one company dissolves into the holding company of another."

"I know all that."

"Fair enough. What did your buddies give you?"

"Commercial passenger lists and customs information on cargo. I got a partial list of anyone who traveled by private jet and cleared into England."

"What you have here is a lot of nothing. I'll give you two weeks to dedicate yourself to see if your hunch pans out into something."

"Two weeks? That's it?"

"That's enough time to learn if something's going to click, and every shred of information you dredge up you have to run through me." He faced her and lowered his voice to a growl. "And, keep your fact spinning to a minimum until we see what we have. I want real, live *on the record* sources. The heat's less if we can point to a lying source rather than a lying reporter. You also have to keep up with your regular copywriting duties. Miss Bartholomew cannot risk being on the air without your words in her mouth. In your free time you can investigate other avenues and see what ripens."

Dally wanted to press for more time, but quickly decided that Don could easily take back what he had given her. If she played nice, she could finally rid herself of the magpie omen. She decided to be happy with what she had.

She started with the passenger lists from all commercial flights for two weeks prior to the explosion. Thousands of people had flooded into the Manchester/Liverpool area because of the sport tournament and she felt a bit ridiculous staring at pages of names as if one would glow neon for her attention. Needing a break, she grabbed a magnifying glass and began to sift through the photos of the bombing.

She had been in such deep thought she hadn't noticed when the office page dropped another manila folder onto her desk. Absently, she pulled out its contents and found enhanced photos of the betting slips. Peering at them through the magnifying glass, Dally was able to confirm the Aintree logo.

The new images were still fuzzy, but clearly showed the dark outline of a horse in full stride jumping over the letter "A." The amount of the wager could be seen along with the odds. Someone had placed a modest sum on a horse and rider with odds that said no one really thought that pair had a chance in hell of winning. She could not see the exact amounts, but looking at the smudged numerals, she could make out the symbol for pounds and a decimal, '*Pounds sign. Blur. Blur. Decimal. Blur. Blur.*'

The name and number of the horse were an incomprehensible smear of spilled coffee and bled ink. The name of the jockey was barely decipherable. For one of the initials, Dally could make out a long downward stroke crossed over at the top. She had no idea if the letter was a "T," "I," "J" or something else. The last name was short and could have started with "N," "W," or "M."

The newsroom was full of stories about leads that broke on major news when the most inconsequential of facts were followed through on. Better yet were the stories that emerged serendipitously. Tracking down a vehicle theft ring? Icing on the cake is learning that a politician's stolen Aston Martin was lifted in front of Miss Sukyurwhistle's abode for wayward hussies. Having the name of a jockey might not lead to the big fish, but she could probably whittle a fifteen hundred-word article from their conversation whether they talked about the bombing or not. She could hear the interview now:

'*Ahem, Mr. Jockey. How does it feel that money from the stinking terrorists was placed on your hack?*'

Or,

'*I heard from some of the other stable hands that you were bragging about fixing the odds on this race.* (A complete lie, but nerves get people talking.) *Too bad it backfired on you, but now you can tell us who you were ringing in.*"

Or,

'*Mr. Jockey. I heard only your buddies bet on you. What were their names? Why do you think they wanted to blow up the Arndale Malls?*'

And when all else fails:

'*Mr. Jockey, who's your boss? Who's he sleepin' with?*'

Dally doubted she'd get much of anything from some jockey about the bombing, but the stories that would inevitably spill would be interesting enough. Jockeys were a lowlife bunch, willing to snog your grandmother if it would buy them a pint or two. They usually hung around in clusters in the same old musty pubs and farms so this gent, if he could be considered such, should be easy enough to find. That is, if he was an English or Irish boy.

With the private race pulling from all corners of the world, perhaps he flew in for the festivities. Dally made a note to ask the sports editor about the favored haunts of the jockey crowd and resolved to start pounding the pavement to the pubs tonight. Who knows? Maybe she'd get lucky and get snogged herself.

Having some kind of filter and framework to work within made reviewing the passenger lists less daunting. She quickly sorted the lists alphabetically and methodically drew a line through each name that did not remotely fit the possible initials. It wasn't long before she had a list of one hundred and fifty names from the commercial flights that she would check against the jockey registry being sent up by her buddy in Liverpool.

The passenger lists from the private jets were much shorter and made her wish she had started there instead of dismissing it. She had barely spent a half hour looking at the names when one began to glow. Dally sniffed and wiped her tearing eyes as she put an asterisk by "J. Wyeth. Citizenship: USA. Country of Travel Origin: Ireland."

Maybe she wouldn't need more time after all.

BALLYRONAN, NORTHERN IRELAND

JESSICA WOKE TO a room full of sunlight. She stretched her arms overhead and languished in the warmth of the bed cozy against the slight chill of the morning air. Leaded glass panes cast crisscrossed shadows along the floor. Rain promised to hold off long enough for some exploring.

She threw on a pair of jeans and light fleece and padded barefoot down the long hallway and curving staircase to the kitchen. As much as Michael encouraged her to have his help prepare and bring her breakfast in bed, she refused, feeling awkward and self-conscious at all the fuss just for her. She was a do-it-yourself woman and felt more comfortable when she toasted her own bread, thank you. But when she pushed open the hinged door and found the central wooden table set for one with flowers, a pot of steaming coffee and the scones she complimented the day before, she knew she was fighting a losing battle.

"Mornin' Miss Jessica. Good to see you up and about today." Murray, Michael's portly and cherubic butler and general man-about-the-manor, greeted her warmly. He was infinitely easier to be around than the bristly Nan. Jessica welcomed his company.

"Good morning. I could smell the scones upstairs. Thank you for baking more." She settled at the table and allowed him to pour her coffee, not knowing how to decline politely his attention. "All I did was eat and sleep for two days. I'm not usually such a slug."

"Not to worry. Michael said you've been through the ringer and needed your rest, but if you're feelin' up to it, I'd be glad to show you around."

Jessica looked out the kitchen window over manicured gardens. The beds directly in front of the house burst with color—violets, thistles, poppies, clover, and daisies. Precisely clipped hedges formed intricate patterns when viewed from above and meandering paths when strolled. Larger beds located on the sides were a tangle of unpruned shrubs and untamed vines. The waters of Lough Neagh, flat and smooth on the windless day, reflected scattered patches of blue sky amid billowing clouds. She was anxious to walk the grounds. A wet gray curtain had obscured the world when her jet landed at a private airstrip, so she didn't have a mental image of what the countryside looked like. As soon as her feet had hit the tarmac, a car pulled up and drove her over winding roads to Ballyronan.

She had been vaguely aware of turning up a driveway through tall gates set in an imposing stone wall as the drive wound around another hill. Two wings, each with a peaked roof slightly lower than the central one, flanked the main part of Michael's stately home. By her standards, it was a mansion, but Murray said tradition considered the home a simple hunting lodge. Each room had a view of gardens, sweeping lawns, or the lake. Even with the misty days, Jessica knew the home was nestled away from probing eyes.

"Michael is the third generation of Connaughts to own the grounds," Murray said, answering a question she didn't ask but wanted to know. "Some say his grandfather purchased the home from an Earl of declining means during the Great Depression. Others say he swindled it. No matter," he said with a dismissive wave of his hand, "the families never used Ballyronan as a main residence. Magnus preferred living in the States and only stayed here during his infrequent trips to check on business. Michael spent summers and school breaks here."

Jessica nodded as she sipped her coffee. "He said they were the best times of his life." The memories held and conjured by the sloping lands and crannies of the estate were good ones for him, even with their bittersweet tinge. "He said he started some renovations?"

"Aye. Some. Seems he wants to erase his father's presence and put his own imprint on it. The name 'Connaught' is descended from a line of Irish kings. Magnus wanted to reclaim the destiny. Michael wants to erase it." Murray softened his expression as he spoke, acknowledging the difficulty of the direction Michael wanted to take.

Jessica relaxed when she sensed Murray's camaraderie with Michael. Destiny or not, this was a far cry from the family or history Jessica envisioned when she first met Michael. With the slow reveal of his background, she wondered what other secret gravities continued to pull them together. She knew Michael was introducing her to his world in incremental steps. Each revelation carefully calibrated. Each story carefully drawn.

Murray spoke of Magnus' history cautiously and did so only when asked. He responded with measured phrases and assessed Jessica's reaction. Michael hated his father, surely, and spent years estranged from him, but the rejection hinted at being one-sided. Murray inquired about Jessica's family in a way that suggested he knew more about her than she told him. She began to wonder if Michael's and her alienation from their families was part of their deep connection, or something else?

She grabbed a second scone from the basket and dabbed butter on it. Murray refilled her cup just as she reached for the pot to do it herself, bumping into his hands. He chuckled and offered her the cream. "Michael said you were independent." He let her finish her breakfast without interruption, then returned, jangling a ring of keys. "Each one is labeled. You can explore as you wish."

"I'd like it better if you joined me."

Murray beamed. "Thank you, Miss Jessica. I'd enjoy that."

With Murray as her guide, she explored the interior of the home with the same determination a child has in the weeks before Christmas when the Santa jig was up and the mother lode of presents was aching to be discovered. Same determination yes. Same excitement no. Rather than fueled by greedy anticipation, her search was pushed by a nagging drive of self-preservation. For the first time in her adult life, she relied on someone else. The experience created an odd push and pull. She wanted to stay wrapped in Michael's cocoon, yet she couldn't fully relax until every corner of his life was exposed. Opening his home, she knew Michael was trying very hard to win her confidence.

They started at the top and worked their way down, checking doorknobs, poking into dusty closets, and opening drawers. She was happily surprised that nothing was locked or off-limits to her. Murray equally enjoyed the exploration of spaces he hadn't bothered with in a long time. Some attic rooms were empty or used for storage and not disturbed in years, while others held an assortment of furniture and boxes. The next floor down was predominantly bedrooms, all were well appointed and comfortable. Fireplaces and sitting rooms sat empty and waiting.

The master suite she shared with Michael was recently renovated. The smell of fresh paint and new carpets distinct against the musty and closed-in smells of the other rooms. A large bath, sitting room, huge bedroom, and closets the size of horse stalls comprised the suite. The brief exploration of the servants' wing showed modestly appointed rooms, looking more lived-in than she expected. The main floor of the home held a library and office as well as larger rooms once used for entertaining groups of people. Most of those rooms were sparsely furnished, if at all.

Her favorite was a glass-enclosed area off the living room. The pavilion-like structure was appointed with deeply cushioned sofas and rattan chairs.

"This is beautiful!" The semi-circular room provided unobstructed views of the grounds. An ancient looking door opened to a graveled path and garden, and a small fieldstone hearth was at the center of one wall. "Mmm. What's that smell? It's wonderful."

"It's peat. Even mid June, mornings can start chilly. I like to keep a fire going and the dried peat has a sweetness to it."

She poked the glowing lumps with a brass rod, sending a scattering of sparks up the flue. A rustic basket held more of the earthen clumps. "Family heirloom?" she asked, eyeing the dark woven branches.

"Aye. From Michael's mother. It's a cherished bit of her. He says it reminds him how her presence always warmed a room." As vast as the house was, and as thoroughly as she had looked, precious little of what Murray said belonged directly to Michael could be found.

"I'd like to see more of what Michael feels is important."

"Fair enough. Let me show you his den."

Aside from the master suite, the den was the only other room where a faint smell of new mixed with the old. Plush carpet cushioned their steps in the darkly paneled room. Framed and fading photos of the Connaughts, deceptively happy, covered one wall. She studied the faces and could trace Michael's intense stare and strong brow through his family's line. Once cherished photos showed the sepia-toned humble beginnings of stern-faced men on ox carts. Others showed stoops—crowded with men, women, and ragtag children—in front of brick flats.

The pictures progressed to full color photos displaying all the spoils of wealth and power. Slickly suited politicians and rosy-cheeked clergymen dotted the pictures. Jessica was not familiar with her Irish history. If she were, more of the faces would have looked familiar to her. Even so, she was stunned to see a smiling and young Magnus Connaught—looking like a stiff and formal Michael—standing in a crowd surrounding the dazzling John F. Kennedy. Jessica was unclear whether this photo was from JFK's presidential years, but even the suggestion of the proximity of power was clear. Another showed a bishop, resplendent in the tall hat, vestments, and crosier of religious power, raising crooked fingers in blessing over a young Magnus' bowed head.

"What's this," she asked, looking at a picture of Magnus with a huge scissor in his hand, poised over a long ribbon.

"Magnus was the money and the power behind schools, churches, hospitals and many, many jobs. He created a legion of men with fierce loyalties who would do anything for him. He fueled small businesses, too, with a steady influx of cash until they were strong enough to stand on their own. He gave the appearance that he shirked attention by donating anonymously or in the names of his sons, but everyone knew where the money came from. Michael was not alone in being blinded by the light of Magnus."

"Are there pictures of Michael when he was a boy?" she asked, eager to see them.

"Not many," Murray replied, uncomfortable with the truth.

He rummaged through a drawer and produced several photographs. One showed Michael, about ten years old, with two other boys, each astride a lathered horse. One was clearly his brother. The other was vaguely familiar with sandy hair and deep-set eyes. Tim. The thought made her squirm.

Murray continued talking. "Michael was not Magnus' favored son. His older brother, Liam, was Magnus' favorite." He looked at another photo that showed Magnus' arm draped proudly over the shoulder of his older son. Michael stood stiffly to the side. No photo of Magnus with Michael showed similar pride.

"Liam? Isn't that Michael's uncle?"

"Yes. The firstborn son was named after Magnus' younger brother." Dusty and forgotten behind a row of books sat another photo of Liam as a young man. A yellowed mass card tucked into the heavy frame showed the dates of his birth and death. "He blew himself up mishandling unstable explosives," he said, uncharacteristically blunt. "Some say Magnus planted the bad chemicals after he realized Michael had the greater talent for management."

"Do you believe that?"

"When it comes to evil, I'd believe any story that relates to Magnus. We have no photos here of Michael after he reached his early twenties, the rift between father and younger son was deep and wide by then. You're not to worry though, Michael has the soul of his mother in him." He produced a picture of a beautiful woman, arms hugged around herself to protect against the chill wind that swept her hair back from her face. She looked out to the distance, a radiant smile on her face. In all the pictures, Michael's mother looked like a lovely and gentle soul, and she was the parent who stood next to Michael with obvious parental love.

Another photo of her and a mass card occupied the corner of Michael's desk. "Michael said she died tragically, too."

Murray's face clouded in pain. "Magnus said she killed herself when she thought Michael had agreed to join the Charity." He quieted Jessica's gasp with a raised hand. "I don't consider any of it to be true."

One last photo sat in the center of the massive desk, marking a place of honor, showing Jessica and Michael together at a formal event in Kentucky. Jessica picked it up and studied it, carefully examining the imposters staring back at her. The memory of the Harvest Ball and the scheming Electra did to play matchmaker made her smile.

"Michael told me about when you first met. He said you were the most beautiful woman he had ever seen. He was gob smacked."

She could feel herself blush. "I didn't know you were in the States," she said, trying to deflect attention.

"He would call me frequently to keep in touch. He never suspected how the two of you were connected. You were Miss Tess White then, a newcomer and a horse trainer." His voice was gentle and without reproach. She liked him more for it.

"And he was *Sheriff* Michael Conant, the respected and well-connected lawman of backwater Kentucky." She smiled at the rush of potent and complex memories from that night. Despite both of their attempts to be someone else, they could not hide the essence of who they were. The private code of wealth was tattooed into her as well as its sensitive radar, and when they met, finding each other felt like the missing puzzle piece clicked into place. "He couldn't fool me. He may have been a lot of things, but a southerner he wasn't." They laughed. Michael fit the bill for an old New England family. The right prep school. Ivy League college. Their mutual attraction was instant and red hot.

"Now he's learning to be Michael Connaught." Murray went to a drawer and produced a photo of five people. Michael was about thirteen. Magnus and his brother stood behind Michael and the younger Liam. Seated in an ornate chair was a much older man. The similarities of the brows and eyes were unmistakable, as was the bond of three generations of family pride.

She nodded weakly. Murray meant no harm, but his observation jolted her in a way she didn't understand.

They had been exploring for hours and Jessica returned to the glass pavilion. She sat enveloped in the sweetly pungent smell of the peat fire, and mulled over each piece of Michael's life as if it held a clue to her own. From the first moment they met, Michael was a powerful factor in her life and was relentless in his efforts to keep her safe. As transparent as he wanted to be, there were still things they were blind to. She questioned whether the unseen was as dangerous as the seen.

The clouds had tumbled back in and rain pelted down on the thick glass. Regardless, the colors and smells were intoxicating. The mists rolled in from the lake, obscuring the shoreline and transforming the wooded area into a hobbit's home. The gray wisps of fog thickened into the shape of a human and moved with slow precision along the shore. She froze, thinking again of the mists at the stone circle. She tensed as a man emerged cradling something long in his arms, a dog at his heels. He paused at the shore, looked out over the lake and up to the house, and continued walking. That was her first sighting of the armed guards that surrounded Ballyronan.

JUNE 1966
BELFAST, NORTHERN IRELAND

ANNA MARIE SECURED her kerchief around her head and adjusted the huge belly that hung by straps from her shoulders. Readying herself with a deep breath, she pushed the huge pram up to the Royal Ulster Constabulary officer. A round-faced baby with brilliant red curls peeked over the tall sides of the huge baby carriage.

"Where to?" the RUC officer asked, too young to know better.

"I live down to Ardoyne. Let us pass."

"Sorry, Missus. You can't walk down Shankill Road. Take yourself around to Falls Park and up," he said, motioning with his rifle in the opposite direction.

"You're asking me to walk all the way around? That's another six kilometers, my back is aching, and my Johnny needs a new nappy. Me and my friends just want to get on home," she said, motioning to the group of women behind her.

"Sorry, orange parade is on and we don't want issues."

"Jaysus! Of all the stupidity. What's the fear with a group of mothers?"

"What's the problem, Georgina?" Bridget said, stepping forward and bouncing a baby boy on her hip. "What's this young man sayin'?"

"He's tellin' us to walk 'round the parades. Says he's worried about issues arisin'." Anna Marie creased her brow with distress and rubbed her swollen belly. "I just don't have it in me, Judith," she said, voice crumbling.

Bridget gave Anna Marie a gentle rub on her back and looked at the young officer. "She's a week away from being a mum of two, and with this stress she could drop that new baby right at your feet." She looked at the group of three other women and various children behind her. "We can't go our separate ways. Safety in numbers and all that." Standing closer to the officer and lowering her voice she asked, "What is it that your superiors are afraid of? Surely it's not mums and babes."

The young officer stammered. "I . . . I need to keep the Crumlin area clear of civilians, M'am."

"The whole area?" Bridget looked up and down the street in exaggerated concern. Armored trucks and groups of soldiers milled about, checking papers on other pedestrians and letting some through. "Look at us, officer—um, Officer Smythe," she said, looking at his tags, "Check our papers. Search our prams. Do what you need to do, but let us through. You don't want to start an incident because a clan of irrational women wanted to protect one of their own and charged your blockade, do you?" She said this with a disarming laugh and the other women chimed in, chiding the young man. Some of the women rustled identification papers under his nose, others paraded ample bosoms and bums asking to be frisked. More laughter bubbled up.

He flushed and looked around for another officer to help. Without one close by, he relented. "Let me check your papers and parcels and be on your way. Don't dawdle."

"What's that you say?" Anna Marie asked in mocked insult. "I can't keep me movin' except in a waddle."

The women erupted in laughter and the RUC officer's color deepened. Each woman opened her shopping parcels for inspection with great ceremony, pushing one another aside teasingly wanting to be the first to be searched and bashing prams together in a gentle roller derby of "Me, first!" Toddlers gaped wide-eyed with fingers in mouths at the sudden activity. The soldier poked about the prams, handling the soiled nappies like snapping turtles and visibly beginning to shake when the tots began to wail at his invasion of their space.

"Fair enough, Missus. Be on your ways and take care. Be alert." He tapped his helmet with two fingers, as if tipping his hat to them. They all smiled and walked on.

A few blocks later, they rounded a corner and slipped down a narrow alley. False bedding bottoms were lifted up and goods consolidated into two prams. Long sashes of brass bullets and green fist-sized grenades were carefully repacked. The three women gathered up all the children and hastened out of the alley and down the street. Bridget helped Anna Marie unstrap her belly and place it in the childless pram, gently tucking the blankets around gauzes, sutures and other medical supplies they fervently hoped they would not need. They walked slowly and deliberately out of the alley and back onto the street, chatting and laughing with ease, nothing noteworthy about two mums out for a stroll with sleeping babies in bouncing prams. Three more streets up and they were joined by two men.

Bridget kept the smile on her face, but brought her voice to a whisper. The urgency in her eyes was clear. "Get everyone and everything out of the Crumlin Road flats. They've been tipped." The men nodded their understanding. "Are we safe ahead?"

Once assurances were given, the men smiled and gave them each a quick peck on the cheeks. One man leaned over and said good-bye to the belly contents nestled in one pram and gave a bounce of the handles on the other. They all smiled and relaxed a bit with the humor and walked on.

Three more blocks and Anna Marie and Bridget opened the door of a brick tenement and hauled the prams inside. As soon as the door shut behind them and they were certain of their privacy, Anna Marie gave a shrill whistle in three short bursts. Doors opened and soon the prams' contents were spirited into the bowels of the building. Guns, ammunition, gas masks, food tins, cash, and more were delivered safely.

They gratefully accepted a hearty meal and a safe bed for their labors. Anna Marie barely finished half of what was served. When she caught Bridget eying her leftovers, she offered the last bits of cold meats and bread and smiled when Bridget hungrily ate them down. The next morning she woke to Bridget hustling to the loo. When she joined her at the breakfast table, Bridget nibbled at her weak tea and toast.

Anna Marie waited until they were back on the street to ask. "Gus?"

Bridget looked confused. "Excuse me?"

"I figured there is no Mr. Harvey either alive or dead, so it must be Gus's."

Bridget's steps paused only slightly as she kept moving forward at her usual clipped speed. "You're bein' daft. I can't believe what you're saying."

"Don't make me eek it out of you. You're pregnant, and I want to let you know how happy I am for you and Gus."

Bridget fought the rising panic mixed with morning sickness and did her best not to puke on the street. She was furious with herself. Everything that she had planned for and steadily worked toward started to teeter. Being a mother was something she never wanted to be, especially in this city. In this hell. They had been so careful. The love they had for one another could not be stopped, and their passion for each other burned too hot to be doused by reality. She did not want this baby, or any baby, and knew the father would feel the same. But even as she thought those words, a filament glowed, lighting a love she willed to stay dark. Bridget knew that fighting the blossoming love she had for the life inside her would be a wasted effort. She didn't want to love him or her, but every moment proved that impossible. She loved this baby with a fierceness that frightened her. She gave herself no alternative but to swell and birth. Anna Marie was right. Mr. Harvey's existence could not be confirmed—or denied. She had sussed out the facts and landed on Gus.

Anna Marie reached over and gave her friend a hug. "Congratulations. Gus is crazy about you, and you both deserve the happiness."

Bridget accepted the hug stiffly, swallowing hard against a wave of nausea. She steeled herself and put as much authority into her voice as she could. "I don't have to tell you of the risks to our men when they are made vulnerable by protecting their women. You can think what you want about who the father is, but neither Gus nor I will ever say."

She stopped walking and faced Anna Marie, drawing herself up to her full height and bringing her face as close to her friend's as possible. "And let me make this clear. You are not to speak of this to anyone. I am not pregnant," she said, wishing the words were true, "and I'm going to need your help."

And with that, she let herself be wrapped up in Anna Marie's arms and wept.

ANTRIM, NORTHERN IRELAND

MICHAEL SAT IN front of his computer screen staring at a truth he desperately wished didn't exist. The spreadsheet had headings and numbers, some bold black and others red. He traced his finger through the columns representing the pipeline of holding companies and offshore accounts. Pausing, he double-checked dates off a second document, cursing when the information stayed the same as when he last looked. No matter how he tried to disprove it, the Charity's money funded each step of the Arndale bombing.

A thick paste of fear coated his mouth as he explained his findings to his uncle. The older man leaned over his shoulder, the white of his hair and brows cast blue by the screen. Entries showed purchases of the truck, cars used for getting to the job and away from it, rental of the flats, and the payment to the soldiers. All tracked because Michael had an odd luxury of knowing what to look for in the numbers.

To Michael's trained eye, the masterful shell game of shelters and accounts that closed after they served their purpose made tracing the money outward from the source intuitive. An investigator coming into the numbers cold and tracking the money inward from the point of purchase back to those corporate accounts would have an almost insurmountable task. In such an investigation, the blind alleys would stay blind.

But the trail existed whether it was cold or not. Money flow could be followed easily enough if investigators had enough of the pieces, knew what they were looking for, or knew where to look. Then the trail would heat up again. Each piece of information was a domino carefully placed; one lucky flick and the entire serpentine path would clatter to his door. Michael did not set up the network, so he had no way of knowing whether someone had carefully placed dominos crosswise to bring the progression to a dead stop, or if it would be too late by the time he figured it out.

"I don't know what to do," he said as he pushed himself away from his desk.

Liam settled himself in a thickly padded leather chair, accustomed to its comfort. He tented his fingers and assumed a professorial tone. "Men who claim to feel no pressure cannot assess risks properly. Their character is best weighed when measured in crisis." He studied Michael's face carefully.

"I know. I'm doing my best." Liam's expression took on a new life that had been missing since his brother died. Liam was expert at determining a man's breaking point and counseled Magnus accordingly. Michael wondered if the years spent on the sidelines quietly watching and assessing Magnus could help him now. "You once said, 'Men of greatest interest were those who bore the weight until their legs buckled.' I'm still standing."

Liam smiled and nodded approvingly. "What do you see as your options?"

"The MI5 is going to be combing through all the information they can find about the truck. One scrap of charred metal, and they'll trace the truck's VIN, figure out where and when it was purchased and by whom, if they can, and go from there. I only have enough information to see whoever set this bombing up wasn't stupid enough to have red flags waving over the transactions. There's a bit of smoke and mirrors with the money, but I'm concerned efforts weren't deft enough. It seems like whoever used to run the books for the Charity completely forgot how to wash cash as of five months ago."

"And before then?"

"Masterful. A simple God-damned genius was at work."

Liam rested his chin on this thumbs and batted the tips of his fingers together. "That's the first compliment you've ever given to your father's work."

"Meaning?"

"Magnus died five months ago."

"So you're saying his death triggered these events?"

Liam's eyes darted to the side then he cleared his throat. "I'm saying he had a tremendous amount of foresight and no one was waiting in the wings to fill his shoes."

Michael suppressed a grimace. "It's maddening. I know what I'm looking for so it's not so much of a needle in a haystack. One good thing is that when I follow the money backward—for example, if I trace money from the flat rental back to me—there are enough blind alleys and false leads that it will take some effort to connect the dots back. But, a few transfers happened after he died. I need to find out who in the organization made them."

"And when you find out?"

"I'll figure out if we're working for the same team or not."

Liam considered the strategy and prodded. "Do you think someone would risk exposure of the Charity?"

"No, actually, I don't. The final payments were made the day before the blast. I'm pretty sure the transfers were supposed to be invisible."

"How?"

"Someone counted on replenishing two of the accounts before anyone—namely me—could notice the balances drop. My hunch is that the positive spit test was a surprise. Whoever he was wanted to use the purse to cover his tracks."

"You have to consider two scenarios. If you're saying you see a marked difference in the skill of who set the transfers up, then two people may be involved. If it was the same person, he may want the trail to lead back to you."

"I've considered both possibilities. That's why I want to see the betting ledgers."

"My brother knew exactly what he was doing, Michael. He wouldn't be so stupid as to leave any telltale signs on truck purchases, and the dead don't bet." His manner bordered on antagonistic.

Michael cursed himself for not seeing the whole picture. The answers were there if he could just understand what each clue meant. "Where else should I look?"

"The race purse proceeds. Who were they intended to fool?"

"Anyone looking at the money trail from the corporation end."

Liam was openly irritated. He gripped the arms of the chair. "I marvel at how someone so similar to his own father would have so few of his innate skills. You still haven't told me what you see as your options."

Michael ignored the barbed comment. "It's pretty straightforward. I could wait until I get a knock on my door and handed a subpoena, or I could do a preemptive strike and go directly to MI5."

Liam exploded. "You're not a fecking fool, Michael! Do you honestly believe that waltzing the MI5 through our books is going to do any good? What's the purpose? You came into the Charity against your better wishes. But you *did* come. You came because you wanted to continue your work—your *charitable* work—with Magnus' wealth. There's another layer going on here. You've judged him and his organization as not being worthy of you, and you want to destroy it. You turn up your nose at how we get things done and arrogantly act as if you're the better of us. But you can't destroy the organization without jeopardizing the very thing that you want—the money. The power."

"You don't know what you're talking about," Michael growled, keeping the shock out of his voice. "I'm trying to set a new course here. I've seen the transfers. Magnus was closely affiliated with Sinn Fein, some would say too close. The Charity used its money to fund violent campaigns intended to destabilized governments. It . . ."

Liam stood up so quickly that the heavy chair tipped backward, his face red with anger. "Be careful what assumptions you make. The Charity funded people and organizations. It did not, as you say, fund violent campaigns."

"Then what the hell is Arndale? *Christ*, Liam! If that isn't an example of a violent campaign, I don't know what is."

"No one died. They made sure of that."

Michael sat back, stunned. His body sank as if all the air were leaked from it. "You *knew*."

Liam's eyes grew round and he wrung his hands together. "If you can only imagine how sick I felt when I learned of this. Those that want violence are feeling stronger without anyone to tell them otherwise. I could do nothing to stop it." He projected the very image of a saddened and contrite man.

"How? When?" Too many questions needed to be asked.

Liam hung his head and heaved a dramatic breath. He looked at Michael from the corner of his eye. "Last week. Just before the race. You and I were meeting with many people, and I sensed then something was in play, and was imminent. I thought perhaps if you sensed it, too, you'd ask me. I didn't grasp the extent of the plan or I surely would have told you. But, you left to be with that girl, so I thought I was wrong." He gave an offhand shrug.

"But you could see that the trail leads back to the Charity."

"The trail leads back to *you*, Michael. The Charity is not a separate entity from you."

Michael rubbed his face with his hands, as if the gesture would rouse him from a dream. "Me." His voice was barely audible. "For how long?"

Liam began to pace the floor as if doing so would help him think and put together the pieces. "The plan must have been made long before you arrived in Ireland. It's no secret Magnus and I wanted you out of the States and back here where you belong. I can only imagine this was part of his plan." He looked at Michael and gave a helpless shrug.

Conversations Michael had with his father after his brother's death came back to him in stark detail. He remembered how Magnus approached him, head bowed and solemn, grief stricken certainly, but assessing the chess board for his next move. "Just before Liam was killed he said the Charity would be mine. That he was proud to have a son follow in his footsteps. It's true, then. He killed Liam." His skin was ashen.

198

"Young Liam never had the innate smarts to run an enterprise as sprawling as the Charity. He was a brilliant strategist on the streets, but never had the ability to make money the way you do. Magnus crowed about your investments in lumber and land in Kentucky. He even went so far as to opine that your career in law enforcement was merely a clever ruse to position yourself inside communities to learn who the players were, who was in financial distress and ready to sell at bargain basement prices."

"That's . . . that's a lie. I-I never hid like that."

"No? Your father was never of the opinion you would shun a fancy education and world-class connections to hide out in a backwater hollow. But you were never far from the Charity's reach. He never believed that you hated him. In the end, he was right."

The scope of the plan became clear. Magnus created a situation that would torch Michael's chosen career in the States and make it feel like returning to Ireland was a free choice. A law-abiding pillar of the community needed to fall from grace. Magnus knew he had enough loyalty not to expose the Charity. The only gamble was whether Michael's love for Jessica was greater. In Magnus' eyes, she was a disposable and inconsequential item. Michael couldn't see that Liam viewed her any differently. Or that he was as innocent as he pretended to be.

Liam righted the chair and brushed the dust from his sleeves. "I've no doubt in our choice of you."

Michael braced himself against the table as his world spun dangerously out of control. No one was safe from the tentacles of his father's and uncle's manipulation. Through either greed or love, the unthinkable happened. Liam still protected Magnus. It was one thing to harbor a man known to kill, it was another to be the man that killed. In the hollow of a man's chest where hearts lay, the Charity found the space to corrupt.

His challenge wasn't simply proving his leadership or that he was in control. It was in accepting how the world worked.

BELFAST, NORTHERN IRELAND

AOIFE SPENT THE week picking up the charred pieces of her life. The flat that was once her home now lived up to its name. Neighbors stood with hunched shoulders and mutely watched as bulldozers scraped the picked-over remains of homes still cherished, nothing more than memories. Plastic milk crates of salvaged odds and ends sat at her feet. Neighbors offered the occasional pat and rub on her back as empathetic strangers offered whatever weak solace they could. After the second dump truck of debris rumbled away, and while the bulldozer still did its undertaking, Aoife shook her head and rallied. With barely a nod to others, she gathered her crates, turned, and trudged down the street.

The cramped room in cellar of Saint Peter's was cold and damp. Pipes ran the length of the ceiling and light bulbs in cage-like fixtures dangled from black cords. The room was infrequently used to house people in urgent need. Even the shelter where Aoife volunteered used it as a last resort. The oval braided rug tossed over the center of the linoleum floor failed to provide cheer. Cinderblock walls framed rectangular windows wedged close to the ceiling. If she bothered to look out, the view would be of a herd of comfortable shoes and thick ankles clomping by. The moldy smell hinted the room did not enjoy even the brief moments of sunlight that had graced her flat.

Aoife hoisted the crates on the creaking metal cot and immediately cursed the soot and grit she had neglected to dust off her belongings. The process of recovery was exhausting, and she let her head sink to her chest for a few precious seconds, gathering the strength to move the crates again. With more effort than she thought she had in her, she brought the load down the hall and into the ladies' loo.

One by one, she took out the odd china plate, teacup, and figurine and gently washed the soot down the drain. When the crates were empty, she did the same to them. Only after she received an odd look from another woman did she glance in the mirror and see she needed to give the same care to herself. The only identifying clues to her former self were the streaks of pale and freckled skin revealed by tears she struggled not to shed. Pity for herself or others was intolerable.

A sudden movement startled her. Aoife crouched down and reached for the knife strapped to her inner leg before she realized a woman had simply burst into the loo for a quick pee before the start of the afternoon's service. Her nerves were shot, and she calmed herself with the tasks of settling in. She put her cleaned world on top of her cot, pulled the curtain around, and trudged up the worn stone steps to the sanctuary.

Barely two dozen people waited, a bigger crowd than usual. Women with rosaries laced through clasped hands dotted the sanctuary, kneeling in pews. A few men sat fidgeting with hat brims soiled from years of Sunday wear. Aoife didn't have to hear them to know they came praying for better days. From the side entrance, she saw a group of nuns from the nearby Sisters of the Holy Cross Convent huddle together with rosaries rubbed by arthritic fingers. She looked at their smooth faces made round by their wimples and was glad for her choice not to be one of them. Their lips moved in a chorus of silent prayer and Aoife knew that this rare excursion to the outside world was testament of the love they had for Father Storm as he approached his retirement. Aoife genuflected, blessed herself with care, and took her place in the front pew on the right side of the aisle.

A bell chimed announcing the beginning of the mass. One boy and one girl dressed in matching albs entered from the vestry. The congregation stood as a stooped and shrunken Father Storm shuffled to the altar, paused in momentary prayer in front of the giant gold-hued crucifix, and turned to greet the altar servers. The reason for his imminent and requested departure from the pulpit was again made obvious when he startled at seeing the young girl. He stood, hesitant and confused, blinking in disbelief for too long before he remembered himself and the changes that had crept into his church as he aged.

Recollecting his purpose if not the year, he raised his right arm to bestow the opening blessing. The curvature of his back, an inevitable result of age and chronic lack of calcium, made it impossible for him to raise his arm any higher than his head. His head seemed to protrude more from the center of his chest than sit atop his neck.

"In the name of the Father, the Son, and the Holy Spirit," he intoned moving his hand through the air in a valiant attempt to make a cross.

"Amen," Aoife replied and blessed herself in unison with Father Storm.

"The grace of our Lord Jesus Christ and the love of God and the fellowship of the Holy Spirit be with you all."

"And also with you." She took comfort as her voice mingled with others.

"Today, as you know, is bittersweet. The last that I will be on the altar alone with you, for soon the Bishop will be here and I will have the honor of saying high mass with him as I bid you all farewell."

A light murmur rippled through the nave as the congregation acknowledged his announcement, punctuated by a loud sniffle from one of the sisters. His voice was strong and did not hint at a waver as he continued. "The next week's services shall be celebrated with others as I am honored so many wish to share the altar with me before I retire. I shall miss you all, as my work here is not yet complete. Only this very week was the need for my calling made even clearer. The destruction of homes and displacement of some of our own brought so much sadness."

Aoife stared at her hands, hoping no one turned a pitying gaze at her. Her well of tears was dry, and she wondered if feelings of revenge would fill it. She fingered a tissue and listened.

"The refrain I hear again and again from tired and hurting souls is, 'Why, Father? Why does the Lord allow such destruction and pain?'" He paused for a moment, making sure he had the attention of all before continuing. "I answer them with what men of God have been saying since the beginning of time. 'Because Satan never sleeps,' I say, 'Satan's powers are stronger than we can imagine and sometimes the serpent wins the battle, but God will win the war,'" he proclaimed, pointing a shaking index finger upward.

"Let no man question that Satan sleeps beside us at night, waiting for us to doubt the Lord Jesus Christ within us. God made man in his image and gave us the power of free will knowing that our faith is strongest when chosen *by* ourselves not *for* ourselves. When we doubt, Satan slips inside our flesh and tarnishes the perfect reflection of God's image.

"Jesus was God's incarnate on Earth and we truly love Him by name, deed, and face. But Satan does not want us to know who he is because once we do he fears we will reject him, so he changes. He changes his form to suit his means. He transforms into flood, fire, disease. These we can see. And, he transforms into powerful forces of temptation and greed. These we cannot see as they manifest in the hearts and souls of men—but they do manifest—and separate us from God.

"Be aware of the Angel of Darkness, for he will come cloaked as the Angel of Light and win your souls through his sleight of hand. Did the serpent prod its way into Eve's womb while she slept, or was he captured between her welcoming thighs? Beware! He is among us. He lives with us, breathes with us. He has tricked all of us, even me, into doing acts we thought were good but were evil.

"Did we help an innocent man escape persecution, or did we help a murderer escape capture? Did we help a mother protect a child, or did we let a father shirk his duties? I have been fooled! I have been tricked so you, too, must be ripe for his harvest. Beware!"

These last words echoed over the small congregation, stunned into silence. Sounds of wooden benches rustled, bodies shifting in physical and spiritual discomfort. The priest's uncharacteristic tirade prompted Aoife to steal a glance at the sisters, each with mouths open, not in prayer but in amazement.

"As we prepare to celebrate the mystery of Christ's love, let us acknowledge our failures and ask the Lord for pardon and strength," Father Storm seemed to catch himself and brought the service back into focus, reciting the Penitential Rite.

"Amen," she answered, weaker this time. The ceremonial mass continued and comforted her as she knelt, stood, blessed, responded. She sat silent in rote acknowledgement of age-old cues.

The fluster of the parish had calmed from the aging priest's lapse and she watched as men and women file up to the altar to receive communion. A round white wafer dubbed "the Lamb of God" during the Eucharist blessing culminated the most solemn moment of the mass when the average person is said to become one with God by ingesting a piece of Christ's body—bread for His body and wine for His blood. At this weekday mass, most of the women were older, but a few younger ones carried a baby on one hip while holding the hand of another squirming to be free.

Without exception, heads were bowed and all were silent in their prayers, seeping in the closeness of the Holy Spirit. Male communicants dutifully stepped aside, letting the women go before them, politeness and tradition winning over impatience and fatigue. The sermon had droned on longer than usual with Father Storm's thanks to the ladies and men who helped with every aspect of the church and his meandering reminiscences of them.

Mentioning her by name, Aoife accepted her acknowledgement with a slight nod of her head and a smile that kept her from nodding off. The crackly feeling of nerves and concern she had at his earlier rambling faded into the folds and shadows of her exhaustion and she waited, as was her custom, to be the last to receive communion.

"Body of Christ," Father Storm intoned, holding a round wafer in the air in front of a communicant's face.

"Amen," would come the inevitable reply, and then a wafer would be placed on their tongue or into their cupped hands.

She was close enough to the altar to hear the blessing and acceptance repeated for each person. The repetition and tradition lulled her. A few minutes later a gentleman tapped Aoife on the shoulder, indicating her turn to enter the aisle in front of him. She nodded but motioned him to go before her.

"Body of Christ."

"Amen," he replied, blessed himself, gave a slight genuflection, and returned to his seat via the side aisle.

"Body and Blood of Christ, Aoife, my child."

Aoife's eyes snapped open. Father Storm had broken the round wafer in two equal pieces and placed the half circles together in such a way that they formed the outline of a fish, oval body and two tail fins. The verbal and symbolic pieces of the venerable code demanded her response. He looked her directly in the eye and waited.

"A-amen, Father," she said, voice shaky, and accepted the wafer on her tongue.

She knelt back at her pew, and clasped her hands together both to pray and to hide their tremor. The sounds of the concluding service surrounded her.

"Go in peace to love and serve the Lord."

"Thanks be to God."

Mass concluded, a few congregants approached Father Storm, bidding him love and best wishes for his long overdue retirement. The sisters flocked around him in tribute. Their simple gray knee-length dresses and modern, abbreviated wimples gave them the appearance of hens fluffing their plumage, even though such an unhumble act would never be their intent. Father Storm bestowed blessings and acceptance of their unspoken wishes.

Only the Reverend Mother had authority to speak in their order. All others had taken the vow of absolute silence. Older, but not as stooped as Father Storm, she gave their promise that they would see one another again after the Bishop's visit. Father Storm assured them that he would be in town for another few weeks while a suitable retreat was found for his retirement, and he would welcome a chance to visit them at their seaside convent.

Half an hour passed before he could approach her. "Aoife. How are you faring?" he asked, sitting in the pew in front of her. He situated himself sideways, his hunched back making it nearly impossible to sit in the pew correctly. He turned his head to talk quietly with her and to keep an eye on the door.

His concern touched her. "I'm doing well enough, Father. I'm waiting for another housing voucher and will soon be on my way again." She nervously looked at the altar and side entrances, tuned to any movement.

"Mrs. Reynolds has been assigned."

She hesitated, unsure of where the conversation was heading. "I heard. It's been a good week for her in spite of losing her home. She found her cats and her photos and now a home. Prayers answered." She looked around the empty cathedral and back at the priest. "You wanted to speak with me, Father?"

Father Storm's eyes moved back and forth as he scanned the back shadows of the nave. "I retire in a little more than two weeks time and have heard they do not have a suitable replacement for me yet."

"You will be hard to replace, Father. You *are* this church."

He chuckled and patted her hands with fingers gnarled with arthritis.

"You were not the target, Aoife."

His directness took her aback. "I know that."

"The Bishop does not know who to place here. He kept me here for as long as he could, but I am long past my welcome."

"You've done great things here. You've saved many a soul and many a life."

The old priest closed his eyes and a look of pain flashed across his face. "I'm not sure all I've done has been in His name. There have been times when I have been used. I have been the agent of evil even while praying every night for purity and guidance." The afternoon sun angled through the stained glass windows, peppering the interior with multi-colored flecks. The Virgin Mary stood over them, arms forever outstretched in offering a mother's welcome and instant forgiveness for a child's thoughtless acts. Jesus rose close by, bare feet stepping over the stones of his intended tomb.

Father Storm looked past them to a distant point.

"I have been here since before the Troubles began. It was a young man's game then. Even a green *sagart* could pour his passion into his faith and build a life. I did that here, in this cathedral. There are two roads to take when you marry the church. One is the road of words and ideas. Living by scripture and the word of our Lord has brought me much solace. I have been lucky to share this peace with others. The other path is the path of man struggling to do God's work on Earth. That path, I've since learned, is fraught with Satan's tricks."

He grasped her hands and looked into her eyes. "Satan walks these aisles. He wears our cloaks and drinks our wine while he schemes to take our souls. I've *smelled* him. I've *seen* him. He wants my soul. I don't know how to stop him from getting it."

Aoife could hear the panic that etched the old priest's voice and tried to quell her own. She had been attending his services ever since she was a baby. He christened her, gave her first Holy Communion, and confirmed her as a soldier of Jesus Christ. The church had always been at the center of her life. Father Storm was a rock and a comfort to her as he was to so many others. But recently, she could see something soften and break inside of him. A quaver, a doubt had trickled into his thoughts and drained out in his sermons.

The confidences of others he vowed never to betray floated like dust in the air. The mind that was once a vault was now a sieve, and she knew the price they would all pay if he broke completely. She tried to redirect his fear. "You, above all others, are safe from Satan. Are you afraid that an idle mind is the devil's playground? You mustn't worry about your soul. What's bothering you, Father? Is it that you are afraid there will be empty days after you leave here?"

"I thought I was doing God's bidding, but I have sinned. I will burn in hell for what I've done. I must confess."

Aoife pulled her hands away and gripped the back of the pew, knuckles white with effort. "Nonsense, Father. You've told me yourself that the Bishop has heard your confession many times and that his absolution comforted you on many nights."

"The Bishop!" Father Storm spat on the floor. "He is nothing but a *man*! He knows only about matters of this world and not of the next. I must confess to someone who understands what it means to seek purity."

"Why are you telling me these things?"

He began to weep. "Because when I confess I fear they will come after you."

A movement caught her attention and Aoife turned her head to see one of the nuns craning her head around a pillar, undetected until now. Aoife looked at her, eyebrows raised, and rolled her eyes upward in an exaggerated expression of exasperation. The nun leaned forward and bobbed her head with understanding, tapping her finger to her temple, and looking at the aged priest as she did so. Aoife gave a look of sadness and shrugged her shoulders.

"What is your plan? Who are you intending to talk to?"

Confusion muddled his words. "Well, I . . . er, the Pope. I should most like to speak with the Pope. He would understand."

"The Pope himself? He's a very busy man, and I'm not aware of him coming to Belfast any time soon." Aoife stood up and helped the priest to his feet, walking him slowly to the vestry. "How about you tell me what you want to say to the Pope. Then I'll have a better idea of how I can help you. What can I do for you? I'll do it as I always have."

Tears ran down the old man's face. "You're a good soul. You know everything about my life here and all that I've done through the years. You must get out now. You must leave before Satan claims you."

"Thank you for your concern and protection, but it's my turn to protect you as best as I can. Don't talk of this again to anyone. You get some rest and we'll talk more in the morning."

"Yes. Yes. Thank you. I trust you more than you know. You're not ambitious or greedy. You don't have the wits to scheme and climb like my brothers do."

Aoife kept the wince from creasing her face. "Thank you."

"I can trust you to hold things in safekeeping. Men can't grip shoe leather without wonderin' how they can wield it for more power. But you," his voice trailed off, "you've never been out for your own gain."

"I helped all who accepted solace from you."

She was surprised when he placed a dry kiss on her cheek. "Thank you, Aoife. I feel better knowing you are watching out for me." He brought a gnarled finger to his lips and shut the doors and shades to the vestry. The room was where the priests changed into the holy vestments for the service. It contained a tiny closet built into the wall, a spare wooden table with two chairs sat under the single set of lead-paned windows, hinges oiled but slightly reddened with rust. An ancient rose-wood armoire, ornately carved with Celtic and Christian symbols, and darkened with age, dominated the room.

Aoife was more than familiar with this room. She had started cleaning and polishing the wood and floors when she was a teen and felt there was not a dimple or cracked stone she wasn't familiar with. Her curiosity had driven her to explore the back corners of the closet and even the musty drawers of the armoire only to be disappointed when the treasurers unearthed were moth eaten robes or wrinkled vestments yellowed with neglect. At one time, she was driven to snoop around the private rooms of the cathedral and the priests' living quarters in the adjoining rectory, thinking she was gaining some insight into their secret lives. She soon learned that priests were simply old men with an isolating job and baggy knickers, and who maybe partook in a discrete nip of whiskey or two. In preparation for his retirement, half-filled boxes of faded albs and cassocks lay open on the floor, ready to be packed and moved.

Father Storm stood in the middle of the room, looking from side to side as he repeatedly worked his fingers together and apart, rocking his body slightly as he did so. He looked nervously around the room toward the window and up at the armoire.

"It's been years. Years," he said, more to himself than to Aoife. "I . . . I'm not sure, not sure." He looked Aoife up and down. "You'll do. You'll do."

"Are you quite fit, Father?" Aoife said, betraying neither her impatience nor growing concern.

"Yes. Yes. Yes. I'm brilliant, actually. Such a relief."

"Father?"

He hobbled over, gripped a wooden chair by the back rung, and dragged it across the floor. With an effort, he placed it in front of the armoire. "Climb up," he said.

Aoife did as she was told, balancing herself as the chair teetered on its worn and uneven legs. Carefully she stood upright, her head almost even with the top of the heavy doors. Above her was a large oval relief carved of a Celtic cross and flanked by figures reminiscent of the Apostles in the Last Supper. A faint layer of dust had settled, bringing the features of the seated apostles into grotesque focus. She absently wondered when was the last time she dusted there and made a note to herself to do so before the Bishop's arrival.

"Place your hand on the left corner and feel for a wooden block."

Aoife reached up and felt along the top edge she had become familiar with during her explorations long ago, but had since ignored for it held no enticement. She followed the priest's precise directions and pushed the block with her fingertips while slightly pulling on the heavy door's latch. A hairline crack appeared around the moldings framing the oval. Had she noticed the cracks before, it would not have registered to her as anything interesting to pursue because it simply looked as if the wood had aged and dried, shrinking slightly from the other pieces that anchored it into place. Father Storm then directed her to reach into the right corner and slide a fragment of wood to the side. The combined actions allowed the oval to protrude enough that she worked the rest out with her fingertips. She gently pulled the oval from its mount, revealing an area eight inches across by six wide and four inches deep filled with a perfectly fitting box.

"Please hand that to me," Father Storm requested, visibly relieved. He gave her careful instructions on re-locking the empty compartment.

He stood, stroking the box and smelling the wood, fragrant of roses, which gave the wood its name. He bowed his head in prayer and waved the sign of the cross in the air with a rote motion that could have doubled for shooing flies away.

"I must give this to you for safekeeping, Aoife. Through the powerful intersession of the immaculate heart of Mary, he spoke to me. Her Son wants this in the hands of a woman, for in it is the evidence of man's failure to resist the temptations of Satan. Go, now, my child. Go with God's blessing."

Aoife took the box, lighter and more plain than she would have thought for something so cherished. She looked at him with a question.

"You will know what to do with it when the time comes," he said and left.

Aoife watched him go, standing silent, deep in thought. She wanted to go back to her flat and curl herself around a steaming cup of tea, but knew she could not. Going back to her cot and her electric kettle was all she could do. She hardly needed the hardness of the stone steps to remind her of reality. They made her knees ache and her heart heavy. When she pulled the curtain back, only the two milk crates upon her cot greeted her, her life relegated to their control. She thumped down with a creak of protest from the rusty springs and fumbled with the box's latch long enough to learn it was locked. Hugging the box to her chest, she dreaded knowing who had the key more than she dreaded the secrets it could unlock.

MANCHESTER, ENGLAND

DALLY PUSHED THE phone up to her ear and sat back in her chair, not bothering to close her mouth or blink. A clear river of snot ran out of her nose, over her upper lip, and unchecked down her teeth. The slight saltiness prodded her out of her thoughts, and she automatically reached for a handful of tissues and blew, not yet focusing on her present world. Instead, her mind whirled away at the ramifications.

On the other end of the line was an American reporter from Boston, Massachusetts. Colleen Shaughnessy-Carrillo's elongated "r's" and sultry voice belied her intensity and exposed that she was a driven woman who hammered away at the facts until she forged an ironclad story. While Dally would have woven a story with the weakest of threads, Colleen would not put one word on paper until the facts were checked and double-checked, evidence of the law degree she chucked to pursue a life in journalism. The story that poured from Colleen bested anything Dally could have dreamed up on her own, even after a few pints at the pub.

"I first met Michael Conant in Boston while I was covering the 'Murdering Heiress' story." Colleen pronounced her city *Bah*-stin.

"You g-got the picture I sent of Wyeth snapped at a horse race, right?"

"Yeah. That's definitely Wyeth."

"So why tell me about Conant?"

"He's the guy standing next to her. Wyeth was headline news so anyone connected with her was, too. I'm not sure who hated the attention more, him or her. I admit I got obsessed with the two of them and followed them back to Kentucky. You heard about the hoax search, right?"

"A bit." Had she? No matter, she fished for more. "Refresh me on the details."

"Conant was leading a search for a special needs boy lost on a mountain. He called in Wyeth to expand the search on horseback. A late season blizzard closed in. They never found the boy, Wyeth was critically injured, and a man ended up dead."

"A b-bloody mess."

"That's not all. There was never a missing boy and the body found on the mountain did not die of exposure as the official medical examiner's report claimed."

"I didn't hear a whiff of that! How'd he die?"

"Two bullets. One to the head and the other through the heart. A confidential source provided me with photos and the bullets used happened to be the same nine-millimeter caliber used by the favored Glock revolver of Sheriff Conant. Conant went missing, well, not missing as much he went on an 'extended leave' right around the time Wyeth decided to tour the world or something. You got my pictures, too. Right?"

Dally pulled an image up on her screen. Colleen's snooping uncovered photos of Wyeth and Conant looking rather cozy at a formal event, dressed to the nines. Sheriff Conant had a distinctly proprietary air over Miss Wyeth.

Colleen continued. "I heard the whole county was at that event. I interviewed the hostess of the party and other guests, but the lips of the dear citizens were sealed tighter than a squirrel's arse." She gave a little laugh. "At least, that's how the hostess would characterize it. Electra Lavielle is a gatekeeper of sorts, and no one dared speak to me in fear of her wrath. Lavielle lives off her father's media fortune that's enough to make Rupert Murdoch proud. It seems her presence had a chilling effect on my learning enough to nail down details and sources. My editors refused to print without confirmations so the trail stopped there."

A lowly horse trainer leaving the country in the dead of night would merit a few hundred words at best. But any updates on the Murdering Heiress would be enough for Grandier News to churn out stories about Wyeth for months to come. After all, lesser personalities had become minor celebrities on dust specks and drivel and Wyeth's story was meat and taters. As Colleen spoke, Dally looked at the smiling people on the screen. At first, her whole attention was on Wyeth. Then her attention shifted to the sheriff. Dally rubbed her eyes in disbelief, but she could not mistake the iron stare and strong brow. Miss Jessica Wyeth had begun a romantic entanglement with a Mr. Michael Conant, a.k.a. Michael M. Connaught of the Magnus Mikevy Connaught fame.

There wasn't a self-respecting Englishman in all of the United Kingdom who did not know Magnus Connaught. Although he never ran for an elected office, the newspapers' archives were full of images any candidate would die for. She closed her eyes and remembered some of the more popular snaps. Many were of Magnus, sitting bedside in a cancer ward, head bowed in prayer for the cure his companies would invest in. Others showed Magnus, surrounded by smiling women, kissing a laughing baby, happy their nappies wouldn't leak because of his newly patented design. In many, his young sons were beside him.

She took a deep breath and spoke in the tune of Spice Girls' *Wannabe*. "So, tell me what you want, what you really, really want." She winced.

She heard a slight pause and chuff on the other end of the line. "I want to know what happened to them. Are they together? Wyeth skulked out of the U.S. to points unknown over two months ago. Most people assume she fled to some remote tropical island and is waiting until the world's interest in her dies down so she can avoid the swarms of paparazzi. What is Wyeth doing and why have you contacted me?"

Dally worried that Colleen's obsession with the case would create an irresistible urge to travel to the U.K. and stomp all over Dally's turf. Buried beneath the stacks of printouts and notes that had become Dally's life were more pictures of Jessica. Dally retrieved the one she had emailed to Colleen. Jessica was dressed in jockey silks covered in mud leaning against a tall and dashing man as if her legs would collapse if he weren't there to prop her up.

The man at the Aintree track and the man at the American event were certainly one and the same. Michael Conant had been busy indeed. Connecting him to that private event at Aintree meant that he was clearly stepping into daddy's shoes. Only the richest of the rich were there, and sonny-boy was doing his best to fit in.

She wanted to keep Colleen as a supportive source but didn't want to be scooped. Being caught lying to Colleen's direct questions would cost her job, but omissions weren't lies. "Wyeth might have been spotted in England, and my boss wanted to run a few column inches with an update on her."

"That picture you sent, which racetrack was she at? Who else was she with? Is she still in England? Who was she training for? Why is Conant in England, too? Wait a second, didn't you guys just have another bombing?"

"I've nothing more than that, but I promise I'll c-call you as soon as I hear more."

"When was that picture taken? Who took it?"

Dally wrinkled scrap paper by the phone's mouthpiece. "Sorry? We're losing our c-connection. Hello? I'm sorry, I can–" She disconnected their call midsentence with a flourish of her hand, pinky up.

Every nerve in Dally's body twitched with excitement. Not only was she on the trail of the face that would sell ten thousand issues, but she had a corker of a story that was better than anything she could have cooked up. This could take her from the cesspool of the tabloids to the hallways of real journalism. She might actually get some respect and loose the magpie for good.

Dally liked Jessica's spunk and looked at her as Dally's ticket to legitimacy. Multiple story ideas popped into her head. The one she ruminated on was how oh-so-sweet and innocent Jessica Wyeth regained her freedom by lynching Magnus Connaught for murder and lassoed his son in the process. Dally had to tip her hat to the beautiful American, who had done what legions of English wished they could do—string Magnus Connaught up by his thumbs with his head resting beside him on a spike. But why would such a girl continue to be enmeshed with the Connaught family? She must have been duped into it. In spite of herself, Dally began to feel the stirrings of an allegiance with her.

She looked at the papers on her desk. The Arndale bombers were connected to the Aintree racetrack by betting slips connected to Jessica Wyeth, who was connected with Michael Conant, née Connaught, whose father is Magnus Connaught, king of love/hate media buzz. The details were circumstantial at best but had all the makings of an epic human interest story.

The angle Dally would work was of prey and predator—how a deceitful rogue led the fragile and vulnerable Miss Wyeth astray. Normally she would have begged to run with that slant, pleading to add another concocted tale to the list of many Don defended. Maybe owing some debt to Colleen's influence, this time she knew she needed solid and verifiable facts and on the record sources before she started writing. She hadn't had this much fun in a long time.

Dally dabbed her nose with a tissue. She felt another sneeze coming on as she got back to work.

NORTH CHANNEL, IRISH SEA

TIM PRESSED AGAINST the curve of the hull to make himself as small as possible. It stank like dead fish. He knew he would too. He would stink like that stupid man who piloted the boat, and he was angry about it. Telling the man he stank didn't help. When someone tells you that you stink, you wash your clothes and bathe. That man didn't bathe. He didn't even wash his hands, just snarled and squirted a brown stream of spit over the deck. It looked like tobacco colored seagull shit. Seagull shit smelled like fish, too.

Tim wanted to wash his clothes. His face contorted in spasms like it did when he smelled bad things and wanted to stop the smell from getting in his nostrils. He wanted to get clean. Now. No waiting. His upper body started to rock, but he hardly moved. The walls of the confined hiding space held him in place.

Liam taught him how to be very quiet. He had practiced with him and showed him how to move and breathe so he wouldn't be heard, but he didn't teach him how not to smell. Liam taught him how to talk the way other people talked. Not all rushed and chopped but smoothly with a grin on his face. Liam helped him to stop rocking, too. The lessons were hard but worth it. Afterward, Liam let him read his books or play with the dogs for as long as he liked. But the best reward was the girl.

The dogs didn't like Liam. They put their ears back and made their eyes round whenever they heard his voice or smelled him. But they liked Jessica. The corners of their mouths went up. They wagged their tails when she was around. That meant she was a good person and it was okay for him to like her too. He tried to show her how much he liked her but she yelled at him. He told Liam and Liam said she was surprised, that's all.

Liam said he should try again. Jessica would be nice like that girl in the village Liam brought over for him when he was good at learning. The girl said no at first too, but Liam said she was pretending. He was right. The girl said no but reached for his pants. Tim practiced and practiced his lessons, and soon the girl was doing things to him that felt really good. He was going to try again with Jessica, but then Michael showed up. Jessica let Michael do the things Tim wanted to do. He hardened against the confines of the tight space.

He could hear voices and footsteps on the deck. Two people were on the deck now. Now three. Was that scratching noise the sound of a dog's feet? The stupid stinking man was walking to the left side of the boat then to the right. He called it port and starboard, fore and aft. Why didn't he call it left and right, front and back? His rubber Wellies squeaked and made a slight squishing sound. The other feet wore shoes with harder soles. Those feet thumped and were heavy when they walked.

He dipped his nose inside the collar of his shirt and tried to breathe. He wanted to get clean, but the stupid man shoved him in the fake door behind the galley and told him to stay next to the freezers and the frozen dead fish until the other people got off the boat. He was cold. If he made a sound, the stupid man was going to make him scrub out the fish guts with his hands. Tim stayed remained still and listened.

"Started off in England at Hinckley Point on Bridgewater Bay. Been out here a bit. Catch has been good." There was a slight pause as the Wellies squeaked. "Here's my papers."

Another voice, not as gruff. "What grounds you been fishing?"

"Been chasin' the cod run through Saint George's Channel." A heavy metal hatch began lifting. The grating sound vibrated in his ears. "Taken me nearly a week to get a full catch. You'd a think there wouldn't be another fish left with all them boats out there. Small outfits like meself are gettin' pushed to the limit. Me wife would get the divorce for the time I spend out here except for the fact that she likes it when I'm gone." A lighter thump then a squish as he took a step. "Say now, why I been seeing you Coasties dashing about?"

"We've been asked to perform standard sweep protocol for all ships coming in from international waters as well as monitor catches."

"I been fishing these waters for thirty years and I never seen anything like it. I'd a thought you were looking for somebody or something."

"Standard monitoring. Nothing more."

"That's good. I'd a thought yas were looking for something to do with that bombing. Terrible business, that. Any leads yet?"

"Standard monitoring. Nothing more."

More grating and slams as hatches were opened and shut. "Take a look around and suit yourselves."

Tim felt the vibration of more footsteps and the boat rocked to the side. "Thank you kindly for your cooperation. Where you selling your catch?"

"When I refueled on the Isle of Man I heard prices were good up north. Thought I'd take my chances at the auctions in the Belfast ports."

"Best be going then."

The boat gave a bigger rock as the passengers disembarked. A few minutes later, the other boat's engine faded and light flooded the stinking fish hole. Tim could feel someone pulling at his ankles, and he shimmied free, gasping, rocking, his face sputtering in spasms as he ripped off his clothes.

The stupid man stood there with a hose, soap and neatly folded shirt and pants. He studied Tim's contorted face and snickered.

"Here you go, Tik."

BALLYRONAN, NORTHERN IRELAND

THE TRAIL SURROUNDING Michael's home started at the edge of the great lawn and meandered through wooded thickets and along streams. Fallen trees or mossy planks haphazardly hammered into place long ago bridged the water. On the top of a rise, the path provided a clear view of the winding drive and gatehouse, quiet with the morning's shift changes done.

The surrounding hillsides were a collage of deep greens checkered by fields lined with stone walls. A few homes and cottages dotted the hills and the gray stone husks of castles reigned on hilltops. To an American's soul, "old" and "historic" meant brick or wooden structures dating back several hundred years. In the Irelands, those words were rendered quaint against piles of rubble that dated back centuries more.

Americans also claim to feel a startling sense of connection when they set foot on Irish soil, as if some sort of invisible plug existed on the soles of their feet that connected to an Irish source of history and sense of self. Many a tourist walked down the streets of an ancestor's hometown and fancied a connection to it. Shoulders squirmed with feelings of déjà vu and a sworn kinship with the people.

Jessica thought them fools.

Reluctantly, she admitted she yearned for roots. Even so, she wouldn't let herself be deluded into thinking she belonged somewhere she had never been. She was born in New England and raised a Yankee. The stirrings of her soul or the needs for a connection were nothing more than her picking up the baggage of her life and moving on. Walking with her hands shoved deep into her pockets, she let the colors of the land and calls of the birds ebb through her as she let herself be pulled to the shores of Lough Neagh.

She bent down on the yellow sand and traced her fingers through the same waters her mother had known. The water was cool, its smell and taste unremarkable. A pang of homesickness, rather than the pretention of connection, flickered alive. At least, this is what she told herself. The once clear direction ahead blurred because all that trailed behind had changed.

Her walk took her through wooded areas and walled gardens. At one time, the gardens of the two hundred year-old estate must have been spectacular. Only those adjacent to the house were tended. Outlines remained of flowerbeds and paths designed to capture different vistas and provide sitting or picnic areas. Her route was often marked by stones slick with moss, other times by scrubby vegetation determined to take hold. The trails beckoned her forward. At least she had that.

The path meandered its way to the old stables. Outside, the turnout areas were marked with broken fences and fallen stones. Down the hill was a flat area that would have served as a schooling ring. The surrounding fields were perfect for jump training with wide-open areas and natural obstacles. Inside, the stable's bones gave evidence to well cared for horses—a broad cobblestone aisle and box stalls with doors that swung on hand-forged hinges. Four of the twelve stalls had been converted into a garage some time ago—showing a bias for horseless carriages over four-legged versions that marked supreme wealth at the turn of the century. The loft showed evidence that the leaking roof no longer offered protection. Dampness threatened to consume everything with mold and rot if left unchecked. She looked down at the hard-packed floor and noticed recent footprints. Her heart skipped a beat as she quickly scanned the interior. Knowing she was in the middle of Michael's world helped her push away a moment of worry.

The path continued to the other side of the sloping lawn. The smooth green carpet stretched up to the house and sparkled with drying dew. A slight movement caught her eye. A man with a dog appeared a discrete distance behind her. He touched his forehead in a salute and continued his patrol.

She had been out longer than expected and began to hurry, looking forward to the breakfast Murray would have waiting for her—still warm scones and soda bread and a choice of tea or coffee. He was determined to amend her heathen ways by encouraging adoption of tea as her preferred beverage, insisting tea was as important as oxygen to the Irish. Taking a shortcut through a garden, she walked directly to the solarium. The heavy doors, unaccustomed to any use, screeched open. A tray waited for her.

Murray gave a discrete cough as he stood in the doorway connecting the solarium to the rest of the house. "Good mornin', Miss Jessica. Glad to see you up and about on this fine day. That door's protesting its use. I'll have it tended." He turned to look over the pile of photographs and journals and the stack of Jessica's recent notes. "Shall I pour you a spot of tea while you ready for more research?" He filled a china cup with steaming reddish-brown liquid.

"Thank you." Jessica took one sip, and placed the cup back down. At least she tried. Murray had the good grace to pretend he did not see. She motioned for him to join her.

They chatted about her walk and discoveries. "What's up, Murray?" she asked, knowing her American phrases would give him momentary pause.

"I'm more curious to what's up with you," he replied, pleased with himself and enjoying the volley. "I'm not surprised you were drawn to the stable and waters today. Horses and love are even in the myths about how the lough formed."

"Seriously? Tell me."

He beamed, happy to have an audience. "A young lad named *Eochaidh* fell in love with his stepmother and they eloped. His father took an understandable exception to that act and killed all the horses used for their escape." He rounded his eyes and lowered his voice for emphasis, obviously enjoying the tale. "A sympathetic *Aonghus*, the Irish god of love, gave the elicit lovers a huge horse, instructing them to never let it rest for all would die if it did. But *Eochaidh* didn't listen and let the horse rest because he couldn't wait to snog his stepmother. The exhausted horse peed and a huge spring erupted on the spot, drowning all."

"Well, the shore here is just about the right color to have me believe that."

He sat down beside her with the comfortable air of settling down next to a friend. Their kitchen talks and mutual enjoyment of the top to bottom explorations of the manse helped establish an easy rapport.

"I took a look at the pictures you gave me. I've identified where a few of them were taken."

Jessica tried to temper the excitement in her voice. "I knew it! What did you come up with?"

Murray placed a few of the photos on the low table in front of them. "As soon as you told me your mother spent happy times on these shores, I had an idea of where that cluster of cottages might be. Looking at the photos, I found one that confirms it." He pulled one picture from the pile—colors faded to browns and yellows with a surface cracked and curled—and produced a tourist brochure.

The picture was one of Jessica's favorites. Bridget's head was thrown back with laughter, a huge smile on her face, expression radiant with happiness. One leg was propped up on the fender of a dilapidated lorry—wooden sides leaning precariously outward—and she rested her arm on her knee. Behind her, a dirt track wound down to a lake.

The coastline and small rocky island were very distinctive. The tourist brochure had a picture of a beach with a rocky island not too far off shore. The islands matched perfectly.

"The cottages were a favorite spot for folks from inner Belfast to summer. Back then, different families owned them, but they were purchased and made into a resort. The island is called Ram's Island. Being one of the few in Lough Neagh made it easy enough to identify."

"Is the resort still in business?"

"This is an old brochure. I really don't know."

"How about a caretaker? Would anyone be there who would remember those cottages and the families who stayed there?"

"I really don't know, and I'm not sure it's wise to appear on someone's doorstep and start asking questions."

Jessica fingered the brochure. "How do I get there?"

Murray pursed his lips. "You're too predictable for your own good, Miss Jessica. It's about two hours drive from here."

"I'll take you."

Jessica was surprised to see Michael standing in the doorway, hands shoved in pockets, and shoulder leaning against the jamb. He walked over and gave her a kiss on the cheek. He wore buff colored chinos and a shirt of thickly woven linen the color of peat that set off his dark hair and made his eyes shine navy blue. His casual attire signaled he had no plans for more meetings that day.

"Murray told me about his discovery," he said. "Those cabins are a short drive south of the school. I thought I could take you there, let you explore, then show you around the campus. Interested?"

"Yeah," she said, giving another look at the brochure before placing it on the table. "That would be terrific. Tomorrow?"

Michael looked at Murray, who gave a barely perceptible nod. "Tomorrow works. It should be fun and I can guess you're getting cooped up here." He poured himself a cup of tea and took a thick slice of soda bread.

Murray got up to leave, but Jessica stopped him. "I feel like you want to tell me more, right? You've taken a look through all of the papers too, so . . ." She let her voice fade.

"I'm not sure if it's important, but if you wouldn't mind, I'd like to keep reading her journals and letters and find someone who can translate the Gaelic for you. Your mother was quite a woman. I can see the resemblance."

Jessica blushed. Murray's compliment was the first time someone told her she resembled her mother—her real mother—and she was rattled by the effect those words had on her. "Thanks, Murray. Of course you can. But the deal is you have to tell me everything you learn."

"Most certainly." He loaded a tray with discarded cups and saucers. "We wouldn't have it any other way," he said and left.

Michael sat down on an oversized sofa closest to the window. He adjusted some pillows and motioned for her to join him.

"We?" she asked.

"Murray's keeping a watchful eye on you and making sure I'm apprised of what's on your mind. I've been busy this past week. I'm happy for his help."

"He's been terrific at making me feel welcomed. Quite a contrast to Nan."

"He's been a part of this home for as long as I can remember. His father worked for my mother's family, and my father hated him."

"Hmm. That makes me like him even more."

Michael chuckled as he pulled Jessica beside him. "You've certainly received his approval. Not everyone gets to crawl around this house like you have."

"Walking the grounds and exploring the house helps me get to know you, too. I'm excited to see the school. I feel like I'm being rewarded for good behavior."

"Very good behavior." He wrapped his arms around her and reclined. The length of his body pressed against hers. Tension drained, he grew content. "It's been a crazy week. I'm sorry I've been gone so much. Murray tells me you've been up and around more. You must be feeling better."

"Mm hmm," she affirmed. "I needed the rest."

"How are you feeling?" He brushed her hair aside and opened her shirt collar far enough to see the round bruise, now dappled with hues of yellow and faded purple.

"Good," she said, rolling her shoulder around, judging its stiffness. She screwed her mouth to the side. "Any idea who wants to kill me?"

Her directness startled Michael. Recovering, he shook his head. "No. Doherty said animosity about you was at a boiling point, so it could be related to the race. No one has learned anything more."

She pressed. "I saw fresh footprints in the dirt in the old stables."

"Footprints?" Michael looked in the direction of the stables. "Most likely one of my men, checking the outlying buildings. I'll mention it, but I'll bet they were just being thorough. The stables haven't been used in years. We always had horses during my summers here, but they were in need of care even then."

"Restored, they'd be amazing. Even the grounds look perfect for steeplechase training."

"They are, or at least were, when I was a kid."

She sat up in surprise. "Seriously? You raced here? Who won?"

He smiled. "I did. It was one of the few things I did better than my brother, and I took a profound amount of pleasure beating him at something. My mother would help me. She'd cut off Liam's line and slow down just in time for me to take the lead. After a while, I could see the strategy for myself and cut both of them off."

"You've been holding out on me! That explains why you weren't wiped off Planxty's back."

He shrugged, enjoying her surprise. "Most jockeys are under six feet tall, so a pretty safe assumption was that I'd find another career. I rode with Tim, too. I mentioned before that our fathers were business associates."

She chewed on the inside of her cheek, weighing how much to say. "Yes, you did. You were a bit short on the details, though." She shifted herself around and hugged her knees to her chest. "Go ahead. Fill me in. I've got time." A smile grew on her face, but an edge crept into her voice. "He's different."

"Tim's loyal to the Charity. He's always been tough to understand."

"There's more to it than that, Michael," she ventured. "With animals he's great. With people, not so much."

"Yeah, I know." He hooked his finger under her chin and pulled her face up to read her expression. "You get tense every time his name comes up. I wish you had asked me about him sooner. Tim is a few years younger than me, but was one of the few kids allowed on the estate when I was younger."

"Allowed?"

"My father would say that money attracts more money or flies. He was cautious who he let close to us. Not every parent wants their kids playing in a sandbox surrounded by armed guards, either, so the locals kept their kids away. You see, my father always had mixed reviews." He shifted, uncomfortable.

"But Tim's parents were okay with him being here?"

"Tim's mom died when he was very young and father was incredibly skilled at handling horses. Must be where Tim picked it up. Anyway, his father established the network of trainers, vets, and jockeys who knew how to work the racing system. He stayed away from anyone directly involved with management of the tracks and used people he knew he could control. He was involved with farms that raced at Suffolk Downs, Belmont, and Churchill Downs."

Jessica could feel her eyes sting, and her face grow hot. She picked at a worn spot on her jeans. "If that's the case, then his father could be the link between Wyeth's Worldwind Farms and the Charity? Maybe he knew Gus Adams, too?"

"It would fit."

She puzzled over the new information. "If his father knew how to dope the animals and fix races, Tim probably learned to wield a needle at his father's knee. That would explain why he was so competent at sedating the horses for transportation."

"Tim idolized his father and did whatever he asked. In fact, I have to say that Tim was hungry for any approval he could get. When we were kids, I would sneak out of the house and meet him at the stables. We never planned a time, but there he'd be, just waiting for me. He would sleep there as often as he could, making a bed from the horse blankets and curling up in a corner of a stall. That reminds me of someone." He playfully touched the tip of her nose with his index finger. "You're right. He's always been one of those people who got along better with animals than humans.

"Tim actions make me think he had some kind of brain injury or maybe he's a bit autistic? He's great if he's practiced doing or saying something, but if he's presented with new information, he gets flustered. I can tell he's been taught to react and behave in certain ways. I've watched him stare when trying to read body language then flip out when he doesn't put the pieces together correctly."

"I never learned if his behavior resulted from an injury or if he was born that way. He was always an odd duck. We got along because we did things he liked to do like riding horses or playing in the woods. You're right about him learning how to interact. With games, he would study the rules and learn different strategies, but once he did, his game never varied. When he learned to do something, he would do it the exact same way again and again. He is extremely reliable."

"Which would make him perfect for schooling horses. Flawless execution of repetitive drills."

"It's hard to tell what's on his mind, but if he gets rattled, he can't stop his actions or his words before they happen. It took me a while to figure that one out." He rubbed his jaw at a memory. "When we were fifteen, Tim landed a left hook during a disagreement."

"But you've stayed friends?"

Michael sensed she was probing around, trying to understand something. "Not really. After that we drifted apart, but our relationship was always a bit one sided. We're only recently back in touch. I admit I felt sorry for him."

"Why?"

"He struck me as gullible. As kids, he would latch on and follow me everywhere. He was always turning up. The store, a local dance, beach.

Wherever I was, he was, doing the same things as me. He was annoying and kind of pitiful. The only break I got was on Sundays when he wasn't around. But, my mother told me to be patient with him. She said he was expressing steadfast loyalty to the family and she showed him a tremendous amount of kindness. She welcomed him in the house, made sure he had enough to eat, and even gave him clothes. He didn't need the charity, but accepted her kindness just the same.

"He was definitely happiest when surrounded by things I either owned or had owned. He had the toughest time with my brother. Liam figured out that Tim would accept whatever tale he was told as true. He tormented Tim. Liam fed him everything from ghost stories to conspiracy theories and laughed when Tim would jump a guy and rough him up because of something Liam said. His fights always ended in Liam's favor. As soon as Tim learned I'd never do that to him, the following, or what felt like hounding, began. He was a lot like his father in the way he attached to people. His father said he would never betray Magnus and killed himself after being arrested for smuggling."

"How sad! Was he smuggling drugs?"

"No guns. He used the transporting of horses to tracks in the States, the Irelands, and Europe as a cover for gunrunning. My father made sure I didn't hear many details, but my sense was that Tim's father handled a complex operation. I guess he felt killing himself was the best way he knew to keep his word of loyalty and silence to my father."

She shook her head. "Tim must have been crushed."

"Yeah. He completely crumbled. I was back at college, and he must have called me five times a day to talk for hours. Listening to Tim go on about what his father was involved in—and knowing his death was because of my father—I couldn't take it anymore. I was sorry his dad died and all that, but that was the final straw for me. My college years were," he rubbed his head in thought, "tumultuous. That's when I was realizing what the Charity was and broke ties with my father. I eventually had to stop taking Tim's calls."

"That must have been a double loss for him—his father, then you."

"My uncle took Tim under his wing. I'm glad I had an ocean between us. Uncle Liam told me he went a little off the rails and would have been completely lost if he didn't have Liam as an anchor."

"I'm not sure he's found himself either, though. Funny how he ended up back at his beginning."

"Hmm?"

"You know—working horses, the Connaught family, that full circle thing."

Michael pulled back the curtain of hair that obscured her expression. "Okay. Out with it. Why all these questions about Tim? It's more than just the tattoo."

Jessica gnawed on her lip and kept her head down. "The day I saw the tattoo . . ." She averted her eyes. "He was giving me a ride home from town and made a pass at me." Each word carefully chosen and spoken slowly. "It felt like he wasn't going to stop."

"You're okay?"

She picked at a fingernail. "Yeah, definitely. The whole episode was weird. One second he's all over me and the next he's nearly bawling and asking for forgiveness. Clearly he imagined it would happen one way, and when it happened differently, he got all flustered. He begged me not to tell anyone."

His hands closed into fists as he listened. His voice strained with the effort to remain even. "Why didn't you tell me this before?"

"Because I could tell that something was off with him, that he might have been like my cousin." She held her head against the flow of memories. "He knew he had made a mistake and afterward made a point to stay away from me. Besides, I needed the help before the race and obviously he was at the cottage as a bodyguard. He just took that role too seriously for my taste," she chuffed. "Now that I'm at Ballyronan, I want to get a sense of how he fits in."

"From this point forward, he doesn't."

Jessica heard the menace in his words but was relieved that Tim's behavior was out in the open. It was one less secret between them.

"He's probably never had a girlfriend," she continued. "If he was taught about women by some drunken sot at a pub, no wonder he acted like he did. Until he learns some manners, I'd prefer he not be around."

"Consider it done."

Michael's body, fluid and warm when he first arrived, was now heated and tense. His shirt pulsed over his pounding heart. He stood and walked around the room. A few minutes of staring at the lake helped him unclench his hands.

"My uncle has him working at Tully Farm until the last of the horses are transported. I'll make damned sure Tim won't be back." He went back to the sofa and gathered her in his arms. "I'm so sorry that happened to you and I'm grateful you're okay." Slowly, they entwined again, taking comfort in the other's presence.

Her thoughts drifted as she enjoyed their easy silence. She could see why the room had been the favorite lounging area over the generations. Rattan furniture with deep cushions welcomed a person to idle there.

Sunlight poured through the glass walls. Hinged windows opened to catch the warm summer breeze. Just beyond, the waters stirred, barely rippling the mirror surface. A couple of sailboats and a motorboat took advantage of the perfect conditions.

"It's beautiful here, Michael. I had no idea you had a home like this. Why didn't you bring me here from the start?"

He raised his index finger. "One: armed guards. It's not a detail most women go for." He grinned at her light trickle of laughter and raised a second finger. "Two: the master suite renovations needed to be completed before I would sleep here again, and it certainly made it more comfortable for you." He raised a third finger. "And most important, number three: no stable means no horses—a fact I plan to remedy immediately. The cottage and lands were perfect for the training job, plus I had no way to keep a half-wild woman out of trouble here." He raised her chin and brushed his lips against hers. "I'm glad you wanted to come. I know your plan was to be closer to places your mother visited, but I feel better knowing you're under some very watchful eyes."

She couldn't remember the last time she had felt so at ease. Her worries and fears felt very far away.

He unbuttoned her shirt and slipped his hand inside. She pressed her body against his.

MANCHESTER, ENGLAND

THE EYE OF a security camera hung in a corner of the employees' lounge at the Manchester Airport, dingy and glazed with lack of attention. Dally noted the money budgeted for airport security went to the public areas of the terminal or areas with lots of comings and goings—like the tarmac and cargo hangars—not to employee areas where everyone's background and affiliations had already been checked. The only security interest was in the occasional rifling of lockers. Nothing there warranted government surveillance.

She had to pass through three different check points—one to drive onto the grounds, one to enter the airport through the back gate, and one to enter the "Staff Only" areas. By the time she was escorted around the maze of cinder block walls and employee lockers, nefarious intent would have long been sniffed out and summarily dealt with. Anyone sitting at the mismatched groupings of faux-wood tables and plastic chairs in the lunchroom would be of no interest to security.

The yellowed and green linoleum tiles were gritty with years of wax build-up and nicotine. Vending machines, serving an assortment of caffeinated beverages and a few flavored mineral waters, flickered and hummed along the walls. The pervasive stink of jet fuel mixed with old cigarettes should have driven her to distraction, but the copious amounts of snot running out of her head flushed the smell out before it had a chance to fester.

She took another handful of budget brand, rough tissues, vowing that when she made it to the top she'd buy only the softest. The skin under her nose was reddened and raw from the relentless assault, but she hardly cared that she had become a red and soggy fountain. What she had in front of her was everything she had ever dreamed.

The sound of someone clearing his throat and shifting in a nearby chair startled her into remembering the mate who had signed her in as his sister. He sat grubby and hunched by the window, taking a smoke, and picking at a Styrofoam cup filled with black goo.

"Did you get what you wanted?" he asked, impatient to get his payout.

"Perhaps," she replied, keeping the excitement out of her voice. "Will take a s-spot more spit and polish before there's a story here."

He grunted and took another long puff off his cigarette. "I did my bit."

"What's this now? You sign me as your beloved s-sis, hand me a bag of snaps, and act like you're all the better for it?"

He wiped his stubby fingers on his oil-stained shirt. "I did my bit," he repeated. "Now you do yours. They said you'd pay in cash."

If her mates in customs had known how big a scoop their pilfered security images were, she never would have been able to afford them. Britain's tabloids had an unquenchable thirst for pictures that would spark a few thousand impulse sales by ladies and gents in the grocery cues. To the customs blokes, a few fuzzy images of a pretty girl getting on and off a private jet didn't matter. They had seen enough of the rich and famous to know that pretty girls with blonde ponytails were a dime a dozen, and this one, although arguably prettier than most, was no one they paid particular attention to.

But to Dally, the brown paper bag filled with curled pictures was gold. Pure feckin' gold. The series of images documented Jessica Wyeth's arrival in England. The first black and white image was enough to keep her stories flowing for weeks, but she knew she couldn't stop there. This was Miss Wyeth. Hair tucked up under a baseball cap. Aviator glasses with dark lenses. Disembarking from a top-of-the-line six-seater Cessna 525B CJ3 Citation Jet. Tail markings "MMC, Ltd." Registered to Magnus M. Connaught Enterprises, Limited. Time stamped 4:00 pm GMT. Woman saying something to airport employee. Forklift and mini lorry seen in background pulling up to jet. Time stamp 4:01 pm GMT. Woman gone. Assortment of baggage and wooden crates, some with unclear markings, unloaded from jet. Time stamped 4:21 pm GMT. Another set of pictures. Same woman. Standing in the large hangar dedicated to receiving and clearing cargo. Large crates emblazoned with "MMC" logo. Time stamped 4:30 pm GMT. One crate stood opened. Her head craned to look inside. Time stamped 4:35 pm GMT. Head bent while writing something on clipboard, most likely signing for cargo. Time stamped 4:37 pm GMT.

Dally gave another look at the security camera. She folded up the paper bag of pictures and shoved it into her canvas satchel. With great show, she rummaged for money, purchased a can of pop from a vending machine, sat down, and produced what looked like a flattened sandwich wrapped in wax paper. She offered it to her companion. When he refused, she pushed it further in his face.

They watched a few more jets land and take off before he stubbed out his cigarette. He slapped his hand down on the sandwich and shoved it into his pocket, shaking his head with impatience and disbelief.

She watched him give the wad of cash an unconscious pat as he walked out the door.

Dally's mind was in full gear as she drove back to her office. Her head held clearly articulated stories. Every illusion and innuendo was perfectly crafted by the time she sat down to write. All she had to do was blurt it out through her fingertips and press send. She wouldn't just write one article and drop it like a nuclear bomb. To keep the momentum going, she determined to write a series of articles. Each would evoke the readers to ask the very questions the next article would answer. She'd become a veritable Scheherazade of rag journalism.

The series would start in the bowels of the paper on page ten's grave-yard of retreaded news. Each segment would work its way progressively up in stature to Page One by the time the week was out. Increasing interest in her stories would increase readership and her own value.

Gaining readership was a one-sided game that the news rags wrote the rules for. The object of the game was to lure as many people as possible to buy your paper. Truth was a tool to be used only when needed. If it were a slow news day, even a headline of "Aliens Invade Buckingham Palace" over a picture of oval-eyed beings fingering a Beefeater's button would do nicely.

The news cycle at Grandier News was a neatly orchestrated event. Gone were the days where the papers would be printed in a central location and shipped by truck or boat to all corners of the UK. With a simple press of a button, the content would flit to presses sprinkled throughout the Kingdom and printed where the readers were. The morning papers would have instant distribution and be in the readers' hands within hours.

A close eye and ear were kept on which stories garnered the most interest. By the time of the evening broadcast, the stories that held the most interest were culled and placed into TV format, updates included if necessary. This fit perfectly into Dally's plans and her headlines read like a steady drum beat. Once the editors saw how her stories sold papers, she would certainly be asked for a live on-camera report. Her nose tickled at the thought.

She wrote Monday's headline and article immediately after her conversation with Colleen Shaunessy-Carrillo. Don already approved it to run in the early edition.

Man Dies in Mountain Search. Murdering Heiress Sought for Questioning

Part One of the game is to refresh the British memories, build the foundation for future stories and to whet their appetites for more "news."

Dally used the information gained from the American reporter and splashed in a few of her own details, veracity notwithstanding. Loosely cited quotes pilfered from other articles on Sheriff Michael Conant were liberally peppered throughout.

Colleen provided the scintillating images. Photos showed Conant in a tuxedo and Wyeth in a too-tight dress with her boobs popping out in a cozy embrace. Others of Conant showed him as a grave but very handsome Kentucky lawman. One image showed Wyeth—with a deer in the headlights expression—on the courthouse steps after being exonerated of murder. Displayed together, identities and connections were clear. Today's news would be the last time Dally would use the phrase "Murdering Heiress" to describe Jessica. The first headline was a cheap hook to grab readers. The brave girl risked her life in a blizzard to save a young disabled boy and deserves to be called by her given and reclaimed name. Greek tragedies didn't get any better. Sympathies would build.

Tuesday's Headline: *Death and Hoax Search Covered up. Wyeth Flees U.S.*

Dally imagined her readers clutching their hearts.

This second article, concept and outline submitted and approved by Don, begins to create the image of the poor girl as a skittish and misguided waif who misplaced her trust in Sheriff Conant. Did the sheriff save her life as many claimed, or was he the one who inflicted her terrible injuries? So much speculation! Who could blame the poor thing for running again? But, to where? And who is that dashing but dastardly sheriff anyway? He certainly looks familiar. Dally sniffled and smiled to herself anticipating the letters, emails, and phone calls that would come rolling in as readers undoubtedly recognized his face and wanted to be a part of making the identification.

Wednesday: *Jessica Wyeth Spotted at Aintree*

Ah! England's beloved racetrack filled with a colorful history and even more colorful characters. A perfect backdrop. Who could blame our poor confused heroine for falling for the trappings of wealth and power by selling out her formidable equestrian skills to the highest bidder? Poor thing is even wearing silks with corporate logos. MMC, Ltd no less. But wait. Who's that man strong-arming her into a standing position after that zillion dollar claiming race? It's that Conant guy!

Hold on a second. Mega money? MMC? Jumpin' Jehosephrat! Thanks to a sharp-eyed, but unnamed reader, a question would be raised that Sheriff Conant is a dead ringer for Michael *Connaught*, Magnus Connaught's only surviving son! A sidebar would refresh the reader's memories of the suspicious dealings and terrorist campaigns the Irish scum Connaught senior supported and how—*gasp*—our sweet, brave

Jessica single-handedly brought down that mighty crime empire. Could his son be out for revenge?

Dally jotted a quick note to get some archival photos of the Wyeth family's thoroughbreds and run them side-by-side with recent pictures from Aintree. How perfect if she could get some snaps with that trainer Jessica was supposed to have murdered, Dally thought. She wrote the name "Gus Adams" in bold letters and underscored them for emphasis.

Thursday: *Michael Connaught Seduces Jessica Wyeth*

A bit of soft news on the emotional side of the story will grab a few more readers who may have been hiding under a rock for the past days and not heard the news. Everyone picks up a paper when the headlines scream "Sex!" The images would be of a beautiful woman and handsome rich guy. All the better that they're young. Dally had her fingers crossed that the photographer she sent out would get some decent pictures of the two of them together in time to run with the story. This wasn't speculative fiction; this was hard-core journalism!

Current photos and interviews with people who may have seen them together would bring the readers to a fever pitch. So, the game continues. Oh, woe of woes! It's true! Poor Jessica is entangled with the most evil of families. Michael Conant is indeed Michael Connaught. The dapper and duplicitous gent charmed his way into our lost girl's heart and brought her closer to the evil world she was trying so desperately to escape. Where is she now? Does she realize the kind of danger she's in?

Friday's issue would be when the real fun begins.

Connaught and Wyeth Connected to Arndale Bombing

Voila! Dally planned to dump the details on the betting slip and cargo arrival in Manchester. Wyeth's horse was sure to be a loser but it won. Nobody is really going to care about that, but her name—well, at least what looked like her name—was on a betting slip in the truck. Dally's efforts to trace the money trail on the truck's purchase went nowhere. Even her investigator buddies couldn't trace as much as a rat's fart saying the trail was too convoluted. Dally wasn't going to let a difficult, pesky fact get in her way of a good story.

She intended to plaster the pictures from the airport and use the "It's common knowledge that . . ." trick to insinuate that Conant or Connaught or whatever his name was perfecting his family's tricks and was the money behind the new truck. Dally could weave a good yarn that Jessica was tricked into smuggling bombing materials into England. The fact that her flight originated from the Republic side of Ireland was that much sweeter. But the holes in Dally's story were gaping. Don would need more to stand on if he was going to walk the plank with her.

If all goes as planned, she'd be able to whip up a feeding frenzy for any shred of information in time for the massive uptick in newsstand purchases usually enjoyed on weekends. Any newspaper reporter worth her salt—or any tabloid hack wishing for more—knows having her story be on the cover, visible as the papers sat folded and ready in the newsstand, was a status symbol.

The lofty space, referred to as "above the fold," was the space she hungered for. Decreasing in importance were the stories on the right hand pages of the paper. Pages three, five, and seven—in descending order—were the pages readers scanned before they viewed the even-numbered ones. Stories on the front page but below the fold guided readers deeper into the paper.

Dally's sole goal was to be Page One. Above the Fold. Continued on Page Three. With pictures. Friday was the final testing ground to see which stories had ripened during the week. Friday was when she would get her on-air debut, with her words being in her own mouth and not Millie's. But for that to happen, she needed a live source, someone who could give her tale some credence and serve as the catalyst for certain assumptions.

That American reporter said the quality of her sources helped her climb the ladder, but Dally didn't want to be hampered. Once, she had the best inside source a girl could have inside her knickers, and he bailed on her. Next time, she'd make sure her source would have more of a reason to stick with her and the story. No more magpies for her! She gave a whispered "whoop!" when she envisioned her series would be more than simply ripe—it would be rotted to the core and stinkin' to high heaven.

Writing for a paper dubbed "United Kingdom's Source for News" did not dampen Dally's enthusiasm for writing for her British audience and only her British audience. Those feckin' micks across Irish Sea and the North Channel were not worth a moment's breath, and she certainly wasn't going to tailor her news to their interests. This story was her stepping-stone to be a news presenter and Irish sympathizers or perky-titted Millie Bartholomew would no longer stop her. Dally's writing was top notch, now her research skills and connections would be on keen display. Not even the Bishop's celebration of a priest's retirement in Belfast would be enough to jar her precious baby off the front pages.

SEPTEMBER 1966
DERRY, NORTHERN IRELAND

GUS ADAMS THREW his pack on the cot, kicking up a small cloud of dust. He should have been tired from his travels, but he quickly bathed and changed and was back outside walking down the dirt road. He didn't bother to hide the spring in his step. A wooden sign with peeling paint pointed his way toward Londonderry, or Derry as the locals preferred.

Strand Road followed the banks of the River Foyle, and he listened to its waters burble over rocks and logs. The river was full with recent rains and its water brown with turmoil. The road, too, was punky with wet, and he kept to the sides as much as he could, avoiding slick patches and puddles with agile jumps and leaps. He inhaled deeply and let warmth and calmness come over him. The air in the States was sharper, drier. He didn't like it.

Hamilton air smelled like pine trees and Boston air stank, just as the waters in its cherished Charles River did. The air he sucked in hungrily smelled like moist moss. The river was the color of mud, but he hardly cared. He was home and he loved it.

Hope had been a stranger to him, but not anymore. His trips to Boston were becoming more frequent. He was staying stateside longer with each visit. He knew his work mattered. He had a chance and a calling to make a real difference and wasn't going to blow it. He quickened his steps knowing he was soon to see Bridget.

When they left the cottage in April, each had promised not to contact or see the others until after the protest marches had begun. The knowledge that they were at their most vulnerable made him wince. Those who knew the complete plans and who was involved with organizing the insurrection were the most valuable before events happened.

Once the parades started, the RUC would have too many targets to run after to be bothered with the likes of them. But until the rebellion spread, the leaders were the easy marks. Any leak hinting at their disloyalty to the

Kingdom would guarantee their arrest. They'd be thrown into Long Kesh prison, or worse—Maghaberry.

As happy as he was to see Bridget, he knew doing so put her at risk. She had sacrificed too much, cared too deeply, and come too far to be stopped now. But he had news from Margaret that could help their cause, and he knew Bridget would want to hear her news.

Messages were painstaking passed weeks ago according to a strict discipline. A series of communications and events was set up as a code. A classified advert in a local paper for nanny help with twin boys set off one series of events. A lace hanky on a light pole on a certain street on the first Monday of the month set off another. To mobilize large numbers, the *Sagart* would preach particular sermons and gospel readings to tell of something afoot. If anyone had found a single direct communication, that one message would not disclose the date and the meeting place together. One meeting required three or more coded communications for confirmation. He felt safe enough, but knew he would have taken any risk to see her.

Black horse grit was still embedded under his nails and in knuckles that his hasty bath did not dislodge. He scrambled down the banks and vigorously rubbed his hands together, employing a broken stick for extra help, smiling as his mother's voice rang in his ears, 'You could grow 'taters under them nails! Go wash up!' He yearned to scoop up a palmful to slake his thirst, but the brackish water and promise of a pint stopped him. He splashed his face, giving himself an extra go.

The fact that he was only minutes away from seeing her was a minor miracle. He was almost late by days. Shipping horses internationally was common for breeding and world-class competitions from racing to Grand Prix jumping. He had a strong preference for air travel, as the hours spent in flight were less stressful on the animals than the weeks aboard a ship. But, he never dithered when an owner decided to float or fly the beasts over the ocean.

Both methods put horses into close quarters. Each horse had to have a meticulously documented clean bill of health and was subject to standard quarantines. Recent outbreaks of the potentially fatal equine infectious anemia exposed four-legged investments to too much risk. Syndicates and owners needed to prove the animal's health at the border or entry to the new country would be denied.

His return passage to Sligo was complicated by the medical forms he needed to obtain for several horses under his care. He smoothed out the details in record time. He knew his way around paperwork, shipping containers, and customs. He could ship anything into or out of the country. Including humans.

He was good with money and knew how to keep his mouth shut. The latter trait endeared him to Bridget even more.

"You're never one to make a peep, are you?" she had asked.

His memories swelled with a summer years ago at the lake cottage. Bridget was twenty-four and in the full bloom of beauty that made his heart ache just thinking about her. He remembered how the sun made her freckles stand out against her pale skin and how the thin blue cotton of her dress stuck to her crossed legs from a mixture of humidity and sweat. They sat on a large flat rock surrounded by scrub and trees, overlooking the oddly shaped island. He liked it when they were sitting down. The difference in their heights was less obvious.

"Not unless I have something to say," he answered. He remembered her smile and the way she reached over and patted his hand.

They had already been through so much together. Growing up in the flats in West Belfast without fathers or a pound between them made them lean on one another for support. She was devastated when he moved to the country to help a horse farm there, but they stayed connected, meeting at the cottage whenever they could. He remembered how she fretted when he began his trips to America.

"I need you to listen for a few minutes. Whether you help me or not, you mustn't speak a word of this to anyone."

How could he do anything but agree?

He remembered how she took in a big breath as if bracing herself against an unseen force. "There's nothing for Margaret here. She's nearing fifteen years old. She's educated. Hardworking . . . and Catholic." She rustled through her pockets and produced a yellowed newspaper clipping. "Here's a service in the United States that helps girls find work as governesses. I've written them and found a family in Boston that is interested in having her there to work."

He could feel it, then. Her desperation to have him listen and not question her. "We've spoken of this often. It's not just your sister who could have a different life," he wanted to say that she could have a different life with him—that he would share his life with her. "Americans would accept you. You needn't change for them." He wished he had said more. She had let him take the clipping from her hands. He remembered how their fingers brushed against one another. How she didn't pull away.

"I've saved enough for her passage. And yours." She held up a hand to stop his protest. "I need you to escort her there, properly," she emphasized, "I want no questions about her legitimate sponsorship and to make sure she's in good hands." He remembered how one tear began to descend her cheek before she quickly wiped it away as if it had never appeared.

Her voice did not quiver as she talked. He was constantly amazed by her strength. Her unwavering conviction.

"You can't leave from the Belfast ports. Too many friends there with big eyes and bigger mouths. Dublin's out of the question, too. Crossing the border to the south is too risky and those damn robbers would charge me triple if they whiffed my concern. I've chosen Sligo. The cargo ships have limited passenger berths—and I can pay. You said your farm transports horses to the United States, right?"

He nodded, knowing she had done her homework.

"You're familiar to the Sligo officials, so they'll take my money and not ask too many questions."

He wasn't sure why he sat silent for as long as he did, but what happened next changed him forever. It was as if all the strength in her body drained and the desires she held in such close check were set free. Her fingers started entwining in his, a simple gesture they shared so often. When she looked at him, he saw an expression in her eyes he had longed to see but had resigned to stop looking for. Disbelief made him pause even longer, and that moment of hesitation was enough.

Her mouth was on his before he could move. Her lips and tongue played over his, and she brought her body over him, pressing into him. He remembered how she tasted, the salty tears and a sweetness he had never tasted before. He sampled her, cautious that he would move too quickly and rouse her to her senses. The cotton of her dress was smooth under his hands, and he dared to grip her thigh to pull her closer. Instead of pulling away, he felt her open her heart to him.

He gently settled her onto her back, and made sure his eyes asked the questions he was afraid to voice. "Is this alright? Are you sure? Is this what you truly want?" She answered him by not pulling her eyes away from his as she undid the front of her dress. He slipped her shoulders free and cupped her breasts in his hand, tasting her and kissing in a way he had only dreamed of before. She held his hand and guided it up her thigh and under her dress, letting him touch her and explore her soft folds. He was feeling her, caressing her, frightened that the hold on his own desire was going to break. He pulled back, not wanting to lose control and wanting the moment to last.

Where he pulled back, she moved forward. Slipping his pants down over his hips, she let him kick his legs free before she explored him with equal passion. Somewhere, he found the courage to ask. He wanted to remember that he was noble enough to have risked ending what was happening between them, but he knew the truth was that they were far beyond stopping, far beyond a point where consequences and future mattered.

"Are you sure?" he had asked, voice barely a croak.

She lay underneath him, legs straddled and wide and gripped him, kissing and pulling at him with her mouth. He moved her hand, circling himself around her, knowing they were ready. He slipped inside and she arched her back to meet him, locking her ankles behind. He moved slowly, letting her set the rhythm, kissing her face.

"I love you," he whispered into her hair as she shuddered.

She didn't open her eyes as she rolled him over. He held back, sensing she needed and wanted more. He remembered looking up at her and seeing her head thrown back, mouth open and eyes squeezed shut, thin tracks of tears running from their corners. She moved on him with an urgency that finally shattered them both.

He hardened at the memory and shifted himself in his trousers as he walked the mud-rutted path. That was the first time they were together, but after that, they would slip away whenever they could. He felt sealed to her from that moment on, and nothing would ever tarnish his love and loyalty to her. Not long after that, before he took Margaret to Boston, he lay entwined in Bridget's arms again and promised her his heart forever and that no legal or religious convention was needed for him to be hers. How lucky he was she shared his passions and understood its risks. No other woman would tolerate his long trips or the need for secrecy, but Bridget understood, and he was her champion for it. He couldn't keep from smiling knowing she was barely a mile away, waiting for him and, he hoped, having the same memories as he was. Could their first time have been almost ten years ago?

The last time he saw her at the meeting on Lough Neagh, soft lines creased the sides of her eyes and mouth. Gone was any self-doubt she may have had in her younger years and any questioning of who she was. She had chosen her life and forged a new path for herself, knowing in her wake were other young women hungry for a chance of more. He knew they would accomplish more than Bridget ever could have imagined because of the trail she blazed.

Gus' heart ached at her bravery. He had wanted to take her then, to make love to her, and consume her in the way he knew she loved to make up for his long absences, but she had adopted the persona of Mrs. Harvey, and there were too many eyes around. He had learned to be patient and cautious to ensure their secret. They had greeted each other as close friends and comrades, and he had moved about her discretely, with hardly a brushed fingertip to give them away. Odd as it seemed, Bridget more freely gave her attentions to other men when they were in such gatherings, deftly deflecting any hint or rumor.

The road changed from mud to stone to coarse pavement the closer he got to town. The ancient walled city appeared in front of him and he never ceased to be amazed that a wall so old could still stand in a city so young and stupid. He passed a few closely set brick flats, stacked on top of one another, and turned up Waterloo Street, stopping to gather himself and assess the area. Locals called this area the Bogside. He could feel the distrust and tension in the air. Catholics and the RUC were butting heads. He knew it was only a matter of time before the lid blew.

The streets were mostly empty this evening. Even though he felt secure, he walked over to a phone booth, took a cigarette from his pocket, and lit it. With one hand shoved in his pocket and the other bringing the butt to his lips for long thoughtful drags, he watched the pub across the street. He used the motion of stubbing out the cigarette in order to see if a piece of red paper shoved into the dial of the phone, a signal that it all was clear. He forced himself to walk slowly to the pub.

In the moment it took for his eyes to adjust, he knew immediately she wasn't there. He couldn't feel her presence. The smell of the place was all wrong. A movement in the back corner saved him from showing his disappointment too clearly. A red felt cap pushed to the end of the table ensured he didn't question the owner's identity. As he walked back, his eyes met with the red-rimmed eyes of Anna Marie. She looked from him, over the table, back to the door. Gus' heart dropped as he began to fear the worst had happened.

"Gilchrist," she said, standing and holding both his hands to her chest in greeting.

He chuffed with warmth at her formality. "Miss Molloy," he replied. He moved to sit at the table, but Anna Marie guided him to another farther toward the back. Gus didn't question her discretion. He raised two fingers to the barkeep and waited until the pints of black stout with a creamy froth were set in front of them to begin talking. He used the time to slow his breathing and gather a facade of cool. Regardless, he could not be calm until he knew.

"Is she alright?"

Anna Marie's eyes darted to the side and she bit her lower lip, slightly skewed because of her broken tooth. "Aye. She is."

"And she's safe?"

"She is that, too."

Gus couldn't hide the wash of relief that spread over him. He took a long pull of stout, considering his next questions. Bridget had sent Anna Marie in her place for a reason.

"I heard about the raid on the Ardoyne flats. Papers said the RUC caught a few women, but their names weren't listed. They thought they had identified two of the leaders, Daniel Heinchon and another man named Harvey. They were looking for them both—plus Harvey's wife."

A spilled pool of light caramel-colored foam puddled on the table. Anna Marie fidgeted her index finger through it and took a few nervous sips before she spoke, her voice low and quiet. "Aye. Someone inside doubled us to the Brits. They heard that one of the women was getting orders from her husband. They've put a net out for them both."

Gus wasn't sure whether to smile or shout. "Figures the feckin' tans wouldn't conceive a woman was thinkin' up these plans. So they're looking for Mr. *and* Mrs. Harvey?"

"They are at that, but we know better. The soldiers went door to door last week in the dead of night. They rounded up a few of the men, no women. Those were horrible nights, Gus. We had to bury three of our men because they barred their homes to stop the soldiers from entering, and were shot for it. It was all the leaders could do to keep the riots from breaking out then and there. But she's gone under and sent me to tell you that she's fine and will contact you when the pressure is off."

She twitched around in her seat, picking at an invisible pill on her sleeve. Then she looked at the faded watercolor paintings of bucolic fields that dotted the walls of the greasy pub and surveyed the overhead lights, still off in the afternoon light. She looked everywhere but at Gus.

He nodded his head slowly as he understood the situation, if it were real, would warrant no less caution. The bundle of nerves in front of him did not put him at ease.

"There's more." He didn't bother to frame it as a question.

The fidgeting stopped as she drew in a deep breath. Anna Marie drew back her shoulders, raised her chin, and finally looked him in the eye.

"No. There's nothing more. Be assured she's safe and in hiding until it's clear for her to come out. If everything's settled, she expects to be back in touch after the first of the year. She knows how to reach you when she's ready." Dictate delivered, her head nodded once with feigned conviction.

Gus couldn't be sure if he heard hoarseness in her voice. She blinked her eyes rapidly and looked around the pub again, suddenly remembering more.

"Do you have word on her sister? She's desperate for news."

Margaret was equally desperate to get news to her sister and had begged Gus to accept her scheme and made him promise to at least tell Bridget her idea. But on the passage back he had time to think. It dawned on him that acting on Margaret's idea would be the only way for Gus to have Bridget in his life. Bridget was all he wanted, and he could feel his heart overtaking his head. For a brief moment, in that stinking pub and in front of the only link he had to her, he allowed himself the indulgence of yearning for her.

His shoulders dropped as he conveyed the plan. "Margaret convinced her new husband to purchase a horse farm north of Boston." He saw Anna Marie's eyes widen as he continued. "Jim is a top notch mate, and he's hired me to help him raise thoroughbreds. Margaret is very, very happy," he said, surprised his own voice thickened, "and she pleaded with me to convince Bridget to come live with her. I'll be able to move money and make the occasional supply run from their farm to help our cause, but Margaret is adamant that all efforts be made to get Bridget out of Northern Ireland as soon as possible. Margaret says there is a growing network of support for reunification in the Boston community and Bridget can continue working from there. She'll be safe there."

He looked at the young, fresh-faced rebel in front of him to make sure the message was delivered loudly and clearly that another life awaited Bridget if she would only allow it. To leave no doubt, he added, "And tell her I'll be waiting."

Anna Marie could not stop her eyes from brimming over. She hastily wiped her cheek with the back of a shaking hand. "I'll tell her, Gus. I will," she said in barely more than a whisper.

Gus finished his pint in one downing and put a few pound notes on the table. When he walked out the door, it was with the heavy knowledge that the walk back to his room would be far longer than the walk there.

When she was sure he was gone, Anna Marie finally let the sobs escape.

BALLYRONAN, NORTHERN IRELAND

MICHAEL WAS EXCITED to spend the day sightseeing with Jessica. He decided to drive Lough Neagh's entire circumference counterclockwise, taking in as many nooks and coves as possible. Even Murray was more animated as he packed a lunch and gave last minute instructions on best routes to take around the lake, quietly remarking to Michael that help would be out of sight but close-by if needed.

Ballyronan sat on the northwest shore, and Michael decided to start by driving south, making the longest drive first to get to Aghalee. The town where Bridget spent her summers was roughly directly across from Ballyronan. From there, they would head north to Antrim and leave the shortest leg of the trip back to his home. Driving the entire shoreline of the lake with their planned stops would take all day.

The most traffic, if one could call it such, was waiting for the churches to empty or for a farmer and his dog to herd cows from pastures to milking sheds. Judging by the copious amounts of flat cow pies stinking up the road, this was a frequent occurrence. At one crossing, a border collie with its shaggy black and white coat, didn't move its ringed eyes from the herd and stayed focused while he worked. The farmer, on the other hand, stared at the gleaming car and its decidedly American occupants. He leaned on his staff a long while to get a good look in, tipping his cap slightly when they passed.

The cluster of buildings that called itself *Aghalee* gave a feeling that time had stopped. If it weren't for the modern cars dotting the streets, any picture could easily be mistaken for one taken years ago. A dilapidated mix of stone and wooden buildings lined two streets that intersected at a town green and a church. Jessica leafed through Bridget's pictures and found two with the church featured in the background. In the foreground of the first picture were two men, arms around each other's shoulders in the age-old stance of brotherly love and kinship. One face she clearly recognized as a young and robust Gus Adams. The other man, dressed in the long cassock of the church, was familiar to Jessica in a way she couldn't pinpoint, and she wondered how many other pictures he was in. The second picture was clearly taken at an earlier time showing the same scene and the same two men. This time, the other man was dressed as Gus was dressed—a pair of trousers held up by thick suspenders over loose fitting shirts with the sleeves rolled up on. The happiness and camaraderie of the two men was obvious.

Michael took a handful of odd photographs into the small store, hoping to learn more about the island Murray identified. Behind the counter sat an old woman wearing thick-rimmed eyeglass and a red cardigan sweater that had seen better days. He asked if she knew anyone who may have lived at the cottages. The woman began chattering away at him with such a thick brogue, he could only pick out bits and pieces. He caught enough to learn that a company bought out all of the cottages decades ago to make a resort. They went out of business a few years ago. No one was left who used to live there. The shopkeeper repeatedly jabbed her finger at the pictures and pointed at the church. The most he could make out was that the church's name was something like Saint Artues or San Garthues.

He emerged with a bag of crisps and written directions and told Jessica the bits he had learned.

They passed a sign that proclaimed, "Solstice Beach Cabins! Where Families and Memories Are Made," and burst into laughter. The resort never caught on with young city-dwelling families for good reason. If the road weren't problematic enough, the cottages themselves would have had a chilling effect on all but the most determined couples. Contrary to what a family resort would normally boast, the cluster of buildings did not have a central meeting place, playground, ball courts, or any of the other amenities expected and needed by vacationing families. The buildings were sprinkled throughout the grounds, evidence that they were initially built by families wanting privacy from one another, away from inquisitive eyes. The beach, although beautiful, was rocky and had only a small sandy area. Evidence of paths could be seen winding up into the surrounding fields and wooded areas. The property sat, boarded and empty.

Jessica looked around with a mixture of melancholy and amusement. The gaiety and laughter she enjoyed earlier faded into an unreadable mood as she settled herself by the shore.

"Not what you thought you'd see?" Michael asked, sensing she may need some prodding to talk.

She smiled weakly. "I'm not sure what I was expecting. I keep thinking that I'm supposed to have some sort of epiphany about my family roots, where everything makes sense and I feel connected to the larger world. I keep waiting for that one moment, but it never comes. I'm sitting in the very spot my mother sat, looking at the same island she saw, and breathing the same air she breathed." Jessica settled herself on a rock by the shore, and dangled her feet into the warm waters. "I'm empty."

"You're being too hard on yourself," he said, rolling up his pant legs and sitting beside her. He let his feet stroke hers, warm water inviting. "You have a kind of freedom that will let you move forward without feeling like you're letting somebody down all the time."

"But you know how you're connected, whether you're happy with it or not."

"I'm happy with you. We fit." He raised his eyebrow to telegraph exactly how he wanted them to fit, again. The sooner, the better.

Jessica raised her eyebrows in a knowing glance. He couldn't help but pull her closer. He loved the sound of her laugh, a light throaty chuckle that seemed to flow out of her, like the sound of water bubbling through a brook. Her cares vanished and she seemed open to the world, not tentative or hidden. The few glimpses he had of that Jessica—the Jessica without worries and simply happy—stabbed him with a potent longing. He wanted that. "You'll be okay. You'll get through this."

Jessica kissed him deeply, then settled her head on his shoulder. "You, too." She hopped down from the rock into shin deep water and picked her way over the rocky bottom, keeping her eyes on the shore.

Michael watched her. The light hitting Jessica made her stand out in sharp relief against the rich blue of the sky and the bronze of the rocks. The pale skin of her legs, untouched yet by the summer sun, shone almost white as she balanced and easily made her way through the water. The outline of her body shone through her cotton shirt, one hand stuffed in the pocket of her cutoff jeans, the other holding back her hair. He hopped down and waded after her, knowing he would follow her anywhere.

"Looking for something?"

She scanned the shoreline ahead of them and pointed to a large, flat rock surrounded by an outcropping of trees. She nodded her head in their direction. "There," she said and scrambled up the bank.

At the top, a natural path hidden between rocks led her to another clearing. Tree stumps formed a circle around an old firepit. She sat down on one stump and motioned to the other for Michael. "Bridget's journals talked about this place a lot. She and *Gean Cánach* fell in love and she . . ." Jessica hesitated, "she lost her virginity here and had other lovers, too."

Michael registered surprise as the information sank in. When he felt she was ready, he brushed the hair from her face, kissed her forehead and the tip of her nose, and led her by the hand back to the car. He sensed how her confusion and yearning to learn collided. In one sense, she needed the information to become whole, but each new nugget of knowledge brought with it an awkward awareness of invading private spaces. He knew exactly who his father was and wished he didn't. She had huge gaps in knowledge about her mother and no knowledge of her father. He wondered who was better off.

As the day progressed, he noted she became tense each time the security detail came into view. Even maintaining a discrete distance was not enough to keep her from noticing. Michael kept up a steady stream of conversation on topics he knew would keep her mood light. He mixed memories of growing up in Massachusetts with the foreigner's confusion of being a child summering in a foreign country—horrified by things called bangers and mash that the locals seemed to love and being perplexed by tuna fish sandwiches with flecks of canned yellow corn in them. As long as she was enjoying herself, he kept the stories flowing.

By the time they reached the school, Jessica's cheeks were pink with laughter. She hugged his arm as they walked along the brick paths that connected the buildings.

"The board members who were opposed to my ideas have been asked to retire. Last month's meeting was tense and the headmaster proved himself an ass."

"Why?"

"The school was his fiefdom long before I started funneling money into it. Liam had the idea to invest in it. He knew I wanted to undo some of the damage my father did to children and families—like what happened to your family. Many Charity holdings work well with what I want, but the headmaster couldn't adapt. He was fired."

"I never knew it was your uncle's idea for you to buy the school." She let go of his arm and took a step back. "Is he here? Can I meet him?"

It's what he wanted, too. He had asked Liam to be at the school, to meet Jessica and to see for himself why Michael was so taken with her. The typically warm and social Liam froze solid whenever he heard her name. Liam was adamant. Michael's focus should be on business. No room existed for anything else. Even if Liam tried to bluff his way through formalities, he couldn't hide his displeasure. "He's not here. A prior commitment," Michael said with his voice tapering. "I'm sorry."

"Don't be if he's not. All of the talk of gun-running and smuggling, and making it sound like investments and business? I hate it." She shook her head forcefully. "I hate hearing about a bombing and wondering if it's connected with you. The vision you have for the school, to help and give back, I love that part of you." He watched her as she looked up at the buildings and down the walks, as if planning her escape. "I'm trying to make sense of all of this . . . this," she waved her hand as she spoke, unable to finish her sentence. "You're close to Liam, but I don't under-stand why he's so involved with your affairs."

"He's a vital link. Without him, the organization would not be stable." He hoped his voice conveyed more confidence than he felt. "Magnus had plans in place before he died. Liam knows I need to get support before I make changes."

The endless meetings he had with the organizations operating under the MMC name were fruitless. Liam made sure to introduce him only to organizations like hospitals, relief organizations, or biomedical research firms. Each time he pressed for details on other holdings, the informa-tion was so vetted, he learned next to nothing.

Liam's strategy was to build Michael's public image with humanitar-ian organizations and didn't want to compete against Jessica's fame. Michael felt Liam's resistance to meet her was more that Liam didn't want a constant reminder of what desperate men were capable of. "I need to quietly get control of who supports the unrest. It's a balancing act. I need time."

"Time you don't have. Good organizations don't bomb or kill. The risk is not with MMC. It's with the rest of the Charity . . . or your uncle." A slow stream of breath escaped her as the recent warmth between them cooled.

He was afraid of what was in her silence. Knowing she had no choice but to move forward was very different from supporting him or wanting to be a part of his life. A fluttering desperation gripped him as the need for her approval grew. "I know," he said, desperate to explain himself. "My father was incredibly connected. It would take time I don't have to forge my own relationships with his contacts. Doing an end-run around them by bulldozing my way into new relationships will only create enemies and solidify the impression that I'm an outsider. I need Liam."

He could see her standing beside him, three-dimensional and whole, but something had fallen away. In some cruel trick of the shimmering light, he felt that his outstretched arms would pass right through her, as if she had become an image reflected on mist. It was his fault she was in Ireland, and that evidenced his weakness. He wanted her to feel as connected as he did to this place. If she couldn't feel it, then he wanted her to feel connected to him in the way he did to her, that his entire existence was cultivated and given purpose by her. But she remained more aloof than he could bear.

When Jessica looked up at him, her expression had changed from confusion to concern, then to wariness. He watched as she pulled her lips over her teeth as if biting back words that wanted to be spoken. Finally she said, "We should get back. Murray will be worried."

How could he tell her that having her beside him made the mountain less steep and gave him the confidence that he could change the world? Seeing her on his school's grounds seemed so right, so fitting. Eventually, she would grow to understand his world. He didn't let the change in her demeanor stop him from scooping her up in his arms and burying his face in her hair. Sad the day was ending, he drove them back to Ballyronan, ignorant of what awaited.

MANCHESTER, ENGLAND

THE JOCK-EYED CLUB was a greasy dive located in a cinder block building on the outskirts of the city. As its name hinted, the second favorite activity its patrons enjoyed was betting on the ponies. The first was getting lubed up enough to put stupid amounts of money on a win, place, or show. Regardless of the time of day, the interior was always dark, weakly lit by humming fluorescent tubes and the flickering closed-circuit screens live broadcasting races from the various tracks. Flat or jump races didn't matter. Betting and winning did.

Despite its humble accoutrements, the Eye, as those in the know fondly called it, was the place to be if you wanted to surround yourself with people who really knew horses, the tracks, and the jockeys. The Eye was the last place any self-respecting woman would go without an escort, and it was the first place Dally went after leaving the Manchester Airport.

She stood at the doorway for a few minutes, letting her vision adjust to the dark. She knew better than to fidget with the thin cardigan sweater draped over her bony shoulders, so she drew herself up to her full height, pushed her glasses up the bridge of her nose. She fancied herself as an investigative journalist on the hunt for a story, but she really was a thirsty tabloid reporter on the prowl for a pint and a snog. She settled herself into a booth by the bar, her thighs squeaking on the sticky red vinyl, announcing to the world that her skirt was far too short. She looked at her watch and stole a quick glimpse at a picture of the man she was to meet. At least she didn't have long to wait for a pint.

A misshapen face atop a body of gnarled muscles materialized out of the darkness and placed a glass of dark stout in front of her. "You Miss Thorpe?" he asked.

Dally did her best projection of confidence. "I am. Fr-Freddy?" she waited until he nodded and motioned for him to sit down with her. "Thank you for meeting with me."

"So, what'd you want?" He was blunt. No matter. She wasn't expecting an earl with manners.

"I heard you r-rode in the p-private jump race at Aintree on the fifteenth."

Freddy's eyes narrowed slightly. "Where'd you hear that?"

Dally waved her hand in the air as if to dismiss any thought of her having secret informants, but doing everything in her power to have him think just that. "I can't d-divulge my s-sources, you know." She gave him a theatric look of apology. "I won't be quoting you or using your name, unless you agree." She rounded her eyes and batted her thin lashes. "So we can talk."

Freddy wiped the back of his hand across his mouth while he checked her out from head to toe, making her feel like a mare given one last look over before being sent to the glue factory. Still, she inhaled and pulled her shoulders back, giving her back a little arch. She started to sing her interview. "A few questions then?" He nodded and she decided to stick with a bastardized rendition of *Do Re Me*. "I heard about a jockey in the race. A famous American."

"Feckin' bitch," he said with more bile than Dally expected. "Dirtiest rider there ever was. Every trick in the book. Said it was her first race, and I'll make damned sure it's her last."

She barely raised an eyebrow. Freddy didn't lose often. He had the reputation as being one of the most vengeful and conniving jockeys in England. Talking trash was part of his persona. The fact that he had lost a race to a woman undoubtedly meant months of undercutting jibes from other jockeys. She didn't expect him to be gracious in defeat and sour grapes were to be expected. Frankly, she wanted the dirt.

"Why was she there to begin with?"

"I'll be damned if I know," he spat. "Seems too convenient, if you ask me. All the jockeys were lined up and committed to the race, and she comes in at the last minute. She insisted on all her own gear, feed, and staff. You name it."

"What did she say when she arrived?"

"Nothing. She was too much of a bloody snot to even look at the other stable hands. She came in all high and mighty, like some goddamned princess. Me and the boys like to have some jollies while we work, you know? A new kid in the barns always gets a hazing. But not her. No sir. Couldn't even have some fun. Her rich boyfriend placed a ring of thugs around her. Couldn't touch her with a ten foot pole without one a'them men threatening to bust our kneecaps."

Dally sat forward. "Are you saying Michael Connaught surrounded her with body guards?"

"Is that the bloke's name? Sounds familiar. But, yeah. That guy must be insecure about his dick 'cuz he made sure she was never out of sight of one of his men." He took a loud slurp of stout and burped. "She had everyone thinking she was a fragile flower. We all thought she'd be turf fertilizer. She even threw her hurdle race to make everyone think she was a goner for the real thing, then she turned into a mighty barracuda. Jesus, that bitch can ride." He shook his head in disbelief at the memory.

Dally fished around in the paper bag, produced the photographs of the cargo area of the airport, and shoved them over to him. Images of wooden crates emblazoned with MMC dotted the table. "You said she brought her own gear. Did you see the crates they came in?"

Freddy sat back. "Yeah. Those are hers." He studied the picture. "Had guards standing over them twenty-four hours a day. Feckin' paranoid lunatic, if you ask me." He turned one of the pictures to the light. "These in customs?"

"Yes. She had gear flown in on a private jet from Ireland."

This time when he looked at Dally, he barely concealed the wheels turning in his head. He leaned forward, working his tongue inside his lower lip. "Hmm. Seems to be more crates arriving in customs than I saw at the stables." His thumb gently massaged his jaw as he thought. He lowered his voice as he spoke. "Did you say her boyfriend is a Connaught?"

Dally nodded, holding her breath.

"Funny how the race and the bombing were on the same day," he said, pushing himself back into the booth with a satisfied grin. "And you can quote me."

BALLYRONAN, NORTHERN IRELAND

MURRAY GREETED THEM at the door and the aroma of a fine meal hung in the air. Jessica hurried upstairs to quickly shower before dinner.

Michael immediately knew something was wrong. Murray had been by Michael's side through the best and worst of his life's events and was the only person Michael truly trusted. Ever discrete, Murray never betrayed a loyalty even when sorely pressed. Occasionally his official neutrality over-lapped with the edges of his personal convictions, but he never compromised himself. More importantly, he never betrayed Michael. Murray was far more than a butler. He was an indispensable friend.

Murray handed Michael a newspaper folded to reveal a story with bold type declaring, *Man Dies in Mountain Search. Murdering Heiress Sought for Questioning.*

"Damn it!" Michael said and threw the paper back at Murray. "What the hell is that?"

Murray didn't betray any emotion. "One of our men at the presses saw the story."

"No. No. No. No." The words sounded more like a moan than a request. "Who's behind this?"

"We're checking. The reporter, Dally Thorpe, is not an investigative journalist that we've seen working other stories. She lives and works in Manchester, England. Her father was killed when a bomb exploded at a hotel in Brighton where he worked as a bellhop."

Michael bolted upright. "Did you say the Brighton Bombing?"

"Yes. Your brother planned that attack."

Michael wondered if the connection was more than a coincidence. Members of the government's Conservative party, namely Prime Minister Thatcher and her husband, were attending a conference at the Brighton Hotel. They narrowly escaped, but five members of their party perished along with a handful of hotel employees. The bombing gave Thatcher the nickname "Iron Lady" for her unrattled demeanor immediately afterward. The IRA claimed responsibility, and Michael's brother had almost earned enough power and respect to take over the Charity then and there. Young Liam's failure to kill the prime minister drove him to take bigger chances. He had just finished plans for another campaign when he was killed handling inferior and unstable explosives. Michael absorbed the information and played it against what he already knew, moving his shoulders in an unconscious way as if to see how much room he had to navigate.

"Arndale," he said, bringing their attention back to the present. "Any word on how the investigation on the bombing is going?"

"Your uncle's sources say the investigation is at a standstill."

"The truck?"

Murray provided an update. "Pieces of the truck have been analyzed for identification numbers, fingerprints, explosive residue, anything you can think of. The government is enraged at its inability to trace the evidence back to the bombers. They found no leads to the identity of the men or the source of the materials. Once again, the trail runs cold through a Medusa's head of holding companies."

Michael knew the game. Lack of eyewitnesses, reluctant or unreliable sources, and the usual dead ends contributed to the stall. What solid evidence would authorities have? The streets' surveillance cameras . . . stores' security . . . the phone calls to the police and news stations . . .

"How about the phone calls?"

"They traced one call to a flat, and we're waiting for word on that piece of the investigation. Every lead they've followed so far has turned up nothing, and they are expressing frustration privately, feeling that another investigative defeat is close at hand. All that shouldn't bother you, should it?"

Michael was unsure how much of his recently acquired knowledge of his father's books he should share. "It should and it does."

Murray picked up a cloth and began to wipe off the counters. "It's good to be concerned about the details."

Michael's jaw muscles pulsed as he thought. "What about this reporter?"

"She's a tabloid journalist, who nearly lost her job for an incident referred to as the Magpie Caper. She wrote a series of articles claiming certain members of Parliament and the Royal Family were involved in homosexual trysts and were selling political favors. Her 'off the record' source failed to materialize so the claims were never substantiated. She stood by her story until her editors recanted on her behalf. It was either that or be buried under a settlement so huge they would have gone under. She's been trying to rebuild her reputation ever since."

"No real news so take the next best target. A simple update on Jessica would sell a few thousand papers, but creating another level of intrigue would send circulation over the edge." Murray cleared his throat, prompting Michael to continue, "And giving an update on the Connaught legacy is too good to resist."

Murray waited patiently.

"She's coming after me."

"It certainly appears that way."

Michael paced as he considered his options. "We have a hungry tabloid reporter with a reputation for lying. That doesn't bother me as much as the increased exposure around my name might fuel closer examination of some of the money trails. My uncle's sources are very good, so if they say the investigation is at a standstill, it is. But he knows my concern that one lucky guess is all it would take to lead back to us."

"So, the story?"

"I don't want Jessica dragged through this. We need a pre-emptive strike to stop them from producing any further stories."

"Unfortunately, she's the bait the readers will latch onto. I'm sure you're aware you can consider having an injunction order drafted against the newspaper and reporter to stop more articles. It's very standard business practice here."

Michael nodded. "How quickly could we get that in place? Would it be enough to stop additional stories?"

"Newspapers are cautious about what they print if they fear the plaintiff has the means to come after them, like the Connaughts. In the States, you are well organized with good connections. That's why you've been successful in suppressing stories about the search."

"Yes. Electra helped with that."

"It's different under U.K. laws. To get protection here, the statements are considered false and have to be proven as true—or at least proven that they were written with enough fact to support the slant of the story. If the story is considered false to begin with, and if a fuss isn't made, then it will all fade into the distance, right?" Michael nodded, seeing the strategy. "This first story is true, although very heavy on innuendo. The reporter's sources are mostly other newspapers, so she'd be able to verify facts quickly enough to prove her stories weren't capricious and had enough truth to support them. I wouldn't wage war on this one article. Doing so would raise unnecessary flags and may even become fodder for another line of stories. Certainly more are coming, but it's interesting Miss Thorpe started tying Miss Jessica to you with a focus on the search. Is there anything else on that search I should know?"

"I killed a man to save her life and covered it up."

"I know that. What else?"

"The search was a setup by my father. He knew I would risk my position as sheriff to keep the connection to the Charity secret. Magnus set up a test of loyalty for me to kill Jessica or the man who held her hostage. Either way, he knew the resulting cover up would force me to leave the U.S. and come back here until the story faded and died. Time is all Magnus needed to draw me in."

"Time?"

"I can't help but suspect Magnus' hand is in all of this. None of this is a coincidence. His death set off a series of pre-organized and orchestrated events. He knew, inevitably, I would come back to Ballyronan. The bombing and all of the transactions that led up to it will point to me if I don't step in and start directing people's actions myself. It's either step directly into his shoes or go to prison."

Too many years of watching how Magnus conducted his affairs stopped any need for Murray to question that what Michael said was the truth. "These articles are clearly involving Jessica in this."

Michael raked his hand through his hair. Lines of concern and fear creased his face. "It's not a coincidence that the timing of the bombing happened when it's easily proved she was in England, less than an hour's drive from there. I have to figure out if anything more is planned and stop it before it happens. Even from his grave he's manipulating me."

"There are no facts to find against her."

"I can't be sure of that." His head fell forward as if the weight of it suddenly became too much, and he sunk onto a stool. "She's fed up with this, Murray. She hates the Charity and everything it's involved in. If I don't fix this, I'm afraid she . . . that I'll . . ." his voice trailed, but his desperation was clear.

Murray listened for a moment to the sounds of the shower running upstairs and closed the swinging door to the kitchen behind them. Piles of Bridget's letters and journals littered the long wooden table. He waved his hand over the papers. "She has bigger problems."

DECEMBER 1966
SISTERS OF THE
HOLY CROSS CONVENT
BELFAST, NORTHERN IRELAND

THE CONVENT OF the Sisters of the Holy Cross sat on a rocky bluff overlooking the North Channel of the Irish Sea. The location was perfect because all who stayed there experienced the misery and the mystery of God. The expanse of the North Sea would glitter like a thousand stars on rare perfect days then plunge into bone chattering cold, testing the resolve of even the most dedicated souls. According to legend, those who worshiped there better understood God's mercies. If they held the glory of His creation close to their hearts, they could sustain themselves by bearing witness when their faith waivered. For those who did not hold such knowledge, the desolate and rocky outcrop became a forsaken place scoured by an unceasing wind. The huge brick structure with its peaks topped by white crosses and small windows did little to inspire any souls who visited and even less to pique the curiosity of those who didn't. The nuisance of a visitor rarely interrupted daily vespers.

The sisters who considered the convent their home acknowledged they had a special calling and were loathe to share themselves with the outside world. Their vows included one of silence whenever they ventured outside of the convent's walls and even the privilege of speech among them was earned with painstaking ritual, which few sisters ever mastered. That peculiar aspect of their lives made them particularly useful.

Their loyalty was legendary, perhaps in part because few could speak, reducing the likelihood that any ill words could be spoken at all. Their needs were few and the resilient women were self-sustaining, but their allegiance would be forever tied to anyone who provided them support. The relationship worked for all involved. Benefactors, needing loyalty and discretion, were generous. The sisters, dependent on their gifts, grew even more discrete. Reverend Mother Cliona Flanagan knew better than to shun her patrons and was even less inclined to judge them.

She looked at her visitor with a face pinched as much by suppressed emotion as by the starched white wimple that surrounded it. The narrow bands of fabric framed her cheeks and rose up to an imposing fez-like crown of white, giving the short woman another five inches of desperately needed height. In a minor wonder of tradition and engineering, the heavy black gabardine fabric that cascaded from her head was somehow held away from her, framing a body stooped with age and prayer. The rest of her habit enveloped her in layers needed for comfort in the cold halls. A rosewood rosary draped at her waist. Her visitor dressed in black as well, but any similarities ended there.

Before she answered her calling, the priest who stood in front of her would have caused tremendous consternation. His height and strong features made him *devilishly* handsome, a phrase she used to connote the turmoil such a presence sparked within her withered womanly soul. It hinted at what could only live within the heart of someone so perfect. For God does not give but what He then takes away, and what gift He bestowed on the outside balanced with what He took away from within. She could barely imagine the struggles the man had endured to prove worthiness for his perfection before God's eyes. She would not add to his burden and gratefully accepted his tithe and food with a head bowed with humility and grace.

Christmas vespers had passed and prayers echoed in the halls to atone for the past year and in hope that the new year would bring them closer to living in perfect spiritual harmony. She ushered her visitor into the humble room off the great hallway reserved for visitors. Another sister, dressed in the all black attire of a novice, waited inside. The novice was barely visible, robes and shadows serving to hide her human form. Only the oval of her face shone in the soft light. Having joined them a few months before, she had not yet vowed her silence and separation from the outside world. She was not the first woman to use the seclusion of the convent for more than simple contemplation. Time spent reflecting on her path could lead to a life devoted to prayer. A life of prayer was not this novice's calling.

"God speed, *Sagart* Hughes," Reverend Mother said, giving her head a slight bow and using his Irish title. She genuflected in front of a large crucifix, blessed herself, and knelt heavily at the prie dieu in the corner. Entwining the rosary in her fingers, she telegraphed being too involved in her prayers to be interested in overhearing what the handsome priest and the beautiful novice said. At least that's what her body language suggested. Her role as chaperone only went so far.

She discretely looked at a spot on the floor as the priest drew up the hands of the novice and kissed them, pressing the long, fine fingers to his lips. She didn't see the looks in their eyes or the way their bodies seemed to pull together, drawn by an invisible force. If she did, she would have understood but would have found it hard not to judge.

Father Kavan Hughes had come to her a few months ago to ask for the convent's shelter during an unwed mother's confinement. She had been surprised that the expectant mother was not a fresh-faced young girl, but a woman in full bloom who should have known better. He had said that the woman was the only family he truly had, and he had promised her dying mother before God to care for her and all her needs for as long as they both lived.

He was earnest with his request and determined to provide for his friend that she could hardly have said no. Besides, his request had come with gifts. Rumors were that this young priest was a rising force in the church, and she would be wise to garner his favor as he rose. She prayed she would not eavesdrop but knew how human flaws could overcome pious intents. Reverend Mother's heart gave a skip at the sound of his voice, deep and steady.

The novice's voice betrayed her surprise. "You should not have come."

The wooden chair creaked as the priest sat down. "Ah, Bridget. It's good to see you so well," he said in the same hushed voice he would use with confessors. "I came to wish birthday blessings."

The slight cough sounded like it covered a chuff. "You'd not risk yourself on account of my birthday. Why are you here?" she asked, her voice a taught wire.

"I came at the wish of a dying man. Daniel wants to see you one more time."

Bridget's breath caught in her throat. "My Danny Boy? What's happened?"

Reverend Mother could hear a rustle of fabric and the chair scrape across the stone floor as the priest adjusted his position. "There was an accident at his, um, work. An explosion," he spoke slowly, each word carefully chosen. "He was horribly burned. I'm afraid there is only prayer left."

Reflexively, Reverend Mother stole a look to witness the young woman's reactions. Bridget gathered her robes around her shoulders, as if doing so would keep the cold reality away from her. "What about Patrick?"

"I'm sorry. Patrick died in the atta—accident. Grace be had that he did not suffer." He reached out—as any compassionate human would—to rub her back in solace, but his touch made the novice jump as if burned with a firebrand. Bridget hugged her arms around herself, and rocked back and forth, whimpers of grief loud in the hollow room. "I see. I understand," she said, barely a whisper. "And Dan? He's in hospital?"

Father Hughes gripped Bridget's hands firmly. "Yes, but there's nothing anyone can do. He's in good care. He's asked for you, and I didn't see how I could refuse him."

"What's word on the Harveys? Anyone see them about?"

Reverend Mother put extra care and attention on running her fingers over the decade of beads on her rosary, averting her eyes when he looked over at her. He continued speaking thinking his veiled meanings were enough not to rouse her curiosity. "They sent word of their travels across the border. It seems that Belfast wasn't to their liking, and they've moved on."

"So, word is they're no longer in Belfast?"

"That's right. Anyone hoping to see them has moved on as well."

Bridget sat back, assessing her options. "How much time does he have?"

"He's hanging on to see you."

Reverend Mother let a gasp escape and quickly tried to cover her eavesdropping by attentively working her rosary. She couldn't help herself. She was embarrassed to be caught listening, but the temptation to see raw emotion was too great. The hours spent praying over the world's worries and cares kept her isolated. To be a spectator of immediate and real suffering was rare for her, and she considered it a gift to bear witness, even if listening in was one of the lesser human qualities. Prayer requests would come from people who had already come to grips with their problems and concerns. Worries from the outside would be brought to her for prayer, but any emotion duly wrung out by the time it was told to her.

The unfiltered reactions of those impacted with shocking news were more of a window into a person's character than any rehearsed request. If she were to pray for a sickly husband, it was after the doctor visits and the handwringing and sleepless nights. The emotion was gone—or at least numbed over—filtered by time and acceptance and replaced with a beseeching that seemed to accompany every prayer request, regardless of reason. She lowered her head and hoped that the drape of her headwear would hide her inquiring eyes. Asking for forgiveness would happen tomorrow.

Bridget stood up and walked over to the window, barely more than a slit in the wall, and looked out over the barren landscape. She smoothed her hand down the front of her robes. The folds of fabric billowed around her figure. Combined with her height and slender build, the swollen belly would be evident only to those who knew.

"At evening vespers, Reverend Mother asked us to keep certain souls in our prayers. She said the funerals of a few men who died during a raid on their flats sparked riots. The RUC used tear gas and live ammunition to break up the crowds." She steadied her voice with a dry swallow. "Was Paddy among those to be buried?"

Reverend Mother scrambled to pick up her dropped rosary beads.

"Yes," Father Hughes finally answered. "Do you think you can travel?"

"I can't be away for long. There is only one I trust to travel with."

"I thought as much. Anna Marie will be here in the morning. You should be back by evening prayers." When Bridget hesitated, he hastened to add, "I can see your time is very near. It's only a matter of a few hours to grant his last wish."

"Tell her to be here at seven."

Bridget bumped along beside Anna Marie in silence. Being at the convent for a few months was enough to condition her to the sparse landscape, making driving the coastal route south back into Belfast a feast for her eyes. The gray winter day cloaked the countryside in layers of wind-swept rain, but to Bridget the beauty of the land was there. She placed a protective hand over her belly, determined to make it through one more day. Happy to be out and about, she also needed to pay attention to what was happening around her.

Anna Marie alternated between hugging her tightly and holding her at arms' length to absorb fully all of the changes that had taken place. Bridget's cheeks were noticeably fuller, and she no longer moved with aristocratic grace, but with a stiffened back and smaller steps. With her mane of hair tucked under her wimple and the volume of robes and capes enveloping every angle of her body, only her height gave hint to her identity. Her radiant face showed that she was rested and the transformation captivated Anna Marie. It was hardly consolation to her as they talked.

"I hardly recognized you, Bridget, and I'm pleased at that. You're smart to've gone under until things have cooled down, but I'm worried that a sighting of you will stir things up." She paused and quickly glanced at Bridget's belly. "Especially now."

Bridget nodded and watched the scenery pass from remote coast to countryside to suburbs. They would be in Belfast soon. She seemed not to hear Anna Marie. "Where is Patrick buried?"

"He's at Milltown Cemetery."

"I want to go there."

"No. Absolutely not. Our people are mightily upset and got into open brawls with the UVF and the RUC. There's been a lockdown, and they're keeping everyone away from the grave."

"I . . . I need t-to see . . ." Her voice trailed off as she tried to find the words.

Anna Marie understood. "They have a plot for him next to your Ma, Pa, and . . ." she caught herself before she said more. "I promised not to upset you. I've said too much."

"You can say it. He has a plot next to Danny's as well."

"They've made sure your brothers have a proper spot, not in the poor grounds. Proper headstones, too."

"They?"

Anna Marie hesitated. "Your brothers are a bit of a legend among the IRA for their daring. They won't soon be forgotten. Gus made the arrangements, and Father Hughes paid."

"Gus did this? Is he in Belfast?" Bridget tried but failed to hide the panic in her voice.

"I don't know, Bridget. If he thought for a moment he could see you he'd be here." She waited. "He doesn't suspect anything, Bridget. I've kept my promise."

Bridget patted Anna Marie's hand, and they spent the remaining time going over precautions and cover stories. Danny was at the Royal Victoria Hospital, a place that caused Bridget much concern. The hospital was earning a preeminent reputation in the emergency care of gunshot wounds and orthopedic surgery, especially in the treatment of "punishment" injuries—kneecaps shot off or arms dislocated on those who had crossed the IRA.

On the winter day when Bridget walked through the doors, the expertise Danny needed was for the critically burned. She dreaded thinking what his experience had been like. For any mortally burned victim, the deepest wish is to have died in the flames and not live with the agony his wounds inflict. Every nerve ending in his skin is short-circuited, sending constant signals of searing heat. The agony of the blistering and bubbling of skin cycles on a constant loop. The body reacts by forming a blister around itself, sapping the organs of moisture, and throwing the delicate balance of electrolytes and platelets into cascades of chaos.

The process of dying would be a slow one for Danny, marked only by a swelling of the face and hands, if he still had them, and a steady drowning as his lungs filled up with fluid. If he survived long enough, then the crust formed over his wounds would be scrubbed off until his skin is raw again, an act that is intended to help in later years by creating scars that are more elastic. The abrading of wounds makes victims writhe in pain and beg for mercy, if not death.

As if not difficult enough, the generous amounts of morphine prescribed create addicts of many. Danny might still die from his wounds, but at least the drugs would make his final days pass without pain. Perhaps because pain medications lifts inhibitions and loosens tongues or perhaps because the Irish are very keen on paying their respects to the sick and dying, the Royal Victoria Hospital had also gained a reputation as the premier undercover resource for identifying relationships of wounded IRA soldiers and the network which supports them.

Rumors prevailed of British undercover agents sitting in waiting rooms, peering over old newspapers to see who came to visit whom. Even a nurse or two was said to earn a bit more on the side for the tips she could bring by observing visitors.

Bridget gave many assurances that she was capable of walking the distance before Anna Marie could drop her off, away from the main traffic area and eyes of the hospital. Using a cane as much for support as for disguise, Bridget—stooped, robed, and methodical—made her way through the front entrance and up to Intensive Care. It was all so easy.

Dan's room was small and sparsely furnished. A single bed, a chair, a rolling cart. His bedside table held only a telephone, the numbers on its round dial nearly new with lack of use. The television propped on a high corner shelf was silent and cold. An iron mesh and a paper shade, yellowed from age and sunlight, covered the window. A few machines on rolling poles and squat metal tables beeped steadily.

Bridget sat in a chair and gathered herself before she reached out and held his gauze wrapped hand, making sure to keep the door in her view. Bits of skin she could see were black or sickly red. Too many tubes, bags, and wires tethered her brother, and she resisted the urge to rip them all away to set him free. Someone had wrapped a rosary around his hand, and she reached over to finger the beads as she said her Hail Marys and Our Fathers. Dan was one of the unlucky ones who survived the first hell, only to be acutely aware his life was oozing out of him, never to recover. He was in a haze created as much by drugs as by the lack of life, and it took him a while to rally enough to recognize her. She was grateful for the time. She needed the minutes to gather herself and not scream and wail at his suffering and their loss.

"Rish-it . . .!" he rasped her name and attempted to move his arms, perhaps to hug her. His lips were gone. What remained of his face was slathered in petroleum goo intended to keep the crisped skin from becoming brittle. One eye was gone. The eye that remained began to glisten. There were no more illusions to keep.

She spoke to him of Ma and the days at Lough Neagh and shared their favorite stories of Patrick and Margaret. Danny promised to look after Patrick and find their wee sister, Eileen. Then he apologized for leaving too early and promised to watch over her.

"Ah, Danny Boy. It wasn't to be like this, you know," she murmured, keeping her voice steady and refusing her tears. She could see his eye focus on her as if committing her to final memory. It slowly traced her face and the outline of her robes.

His chest started to heave, and he gave a "har . . . heh" followed by a racking cough. Alarmed, she started to reach the call button for the nurse, but he managed to raise an arm and stop her. It took her a moment to realize he was laughing.

The moment suspended between them. Bridget would be forever grateful that the tears she shed for her brother that day included those of mirth. She wanted to stay, to be there until his very end, but he was clear. He needed to pass in private and in close conversation with God. She could hardly refuse him. With a final kiss to his forehead, she left.

Her robes were the perfect cloak, and a cane served to reduce her identifying height. If it were not for the fact that the man the nun had visited had been pulled out of a building targeted by the Ulster Volunteer Force and bombed with the support of the RUC, she may have gone undetected. As she neared the exit, the hair on the back of her neck bristled. One look at Anna Marie's face was enough for her to fear that she would not make it back to the safety of the convent. Any hope was doused with her words.

"They've been tipped on Mrs. Harvey."

They crisscrossed side streets and alleys and brought the rattling compact car into car parks and out the other side. Bridget guided Anna Marie as much as she could but soon realized the young woman was well versed in the skills of losing a tail. A month before, the RUC had begun a systematic sweep of the streets to bring in persons of interest for questioning, and commonly such persons ended up jailed and forgotten by the process. She feared she would soon be one of them. Anna Marie was in tears as she begged Bridget to enter the network of safe houses that Bridget herself had created. The network was only available for women and was populated and operated by women, but Bridget refused. She had worked too hard to keep herself and her baby in secret these past months and she was not to be revealed now.

"Bring me to the cathedral."

Anna Marie obeyed. Masses were over for the day and the hollow interior betrayed no movements of anyone inside. Anna Marie helped Bridget into the cramped confessional in the back of the nave. Bridget undid the tucks of her wimple and dropped the folds of her habit beside her, revealing a simple thin woolen under-dress. She remained there, breathless, exhausted and with the growing knowledge that things were going terribly wrong.

Sounds of approaching feet echoed and the curtained door to the confessional swung open.

Anna Marie guided her to her feet and kicked aside the pile of robes. "We have a place for tonight."

"No." Bridget's mouth was set in a straight line of resolve. "This is my problem. The RUC is only after me. You've done enough. Keep yourself safe." She smoothed a strand of hair away from her friend's face, feeling the bond of closeness and family more strongly than she ever had. The day's events were moving too quickly and with a gravity that threatened to crush her. She was afraid—afraid for her brother's final hours, afraid for her friend's foolish loyalties, afraid for her baby. Mostly, she was afraid of being an albatross and of being the reason her networks and relationships were discovered.

"You can't drive, and I'm not leaving you."

"I can't risk being followed back to the convent."

"I agree. We have access to a car and directions to a safe house outside the city. But it's a long walk through the tunnels. Hours. I'm worried that it will be too much for you. Will you be alright?"

She gathered herself with resolve knowing arguing wasted precious time. "I have to be. Let's go."

Bridget walked too slowly, leaned too much on Anna Marie. They met each other's eyes without questions and continued down the stone steps, through the darkened hallways of the basement, and down a second set of stairs. At the far end of the building, away from any windows or vents, they entered a room only visible when a table and picture was moved away from the wall to expose its entrance. Shadows in the corner swept toward them and Anna Marie stifled a gasp.

Kavan rushed to Bridget and enveloped her in his arms, kissing her face and running his hands down her shoulders and over her belly, using his sense of touch as if to see her fully in the dim light. He seemed to marvel at her changes and not know how to respond to her, but only knew he wanted and needed to experience her, this changed woman. He brought her hands up to his mouth, kissing her palms and up to her wrists. His hands never stopped moving, feeling, committing to memory what his heart said was impossible.

Anna Marie cleared her throat, and he stepped back, remembering himself. He gave them a pack of food, water, and a flashlight, ushered them through a narrow door, and told them to stay in the main passages.

"A car is hidden at the end. Other safe havens would be clearly marked," he said. Anna Marie walked through and turned in time to hear Kavan whisper, "I'm so sorry. May God forgive me."

Bridget forced herself to walk for as long as she could. The passage was ancient, carved and bricked by unknown hands generations before. They took care not to talk or make noise. The sounds of the city above them washed and echoed through the walls, carried by a persistent wind that sometimes howled through the chambers enough to keep the stench from overpowering them. At times the floor would incline, and the sounds of the city would grow louder, sometimes accompanied by the smells of cooking or diesel, a welcome change from the stench of sewage. Other times the floor would slope, and the only sound would be their soft foot-falls and breathing. By the time Bridget allowed them to rest, the sounds and smells of the city had disappeared.

Around a sharp bend and protected from wind, the narrow passage grew larger and became almost room-like in size. Crude benches were carved into the walls, evidence that they were not the first people to need to flee the city in secrecy. Anna Marie swept the light around and walked over to examine a section more carefully.

Chiseled into the wall with great care was a series of images. Curved lines depicted hillsides or lakes, and a circle with radiant lines marked the sun. The images were set in distinct groups, and the women determined that it was a map segmented by a day's travels. At times, the travels were through tunnels like the one they were in. Other times, the trail passed through woods and the outskirts of rural towns. Friendly homes were marked, and a plinth of rocks designated the entrance to the next under-ground passage.

The trail started at a crude rendition of the eastern coastline of Northern Ireland, Belfast and its cathedral clearly marked on Belfast Lough—more a mouth of a bay open to the North Sea than a lake in its own right. Lough Neagh was clearly drawn at the center of the map with a northern or southern route around it. The northern route showed a circle made of dashes and odd rectangles, a crude impression of something like Stonehenge. Over this marking was an open-ended square with a cross on its top, clearly denoting that safety would be found in the cathedral by the stone circle. The markings showed each church that would also afford haven. Both routes ended at the western coast, at the port of Sligo. The

263

map was simple and easily remembered with a glance, giving comfort and direction to those who fled.

Bridget felt Anna Marie's worried gazes. She smiled and rubbed her belly trying to give assurances that all was well. Bridget yearned to go back to the stone circle where she imagined Gus waiting for her again but kept her flight of fancy to herself. Anna Marie wondered aloud how long they had been walking, deftly marking her concern. Neither had any idea if it was day or night, but only that they should eat and rest. They huddled together as best as they could and allowed themselves a fitful sleep.

Anna Marie woke first, giving Bridget whatever additional rest she needed. They ate a few mouthfuls of bread and continued their trek. It took another hour's walk before the air began to freshen and the sounds change, telling them that the end of the passage was close.

"Wait here," Anna Marie demanded and disappeared around a corner. Bridget had no time to worry because Anna Marie quickly poked her head around the corner and motioned for her to come.

The two women were stunned when they finally emerged. The passage had ended on the outskirts of Belfast in a forgotten section of the city. Rows of empty warehouses and abandoned factories sat as a reminder of economic fortunes that never filtered down to them. Gutted buildings with rusty doors and broken windows told any number of stories but didn't tell them which way to turn. Down the center of all of the buildings was a road, much wider than it needed to be for a double lane of trucks or cars. Unlike most of the infrastructure she could see, this broad stretch of pavement was swept clean of glass, debris, and even weeds. On top of some of the wider buildings perched tubes of remnant fabrics, fluttering in the light wind.

Bridget looked around anxiously. "Where's the car at?"

"Father Hughes said it would be inside a nearby building. Will you be alright to wait?"

Bridget nodded and settled down on a stack of wooden pallets, tolerating Anna Marie's fussing, nibbling on food when asked, taking sips of water, and obediently rubbing her swollen ankles. She watched as Anna Marie took off at a fast trot around the concrete and weed pocked roadway. A few minutes later a battered and rusty car careened around the corner and the door flew open for her. They allowed themselves a smile at their good fortune and drove off.

Anna Marie assessed Bridget carefully. "You're looking too drawn, Bridget. I'm getting worried for you."

Bridget put her head back against the seat and moved her hand in a circle around her belly. "I'll be better when I get back to the sisters. I'm not sure how patient this baby is going to be."

"The plan is to stay until nightfall at the house and only travel if it's safe. I'll sleep when I get you back to the convent. You look like you're ready to go."

"I need to rest, then I'll be fine. Thank you." She gave Anna Marie her most convincing smile. "It's not been easy on you to keep my secret, but it's been for the best."

Anna Marie drew in her breath as if to say something, then thought the better of it, keeping her eyes on the road ahead.

When they arrived at the safe house—a small and unremarkable wooden row house indistinguishable from all the others on the narrow street—the mark gave her comfort. A circle inside an open bottomed square topped with a cross was carved into one of the bricks at the top of the chimney, signifying this home was part of the same network depicted on the walls inside the passage. For a few blissful hours, both women rested and felt safe as they waited for night to fall to continue their journey.

She understood perfectly what happened next but did not have the strength or the speed to react. She was wrong to feel safe because the air quickly filled with the flashes and roars of war. A series of clicks to her left made her turn her head in time to see orange-white flashes of light as bullets began to shower where she lay. The gunfire came through only one window signifying one assailant, but the element of surprise gave the needed advantage. Her heart lurched when she heard the distinctive rapid "*thwunk-thwunk*" of gas canisters. Instantly the hell that had been both of her brother's last moments became clear.

The stench of gas was overwhelming. Flames ignited from superheated vapors enveloped her. She could feel her hair shrivel and singe, and the skin on her face threatened to pucker. Anna Marie threw herself over Bridget, shielding her as best as she could. The force of their bodies colliding made Bridget gasp and suck in air that no human should ever breathe. White-hot agony filled her lungs as passageways blistered from chemicals and unforgiving heat.

Bridget was starved for air, but the heat took her oxygen and fed it to the flames. She could feel her baby wake and kick, sensing the change, but was pressed to the floor by Anna Marie.

"Anna Marie! The back door! Quickly!" She yelled but her voice was gone, burned away before she could utter one word. Struggling to free herself, she looked up. The young woman's eyes and mouth were forever stilled wide with shock, rivulets of thick blood poured out over her tongue and lips.

She could feel the furnace heat increase as the flames devoured the thin curtains and threadbare couch. Rivers and spikes of red flames rippled over the sparse furnishings, working their way to her, melting her stockings and blistering her skin. She saw Danny's face again, swollen and roasted, and knew she was feeling his pain. Her spirit yearned to be bound together with him in her last thoughts but hesitated to leave her.

She started to make peace with God. The baby punched. The air fled. Her saliva wanted to boil. Her arm jerked aside. Anna Marie's body rolled away. Bridget's shoes pulled off her feet as her legs dragged along the floor. The pain of birth ripped through her belly to her back. The rough wooden floor changed to smooth linoleum.

Her feet thumped over the threshold and down the crickety wooden stairs.

She was outside.

Alive.

With Gus.

BALLYRONAN, NORTHERN IRELAND

MICHAEL AND MURRAY sat at the kitchen's island surrounded by newspapers, journals, and empty coffee cups. They spent hours tracking down the network of possible sources Dally may have tapped into. From that very short list, they began the process of anticipating the substance for the next articles and what moves they should take to preempt them. When they finally took a break, Bridget's journals provided a good diversion.

"I've translated parts of her mother's papers. She didn't use names very often." Murray leafed through the yellowed pages.

"I know. When you think about it, that makes sense." Michael sat on a stool pulled up to the table. "Most people back then probably used first names or nicknames in their own diaries."

Murray nodded in agreement and drummed his fingers on the table. The movement was subtle, but Michael began to watch his butler carefully. Murray averted his eyes when he asked, "What exactly does Jessica want to know?"

"She wants to find her uncles. I figure they must be in their late fifties now. We should be able to find some public records on them and anything else on the rest of family. I'm hoping to find anyone who could share a memory and fill in some of the gaps for her." He paused for a moment, rubbing the heels of his hands into his eyes. "I really want a way to help Jessica feel connected."

"Anything else?"

"I want to know who this is." Michael pointed to the other man wearing a straw hat in the only picture Jessica had of Bridget and Gus together. "What else have you learned," he leaned over his pad of notes.

Murray coughed and rearranged the papers, making the unconscious tells that killed any hopes of his ever winning at poker. "I learned that her mother was deeply loved," he began slowly, "and that she was a remarkable woman."

A lump formed in Michael's throat, surprising him. Hearing a trait that flowed through her mother to her was tantalizing. "Go on."

"The Irish salutations were the easiest for me to translate. Here," he drew his finger over a line of fine cursive writing, *An bhfuil sé indéanta go breá níos mó?* "This was frequently written in her mother's handwriting and says, "Is it possible to love more?" The other phrase was written in a different hand. The salutation was the same as on the letters hidden inside the book covers. I can only guess a lover wrote them. '*Gach mo ghrá go deo*' means 'All my love forever.' It's quite clear they both went to great lengths to keep their affections private."

"Is there anything that hints at who *Gean Cánach* was? I'm pretty sure Jessica has connected him with this man," he said, pointing to Gus' image, "but I want to be sure."

"You mean you want to make sure that Gus Adams was Jessica's father."

Murray's bluntness was too sudden. Michael gave a wary, "Yes."

"Well, there is enough information here for us to reconstruct her mother's life. Let's focus on her. No need to focus on this *Gean Cánach* character." Murray fidgeted with the notepad, betraying exhaustion and nerves.

Being resistant or evasive was uncharacteristic. Michael paid closer attention. "Okay. Any more ideas?"

When he was especially tense or upset, Murray had a habit of tearing strips of paper and rolling them up into balls. Michael noticed the habit when he was a young boy. Murray would serve him biscuits and tea while the voices of Michael's parents shrieked through the house. Murray would shred the waxy white paper wrappers that the biscuits came in as they pretended not to hear. The row of tightly rolled, perfectly aligned pea-sized paper wads always meant difficult times were at hand. "About Miss Jessica," Murray began, too formally to give him comfort, "are you truly sure you want her to learn more?"

The hopeful warmth slowly seeped out of him, replaced by a feeling of dread. "Yes. Definitely. She's torn up by all that's happened to her. You've seen her, Murray. It's as if she's been hollowed out inside. I want her to have answers about who her family really was."

Murray pushed the wads into a perfect triangle and said nothing.

"Why? What are you seeing there?"

Michael waited while Murray pushed the triangle's dotted sides into three adjoining piles, making something that looked like a shamrock.

"It's just that . . . sometimes mistakes are made. You learn things about an ancestor that aren't true. That family stories might simply be a bunch of malarkey."

"Out with it, Murray. I want to hear it all." Michael could feel himself shrinking. The kitchen counters, walls, the doors grew and slanted around him in the odd angles of his childhood. He swallowed.

"I had one of our men do a bit of research in the newspaper archives, a different man than we used to research Bridget's marriage." Michael nodded in quick understanding. "Patrick and Daniel Heinchon were leaders in the IRA and responsible for the bombing of Nelson's Pillar in 1966. That fact was confirmed in later years as the conflict heated up. They weren't considered the most notorious members by the British but were known to be part of the team that was the heart and soul of the fledgling civil rights movement."

"Daniel and Patrick are common names in Ireland. There could be any number of them. It doesn't mean we're talking about the same family."

Murray fanned Jessica's notes. "I've no questions."

"So the men in the family were involved in the struggles. That's hardly surprising. Most families in both Irelands have some kind of connection. Where are they now?"

"The two men died in a Christmas day raid. Patrick was killed instantly. Daniel never recovered from his injuries. The raid was considered one of the most successful campaigns early on by the British to disrupt the leadership of the opposition. Their funerals sparked a week of unrest that many point to as the beginning of the Troubles."

"That doesn't tell us anything about Bridget."

"No. But there is a connection here." He shuffled through the papers and produced a faxed image. Even with the grainy quality of the newspaper photo, the image of the priest presiding over Daniel's funeral was clear. Murray placed the picture of Bridget and Gus and the unknown man beside it. "The priest's name is Kavan Hughes."

Michael cocked his head to the side in thought. "Would he be called *Sagart* Hughes?" Murray nodded. "That's what the woman at the country store in Aghalee was trying to tell me. I thought she was telling me the name of the church, but she recognized Father Hughes. So, he was definitely in Aghalee with Gus Adams and connected to Bridget."

"It all fits," Murray continued, "and the article makes even more sense. He was quoted as saying he was a childhood friend of the Heinchon family and that he understood why these boys of such promise had taken the lesser path of violence. He stopped short of endorsing them. He used the sermon to instruct on the growing gulf of opportunity and patience."

"So he took the middle road?"

"He certainly didn't fan the flames for either violence or assimilation. But it was enough for me to go back and re-read some of Bridget's entries." Murray cocked his middle finger onto his thumb and fired away at the wads like miniature cannon balls.

"And this priest, is he still living?" Michael wanted to be excited, but Murray's manner betrayed more needed to be said.

"Yes. Father Hughes has led a remarkable and successful life inside the church. He is now Bishop Kavan Hughes."

Murray retrieved the tiny paper balls from around the kitchen floor. Then he began to rearrange the wads into neat stacks, busying himself until Michael spoke.

"Jessica's going to want to meet the bishop."

"I've no doubt on that, Michael."

Michael paced the room, alternately looking at the picture and the newspaper photo. "With her uncles dead, this bishop is the only person who can give Jessica what she needs. Nothing will stop her from going to him once she makes the connection." He stopped pacing. "Wait a minute. He must be living in the Belfast area and—"

Murray put his hand on Michael's arm and motioned for him to sit back down. He methodically closed and checked every window and door, putting on a kabuki theater of security and calm. He wore an expression of empathy, a look Michael knew and dreaded.

"The papers said the brothers were part of a team. I had our fellow do more research to get names of any affiliates or anyone else who could be living and more easily accessible than a rising star bishop."

Michael sat obedient and silent, hunched over his stomach. The familiar feeling of the moldering pit sickened him to helpless waiting.

"Bridget Heinchon Harvey was apprehended by the RUC in January of 1967. She was sent to the Mourne House Women's Unit of Maghaberry Prison in Southwest Belfast where she remained waiting for a trial which never happened."

"My God, Murray. That's when Jessica was born."

"No documents mention any child or pregnancy. That doesn't surprise me. The fact that Bridget never went to trial meant very little evidence—if any—was found against her. If the papers had gotten a hold of the fact a pregnant woman was incarcerated, there would have been a ruckus in the news about it. As it was, it seems that she was held as bait."

"Bait?"

"Yes. The British had identified the key brains behind the civil rights movement and popular opposition as a man, assumed to be a close associate of Daniel and Patrick. Common practice was to watch every visitor of imprisoned activists, although the authorities called them criminals, not political prisoners. They tried to determine networks and then would disrupt organizing by targeting and killing leaders."

"Why zero in on Bridget?"

"According to the paper, they received an anonymous tip that she was the leader's wife and justified her incarceration on the basis of national security."

"So, changing her name to Mrs. Harvey was to blur the lines of connections."

"Exactly. The Brits imprisoned her to see who might visit and lead the authorities to her husband. And it's no surprise that they failed to even turn up a marriage certificate. Evidently they found it easier to believe in a missing husband rather than a woman being the brains behind the movement."

Michael stopped pacing and slowly sank into a chair. "Are you telling me that Jessica's mother was imprisoned out of fear she was an enemy of the British?"

"Yes."

Michael railed against Murray's attempt to soothe away the news with a gentle tone. He kept his own voice in check. "Jessica's uncles were heavily involved—that doesn't mean their sister was."

The tiny white wads were rearranged into a long dotted line. Murray waited until Michael directed the conversation with his next question.

"How long was she there?"

"Five years." Murray stood up and replaced cold and muddy coffee with a steaming mug.

Michael swallowed against the bitter bile that pushed its way up from the pit of his stomach. He looked at the images of Bridget, smiling on the banks of a lake, surrounded by admiring men and laughing women. Young Bridget exuded vibrancy that shimmered right off the surfaces of the black and white photos. He thought of the reserved and sickly woman Jessica described and dreaded the reason for the change. "Someone must have visited. Someone must have cared."

"The conditions at Maghaberry prison were quite trying. Men lived atop one another without space to move. Even their meals afforded them nothing but cramped tables, so they could only wish for space to move about or exercise. Circumstances were even worse for women. Prisons were built with only men in mind. Women were being locked up as an afterthought. Since they knew better than to let men and women share and mix, what may have been a medium security prison for men effectively worked as a maximum-security lock down for women. Word is they had less than one hour out of the cell each day. I shudder to imagine what her experience was like. But we did identify one person who remembered her and cared enough to visit."

Michael raised his head. "Let me guess. Gus?"

Murray frowned. "If Gus had visited her, I doubt very much he would ever have been able to leave the country again. The Brits take their security very seriously."

"So, who then?"

"Our fellow in archives found a three paragraph article buried inside the late edition of the newspaper reporting on the Heinchon boy's sister's release. The conditions were very harsh. Seems her health suffered horribly. She was given a reprieve for humanitarian reasons and was subject to immediate deportation."

"Deportation? But she was a citizen. How could they deport her?"

"She was deemed to be an enemy of the state and a felon. Penal deportation is not new. Just ask a few blokes in Australia. When getting to that country became easier with modern transportation, exiling criminals to the bottom of the earth lost favor. Deportation codes are still on the books. Father Hughes pushed hard for her release from prison on the promise she would leave the country."

"Was Father Hughes was trying to get the family of Gus, Bridget and Jessica back together?"

"It sounds that way."

"But that's not what Bridget did."

"No indeed. Think of it. By that time, a five-year-old girl had another mother and father. Bridget went to live across the border in Ireland."

Michael's excitement faded as he listened. He picked up the photograph of Bridget, Gus, and Kavan and studied their faces, wishing a boy's wish that all could be made right just by desperately wanting it. He must have sat there for longer than he knew. His coffee grew cold.

Murray had finally exhausted his nervous energy. News delivered. Tempest passed.

Michael barreled on. "There's no way she can waltz into the bishop and start asking questions about her mother. A baby was born. A mother went to prison. Bishop Hughes knows what happened. He obviously had more than enough power and resource to reunite them after Bridget's release, but he didn't. He must have felt he had very good reasons not to do so."

"You have to find out those reasons first, Michael. You cannot let her blast forth with an American brashness and start demanding answers to questions that should never be asked. You may laugh at my Irish ways, but my soul is worried for Jessica. She's been thrown up in the air like a bit of chaff, and the first wind that puffs will claim her. Let her know she has a place with you. Hold her to you and anchor her."

Michael's throat clenched in the effort to control himself. "I don't know how."

Murray slowly wiped down the countertops and put their cups in the sink, letting Michael's words hang in the air. He couldn't help but be saddened by the boy who sat on the stool. "There'll be no second chances if she decides to leave you."

Michael patted Murray's back with wordless thanks and walked through the swinging kitchen doors into the hallway. The sky hinted at dawn by changing to a deep cobalt blue. He plodded his way up the stairs, gripping the newel post and railing, almost pulling his body up the long stairway to his bedroom. Catching himself midstride, he first turned away from his renovated master suite, almost forgetting he had erased all of his parents' unhappiness with new carpet and paint. He opened the door and slipped into the room as soundlessly as he could.

Jessica stood at the window, a silhouette against a starry blue sky, hugging herself, head resting against the panes. She seemed so small.

He walked up and wrapped his arms around her from the back, resting his chin on her head. "I thought you'd be asleep."

"I couldn't. I tossed and turned for a while and went down to the kitchen to get something." Shaking fingers brushed under her eyes and the back of her hand wiped against her nose.

"How much did you hear?"

"Enough."

He held her tighter, feeling her warm skin through one of his T-shirts she liked to wear to bed. "I'm so sorry."

He turned her toward him, staying close. Her breasts were soft, and her heart pounded against his chest. He curled her arms between their bodies to stem her shaking. His voice was coarse as he whispered, "I was going to let you get a good night's sleep before I told you."

"I know," she said and rested her head on his chest. "It's what she never wanted me to learn. I feel like I've betrayed her for digging through her life. There's a loop running through my brain, and none of the images are what I want to see. I want to envision her happy and healthy, but they flicker to her being curled up and emaciated in a concrete cell." She rubbed her eyes. "I'm just so damned angry."

"Angry?"

"I'm angry at being lied to by Margaret and Jim. I'm pissed at Gus for facing off against Magnus and getting himself killed. I want to hate you for confusing me even more." She half laughed, half sobbed the last words.

"They did what they thought was best. She knew you and loved you."

"But I treated her like a weak old lady. I never had a chance to show her the respect I have for her now."

"That was her choice. She gave you a freedom she never had and wasn't trying to make you into something you weren't. She accepted you. In my book that's pretty huge."

"She lied."

"She protected you."

"From what? From who?"

He didn't answer right away. She grew limp as her energy slowly drained. One by one the stars began to fade as the day progressed. The flat lake reflected the changing colors, and Michael knew that along its shores two men with night scopes patrolled.

She pulled away and wiped her face on her sleeve. "Maybe I've learned enough and should just stop."

He started to say more, that the truth existed whether she could see it or not, like the pit that remained in his stomach. Maybe Bridget wanted to forget her past and maybe Jessica had learned enough, but whoever made sure those journals ended up in Jessica's hands knew who she was and wanted her to know the truth.

"That's not an option anymore."

BELFAST, NEAR STORMONT
NORTHERN IRELAND

KAVAN FIRST MET Bridget on the shores of Lough Neagh when he was four and she was two. She was seated in the lap of her Ma, banging a spoon against the side of a tin cup. He remembered how red jam smeared her face and how she refused any attempt to clean her up by twisting her head and body away, and threatening to release earth-shattering howls. Ma was beside herself. She wanted her daughter to be sparkling clean when the *sagarts* arrived, as if they had never seen a smudged and wild-haired toddler before. He could still see Bridget's face widened in disbelief as Ma dabbed a hanky with spit, how she screamed in terror as the hanky came closer. She finally wriggled free and broke away, right into Kavan, knocking them both to the ground.

Instead of crying, Bridget had merely gazed up at him. Perhaps it was the instant camaraderie of children in an adult world that calmed her. He remembered how his mouth watered at the promise of the seeds puddled in jam at the corner of her mouth, his hollow stomach grumbling at the discovery. He can still feel the way her body relaxed when he brought his mouth to hers, lipping and licking the last of the jam away. He does not remember how they separated or who may have pulled them apart, but the back slaps, jostling, smiles, relief, and the sweet warmth of Bridget's mouth stayed with him forever.

Eventually, Kavan began to earn the reputation as the one person who could do the unthinkable and bridge the impossible. When he was barely more than ten years old, he had come across two men locked in a seething brawl down an alley by his flat. A crowd of bystanders had encircled them, cheering them on, encouraging their anger and hate. Both men were bloodied and failing, but neither would relent. Kavan had pushed his way into the center of the circle, stepping aside whenever the fighting men flailed near. He simply stood there, watching. Then, when the men seemed to pause for a breath, he had slowly raised his hands, placed them on their arms, and simply said, "Please stop." And they did.

From that moment on, no one ever treated Kavan as simply Kavan. Conversations would hush when he approached. Young girls and their mothers would steal looks at him from under their lashes. Complete strangers brought him in to comfort the sick and, being a young man of few words, spent his time of consolation reading. Doing so allowed him to read more widely than any peer or elder. Some were contraband copies of banned books. Many other times, the classics or philosophy. Most often, the only book in the home was the Bible. But he read each for hours at bedsides of the infirmed. His body of knowledge soon outstripped most teachers. People believed that he was not only wise beyond his years but that his insights were divinely inspired.

Any power he had was given to him freely. The religious say the power was given to him as one of God's chosen. The secular would say such power was given by each and every person who paused to look as he passed them or that it was given by those who clung to and analyzed each word he spoke. The jaded would say he had a shtick and worked it. Whatever external forces gave him his power, his internal force burned with the deep and fervent belief that he was put on Earth for a purpose.

He possessed two inborn traits he silently coveted. One earthly quality he cultivated with an obsession bordering on maniacal was discretion. He never betrayed a person or a secret. That made him more valuable than gold to those who sought his counsel. With neither word nor eyelash flicker, Kavan Hughes became a vault of secrets. As the personal troubles of some became the political problems of all, Kavan kept his promise and never divulged a confidence, at least overtly. This quality helped him with Man.

His second trait was that of an uncanny strategist, the quality that helped him with God. As he made his way through life and early priesthood, his knowledge of the hearts and minds of men and women proved seminal. Without divulging a secret or tipping the slightest hint, he could ask questions of a confessor that would lead to the kind of reconciliation no one thought possible. By boring into the crannies of guilt or belief, through the artful construct of a question or a story, he would build the scaffolding of compromise. He knew the strength of a position because he knew the opposition.

He was a neutral observer biased only by God's light. The weak used him to bring messages to the powerful. The powerful used him to weigh the effect of action on popular opinion. He used them all to bind a way back to unity.

Few ever suspected what he was doing. None ever suspected why. If anyone had known the unabiding hatred he carried for the English or the longing he had for a united Ireland, he never would have made it past being a Monsignor at an insignificant parish.

Even within the safest strongholds surrounded by those who voiced kindred beliefs, he never spoke of his own desires but only helped elicit and strengthen the beliefs of others. Then, he would carry messages of politics and faith to the powerful. He knew he would be safe as long as he was useful.

He learned a harsh lesson, but he quickly realized that secrets traveled faster than the thirsty to a pub, and he saw how long a lie would stick if it hit the right mark. He quickly and painfully learned that not everyone shared his tight lips. Except for Bridget Heinchon.

If anyone could have made the mistakes of a desperate person, it should have been Bridget. Her father died of drink. Her mother went off the rails. Alone, she learned to fend for her family. Desperate people put their needs above all others, using gossip as currency or making mistakes in their own favor. Never Bridget.

From the moment he tasted that sweet jam, he never lost track of her. The flats they lived in were as connected as the people who lived there. Alleys and streets crossed one another the way bloodlines and marriages intersected their people. He thought he was the only one who kept his eyes and ears open and his mouth shut. That was until he saw how Bridget watched and waited. As a woman and not of the clergy, she could go places and do things without watchful and judgmental eyes following her. They were a match made in heaven.

As an altar boy, Kavan was always at Saint Peter's. Bridget went as well, to clean and polish. Bridget cared for her family by caring for others. Through her contacts in the church, she found flats or food for those in need. He watched her as she leaned her head over slates and chalk, helping the young ones with their studies. She, too, was a voracious reader, and he slipped her books of Niccolo Machiavelli, Karl Marx, Socrates, Thomas Jefferson. She gave him works by Henry David Thoreau, Thomas Hobbes, Martin Luther, and Jean-Paul Sartre. They were both clear on their destinies and instinctively knew to keep their growing radicalism in deepest secret. She never asked anything for herself. She didn't need to. She had him and Gus to watch over her.

Gus Adams was the only other person who saw Bridget for who she was. Kavan could not claim her as his own because he was beholden to his vows and the tradition of the church. He would never bring scandal and dishonor to his door, nor could he consider her as his alone. Gus could not claim her for she was beholden to no one and let no tradition define her. She lived her life robustly, without fear of rumor or reputation. Gus respected that and loved her even more for it. Kavan and Gus shared the heart of an incredible woman. The three formed a bond that transcended their time.

The picture in the day's paper triggered Kavan's memories. Somehow, among all of the races won, the pictures chosen to run under the headline *Jessica Wyeth Spotted at Aintree* jarred his memories to the surface. Two pictures, one from the past and one from the present depicted the same scene: a horse in the winner's circle surrounded by its jockey, owner, and trainer. The picture from the past showed the beaming trainer and stoic owner standing beside a gleaming and wild-eyed horse in a winner's circle at Suffolk Downs, a flat track outside of Boston. The stocky stance, curly hair, and broad smile of the trainer from the older photo were of his friend, Gus Adams. He could hear his friend's humor as fresh as ever. The horse was named Dark Irish, a poke, Kavan knew, as much for the horse's color as it was to its heart. For one shining moment, they were together again, laughing at a shared joke. Gus would have enjoyed knowing his jest had people smiling even years later.

Alone and unobserved, Kavan allowed himself to stare at the images of friends long gone. The recent picture showed Jessica Wyeth and owners beside an equally wild-eyed horse. Jessica was the image of her mother. His heart pounded in his chest as he thought of the love and connection he had to them both.

He could clearly see Jessica's athleticism and near-regal bearing came from her mother. Even covered in the slop and mud from the track, she stared at the camera with a combination of daring and aloofness. She dared the viewer forward, then kept just out of reach, squelching any satisfaction to know her better. He let himself remember her mother's laugh and noted Jessica's cool, almost cold, gaze. The wariness that lay beneath the surface broke his heart. He wondered how much she knew about her mother.

Next, he studied Gus' round face and had a pang of nostalgia for his old friend. There wasn't a day that Kavan didn't send up a solemn prayer for Gus' health and wellbeing for living a life of sacrifice and humility. When Bridget and Gus died, a piece of Kavan died with them. He yearned for the joy of sharing a few more pints and laughs at what young men did when they thought they had nothing but time to live. Imagining the *craic* of that moment made him grin at the unsaid jokes and private truths. The breeze of memories kicked up a swirl of envy, for Gus was more of a man than Kavan could ever be. Gus had what Kavan so desperately wanted for himself. He wondered if different choices would have led to different lives.

But his friends were long dead and alternate paths long grown cold.

He had saved each article. The first had been buried deep inside the newspaper near endless columns of stocks and scores. *Man Dies in Mountain Search. Murdering Heiress Sought for Questioning.* He neatly folded the paper, keeping the story on top. Tuesday's paper declared *Death and Hoax Search Covered up. Wyeth Flees U.S.* The byline, Dally Thorpe, was not even a name that was vaguely familiar, but the name Connaught was one all too familiar to him. He folded the paper and placed it with the others. He didn't have to read them to learn the details but was happy that the articles placed Jessica in a favorable and sympathetic light. She had obviously inherited her mother's grit. And from what he could tell about the direction of the series, she was going to need every ounce of it.

Rosalie, his middle-aged housekeeper, quietly knocked on the door and entered. Rather than a maid's uniform, she wore a simple gabardine dress and sensible shoes. A gold crucifix was pinned to her collar. "Excuse me, Your Excellency, Deputy First Minister Bragdon is here to see you."

Bragdon had been a steady presence in the government for as long as Kavan could remember. Unattractive exterior notwithstanding, he always seemed to be surrounded by women with tight skirts and nervous eyes, and men who never said no. Kavan would watch closely while Bragdon maneuvered through a crowd and manipulated even the strongest man with a whispered statement or stony silence.

Bragdon had tried many times to tempt Kavan with women or booze— or once, boys—but Kavan held himself and never gave Bragdon so much as a whiff of a corruptible soul. Bragdon aspired to move beyond his title of "Deputy" and barely hid his ambition to be at the top of Northern Ireland's government with at palatial office at Stormont. He needed to create his own career path despite being hated.

The proposed talks for reunifying the Irelands would restructure the executive branch of the country and annihilate his carefully plotted rise. He had steadfastly cultivated the Minister of Home Affairs and was a key supporter of the Special Powers Act; an act that interred people as security risks of the state until such time they were no longer a threat— with or without formal charges. He found it easier to marginalize threats simply by incarcerating them. Bragdon worked hard to learn the weakness and mistakes of others. He used such knowledge to build his career and didn't care who hated or feared him. Kavan was aware of Bradgon's probing into his background and life and knew that none of Bradgon's hooks had snagged on anything. Theirs was a long and tedious friendship, one marked by a profound inability to let one's guard down.

Kavan rose up from his chair and walked over to the rotund minister. "Reginald! Always a pleasure to see you, but this is a surprise. What brings you out today?" Kavan pulled himself up to his full height and flashed a smile as dashing as any in the movies. Dressed in the casual attire of the clergy—black shirt, black pants—Kavan didn't attempt to soften the effect he knew his presence would have.

Reggie Bragdon was a squat and arrogant man who hadn't quite come to grips with the fact that he was woefully unattractive. Somehow, mirrors seemed to have eluded his universe, so the only indication to him that he was not movie star perfect was the fact he had to tilt his head upward to look most people in the eye. Even so, he found that he could still look down his nose at anyone else with ease.

As a man of God, Kavan was presumed to be above human frailties, but something about the gnome-like man in front of him begged addressing. He took a slight step forward, knowingly that half meter too close, forcing Bragdon to take an uncomfortable half step back. Kavan enjoyed cloaking his welcome in the unspoken language of alpha.

Bragdon gripped the outstretched hand and gave it a perfunctory pump. "Bishop Hughes," he said with his usual formality and pomp, as if someone would reflect it back on him, "I came to offer my congratulations on your upcoming appointment to Archbishop. Long overdue. Long overdue." He looked expectantly at the chairs and tea service.

Kavan raised his eyebrows. "My ascension and move to Rome is not for several months. I hadn't thought the news was out."

"It's not," he said, giving a satisfied smile. "I'll miss having you so close to Stormont."

Kavan suppressed a wince and raised his chin. "Thank you. I've been happy to serve at the pleasure of the Holy See and am humbled by his confidence in me."

"Your appointment comes at a tumultuous time. You have always had the gift of understanding both sides of our conflict and helping others hear consensus when only words of fighting were spoken." Bragdon cleared his throat and took a step toward the empty chairs.

Kavan acknowledged the compliment and remained standing. "It won't change my involvement in the administration of the different dioceses here. This is more of a change of title and address than duties," he waved his hand as if to dismiss a larger thought. "But you seem to have more on your mind." He took a halting step forward and smiled to himself when Bragdon almost invited himself to sit.

"What I am going to say must be kept in the strictest of confidence. No one must hear of this before its time."

"Of course. I have always kept your counsel."

Bragdon coughed nervously into his hand. "I wanted you to hear it from the government firsthand. Sinn Fein will be offered a seat at the negotiating table."

The news shot through Kavan. Without changing his expression or the set of his shoulders, he lowered his head and gave a silent "Thanks be to God." He took in a measured breath. "This change of heart is sudden. What led the British to decide that all parties should have a say after all?"

"With all due respect, Bishop Hughes, you can say that bombs don't make diplomacy but those filthy hooligans know better."

Kavan made sure to carefully etch his irritation with restraint. "Reginald, you know as well as I do that no one will listen to anything if they have one ear plugged by the muzzle of a gun. Linking a change of heart in the British with the bombing of Arndale will only serve to embolden another attack. You and I have had many discussions on this. The only path to lasting peace is for anyone with an interest in the outcome to have an opportunity for input on the process. People must feel their words are heard to stop their fists midair, and not just in Norn Iron. Surely you see it that way." Beaming a benevolent smile, he waved his hand over to the empty chairs and signaled Rosalie for more tea. "This is the first I've heard of it."

Bragdon settled himself in and fluffed his jacket. "We think it's best that the announcement come from you at the retirement service this Sunday. You and Father Storm have had strong ties to the Irish community and hearing it from you will go a long way toward legitimizing the message."

"And they are certain that this announcement so close to Arndale won't be misconstrued as success for darker strategies? The loyalists have long felt that Sinn Fein is the brain and the IRA the brawn of the same beast. The IRA will claim success for their tactics. Won't they be right?"

"Certainly not." Bragdon waved his hand at the thought. "Merely a formality that they overlooked."

Kavan's eyes narrowed as his smile widened. "My church has never been a pulpit for taking a side in politics. I've spoken to the hearts of men and the calling of their souls. I don't meddle in their political bedfellows. I have been very transparent with you in what opinions I have heard and provided insight into what arguments may hold sway, but neither the Church, nor I, have ever been the government's public mouthpiece, and I'm not sure it's wise to start now."

As he leaned in on Bragdon, Kavan had the clarity he had been lacking for so long. Perceived as trodding the middle ground all these years meant that he had listened and given credence to both sides equally. Doing so cultivated an oasis of neutrality, becoming privy to the plans and confessions of many. He used that information and shaped his own agenda, but quietly, never venturing into the open. Publicly he wanted equality for all people and didn't care what government's flag flew over his meetings. But privately, he yearned for his language and history to flow. He could be a

Catholic in Greenland or Italy. But he could only be an Irishman from Irish soil. Neutrality was one thing. Being a tool was another.

Bragdon's offer reeked of manipulation, but the Deputy Minister certainly was not smart enough to work that out on his own.

"Father Storm is deserving of the spotlight all on him and not to be sharing it with a political message," Kavan infused his voice with friendship, even as he was feeling anything but.

"I'm sure he'll want to be remembered as going out on such a strong note."

Kavan remained firm. "I will not tarnish his final service with that announcement."

"I've seen you skirt the edges, Bishop. Wait until the mass is concluded to make your announcement, but do it that day when the cathedral is full of those who need to hear the word." He waited for an acknowledgement, and received none. "Give me your promise."

They had been through too many trials and tests for Kavan not to recognize a trap. Bragdon had never asked for his word before and that seemingly insignificant fact illuminated his desperation. He manifested his most genial demeanor. "I only give my oaths and promises to God."

Bragdon started to press for more and leaned forward, eyes darting as he thought of other avenues to get the answer he wanted. They finally settled on the stack of newspapers, absorbing every detail. Kavan watched as Bragdon took a deep breath and sink into his chair. He could almost see the mental wheels churning that not getting an outright refusal was worth meeting today. Bragdon would think the offer was too tempting to be disregarded.

Rosie set the tea service down and the men made a show of enjoying one another's company, each secretly wishing the amber tea packed a mite bit stronger kick. When enough time had passed that Kavan was finally able to walk him to the door without offense, he went back to the newspapers and culled the pages for anything he may have missed. He read the international section for business deals. He read the police blotters for neighborhood skirmishes. Nothing indicated that Bragdon's offer would have been coming.

He was at a crossroads. Something nagged at him about Bragdon's offer. The timing? This was a chess game he had played for far too long. He yearned to talk to someone openly, freely, the way he used to talk to Gus. And Bridget. They had understood.

He looked at pictures of Jessica and felt the hot stab of loss as he saw Bridget's smile. So alive. So vital. Bridget's child seemed to cling onto the arm of that dashing fellow. Michael Conant? Connaught? He remembered how Bridget would cling to her *Gean Cánach* along the shores of Lough Neagh and for a moment, he was lost in the thoughts of a young man.

He fingered the key hanging around his neck on a long woolen cord and wondered about the path not taken.

MANCHESTER, ENGLAND

DALLY GAVE A muffled "whoop" as she put down the phone. Monday's paper did exactly what she had hoped. Interest in the Murdering Heiress had not waned. Circulation for Tuesday's paper was up, and the tip line started to ring. Wednesday's paper had the good citizens of England all doing their part in Dally's drama. The numbers were modest, but anyone who made a pastime of tracking the beautiful blonde American were calling in her location and offering details—for a price. Whether the details were true or not didn't really matter. The feeding frenzy mattered. Dally was going to do all she could to make sure the pacing was perfect for the upcoming weekend's explosion of demand.

Her story had moved up one page in the paper. The pictures she chose to run of the dashing Sheriff would be instantly recognizable as the surviving Connaught son. Don gave the article a huff-and-buff edit but nothing more because she essentially rehashed everything the American reporter had already published. Everything was going like clockwork. She checked her calendar and penciled in a time to get her teeth cleaned and hair highlighted for her television debut. She stifled an urge to rub her hands together and dabbed her nose instead.

Don's shadow darkened her desk. He threw a stack of papers in front of her.

"Your story got a bit of interest."

"Just like I told you. It's going to be a corker."

Don stared at her until she got the clue that she was supposed to read the papers.

After a few minutes, she raised her chin and peered at him through her glasses. "So what? I was expecting injunction orders. You deal with those all the time. Besides, it's going to help us sell more papers if Connaught tried to stop us." She looked at the papers more carefully and gasped. "These aren't injunctions! They're cease and desist orders!"

"It seems that American reporter didn't take too kindly to you using all of her information and not crediting her. She says that all would be forgiven if you shared your research with her."

"Bloody hell, Don!" Dally said as a sneezing fit kicked in, "this is *my* story."

"No, Magpie, it's not. This is the paper's story, and I can assign it to any reporter I want. You will get this American reporter off my back by calling her and making nice. Throw her a few choice tidbits, then write Millie's copy for tonight's news."

Dally's knuckles were white as she dialed the phone.

BALLYRONAN, NORTHERN IRELAND

JESSICA AND MICHAEL walked along the shore then turned up the path and into the woods. They had been out picking wild flowers, and Michael guided her away from the house. Sounds of saws and hammers could be heard before the stable came into view. The area that had once been the garage and loft had been demolished clear to the rafters. Slits of light shone through the aging roof. A grid of yellow tape and blue lines mapped out more box stalls. A handful of men were hard at work fixing roof shingles and replacing long neglected wood. Sweat slicked pale and freckled forearms. They worked in silent choreography paced by the steady beat of the hammers. Three men, shirts drenched or missing, struggled to put a heavy beam in place. A fourth man, hoodie pulled over his head, pounded a nail. Another carried lengths of wood and threw them down with a heavy clatter.

Michael didn't realize how tense he was until she turned to him. After his conversation with Murray a few days ago, he struggled with ways to help her feel connected and rooted. He searched her eyes for signs he was on the right track.

"I guess this is all for me." She turned a slow circle and took in all of the activity.

"The property needs your touch. Creating your ideal facility will help you feel connected to the Irelands." He tried to keep the eagerness out of his voice. "The barn needs to be upgraded. I was impressed with what I saw at Aintree, and you said the facilities at the cottage were too basic. What will we need?"

"You mean, what do you need aside from electricity, running water, indoor and outdoor training rings, padded shower stalls, and—oh, yeah—horses? Aside from that I'd say you're all set." She tried to temper the bite of her words with an empty laugh. "Thank you. I can see you're trying to keep me happy and occupied while you're gone."

"The architects come again tomorrow to put finishing details on the plans we already roughed out. Meeting with them without me will help send the message that this is your project. I hope you request everything you need." He swept his hand to the south. "There's plenty of land for a track and indoor arena. I want you to design those, too. I, um," he hesitated as he struggled to find the right words, "I want you here with me, Jessica. I want you to feel like you belong here . . . with me." He used his fingers to comb through her hair, gliding the soft strands away from her face. Her forehead was starting to pink in the summer sun. She had true Irish skin. Whether she felt it or not, she belonged here. With him.

She surveyed the activity. "The barn could start with ten horses and I could build from there. The connections made with Tully Farm and others at Aintree would put me in demand immediately. Doherty would put half his stable under my care even without your influence, and Electra would use me to source top-notch animals to sell in the States. It could be very successful."

The excitement in her voice gave him a flicker of optimism. "The life you tried to create in Kentucky you can create here."

"That life was based on a fear and a lie, and the life you want me to create here is the same life that got Gus killed."

His heart sank when he saw the determined look in her eyes.

"Until I'm completely free of any involvement in the Charity, I'm not making any promises. I'll help you design the facility, but I don't know if I'm part of the long-term deal."

Michael's pounding heart betrayed how desperately he wanted this, but he knew better than to press. Out of the corner of his eye he saw one of the guards, rifle draped over his arm surveying the woods. He tried to steer her by the elbow to look in the other direction, but she gently removed herself and followed his gaze to the sniper. "This is temporary. We won't always have to live like this. I'm leaving tonight to access the final papers of my father's estate. I'm going to Switzerland."

"Does your uncle know that?"

"He will when I return."

"And then?"

"And then there will be no more secrets."

It didn't make him feel any more secure when her only response was an aloof shrug.

The worker lowered his hooded sweatshirt, wiped the sweat from his forehead, and watched the retreating figures. Then Tim dropped his hammer and walked behind the barn. Rummaging around his pack, he finally found what he was looking for. The day's rumpled newspaper contained a story that made him nearly crazy.

A headline on the third page screamed *Michael Connaught Seduces Jessica Wyeth* complete with pictures of them together, arm in arm either dressed like royals at some formal event, and other candid shots of them taken at the race. He paced in small circles, opening and closing his hands into fists. He could not hear their conversation, but he could tell that Michael was doing everything Tim could not do to woo her.

Tim had watched them carefully. Jessica's movements were those of a frightened horse. She moved her shoulder away from Michael's touch, taking steps back. Her face angled down, avoiding eye contact. Her body was tense and signaled to Tim she wasn't about to yield. Michael seemed stiff in the way he did as a boy, when he was angry enough to hit something but was controlling himself. Tim puzzled the pieces. Could Michael sense she didn't like the barn? Or did she act that way because she no longer liked Michael? Maybe Nan was right. Tim would try again to get Jessica to love him. He had to make sure his second try didn't fail.

Tim wanted to watch her before she disappeared into the great house. He crept around the side of the barn and looked up the hill. A near silent wisp of branches made him reflexively drop to all fours and look in its direction. The man with the rifle walked toward him, muzzle raised.

"Jay-sus, Tim! What are you doing creeping around like that?" the sniper re-engaged the rifle's safety and pointed it to the ground.

"Rourke!" Tim said with practiced enthusiasm, "Sorry to give you a start, man. What's that you're doing here?"

Athletic and lean, Rourke crossed the opening to Tim in easy strides. "The young Mr. Connaught has me keeping the riffraff out."

Tim clasped Rourke's outstretched hand and gave it a pump, eyeing the cradled rifle. "It's good to see you, my man. Good to see you. How's the missus?"

"The missus and I are parents now. Garrett is four and Caroline is six months."

Tim widened his eyes and shook his head back and forth slowly, Nan's lessons well learned. "Doesn't seem possible that my bunkmate at training is a father. Young Liam, may he rest in peace, was right when he said you were the marrying type. Last I heard you were part of the militia near the Bogside. Good to see you in these parts." He remembered their training— hand-to-hand combat where it always ended with Rourke's face pressed to the mud and Tim holding the wooden dowel used for drills to his throat. He won at that. Lost to him at target practice.

"What brings you 'round? I hadn't heard you were part of the team here." He patted his pockets and produced a folded paper. He read it carefully. "They've left your name off the list, Tim."

Tim noticed the way Rourke tightened his core muscles and lifted his chest a fraction of an inch. The pupils of his eyes grew for that split second long enough for Tim to be on alert. He gave Rourke his most rehearsed smile. "True enough. Seems that Michael wanted a fast start on the barn and brought me in to get things going." As they spoke, he led them inside the barn and motioned to the yellow tape and blue lines. "I plotted out the new stalls and rough marked where the plumbing should be."

Rourke relaxed. "Ma told me that Michael's woman had a way with horses and you worked at the cottage, too. What'd you think of her?"

He gave a slight sputter before he responded. What else had been said? He didn't want to talk about Jessica. He didn't want anyone watching him while he thought about her. "She doesn't have a firm enough hand with them," he said, suppressing the urge to walk in tight circles. Instead, he could feel his back become rigid and the first pulses of rocking begin.

"You were never one to spare the rod. I heard she got great results with the horses you chose for Aintree. Folks at Tully Farm said their stable never's been worth so much. They turned down seven million pounds for that horse she rode and anticipate making a killing on stud fees. Maybe the two of you would make a brilliant team."

Tim could feel his lips involuntarily pull back, baring his teeth like a snarl. He didn't want anyone talking about her. Rourke didn't have the right to talk about her. He tried to remember what Nan had said. People couldn't read his thoughts like he could read theirs. People couldn't see inside his head. Rourke didn't know his secret. Rourke didn't know Tim was going to make her his own. Tim relaxed his lips to form a skewed smile. "My job's with the barn."

Rourke straightened his back and gave a last look around. "Well, it will keep you busy enough. I'd best be going."

"You off now?"

Rourke looked up at the sun, still high. "I've a few hours left before the next shift starts. I'll make note to add your name to the list. You're lucky I'm the one who found you. Otherwise I'm not sure you'd still be standing."

Tim patted Rourke's back, assessing his strength. He would prove to be no contest. "Aye, fair enough. I'll be seeing Michael myself in a bit and will see to the list. No need to worry yourself with it." He embraced his friend, knowing it was for the last time. "*Téigh le Godspeed, mo chara.*"

The bouquet of primrose, bee orchid, and foxglove Jessica and Michael had gathered that afternoon was placed next to the china and crystal recently excavated from the bowels of the attic. She saw a half smile brush across his brow as he traced the stem of a wine glass with his finger. He had requested dinner in the alcove of the master bedroom, and she appreciated the incremental steps he took to bring her into his world. Sitting at the overly long dining room table would have rung hollow and odd, like children wearing their parents' shoes.

Over her favorite broccoli and black olive pizza and Murray's masterful mac-n-cheese, the easy rapport she loved between them surfaced. The wine worked to relax her, and she let herself be beguiled. Being together was easy as long as she didn't let reality interfere. She fingered a silver spoon. "Your family's?" The question was innocent enough.

"My mother's," he answered, a bit more loudly than the close space required. "My father insisted on everything being his decision. She didn't have to try hard to banish him to the States." He tried to make it sound humorous, but neither laughed. They both knew his father made sure his mother never finished putting her mark on her home. The lines on his face deepened. "I'm not like him. I could never do what he did." He tried to be convincing.

She took him by the hand and led him to bed. He started to say more, and she silenced him with her mouth over his, pulling off his clothes and slipping out of hers. She closed her eyes and blocked out everything except the feeling of his hands running over her body. Her only thoughts were of where to kiss him and how hard. They consumed each other with equal hunger, giving as much as they received. Her connection to him was so perfect, as long as she stayed in a bubble.

Her head rested on his chest and she listened to his heartbeat. The pads of her fingertips traced lopsided circles on his skin. He was leaving again and was doing all he could to create a life she could slip into without effort, but with purpose and a future. All she had to do was breathe.

"In exchange for you working on the stables, I promise to take you to see every living person you discover who knew your mother."

If he was holding her with promises and bribes, she wanted the terms clear. "And father," she pressed. "I need to know about Gus, too."

An hour later she lay alone in the enormous bed still warm from their lovemaking and looked around the room she could call home. She could see the last glint of the limousine's taillights as they wound down the drive. Head nesting in a pillow, she let the silence of another Irish night close in around her. She was alone again, and for the first time did not welcome the feeling. As hard as it was for her to admit, a piece of her inner being traveled down the drive, too.

The vise grip around her chest told her, one way or another, their relationship wasn't ever going to be easy. Something organic within her resisted his hold, and then she'd miss him. She stretched and idly looked at the length and silhouette of her arms. As a girl, she would do the exact motion—raising her arms above her head and letting her hands glide through the darkened air. She remembered how her arms had changed along with her body, growing more lithe and strong as she emerged from girl to woman. She would stare at them, committing every freckle and sinew to memory, marveling that they were hers, and tracing their lines up to her heart to make sure.

She let her right hand smooth up her arm, over her shoulder and down her chest, cupping her breast before her fingertips felt that not yet familiar smoothness of skin that she could not deny but refused to acknowledge. In full light, the long scars were still an angry red with edges fading to a shiny white, as if something she had no chance to refuse had branded and claimed her.

She had been tracked and hunted like an animal on that cold mountain, tortured with cold and pain, and brought to the brink of wanting death more than anything. In the age-old and endless game of power and control, she had stared into the barrel of Michael's gun aimed at her head while her captor held a knife to her heart. The decision that took only a fraction of a second, determined what remained of her life. She looked into Michael's eyes and saw he wanted something more for both of them. She had seen that same look in his eyes tonight.

Her mind thrashed with disjointed memories and mismatched fears as the moon slowly arced from one side of the windows to the other. On other nights like this, she would use her insomniac energy as an excuse to pad out to the barn and check the horses. The excursions were a Trojan of productivity. What seemed to be boundless energy in the middle hours of the night always proved to be a sinkhole of exhaustion in the morning.

Tonight she had no Michael to spoon or horses to check. The minutes passed with maddening relentlessness. With nothing to do but toss and turn, she threw off the covers and stood in the middle of the room letting the chill of the night air brace her skin and bring her to seeming alertness. She dressed in yesterday's jeans and fleece and cracked the door open to listen. Hearing only the ticks and groans of a cavernous old home, she headed to the kitchen. At least she could look at more of her mother's pictures.

The air changed as she descended the stairs feeling as if she had plunged too deeply into a lake's cold waters. It felt thick, like the slurry of gelatin immediately before it set, pushing her back up the stairs. She hugged her arms and hunched her shoulders against the growing chill that tingled up her spine and settled into the hollow below her skull. Habit made her movements silent. She reached out and steadied herself on the newel post, quickly recoiling when she thought she felt a light caress down the back of her hand.

Murray left lights on for her nocturnal roaming. The hallway's Tiffany lamp projected her shadow alongside splotches of color from its glassed and leaded shade. The door to Michael's study was slightly ajar showing the green shaded lamp on his desk glowing warmly. The dining room sat silent with bits of silver and glass reflecting the dimmed light on the mahogany sideboard. Everything was familiar from past evenings, except the yellow sliver of light did not shine under the swinging kitchen door. She pressed her ear against it. Silence meant nothing, so she peered through the crack barely more than the width of her finger.

Her eyes adjusted enough to identify each shadow. The door was at the end of the rectangular kitchen and gave a clear view of the length of the room. The kitchen was bathed in the soft blue-blacks and grays of night, flattening everything to two dimensions. Chairs were tucked neatly under the far table by the windows where her mother's papers sat. The pantry door was closed and the long counter was clear of clutter. The glass panes of the cabinet doors reflected the barest of light from a setting moon. The straight lines of the center island held the shadow of a vase of flowers and the breakfast plates Murray always set out for her.

Nothing seemed out of place, so she had trouble assessing the angular shadows at the end of the island. Perhaps the form was a throw rug not remembered. With everything in order, she felt stupid for her caution. Her eyes adjusted more, and she swept them again over the surfaces. Then she recognized the shape as two feet lying askew. Murray.

Panic is irrational even in its pure focus. She wanted to run to his side, to smooth her hand over his brow, and tell him everything would be all right, that she was getting help. Instead, as soundlessly as she could, she pulled away from the door and took two steps back before she turned and ran to the solarium. She hoped Murray would forgive her cowardice.

The seconds it took for her to grab the phone and dial the only number she knew were not enough to sift through what could be with what was. She listened for the connection click through to Michael's cell but heard a sound from within the house instead.

She raised her voice above a whisper. "Murray? Are you okay?"

The only response was a crash and scrambling noises coming closer. She dropped the phone and ran. She pushed through the glass doors with all of her strength, waiting for the wail of the alarm to mix with the screech of the old hinges.

Nothing happened. The door swung open on greased hinges. Alarms did not sound.

Incredulous, she bolted across the lawn toward the gatehouse, hoping that the web of motion detectors would begin their synchronized plotting of her position. The moon had completed its task and set, leaving her in the darkest time of night. She ran to the front of the house, across the drive, and dashed into the cover of the woods and listened.

No warnings sounded. No lights flashed on. A metallic taste she recognized as fear coated her mouth. She had no place to hide until she figured out what was going on.

High-pitched, tingling sounds of metal hitting metal grew louder and mixed with the sounds of snapping branches. Something big was out of breath. Two crashes. Different approaches. Her pursuers were getting closer, not caring if she heard them. Her legs felt featherweight and lightning fast as they propelled her to the gatehouse. Through the trees, she could make out the building. The huge shape loomed in front of her and her heart sank as the darkened windows registered their meaning.

Her legs were still pumping her forward when she tripped over something too soft to be a fallen log. Frantically, she moved her hand along the shape and felt clothes and cooling skin. Even without light, she knew that Rourke's head and body sat at an inhuman angle. She barely had time to get to her feet before she was pushed forward on her face with such force that leaves and twigs packed into her mouth, open for a scream cut short.

She stayed motionless, trying to make sense of what was happening. A dog's snout shoved its way to her face and around her body, its rapid sniffing making the tags on its collar ching in syncopated rhythm. Someone gripped her shirt and pulled her upright. A beam of a flashlight blinded her. Squinting and shielding her eyes with her hands, the clear alert eyes of two wolfhounds watched her every move. Their huge bodies sat to the side, ready for action they were trained to see as a game.

Tim reached around and put his hand over her mouth before she had a chance to move. He steadied his breathing, and his chest pulsed in time with his pounding heart. He brought his mouth down to her ear.

"No sound," was all he said in a whisper that was barely more than the movement of his lips to form the words. He raised the palm of his hand up to his dogs and gave his wrist a flick. The dogs instantly turned and sniffed around Rourke's body and fanned outward. They both stopped at a point about ten yards away, heads raised and tongues out. Tim snapped his fingers, and they followed him as he walked in the opposite direction deeper into the woods, one in front and the other in back.

He kept a grip over Jessica's mouth with one hand, holding her up with his other as her feet tangled on brush. She tried to slow their progress as much as she could by sinking down on his arms, becoming dead weight, but he was much stronger and more determined. He was rough with her, seemingly immune to her stumbles and muffled gasps of shock. A few times the dogs stopped and scanned the woods with their snouts and eyes. Tim mirrored their actions and only started to move again after the dogs had glanced back and received permission to continue. They walked for ten minutes and entered a small clearing. A ribbon of orange began to glow on the horizon. She could feel her blood begin to circulate when he released her. He retrieved something from under a log.

"Tim! What's going on?" She wanted to say more, to ask him what happened to Murray, and to find out if he was all right. What about Rourke? Why wasn't there power for the alarms or the gatehouse? She wanted to say so much more but was only able to draw in a breath when he closed the space between them holding a narrow cylinder in his hands. A pen?

In a practiced move, Tim bent his arm at the elbow and quickly straightened it. She was aware of a bee stinging her thigh before her reality turned sodden and dark.

MANCHESTER, ENGLAND

DALLY'S FINGERS FLEW over the keyboard as her thoughts poured through them. Nothing like a deadline to get the words flowing! She had only one more hour to put the finishing touches on the day's story. The week's series of articles accomplished exactly what she had hoped. Her stories moved up in the paper. Wednesday's story was on page six and Thursday's was on page four—just a smite away from the prime spot in the newspaper world, that lofty region on page one, above the fold. She had almost been there once. She wasn't going to let this chance slip by, and Freddie was going to help put her over the top.

Papers were selling out earlier in the day, prompting larger volume print runs. Pings to the paper's tip lines increased with people convinced they had spotted Wyeth and had proof. For a few hundred pounds, some tipsters offered to produce blurry photographs of couples they emphatically insisted were Wyeth and Connaught. Conspiracy theorists were beginning to weave their tales and post them on the paper's fledgling Web page. The nuts were coming out of the woodwork. Most importantly, reporters from other papers started dogging her trail, hoping to get a grip on another angle to the story and fuel the frenzy. All of that was a sure sign she was doing her job.

The story with Freddie's interview was her bombshell and was the last article she needed Don's go-ahead on. Connecting Connaught and Wyeth to the Arndale bombing was a sure-fire hit. After this story ran, she'd be promoted away from Don and the Magpie shadow. Nothing could stand in her way. She looked over her notes and photos and felt a rush of pride. This was the most important night of her career and soaked in every detail. Fluorescent lights hummed. Air ventilation *whooshed*. She wanted someone to mark the moment with her.

The rows of desks sat deserted at this time of night. She was past the point of fearing someone would scoop her story and looked around the newsroom. Another reporter sat at the far end of the cavernous room. He was so deep into his own story and thoughts that Dally wondered if he even knew she was there. She fancied he would want to remember this night as a witness to the paper's history. He would tell the tale of the conscientious and diligent reporter working until the wee hours to hone her story, all alone and sacrificing everything for the good of the paper. The hell with propriety, she thought. Her big moment was too magnificent not to share.

She sneezed, keeping her head down and cupping her hand to direct the sound over to his corner. He didn't move. She pushed her chair back from her desk, then stretched her arms up, nearly waving her hands over her head. Nothing. She launched her coffee mug off the side of her desk and it fell with a satisfying clatter. Success. He glanced up from his work. She gave him a baleful look and shrug meant to engender his sympathy and chivalry at her working so late alone. He put his head back down and continued typing.

Momentarily thwarted, she returned her attention to her story, biding her time and finishing the last paragraphs. The article was pure genius— parts of it could even be proven as true, and the tale it told was more important and sensational than any recent news.

God dammit. She wanted a witness to her final moments as a nobody. She was no longer going to be the backroom lackey for any newsreader, and her emergence into the world of real journalism was going to happen tonight. She wanted a snog to celebrate. Right there. On the desk. Her legs in the air and his trousers around his ankles.

"What's that you got there?"

She jumped at the voice so close to her. His approach was silent. She swiveled around in her chair, sweeping notes and photos to the floor. "It's history in the making is what it is."

The reporter helped pick up the fallen papers, taking time to read her notes and absorb the photos. He was a head taller than she was and had the rumpled quality about him that said he spent a lot of time indoors sitting down, presumably behind a keyboard. His hair was balding in a Friar Tuck pattern and his thick-lensed, gold-rimmed glasses hooked behind his ears with plastic guards, yellowed from age and scalp oils. A pair of suspenders held up his flannel trousers to a point below his burgeoning gut. His shirt looked liked it had been slept in for a better part of a week, with crumbs from a recent bag of crisps littering his chest. Dirty cuffs flopped open from missing buttons. Central casting could not have come up with a better-looking newsman. He gave her papers back in slow motion, using every spare second he had to read and absorb everything. He looked up at her suddenly as a thought occurred to him.

"You that Dally Thorpe people are buzzing about?"

She could feel the flush of excitement tingle across her. He used her name! He didn't call her Magpie! "Could be yes. Could be n-no. What've you been hearing?" She had to turn her head away knowing that she could not keep the smile from her face.

"Chaps on the tip phones like to line up jars for each story and put pennies in them as the calls come in. They bet on which reporter's going to have the biggest pot at the end of the week and the winner gets the kitty. I heard your stories are filling up faster than anyone's." He paused for a moment, letting the silence be awkward. "I bet on you."

She could keep the flush from her cheeks no longer. "Yes. I'm her," she said, trying to sound modest. She inhaled a bit, arching her back and sticking her small breasts out as far as they could go, barely enough to pull at the buttons of her pink cardigan.

"I heard the advert rates ticked up a point around your stories, too. Could be a real boon for you."

The other measure of a reporter's or a story's success was in how the advertisers reacted. The column inch beside the number one sports story costs more than those beside lesser stories. A strong series would earn the paper bonus revenues, as advertisers out-bid one another for the prime spots in the paper. Her stories were going to net her new admirer a few pounds and the paper a few hundred thousand.

"Derrick." He put out his hand in greeting. His fingers looked like the leftover stubs of chewed cigars, leaving doubt what that meant about the rest of him.

"Dally." She tried to find something pleasant to settle her eyes on as she shook his hand. The fabric around his half-open fly was greasy from frequent checks. The knees of his trousers, baggy and shiny with wear, were the best bet. "What's keeping you here tonight?" She wasn't interested in what he was working on but wanted to fake it until the pleasantries were no longer needed and the snogging could begin.

Derrick looked over to where he was working. "Just got me an assignment about the gypsies killing one of their own in a brawl. Seems that a fourteen-year-old vamped up enough to pass for eighteen and got what she was looking for. Turns out her boyfriend got more than he bargained for when the girl's daddy came looking for him. You know the drill. A few beers, a few more jeers, and a bottle gets broke over someone's head. Only this time the father sliced the boyfriend's throat for good measure."

She nodded with exaggerated sympathy. "I've d-done plenty of those stories. Keep at it. You'll rise up from writing b-bumpers soon enough."

"You're going to be a legend around here." He dragged a chair over from one of the other desks and plopped himself down. "Heard you got exclusives with witnesses, too." He pursed his lips and nodded his head in approval. "Not bad. Lucky break for you the story dropped in your lap the way it did."

The growing bubble of her good mood popped. "It wasn't chucked down in front of me to trip over. I had to dig for what I got!"

"Keep your panties on. You asked me what I heard, right?"

She nodded, increasingly desperate to hide her need.

"Word is that reporter and newspaper in the States just got socked with a huge libel and defamation lawsuit for a story she was working on there. It seems that your Prince Charming is using his deep pockets to squelch the stories before they take root."

"He's not my Prince Charming. He's a feckin' m-mick in a gentleman's clothing. Besides, it would be my luckiest day ever if he came after me with his big bucks. Just filing that lawsuit will be worth page three at the least."

Derrick chuckled. "Blokes on the tip line say Master Connaught has been getting a few proposals for marriage. Seems the ladies like his Hollywood movie star looks and are takin' a shine to him. Doesn't matter to them who his father was. Maybe it would matter to their mothers, but the callers just have eyes for the younger."

"There's no accountin' for taste." She tried to keep the irritation out of her voice.

"Seems, too, that your article is doing his PR work for him. You running the story with these photos?" He pushed a few pictures around until he found what he was looking for. He pulled a picture from the pile of Jessica and Michael, arm-in-arm, walking along the quad at Saint Mark's. The beautifully tended grounds and soaring academic buildings gleamed in the background. Jessica's face was slightly shadowed while the afternoon sun hit Michael's face, showing his expression of pride. It looked like an image from a promotional brochure.

Dally wagged pages of her notes in his face. "It d-doesn't matter what the people see. They'll read my story and end up hating him." She thrust the pages into his hands. "Besides, the picture is proof they're together. It shows him lying to her."

Derrick rounded his eyes and slowly nodded his head to convey how impressed he was at her plotting. "You've got it all figured out. The trap's been sprung and you're ready to gather the spoils. Nicely done." He stood up, placing his hand on the table beside her and leaning over her computer terminal, scanning the screen. "Amazing work. All the pieces fit right together. I'll bet Don's been doggin' your every word."

"He's been giving them a look over. I've been building back his trust in me. He didn't give me a whit of issue with the first couple of articles."

Derrick nodded slowly, clearly impressed. "And you're hoping for his green light for the bomb you want to drop."

"He's as excited about the story as I am. He's been watching my every move."

"Fair enough, but is he watching your every word? I'm amazed he's even kept you on his team. He would have been Managing Editor if it weren't for Magpie."

She bristled. "That's old history. Everyone makes a mistake."

"True, but not one that cost people their jobs and their pensions. Cost the paper a pretty penny to defend itself. Heard they only kept you on to fill Millie's mouth with copy. I'll bet they never do that again."

Dally hunched her back and pulled her sweater tighter over her arms in the sudden chill. "Everyone makes a mistake," she repeated, voice smaller.

"True enough, but you can't afford another one."

"I've got a named source—one who wants to put his name out there. He won't be hanging in the shadows, refusing to be shown like with Magpie. I learned a hard lesson, but the knock was worth it."

"A named source, sure, but folks will fancy he's keen on seeing Jesus' face in the crust of burnt toast. Unless he's the bloody Pope himself, I doubt your story will survive a day. I'd give you odds on even less."

"Bloody hell!" Dally couldn't take the provocation anymore and threw her file down in front of him. "Look at these! It's Wyeth with the cargo containers at the airport! I've got a witness on record who says that Connaught slime surrounded her with bodyguards and I say that move was more to protect anyone from finding out what was really in those boxes than to protect her. Here's the image of the betting slip from Aintree found in the truck with her name on it!" She panted with the effort to contain herself.

"But what proof do you have of what was in that cargo? It's a rich man's right to surround his woman with care. Plus, sayin' a jockey's crooked solely because someone who bet on her is is daft."

Dally jammed her closed hand to her mouth to stifle a sob. "My story's not bollix, damn you."

Derrick looked through the pictures again and gave a low whistle. "Well, so much for what I think. Looks like you're about ready to send your story to the presses. Right after it gets reviewed by Don."

BELFAST, NORTHERN IRELAND

REGGIE BRAGDON STOOD on the corner of Bombay Street and Cupar Way. He hated going to that area of Belfast and only did so when he felt he had no other choice. The deserted street did not give him comfort that he would be unseen. Neither did the odd coat he wore, even with a hat pulled low over his eyes. What was left of the peace line stretched ahead of him, covered in the vile hate slogans of the Catholics, and pockmarked with multiple scars of petrol bombs and live ammunition. No rubber bullets on this side of town. The RUC would shoot to kill any idiot fool enough to step out of line.

He continued his walking and stopped where the towering barrier ended in a twisted and blackened heap. The sheet metal had been pried up at the corner, exposing the support beam. He worked his hand inside and felt up and down the pillar until he found what he was looking for. With a bit of effort, he loosened the metal plate that had the manufacturer's name on it. He huffed once to steam it up and then rubbed it against his leg until the "2100, Ltd." stood out in shining relief against the sooted background. He usually wasn't one for souvenirs, but this one he couldn't resist. He put it in his pocket, flicked the collar of his coat up, and continued on his way.

The peace line was built because of Bragdon. Without his help to navigate through the morass of laws, legislators, and city counselors, Belfast would not have been divided. He was the one who had lined up support and executed a lightning fast strategy that caught the opposition flatfooted. The wall was up before anyone knew what was coming. The weeks of relative calm after its erection proved the wisdom of the wall. The burgeoning balances in his bank account proved that money could make anything happen. His contact at the corporate offices of 2100, Ltd. was more than generous and very discrete. He liked them and worked well with them. Now the wall and defenses had to be rebuilt and his bank balances had to be replenished.

His visit to the bishop came off better than he had hoped. Telling him he could announce that Sinn Fein had its longed for seat at the bargaining table at Sunday's service rattled him. The bishop was no fool, and no amount of spin would lessen the connection between the Arndale bombing and getting Sinn Fein what they wanted. The talks labeled "All Party" were nothing of the sort, and the Arndale bombing solidified the Prime Minister's stance on denying the hooligans from equal's seat at the bargaining table. What the bishop did not know was that the investigation was stalled again and the announcement was intended to do just what the bishop feared—embolden and ignite the passion for more power gained from the use of a bomb.

Bragdon was more than happy to comply with a request that came from the top of his government. The Prime Minister was quite clear in his plan to have a defined starting point for the announcement. The MI5 would be positioned to track the communications of a targeted few. With the proof that violence worked, the weakness in their human morality would motivate them to do more. They would make a mistake. Networks would be exposed. Inevitably, another bombing would take place, and any proposed talks would be cancelled. The invitation was not to the talks but an open door to prison.

He loved watching people squirm, and in the moments of their greatest discomfort he could ascertain their deepest secrets. Bragdon expected Bishop Hughes to postpone the announcement on the grounds the bombing would look like a successful strategy. But, rather than unsettling the smooth and unflappable bishop with that news, he found instead that the bishop was already agitated. He tried to cover it well enough, but the Bishop was distracted.

Their small talk hit on the usual banal fodder of local football clubs and weather. But something was different with the bishop. He was not focused. While they had talked, Bragdon looked around the room to see what his friend may have been doing that distracted him so much. The answer was in a neatly stacked pile of newspapers folded in such a way that there could be no mistaking the bishop's interest. Why was he taking such an interest in a series of articles on that pitiful American girl? Bragdon would have paid no attention to one newspaper opened to that story, but having three papers perfectly folded was too delicious not to poke around further.

What he learned from the articles was purely academic but could be the hook he needed into Bishop Hughes. He'd been trying for years to find something—*anything*—on him and was never successful. Bragdon had no idea why the American girl meant anything, so after leaving the bishop's flat, he dug out his issues from the rubbish bin. The only connection he could see was that the older trainer, Mr. Gilchrist Adams, was a boyhood friend of the bishop. Bragdon still remembered how shaken

Bishop Hughes had been at Adams' death eight years back, and the masses he said for his chum of long ago.

Masses were often offered for the dead, but the Bishop's sorrow was clearly more pointed. Bragdon learned that none other than Magnus Connaught had killed Adams and that the American was sleeping with Connaught's son. Exactly the kind of muddy facts the British tabloids could make into a reeking dung heap without a lot of effort. No doubt the articles were gearing up to target the younger Connaught in a larger filthy scandal. This trajectory was all very amusing, and he wondered what additional shite was going to be thrown.

He fingered the badge of metal in his pocket and smiled. He could make life excruciatingly uncomfortable for the son. The elder Connaught was a wolf in sheep's clothing, and Bragdon hated Magnus without ever having met him. The slippery operator seemed to have something to do with illegal arms or funding operations but always managed to keep his hands clean and remain above the fray.

Bragdon's compatriots at the Security Branch of the Ministry of Home Affairs knew the elder Connaught's activities threatened their tiny country's security and integrity but were never able to pin anything on him. They knew better than to go on rumor and innuendo when building a case. Once an accusation was made, they damned well better have the goods to back it up or face being buried in an avalanche of investigative hearings, due diligence audits and lawsuits. Bragdon tried many times to connect Magnus to terrorists but offshore accounts, European holding companies, and the damn secrecy around the banking policies of the Swiss routinely thwarted his efforts.

The closest he got was discovering that the guns, munitions, and other weaponry used in the conflict were sourced through the same holding company as the metal detectors, airport security devices of all variations, and other protective gear—including the peace line. The selling of the guns did not constitute the crime. The use of them did. Nothing tainted the transactions, and the money flowed. The only sure winners in war were the suppliers. And, the politicians.

It frustrated Bragdon that nothing ever tainted the bishop. Digging around the Adams murder and the goings on of that American girl could yield some information. If nothing else, maybe he could bully the younger son into making a sizeable donation into his upcoming election fund.

Satisfied, Bragdon pulled up his collar and strode down the street.

SOMEWHERE IN
NORTHERN IRELAND

THE ONLY SIGNALS that told Jessica she was conscious again were the discrete chaffing pain in her wrists and ankles and the roiling nausea in her stomach. Being curled into a ball made the pressure in her gut worse. The air was hot and fetid. Pervasive numbness infected her hands and feet, making them sluggish to her command. A wave of black wool enveloped over her and she could feel herself fight against its pull. She tried to wake up, tried to move, but her body had not cleared the tranquilizer from her bloodstream. Everything inside and around her buzzed and swayed. The contents of her stomach inched upward, threatening her to panic, but stayed at a distance. She took deep, steadying breaths and willed herself not to puke. Even muddled through the cloud of drugs, she knew she was blindfolded and gagged. Vomiting would choke her to death.

The bands of cloth around her eyes and mouth did not loosen when she scrunched and contorted her face. She was only successful enough to see darkness surrounded her. As more consciousness crept in, she figured out her hands were not tied to her feet, as she had first thought, but that she was jammed into a box. She needed a few more minutes to realize that the box was vibrating and swaying, not her.

The vibration of pressurized air released from a diesel engine jake-braking rattled her skull against the wooden sides. She swayed as the truck slowed and turned off a smooth road onto a rutted secondary road. The driver must have been in a hurry because he made no effort to ease the huge rig over the bumpy surface. If she weren't wedged inside the crate, she would have been tossed and thrown against its sides.

Her breathing was too fast. Her heart was beating too quickly. She instinctively knew that she was using up precious oxygen and tried again to calm herself. Inhale ten seconds. Exhale twenty. Inhale ten. Exhale twenty. The minutes dragged on and oxygen became scarce. Outside sounds no longer registered as her world shrank down to a three-by-four foot space.

Her knees, compressed against her chest, throbbed against the wooden sides. The air should have run out. She felt she was living on borrowed time. Her focus flagged for that split second too long, and the hold she had on her gut finally released. The burning acid crept up her throat, and she sputtered and gagged, unable to stop her convulsing.

The top of the crate flew open, and someone grabbed her by the scruff of her neck and waist, hoisting her over the side. Someone ripped the gag from her mouth, and she heaved and gasped for air, spitting and choking uncontrollably. The firm grip forced her head over a bucket, causing her cheek to strike against its metal sides. It should have hurt, but her face felt thick and distant. Finally, her stomach emptied and longed-for breaths of air cleared the last of the wool from her head. She needed to get her bearings. A gap formed at her cheeks and the bridge of her nose where the blindfold did not reach. She tilted her head back enough to see slits of light when she was yanked clear of the box and her blindfold removed.

A man about her age stood in front of her. He was tall, well over six feet with a calculated manner of moving that made his actions deliberate and efficient. He had long red hair pulled back into a stringy ponytail. Dirty blue jeans and a sweatshirt that proclaimed him a fan of the Lisburn Distillery Football Association looked huge on his lanky frame. His work boots were caked with dust and grease, with laces untied as worn by simple workmen. Something about the way he assessed Jessica told her he was anything but. He shoved his sleeves up to his elbows and watched her expression as his tattoo of a shamrock sliced by a dagger registered.

If they wanted her dead, they would have had more than enough opportunity. She shrank away from him and waited, slowly working her wrists to stretch and loosen the silver duct tape that bound them, trying for one little rip, enough to let her tear free. She contracted and relaxed her muscles slowly to regain circulation. Her head was clearing, but her body was still sluggish to react. The barrels and scopes of at least two guns rested within easy reach of the man, but she was too uncoordinated to try for them. She took in all the details she could and bided her time.

The man gave an odd snort. "Don't go getting your hopes up that you'll be moving quickly any time soon. Xylazine will keep you from hurting yourself for quite a while." He pointed at her bleeding cheek and laughed. "Bet you don't e'en feel that, eh?"

He was right. Everything was in the distance. Xylazine was a powerful tranquilizer capable of felling a stallion mid-rut and often used to calm animals for transportation. Its aftereffects include lack of muscle control and numbing. Her arms felt like logs when she tried to move them. She nodded toward her bound hands. "Then what's all this?" Her mouth was feeling too thick and funny to form the words correctly and tasted of acidic bile.

"We heard you was a feisty one. Just some insurance in case you woke up too early."

She was in the back of a tractor-trailer. Its large cargo area was filled with wooden crates the same size and shape as the one she was transported in. Rows of crates were stacked to the ceiling of the truck, and her crate was in a hollow, blocked from discovery from the door. As her eyes adjusted to the light, another wave of nausea roiled upward as she read the crates' logos.

Many were of companies she had never heard of, but others were very familiar. Ariat, Dover Saddlery, Crown Bridlework, Equistar were all names she knew as high-end equestrian suppliers. Others had Tully Farm and its running horse logo. She was surprised to see pallets of cases of baby formula and diapers mixed in, recognizing the names. Logos of charities and relief organizations—Red Cross, Oxfam, Global Families, Christian Relief—were mixed in. She was intimately familiar with those that had "MMC" stenciled on them. But something was off. If the boxes were full of baby items or gear for horses and riders, why didn't she smell baby powder or leather? Instead, she could identify only the oily smell of polished metal and something reminiscent of fireworks.

He slung one rifle over his shoulder and carried the other cradled in his arm as he wedged his body through a gap toward the back of the truck. With one leg he kicked open the doors and hopped down, taking time to carefully scan the area. He climbed back up, ripped the tape from her ankles, and shoved her forward, nearly throwing her on the ground. She tried to scramble to her feet, but her legs were rubbery. She wobbled until she sank down to one knee. They were in the middle of emptied and battered warehouses with rusted roofs and broken windows. Weeds grew up out of the pavement. Sounds of a highway and a door clanging against the metal structures echoed in the wind. The huge rig was pulled beside a road that was incredibly wide, enough for a six-lane highway.

He grabbed under her arm and nearly dragged her into the closest building. Instead of entering a cavernous space, they walked down a series of cramped walkways flanked by rows of towering pallets of scrap metal alternating with walls of cargo containers. At times he pushed her ahead through a broad aisle and other times he grabbed her arm as they shimmied through a narrow canyon. In the center of the maze was a trailer of the type used as a temporary office space at construction sites. He unlocked the padlocked door and entered.

The inside was exactly what she expected. Plastic wood paneling, gritty plywood floors, green metal desk. A thick wire mesh covered the windows. Her chest tightened when she saw a mattress in the corner with shipping blankets piled on top. The gap between her emotions and her reactions was closing as movement helped to clear her head. She didn't need a lot of lucidity to understand she was trapped.

"Who are you?" Her voice was flat. She didn't know whether that was from the drug or simply not caring anymore.

She felt eyes assessing her and glared back.

"Folks here call me Paddy." He swooped his free arm to his waist and nodded his head in a pantomime of a regal bow.

She held up her hands. "Cut this off."

He shoved her to the middle of the room, making sure his body was between her and the door. From his back pocket he withdrew a long knife that looked exactly like the dagger she had found in Tim's truck. She couldn't take her eyes off it as he sliced the tape and ripped it from arms. She rubbed her wrists and worked her hands as the feeling returned.

At the sound of a footstep outside of the trailer, Paddy dropped to one knee, brought the riflescope up to his eye, and aimed at the door all in one fluid motion. Three quick knocks, then two and the door burst open.

"Jay-sus Paddy! Put that thing away." Tim put up one hand as if that would be enough to stop a bullet.

"Tik! You're supposed to stay at the rig."

The dogs bounded into the room, eyes bright with the anticipation of another adventure. Tim snapped his fingers, and they sat in unison, watching his every move. He looked at Jessica and walked over to Paddy, seething. "What happened?"

"Keep your knickers on. She puked and hit her face. I did nothing."

"I told you to keep an eye on 'er for that. You need to keep her walking for a while yet. Give 'er some water."

"Christ, man. She's not one of the animals you transport. Look at her." Paddy flicked his head in Jessica's direction. "She's fine."

Tim walked over to the tiny kitchen and grabbed a bottle of water from the cabinet. He broke the seal and handed it her. When she hesitated, he took her hand and shoved it into her palm. "Drink."

She took a sip, concentrating on how to fit the bottle to her lips and not dribble the water down her chin. Her lips felt puffy and fat. She wiped them with the back of her hand. "Tim, what's going on?"

Paddy snorted. "So much for her being clever. Doesn't have a clue, does she?"

Tim motioned with his head for her to drink more. He checked his watch as he observed her carefully for a few moments as she took a series of sips, then turned to Paddy. "I've not said anything. Nor has Nan."

Paddy reached over and pulled back the collar of her shirt. Only a pink and yellow circle remained of the bruise. "Jay-sus! I'm a great shot. Look at that, Tik. Perfect! Drove like a bat out of hell after we positioned the truck but made it to Aintree with enough time to get to my perch. Had her in my scopes for half the race and had less than a second to pull that shot off. Good thing your boyfriend was thinking ahead, eh?"

Her thinking was still sluggish. What was Paddy saying? She wanted to ask more, but Tim became agitated.

"*Níl muid chun labhairt os comhair a.*" 'We're not to talk in front of her.'

"*Ifreann Fola, a deir tú. Beidh mé a rá cad ba mhaith liom.*" 'Bloody hell, you say. I'll say what I want.'

"*An plean a bhí a chur léi anseo agus go raibh tú ag dul a fhágáil.*" 'The plan was to stash her here, and you were going to leave.'

"*Bhí ceaptha againn a cheilt a corp anseo, gan a bheith buartha faoi di reáchtáil ar shiúl.*" 'We were supposed to hide her body here, not to worry about her running away.'

"*Ansin, ba chóir duit a bheith dírithe le haghaidh a cheann nuair a bhí an deis agat. Tá sí anseo. Is é seo a cinniúint.*" 'Then you should have aimed for her head when you had the chance. She's here. This is her fate.'

"*Fuck tú.*"

"*Is é seo an méid atá againn a dhéanamh. Tá tú ag dul anois. Ní féidir leat athrú ar an bplean.*" 'This is what we have to do. You have to go now. You can't change the plan.' Tim's feet began that odd tapping and his upper body pulsed in quick, small motions.

Paddy scowled. "Whatever you do, don't leave any trace of her behind. The cleaning crew in Belfast have their hands full as it is." He gave the room one last check before he left. Jessica and Tim stood motionless until the last of his footsteps faded and the door slammed shut.

Tim looked her over. "The nausea will fade in an hour, and you'll feel more like moving after a couple more. Nothing for you to do but to sit and wait." He motioned to the dirty mattress and blankets.

"What the hell, Tim?" Jessica took an unsteady step toward the desk and nearly fell into the chair. A dull throb started at her temples. She reached for the plastic waste can and puked again, using the time to think. Paddy was a stranger and made her nervous, but Tim she knew. Michael trusted him. Wait. No he didn't. She grabbed her head and rested her elbows on the grimy desk.

He checked his watch again and his steps became more urgent. The dogs, huge in the tiny space, shuffled their bodies to the side to make room for his pacing. His movements took on a rhythm. Pace. Pace. Pace. Turn. Check watch. Pace. Pace. Pace. Turn. Check watch.

A low rumble shook the building then faded. Tim stopped and stared at his watch. A few minutes later the rumble started again, grew louder then faded. The high-pitched screech of a jake-brake joined the vibration of a diesel engine, then faded. It grew quiet again.

The dogs and Tim noticeably relaxed. Feeling unobserved, he sank to the floor with his back to the wall. The rocking continued. "Now, we wait. We wait. We wait."

GENEVA, SWITZERLAND

MICHAEL WALKED BRISKLY through the gleaming corridor of Terminal 3 at the *Aéroport International de Genève*, or the GVA as the pilots liked to call it. He tugged at his starched white cuffs and worked his shoulders further into his suit jacket. He had one last meeting before his departure, and it had to be in the private lounge. The terminal wasn't an ideal meeting place. He hated it actually. But time was of the essence and left him no alternative.

Walking past the perfectly tailored and gracious concierges, offering flutes of champagne for hospitality at what seemed to be every twenty feet, he felt out of place—and watched. His head was crammed with new information and a nagging self-loathing. He should have figured this out before, but with answers came action.

He had no time to plan. He was desperate to get back to Northern Ireland. The answering service radioed just before he landed at GVA that someone had used the landline at his home to call his cell. When the service answered the call, no one was on the line. The line remained open, most likely from a dropped phone, prohibiting anyone from calling the house back.

Attempts to reach the security detail at Ballyronan failed, and another group of men was sent from Antrim to check on his estate. Precious minutes turned to hours as they recovered the bodies of the two guards. Murray was gravely injured but would survive. Questioning the disoriented butler yielded no clues to what happened or who could have been behind the attack. Two things stood out as abundantly clear. It was an inside job. Jessica was gone.

He moved up his departure by hours, catching the ground crew off guard and leaving them scrambling to service the jet and get it ready for departure. If Michael had his way, he would have already charted another flight in a desperate attempt to feel like he was taking the initiative. A brief moment of reflection was enough for common sense to kick in. Charters ask questions. Most could not land at his airstrip without checking its craft size certification. Another risk was he could charter a craft that forced him to land closer to Belfast. What time he lost readying his jet for departure from Geneva, he more than gained on the other end by being closer to Antrim and, he hoped, Jessica.

He tried to keep his exterior smooth as he spoke with Jean-Paul Cousette, a meticulously groomed older gentleman with salt and pepper hair and a weathered complexion. The pale skin of Jean-Paul's upper face and hands gave him away as a skier whose eyes were always covered with goggles and hands always in gloves. Indeed, Jean-Paul's polite banter inevitably turned to the beautiful mountain air of *Bellevaux-Hirmentaz* and the skiing that the locals enjoyed even as summer approached. Meeting the son of Magnus Connaught on a moment's notice at the GVA instead of in the Geneva offices of his bank was the least he could do for a young man who was coming to grips with the wealth that was now his.

"Please accept our deepest condolences on the passing of your father. If I do say, you bear more than a passing resemblance to him." Jean-Paul's face was the image of sympathy.

"Thank you. As it often is between fathers and sons, we had not spoken much in recent years. His sudden death meant he was not able to bring me into the details of his affairs. Thank you for assisting with putting together the documentation on such short notice."

Jean-Paul waved off Michael's concerns. "Not at all, *Monsieur* Connaught. Your father was a brilliant man. I was always in awe of his encyclopedic knowledge of his dealings. You and he are of the same cloth but different, nonetheless."

"Oh?"

"*Oui.* You have the quick grasp of the larger picture and can see where the details fit it, as he did. But you are different because you want to work with one person on all of your dealings. You Americans, you say you like to 'centralize' and 'streamline' your operations. No?" He paused just long enough to get a noncommittal nod. "With him, he was satisfied with a handshake here and a handshake there. No one person knew the whole picture, but we all, um, how you say, we all understood that he was not a man who would take a misunderstanding lightly."

Michael let his eyes narrow slightly as the implication of Jean-Paul's words registered. He forced himself to sit back in his chair and smile, teeth showing. "You're right. In that regard, we are of the same cloth."

The banker adjusted his tie. "Very well, then. I have reviewed the documents you have provided from your father's estate, and they are all in order. I've had prepared for you the account title transfers. At the request of your attorney here in Geneva, I have included the transfer of ownership documents of your father's corporations to you."

"The transfers happen immediately upon signing?"

"*Oui.* All of this takes precedence over the Powers of Attorney put in place by *Monsieur* Liam Connaught."

"You'll communicate immediately with all account holders that no more transfers or requests for information can occur unless expressly permitted and authorized by me."

"I have the notifications ready. All parties will be updated within minutes. I will personally speak to *Monsieur* Liam."

"No. I'll take care of that."

Jean-Paul cleared his throat behind a closed fist and gave a crisp nod. He placed a set of papers on the table, signature lines marked with color-coded tabs. In an unhurried motion, with a slight bit of ceremony, he produced a gold fountain pen and handed it to Michael, using his finger-tips to lightly grip each end of the pen.

As Michael quickly scanned and signed the papers, Jean-Paul looked out at the jet with "MMC" on the tail, taxiing to the jetway.

"I always thought your father was very clever to have the two sides of his business reference one another without being commingled or entangled in any way. Using numerals for his other holding companies was a clear demarcation of the subsidiaries. Your initials are the same as your father's. If I'm not being too bold to ask, will you continue to do the same?"

Michael took an extra moment to review the papers emblazoned with the "2100" letterhead. He finished signing all the papers, clicked the top of the Mont Blanc back on, and waited until Jean-Paul nodded in satisfaction that the transfer was complete and sealed before he answered.

"If my father was not already dead, I would kill him for what he has done."

Northern Ireland

TIM FINALLY LEFT Jessica alone, taking great care to padlock the door behind him. He had spent hours on the floor, arms slung around the necks of his dogs, just staring at her. She finally told him she needed to sleep and wanted him to leave. As soon as her body was able to obey her commands without hesitation, she ran her hand over every square inch of the trailer. No ceiling tile was unexamined. No window was untested. The desk was empty of anything remotely useful and only held an odd assortment of paperclips and pens, which she shoved into her pocket.

The kitchen yielded nothing more than plastic bottles of water and food in cellophane packages. No utensils of any sort were in any of the drawers or cabinets. The tiny bathroom didn't even have a shower rod she could wiggle out of place. Placing herself in time or geography was impossible. No natural light found its way through the maze of walls and stockpiled goods. The only sounds were deep vibrations of heavy eighteen-wheelers that periodically rattled the windows.

Other sounds were more high-pitched, oddly familiar, but not identifiable. She had no idea how long she was unconscious or how far she had traveled in the back of the rig. She had a faint memory of traffic on a highway but wasn't sure if that was part of her semi-conscious memory or if a busy road was close by. She was a prisoner and acutely aware that even if she did escape, she had no clue where to go after that.

High-pitched jingles of the dogs' collars announced Tim's return. The sounds of keys and the sharp pull of the padlock followed. The dogs rushed in ahead of him. They sniffed all along the floor and through the pile of blankets before they came to rest at his feet, sitting with such readiness that their butts almost hovered midair. Tim didn't have to lean forward to reach their heads as he gave them a pat. He wore the simple clothes he always did. Jeans, a cotton shirt, simple belt. His hair was uncombed. He was present with his body but completely absent with his mind.

If he was following a rehearsed plan, she grappled with how to disrupt him. His communication with the dogs was unparalleled. She felt the hours of observation yesterday were an extension of his ability to understand the language of animals and his inability to understand the complexity of people. What had Michael said about him? He was gullible and trusting until he was slighted. He had an unpredictable quality that was unnerving.

He may have been unpredictable, but he was also new at holding people captive. She noticed he did not lock the door after he entered and hung the opened padlock on the door latch. She leaned against the desk, angling her body closer to the door. One of the dogs whined for attention, and the sound roused him to the present.

"You're good with animals, Tim. Look at how they relate to you."

He scratched each under their chins. "They're good pups. They're good pups, they are. Wolfhounds don't have a mean bone in their bodies. They do what's asked of them for a biscuit and a rub, nothing more. You can't get better than that. No sir, not at all."

"Horses, too."

Tim's eyes flickered up to her face and quickly away when he saw she was looking at him. "Good. Not great. They respond to you, though. I show them who's boss. They don't like that."

"Why am I here, Tim? What's going on?"

He was calm today. His feet were planted and hands steady. "You're here for me. Because I want you here."

"That doesn't make any sense. Michael's going to be worried sick about me. You need to take me back to your friend."

His upper body stiffened and threatened to begin its rocking. "Michael doesn't care."

She backed off, sensing that mentioning Michael threatened to shut down this conversation and agitate him. "Well, I do care. I don't like it here, and I want to go home."

"What's home for you?"

The question took her by surprise. She hadn't a clue how to answer him and was surprised how that truth stung. She could only manage a weak, "Not here."

"It is, you know. It's here. The child of *Gean Cánach* cannot live anywhere else."

Jessica tried to make sense of what he said. Had she spoken to him about this? She tried to dodge. "I don't know anyone with that name."

"Liar!" He shouted the word with such force that she took a step backward. "*Cuireadh fucked Do mháthair ag spiorad*" 'Your mother was fucked by a spirit.'

"What are you saying?"

Tim shifted his weight from foot to foot. "I read your mother's papers. She was seduced by *Gean Cánach*."

"You had no right to even go anywhere near my things, and you had no right to read her papers." She wanted to keep calm, to get him talking, and catch him off guard, but the cold fury of being spied upon eclipsed everything.

"No, no, no right. *You* have no right." He put his arms on the windowsill in a conscious effort not to rock. He concentrated on his words. "You have no right *not* to know who your parents are. He knows. He didn't tell you."

"What are you talking about? Of course Michael knows. My mother was Bridget Heinchon. My father was Gus Adams."

"No. No! Not Michael! You're protecting him. Why do you want to protect him, he's done nothing for you. He's followed you around, crept around you, spied on you, and still you protect him."

"Tim?" Jessica watched his increasing agitation with fear. Was he making sense? She hoped a softer tone would calm him. "Michael has helped me find information on my mother. He's not lying to me. He's told me hard truths about her life. She was sent to prison as bait and I . . . I was born there." The conversation she overheard between Michael and Murray echoed in her ears, and she wanted to cry out and scream in denial but couldn't find her voice.

"Your father was not Gus Adams."

"You don't know what you're saying, Tim."

"I do. I do. I read them. I read your mother's journals. I saw what she said. You couldn't read her words. You didn't understand what *Gach mo ghrá go deo* means."

"It means she loved someone and someone loved her."

"And you don't know that your mother was the most hated person in Britain. They hated her because she was like me. And like you."

"What are you talking about?" Thoughts spun around her head and her heart beat somewhere near her ears. Tim was insane. It was impossible for him to know what he was saying. "You're crazy if you believe she was hated. My mother lived a simple life. She helped her friends and others and taught a few how to read. I've done nothing . . ." Her eyes grew hot with tears. Blinking them back, she continued, "I've done nothing but want to learn about her. Her journals say nothing like that." The ground beneath her feet shivered as if threatening to quake open.

The dogs stood up, looking at Tim, wanting a part of the excitement. He commanded them to lie down in the corner with a wave of his open hand pushed downward. They curled up in a corner, well away from his frantic pacing.

"There's more than what was in the journals. Your mother was Mrs. Harvey. Your uncles were Daniel and Patrick Heinchon. She was the leader of the civil rights movement and her brothers were loved for their courage. You have to know this. It's wrong you don't know this."

Tim paced over to her, standing too close in his disjointed manner he had. She could feel how hot his body had become with agitation. A slight sheen of sweat covered his neck and the upper part of his chest. One rivulet rolled down his smooth skin. She tried to focus on anything but what he was saying. The bone of emotion stuck in her throat, making her voice nothing more than a croak. "My mother was Bridget Heinchon. My father was Gus Adams. Please don't do this to me."

"Nan said. Nan said."

"What about Nan?" She spat the words, not intending them as a question but a mark of dismissal.

"Nan said if I told you the truth then you would like me." His eyes had a way of sweeping over her body, no longer as if assessing livestock but keenly aware of her.

There it was again. That shift in the air that says a corner was about to be turned. She angled her body closer to the door, fearing the turn was inevitable, bringing into focus where the door was, where the dogs were. "Nan doesn't care about me, Tim. I'm a job to her. She wants you to do something to me that will hurt me."

"She said I should tell you about your mother and father. She figured it out, you know. I helped her by translating the journals. We figured out who your father is. She said if I told you then you would let me hold you the way Michael does." He put his arms around her and pulled her to him, pinning her arms at her side.

"Stop it, Tim. Nan wants to make a fool of you, and she wants to hurt me. Please don't do this." She craned her neck to the side, avoiding his face, not wanting to see the expression in his eyes. "My father is dead. I watched him die."

He pushed his head down, his mouth searching for hers. His hands gripped her butt, smashing his hips into hers. She tried to push against him, but couldn't wriggle enough room. Her fingertips barely brushed the top of the desk, feeling, hoping to find anything she could use. His arms locked hers at her side while he pulled her closer, making it clear he was stronger. Making it clear this was going to go his way, not hers. Showing her his need. He lifted her up so her breasts were within reach of his mouth. She could feel his stubble scratch against her neck and chest.

"Tim. STOP IT! NO!" Jessica could not keep the beseeching tone out of her voice.

Suddenly, the dogs jumped into the fray, tails wagging, tongues out. Up on their hind legs they were taller than Tim and able to lap and lick at his face. To them Tim's attack was great fun, and they wanted to get in the middle of them. He let her go, and she dropped to the floor, gasping and shaking at what almost was and most certainly would be if she didn't get out of there.

He commanded the dogs to sit and looked back at her as if nothing had happened. He didn't do any of the pleading and crying that he had done at the truck that day. He had rehearsed this, but her begging was part of the scene in his head. Somehow, he had run through this event in his head again and again until he wouldn't crumble. He hadn't figured on the dogs. He looked at them and gave them an idle pat on their heads.

"I have to tell you first. Then you'll have me."

She knew the next time Tim came at her, he would not let the dogs stop him. Her breath came in shaky gasps. "S-so, what does Nan want me to know?"

"Nan figured out who your father is when you got that box. She read the lot when you were riding. She had me read the Irish parts."

"Murray would have told me."

"Nan gave me the papers she couldn't read. She gave me the hidden ones she found that had our language in them. She told me to hold on to them. She said we had a secret and that we had to be smart in how we used it. She said I should use it to get you to like me."

Jessica thought about the books she had stashed in the crawlspace before she had a chance to thoroughly understand what was in them. She never would have known if papers or a whole book had gone missing. "Those were my private papers, Tim. Nan was wrong to encourage you to read them. If there is a secret, then it's my secret to hold. Not yours."

"Murray suspected the truth. He was waiting to find proof before he said anything."

"Did you kill Murray, Tim?"

Tim looked away, puzzled by the question. "I hit him. I found him in the kitchen. He didn't want me to touch the journals. He didn't want me in the house. But he knew that Gus held the secret, too."

Her heart froze. She wanted the truth.

Why was fate so intent on playing another twisted game with her life? The earth threatened to swallow her whole, and she wanted to kick open the fault line and sink through until the heat and pressure of the earth finally erased her. What was the point of resisting? The tenets of her life would inevitably fall despite her efforts to keep them standing. A mere trip of her feet would send them all cascading in their pre-ordained directions. Mustering another fight against fate required strength she feared she did not have.

When the walls of her soul weakened to the point of collapse, a cool breeze floated through the closed windows. The dogs stopped their panting, ears snapped forward and heads cocked. Tim stopped his rock-ing and looked at them and back to Jessica. She didn't have time to process what was going on, only that something was different. She became detached, thoughts floating somewhere above her body, angles of the room skewed and out of true. She gripped the top of the desk, buttressing herself against the coming shockwave.

She heard herself ask in a small voice, "It could only be Gus, right?"

He did not answer, but stared at her, mouth open, for too long. His eyes followed a path around her as if they were following her shadow, connected to her but not. Then he shook his head quickly, made the sign of the cross, and blinked his eyes. The dogs settled back down.

"No. Not Gus. His name is Kavan Hughes."

"Kavan Hughes?" She repeated the name, racking her brain for where she had heard it before. If she had ever read it in Bridget's journals, she would have remembered it. Then she recalled the conversation she over-heard between Murray and Michael and the promise Michael made her make. "The Bishop?" Her muscles went lax with disbelief. She balanced herself against the desk.

Tim nodded, excited to be telling Jessica her secret. "Yes. Yes. Yes. After the box came. Nan doesn't like not knowing what goes on in her house." This time his rocking had more of a boy's excitement rather than agitation.

She thought of her birth certificate, with the frayed bottom edge, that listed Gus' and not Margaret's name as 'Next of Kin.' "There's no proof," she said.

Tim was almost gleeful. "The journals said so. Nan had me translate."

Jessica bristled. "The journals said no such thing. Even if it was true, my mother would never commit that truth to writing."

"Nan is very clever. She's very smart. Bridget and Gus and Kavan had secrets, but Nan guessed that the Bishop must have figured out where you were through the churches you attended so the box knew how to find you. No matter where you lived, you went to church. The parishioners would talk about you. So, Nan tricked Father Archdall into telling her about who asked of you. What was the harm to inquire about a new face?"

Could what Tim said possibly be true? She thought of St. Paul's in Hamilton, the beautiful stucco chapel at Saddle String and Father Steeves in Kentucky. Whether they were priests or reverends didn't matter. They were part of a brotherhood and were more than happy to keep one of their own informed. Did they truly have eyes out for her all of this time? And what was the peculiar way Father Archdall spoke to her? This wasn't a network created solely for her. Countless others must use this under-ground message train. How perfect could it be?

"If it's true, then he wanted to know where I was to protect me."

"No. No. No. He wanted to see if you were a problem, that's what Nan said. Nan said the Bishop wanted to know if you were close enough to harm him by telling anyone he had a child. So we're the ones who have to protect him. That's what Paddy wants. Paddy says you never should've been born, so we should take care of that mistake. But he missed, so Nan said that was because you were supposed to be mine. So now you know."

She heard nothing after 'never should've been born.' An image of a woman accused of being a witch and condemned to death by slowly being crushed by rocks came to her. Each word he spoke was another rock, crushing the breath from her lungs and giving her heart no room to beat. Its pulse was already constricted, encased in scar tissue stiffened from wounds of rejection, disrespect, and deceit. Tim's rant was too much for her to take in. And worse, Tim was waiting for her response, waiting for her to react. This was his act of claiming her, the moment rehearsed again and again until every action was perfect.

"I don't believe you."

The incessant rocking stopped. His eyes unfocused showing that his mental gears were spinning, but not engaging. He had not planned on this. She kept one hand on the top of the desk and used the other to crack open the long, narrow drawer.

She pressed. "Bridget never would have written that. Think about her journals. She never named anyone, even her brothers. *Gean Cánach* could have been anyone, but it was Gus. Gus' real name is Gilchrist. GC. Nan lied to Paddy so he would kill me. Nan lied to you to manipulate you, and now you're lying to me."

Tim remained frozen. One dog raised its head, ears back and gave a whimper as the sea change of Tim's temperament registered.

She felt for anything and grabbed the only things she could find—a pen and some paper clips—and gripped them tightly, slowly inching her body closer to the door.

"Nan laughed at you the same way Michael's brother did. Liam would lie just to watch you fight his battles. Nan doesn't like me. She's using you to hurt me."

He glazed over, but his breathing started to become more rapid. His face slowly reddened.

Her words were having an effect. "Michael never hurt you, Tim. He never lied to you. He put you in a position of trust to watch over me. Nan wants to destroy that trust. You're nothing to her. Michael kept you away from me because of what Nan told you to do. He's your friend, Tim. Don't do this to your friend."

Tim's face turned a deep scarlet. She doubted he could hear anything more she said.

In one motion she threw herself against the door, hitting her elbow against the latch and missing the padlock completely. She fell through, tumbling off the wooden stairs in a greater drop than she expected. The miscalculation cost her a precious second. Only Tim's surprise and lack of a plan kept her from being grabbed. She scrambled back up, shoved her shoulder against the door, and slapped the metal hasp over the narrow metal loop. Her hands shook as she snapped the pen in half and pushed both halves through where the lock would hang. It took her barely seconds to secure it, but it had to be enough to hold—at least until she could get a head start.

A bellow joined a high-pitched bark. Something huge crashed inside. The trailer shuddered. She ran through the dark maze.

The first aisle she chose ended suddenly. Crates and boxes haphazardly piled on top of one another without regard to balance and stacks of sheet metal leaned at precarious angles. If she stayed on the ground, the dogs would easily follow her scent. She looked up at the ceiling, studying the pitch of the roof and trying to figure out which way to run. Some aisles were broad enough for a forklift to maneuver easily. Others only narrow enough for a body to squeeze through sideways. She pushed the crates and they swayed with the pressure. She decided she had to risk it.

Bracing one foot on each side, she inched her way up. Once on top, she paused long enough to hear the continued bellows and jumped over as many aisles as she could, always working toward what she thought was the door and putting as much distance as she could between herself and the trailer.

The size of the building was disorienting. Its layout confusing. She cautiously worked her way along. Either the building didn't have any windows or it was pitch dark outside. Only weak halos of yellow light dotted the walls. She examined the rafters and thought about walking along them, but the only way up was to scramble up the wall. As she hopped from stack to stack, she listened for the panting dogs or jingling of their collars. Only a few minutes passed before it became dead silent. Tim and the dogs were out. Lack of any sound meant they were hunting her.

The stack closest to the wall swayed dangerously from side to side when she landed on it. She flattened her body along the top, hoping it would regain its balance. Something had shifted underneath. The core of the stack had moved beyond its center point, and she became its ballast. If approached from the ground, the aisle appeared to turn but was a dead end. She heard the faint sound of the dog's collars. Tim and the dogs were coming.

As easily as she could, she half crawled, half jumped to the next stack, taking care to brace one foot against the one she abandoned. Soft panting

sounds grew louder. She knew they were only a few feet away. She shimmied herself less than half way down the stack, keeping her back against
the sturdy wall of crates, and her feet against the wobbly spine of the other
row. She reached into her pocket, grabbed the paperclips, and threw them
up and over. She heard dogs' feet hurrying to investigate the sudden noise.
Next, soft thuds of large human feet cautiously followed behind. When
the sounds were too close to bear, she pushed the stack of mismatched
crates and boxes beyond their balance. Tim's startled yell was cut short as
the crates toppled. The dogs yelped with surprise.

She scrambled back to the top and carefully identified each sound. A
confused high-pitched whimpering lingered but no sound of large feet
met her ears. The dogs stayed near the toppled crates, loyal to the owner
who could not move.

She stood upright and noticed an aura of light slightly brighter than the
others at the center of the long wall. She scrambled over to it and jumped
down. The semi-circle of light was enough to see a row of sickly green
lockers, dented from years of abuse. Assorted tools lay the floor, but she
found no door, no way out. Another dead end.

If she were only exhausted, she may have been able to push through.
Doubt washed over her, and sucked her will away with its undertow. Her
head became too heavy to hold up, her body too weary. Gravity and resig-
nation forced her to her knees.

She heard Tim groan in pain and grunt with effort and feared what he
would do when he found her. For the first time crying out for her mother
had Bridget's face and not Margaret's attached to her plea. She offered
a silent apology for not knowing, not understanding, and begged her
mother's forgiveness as she gave her own. She asked for help.

The lockers stood shoved into this distant corner and forgotten.
Misshapen doors hung askew on a single hinge or gripped shut on a
tortured latch. Some had initials scratched into their surface and others
a simple "Fuck you." One had the same symbol she had seen at the
cottage—an open-ended square with a circle inside of it, a crude cross
etched on top. The meaning was lost to her.

She reached out. The lockers swayed, easily put off balance. She
grabbed the first tool she touched—a flat piece of metal about a foot long
with a light curve at the end—and crawled on her hands and knees to
inspect the back. Shadows hid a narrow space. Feeling around, a flat cold
metal surface rose up to a horizontal bar. A door.

She didn't hesitate to press her body into the tight opening. With just
enough room to raise her arms to push against the long bar, she opened
the door far enough to trigger the click of an alarm. Age and neglect kept
it from wailing, making a pitiful mewling sound instead. She paused only

long enough to listen for footsteps outside. Hearing nothing, she squeezed her shoulders through. Once outside, she wedged the door shut and ran.

She zigged and zagged her way through the buildings, diving behind—and sometimes in—barrels and trash bins to keep from being seen, always expecting a small army to respond to the triggered alarm. Every detail of her environment was important, and she was disoriented when she emerged in the middle of a major transportation hub. Huge diesel rigs sat in long rows, running lights on and engines idling, their drivers either asleep or stretching their legs waiting for the next load. Forklifts scooted back and forth.

Away from the busiest section sat huge horse Pullmans—the kind of tractor-trailer rigs that could hold up to a dozen horses and gear—their sides gleaming in the dim light. Three sat cold and silent around makeshift turnout areas used to give the animals a place to walk and have a break from whatever travels they were on. No raised voices could be heard. No calls or shouts of alarm. She continued moving, crouched and low. Each shadow, nook, and bin was used to her full advantage to stay hidden.

What she thought was a wide road was actually a runway, as long as the one Michael's jet used. Prop-engine planes sat tethered near a long building, wheels chocked, and canopy and prop-blades covered. A tattered orange windsock creaked as it swiveled on a pole in the light breeze. The oversized warehouse was an airplane hangar, and the vibrations were planes landing and taking off. As she made her way through the complex, the sounds of a highway grew louder. Chain-link fences surrounded the entire area. Rigs entered through a guarded gate. She crawled around the perimeter until she found a turned-up corner of mesh. She used her hands to dig away the dirt and weeds to make the chute big enough to shimmy through.

She ran inside the shadow of the highway until she came to an off-ramp and used it to navigate onto a side street. She paused only long enough to catch her breath know she had to keep moving. No longer under the effects of the tranquilizer, and her head cleared with a shot of adrenalin, she began to walk briskly along the streets. Several hours and many detours later, she finally became bold enough to try hitchhiking despite the broad daylight. She thumbed a while before a white van, with a bright orange lightning bolt streaking across its sides, stopped.

The driver pushed open the passenger side door. She grabbed it and hesitated.

How many times had she paused, door propped open, and looked at a car's driver or truck's interior and weighed the risks of closing herself behind that door? Another gamble. Another calculated risk. Safety was only remotely hers when she made her own choices and determined her own direction. She had kept herself safe for years until Michael entered her life. For a few brief and perfect moments, she had trusted him and allowed herself to be wrapped in his cocoon.

She would never make that mistake again.

ANTRIM, NORTHERN IRELAND

MICHAEL STOOD AT the end of the long conference table and looked at the faces of the men seated there. He had used the flight back from Geneva to cull the corporation documents for names and radioed ahead to ensure their presence. He summoned the full strength of his father's army to meet. They looked at one another with knowing and surprise. The cherubic faces of the corporate officers of MMC stared at the angular and lean faces of 2100. This marked the first time they had ever met as a group. Identities suspected were confirmed. The two worlds of the Charity looked across the table at one another in mute checkmate.

These men were his father's inner circle. They were the men who held each piece of the Charity in their heads and protected the knowledge with their lives. A few were fresh-faced, barely out of their twenties and did not attempt to curb the look of ambition from their eyes. They were matched in number by the more grizzled, who possessed a sharpness to their expressions that spoke of knowing hard truths.

The energy surrounding Michael channeled that of a young Magnus in those heady early days. Michael knew the fathers of some, the mothers of others. The individuals his father manipulated like pawns, moving them about at will keeping the next sequence of moves a chess master's secret.

What he did not grasp was who had the capacity to betray him because not even blood ties would guarantee their troth. He had no time to orchestrate a Machiavellian coup, locking the men into action with a potent concoction of fear and greed. He could only use the fact that the men did not know what he was capable of. He could cut their incomes or their throats. He trusted they liked their lives and would continue being discrete. From that moment on, no one person could make a move without jeopardizing the other's existence. They would enforce one another.

Michael accepted condolences on his father's death offered with a gentle pat and an assessing look. They were wary and confused, waiting the past few months for him to lead. He knew gathering them on such short notice was a bold move—one many had wanted but none had ever thought they would see.

His first priority was to collect all the information they had on Jessica's disappearance. He suspected one well-trained assailant. Entry onto the grounds happened hours prior. The person killed two guards and scattered papers and documents from his office in the kitchen area. Some were missing. Their disappearance—along with some of Bridget's journals—was more a feeble attempt to make it look like a burglary than a kidnapping. Murray had surprised the intruder and paid for his stealth by being bludgeoned. Jessica interrupted the attack and fled through the solarium. After that, Michael's men found no trace of her. Whoever he was, he knew his way around the inside of the house and grounds.

He considered what her disappearance meant. She would have been killed on the spot if her death provided an advantage. If Jessica was to be used as a bargaining chip, twenty-four hours had already passed to present the terms of ransom. If his punishment for loving the wrong woman was the goal, evidence of her torture would have been clear. It didn't take a lot to figure out that someone wanted something of Michael's to call his own.

Tim.

The thought that Tim had her now, knowing what he had tried to do to her, knowing what he was capable of, pushed him to the limit of control. His hands pressed down on the table. Blue veins roped to his fingers. If ever he wanted the adrenaline-fueled power that came with the fury of unleashed anger, it was now.

He would not be intimidated into inaction by the flat stares of headmasters past lining the walls. He would not let the blazing eyes of his father weaken him from the shadows. No longer would he allow the myth and the truth of his father to cower him. Magnus' legacy, and all of the fear and the love that came with it, would be his strongest tool. He no longer suppressed the hatred, tamping it down to a manageable size. He refused to obey a rational voice. He had no choice but to assume the full mantel of his father's power in order to find her.

Of all the accoutrements of power at his disposal, two were his most valuable: money and knowledge. Money built strength. Knowledge exposed weakness. He would spare nothing to find her.

Another trap of his father's had snapped shut around him, and once again, Jessica was a pawn.

He tugged on his starched white cuffs. The motion exposed the favored gold monogrammed cufflinks of his father. A flicker of recognition rippled through the men. He steadied himself with a breath. "It's clear that the Charity was behind the Arndale bombings. Both the money and the men were sourced through our channels. Each of you knows your part in the plan. None of you knows the whole. If one part is leaked, the dam will burst for all of us. To remain protected, we have to watch out for one other. This is a critical time for us to be unified. The only person here who can decide who is expendable and who is not is me. Anyone who thinks differently puts us all in jeopardy. A betrayal is not to one person but to all of us. Deception will not stand."

He held up a printout with a heading showing *Connaught and Wyeth Connected to Arndale Bombing*. "Our source inside the paper says the alleged connections are circumstantial at best and sensationalized lies at worst. If the editors felt they had a real story here, this would have been today's front-page news, and reporters and investigators would surround us. As it is, this is an advance of what coming in tomorrow's paper. It's not going to make the front page and most likely won't get any higher than page four.

"The reporter made a Hail Mary pass on this story to save her career. Her facts may all be unsubstantiated, but her conclusion was right. We must discredit her and stop the story. Even this low level of exposure is enough to make people curious and begin to ask questions. This morning, I was told that Deputy First Minister Reginald Bragdon called to discuss rebuilding the peace line destroyed in the riots."

He nodded to a sinewy man with a tanned face and crisply tailored suit. "You already owe a debt of gratitude to the General Manager of 2100 for knowing the difference between on-the-books business and off-the-record fishing. Minister Bragdon's activities and curiosities will come under closer scrutiny until we can be assured that no official or unofficial investigation gets underway. You each need to be diligent in managing your affairs to make sure any avenue opened by this article flows to a dead end. My father taught you well. Do it."

Next he threw pictures of Tim and Paddy on the table. "These are the two men who many of you applauded for following orders and executing a difficult task. Whether or not the Charity takes a similar action in the future is my decision and my decision only." He looked each man in the eye, leaving no doubt he would deal with them personally if they doubted him. "But, these men have broken ranks and deserted us. Do what you have to do to stop them and to find Jessica. Let me make this very clear—she is as much a part of the Charity as you are." His voice threatened to thicken as he spoke. He willed it steady as he said, "Find her. Then I will personally deal with these men."

The relief around the table was palpable. They had been waiting for this moment when Magnus' son would not shrink from his father's shadow. He tried to read the looks exchanged around the table. If any gave a clue to a weakness or a conspiracy, he did not see it. This marked a new way of operating for them, and he wished he had the time to plan his next moves in detail. He only had his gut for guidance and hoped his bold steps would be enough to erase his indecisiveness of the past months. Too much was at stake.

The men broke off into groups, greeting each other as old friends, sharing information and making plans. After an hour, the conference room emptied, leaving Michael as the lone figure at the huge table. He knew the mechanisms of a search well. What he heard today impressed him and knew his men would use their best efforts to find her. He had to sit tight until he received word. But sitting still was impossible while his blood coursed with a desire for vengeance.

Walking down the empty hallways did nothing to calm him. The Arndale bombing exemplified the best of the Charity's covert operations. Magnus had laid the plans well before his death. Independent and autonomous actions were triggered—not by a personal communication, which could lead back to a person or business—but by a specific event. If the event happened, then each cell performed a specific action. No one action was criminal or suspect in and of itself, but the totality of the actions were deadly. Acquisition of a small amount of explosives quickly became enough to annihilate a city block when sourced through multiple channels. Purchase of a car or a rental of a flat was lost in hundreds of similar actions when made weeks or months before. Two soldiers arrive at a pre-established time and place, strangers to one another but each with a specific role.

Planning for each step occurred well in advance and in perfect detail. Creation of the cohesive operation included provisions for information dissemination and countermeasures. Then, with eyes watching current events and common news outlets, a pre-established signal would transpire. Maybe a law would pass or an official elected. The catalyst might even be a clergyman, preaching a sermon from the pulpit. The politicians had no idea that their words or actions were the triggers for the very events they loathed. The priests sometimes did. In the case of the Arndale bombing, the flashpoint was the death of Magnus himself.

But something went awry as the final pieces of the plan were being put into place. Although the sequence of events had the usual cunning of Magnus' schemes, they had none of the finesse and manipulative skill. In his mind's eye, Michael imagined two brothers discussing the future of their creation. One, standing proud and tall at the top of his empire. The other happy to coast on his brother's riches without the stresses of responsibility. Both acknowledging that the only real successor was a son whose loyalty divided between the love of country and the love of a woman. Jessica's fate became part of the plan long before the brothers even knew who she could be, only that whomever Michael would compromise the Charity for, could not survive. Magnus declared the goal, orchestrated steps, chose soldiers, set catalysts in motion. No one knew what was going to happen after Magnus died until it did. No one, except for Liam.

Michael's uncle was a man who knew his people and their weaknesses. No hook or motivator escaped his attention. The more primal the urge, the greater the assurance in the outcome. He gave money to the greedy and influence to the power-driven. He provided security for the spouses and children of his men. His words of praise flowed to those who craved acknowledgement and acceptance. No human need went unexplored or unexploited.

The old wooden floors creaked beneath Michael's feet as he entered his office. The spike in his heart rate and breathing somewhat calmed, but the drive for revenge was strong and unrelenting. Today, he would not pause to appreciate the afternoon sun as it streamed in through the leaded panes. Today, the only thing he saw was his uncle's white hair in the shadows of the room. Liam did not turn when Michael entered.

"They've all gone, I see." Liam spoke softly.

"Yes."

"You didn't turn them against me."

"No. That wouldn't have been wise."

Liam chuffed. "Brilliant reading of the players. You've given them a full trough of changes to mull over. Working together on a shared goal while they adapt to your new management was a stroke of genius. Crackling well done."

"Thank you."

"As long as the mission is successful, that is." Liam swiveled his chair around to look at Michael. His gaze held no trace of fear. "You're determined to find her at any cost."

"Yes. And when I do, you will never threaten her life or interfere with mine again."

Liam assessed Michael and nodded with satisfaction. "I kept my promise to Magnus. You've stepped into his shoes as he wished. I'll not stand in your way as you make the Charity your own."

"The Charity is dead. I won't lead his organization. I will make my own."

Liam waved his hand dismissively. "As you wish. Your adroit handling of the opening moves speaks well of you. I've no doubt your next volleys will be a series of equally deft plays. At last you're leading and in full control. That's what your father and I wanted."

"Where is she?"

Liam smiled, showing a row of yellowed teeth worn down to dull nubs. "I don't know. The Charity has its connections in the darker arts of disposing of a body, but it seems that none have been pressed into service recently."

Michael's fists gripped Liam's lapels before he realized he had even moved. His knuckles whitened with the effort to hang on to the tweedy material as tightly as he could, fearing that if he let go, they would find their way around the creped skin of his uncle's neck. "Don't lie to me," his voice nearly a growl.

"Hardly. It seems your woman is a bit of a Houdini."

"But you know what happened."

Liam swept Michael's hands off him and brushed down the front of his jacket, straightening his shoulders. "To a point. But first, please accept my apologies."

Michael waited, unsure.

"I miscalculated. I thought that by getting rid of that American woman, you'd be able to focus on the job at hand."

"Jessica," he said, jaw clenched. "Her name is Jessica."

"Well, your *Jessica* was supposed to be nothing but a chit on the wind by now. She was an unwelcomed fly and never was supposed to survive long enough to even get to Aintree, let alone win."

"You wagered against her."

Liam's chuckle caught in his chest as he gave a phlegmy cough. "Of course. The winnings were supposed to wash the final payments to the crew. No one but your father could have seen the connection, but you did." He nodded in satisfaction. "Brilliant."

"My father never would have been so stupid as to make the payments so close to the actual event."

"Ah, you're right," he said with a theatric flourish. "I thought I was making things simple by using the same man for the Arndale and Aintree jobs. I could transfer the money easily enough, and his transport brought him near Aintree as it was. But, our sharpshooter didn't plan on the use of one of our own vests. Magnus would have seen all those details and planned accordingly." Liam half smiled as he shook his head with forced admiration. "Then, you complicated things by locking her up in that ivory tower. It's all worked out much better than I dared hoped. I'm getting beyond my years, Michael. I miscalculated my own nephew." His expression softened. "She wasn't a distraction to you as much as she was motivation. I should have figured that out sooner. I was pressed into using Tim and was delightfully surprised he was such a, um, *willing* participant."

Liam looked up at Michael from underneath his brows. The look, the timbre of the words, came close to triggering Michael to lose the control he struggled so hard to maintain. Money and power would not manipulate Tim. He thought of Jessica and knew what motivation Liam had found. "What did you do to him?" he said, his voice hard bits of gravel.

"It's always useful to cultivate vulnerabilities in people around us. Tim's idolization of you and his unique needs fit surprisingly well. It seems that Nan had seen something in him and had already begun working him up. He's quite beside himself that Jessica's missing."

Michael pulled his collar away from his neck as he heated. "What did Nan have to gain by turning Tim against Jessica?"

"Never underestimate the power of the faithful."

"Jesus Christ, Liam. What are you saying?"

"Nan and I have been friends for years." He chuckled as the look on Michael's face shifted. "Not lovers. I wasn't her type. She was besotted with Magnus, and he sagely used his resources to cultivate her. His death was quite a shock to her."

"I thought she was one of us. Isn't that why you placed Jessica at her cottage?"

"The network she was affiliated with complimented the Charity. Magnus and I used her many times to hide people or get them out of the country. Taking in your woman was a bitter pill for her to swallow. She didn't turn Tim against Jessica as much as she realized how desperately he wanted to be like you, to do the things you do."

"Tim trusted you. And Nan. Tim . . . he," Michael struggled to find the right words, "he doesn't have the capacity to figure out if he's being manipulated."

"Which is why he was perfect."

Thoughts raced and refused to slow to rational speed. If he could get through this day, the legacy of his father could begin to fade. He clung to the discipline of logic to override his emotions. "I will not kill you," he said through gritted teeth.

"Coded into your DNA is the urge to kill in order to protect. I doubt the genes of your mother are enough to tip balance. You've killed before and will again. The irony is you don't see yourself as the cold blooded type." Liam's stare bored into Michael. "You haven't put all of the pieces together yet, so you still need me—especially through this transition."

Michael was conscious of what he wanted to do, afraid of how much like his father he could become if he lost his tenuous grip on his emotions. "You said Nan had already targeted Tim against Jessica."

"Nan is a deeply devout woman. She suspects that Jessica is a bishop's bastard. It took all my effort to stop her from doing something quite rash."

The words made no sense. "What are you saying? Gus Adams was Jessica's father."

Liam raised his eyebrows and blinked his eyes in surprise. "Nan had Tim translate the mother's journals and letters. Bridget's cleverness was no match for Nan's suspicions. Some might call it a coincidence, others might call it fate, but Nan's goals and mine became shared. We helped one another. You've made your leadership clear," he said with a weary wave of his hand, "and stopped the forces inside the Charity from targeting her, but I'm afraid we have a few friends who would be relieved to see the bishop's secret die with her. Anyway, Nan discovered Tim's crush, and it didn't take much to fan the flames. I really don't care what happens to her."

Michael reached his breaking point. In a flickering image as if watching an old-time movie, his hands opened for a split second before they closed again. Then the faint feeling of the stubbled skin and fragile Adam's apple creased into his palms. With detached fascination, he watched as Liam's face reddened to purple making the shock of his white brows stand out in stark relief. The old man's eyes widened, then bulged. Not even the sound of his own breathing interrupted his thoughts. Three seconds. Then eight. Then fifteen.

He let go, fingers springing open as if animated by an electric shock, and both men sputtered and gasped for breath. Liam braced himself against the back of his chair, stretching his neck upward to open nearly crushed passages.

"Get out." Michael's own voice was barely audible above the rushing of blood in his ears. The terms and conditions of Liam's spared life unspoken and clear.

The older man gathered up whatever dignity remained and walked out of the office without another word.

Michael pressed his hands against his head, rocking his body back and forth, keeping the magnitude of his world from exploding his skull. Cold rage threatened to turn his heart to stone, and he wondered if this was how it happened for his father. Magnus was not born an evil man, but somewhere he lost his humanity. Did it start when his hands wrapped around someone's neck, watching the life drain out on a tide of panic? Michael wanted change but not in exchange for his soul.

Liam was inept. His horribly botched missions seriously jeopardized the security of what was once the Charity but thankfully spared Jessica's life. Now she was missing. The first warm emotion he had felt in hours sparked inside of him as a flash of admiration for her surfaced. He focused on that spark and willed it to spread. Through Jessica, he might be able to keep himself intact.

As quickly as he thawed with the thought of her, anxiety closed in. She was running. Again. This time without money. Without resources. Blind. He knew she would not go back to Ballyronan or the school, and he doubted she would be fool enough to try to cross the border without any kind of document. She might try to get word to him but would have only one chance. And for that, she would have to be at a place safe enough to wait for him to arrive.

Murray's reluctance to talk about Jessica's father confirmed that Liam did not lie. Ever loyal and protective, Murray would not tax Michael with such a concern if it merited no more attention than a rumor. He was waiting for confirming facts. If Jessica was a bishop's child, then that bishop was Kavan Hughes—and he was the only person that Jessica would try to see.

Michael closed his eyes and methodically parsed through all the variables, carefully considering his options. He slid off his jacket and walked over to the small safe in the corner. With a few twists of the dial, he pulled the heavy door open and the smell of machined metal and gunpowder met him. The Glock nine-millimeter felt cold and heavy in his hand, untouched since he had placed it there after arriving in Northern Ireland and unused since he killed the last man who threatened Jessica's life. He grabbed two clips and a box of ammunition. He checked the magazine, pulled the slide back, and squeezed off several test shots, the clicks sounding harsh and out of place in the hush of the school. The leather holster was supple enough to slip over his arm and strap across his chest with ease. He tested the feel of the gun under his jacket, saw that it slightly bulged his precisely tailored suit. He stripped, pulled out his untouched suitcase, changed into clothes he knew he could move in and would help him blend into the background. Dark pants. The holster fit easily over the long-sleeved shirt. Loose jacket. He stopped himself before habit made his hands pat pockets to check for his badge.

Since leaving his post, he had not been to a firing range and hoped he had not lost his touch. He doubted it.

With practiced and fluid motions, he loaded the ammunition into the clips, secured it in the magazine, smacked one into his gun, and checked the safety. Then he did it all again with his eyes squeezed tightly shut, making sure to muffle any potential click of metal. Satisfied, he turned and loped to his car.

Larne, Northern Ireland

AN ASSORTMENT OF utility vans, contractor trucks, and passenger cars lined up at the gas pumps. Drivers—shadowed and weary from hours on the road—stood hunched and mute as men clad in oil-stained coveralls serviced their vehicles. Fluids checked, windshields washed, petrol filled. Cars pulled up, filled, and departed—empty coffee cups replaced with filled, steamy ones. People milled about. Most were half-awake, but their hooded eyes may have signaled more than a need for sleep. A girl tried to hide her underage youth behind thick eyeliner, heavy make-up, and a shirt that put her boobs on display. The rest stop was her territory, and she defended it. A hardened scowl and a flick of a cigarette dared anyone to come near unless they were willing to pay—cash. The sign for "Statoil" hummed and flickered as one fluorescent tube sputtered its last light out. Jessica turned her head away to keep her face in shadow.

"Here. This'll keep you for another while."

A fire-plug of a woman with slicked back hair held out a Styrofoam cup emblazoned with the name of the quick-stop and a bag of food. The frayed ends of her hacked off t-shirt sleeves framed tattooed arms. Embroidered on her dirty vest was "Trish Mackey, Electrician" on one pocket and an Indigo Girls' logo on the other.

Starving, Jessica gave the bag a shake. Its heft surprised her. "Thank you, Trish."

"I don't usually stop for hitchhikers, but you had not a clue about you. If you need to catch another ride, do so from the bottom of a slip road or at a lorry park like this one. The Guarda will snatch you up and slap you with a penalty if they find you thumbing on the motorways like I did."

Jessica took a sip and winced. The scalding heat from the weak tea did not minimize its cloying sweetness. It tasted more like boiling water poured into a sugar bowl than an honest caffeinated beverage.

"To your liking?"

"Yes. Very," she croaked. "Thanks again."

"It's none of my concern, but that man you're running from isn't worth the trouble. You can get the help you need to get away from 'im.'"

When Trish had picked her up and asked, "Where to?" Jessica had answered with a shrug and said, "Not back to him." A shower, clean teeth, and sleep were what she wanted, but she got the protective capsule of Trish's cab instead. Trish's eyes looked her over and settled on the large bruise on her cheek. With a disgusted snort, she pushed the van's door open. She had tried talking, but Jessica feigned sleep to avoid conversation, knowing that the more she spoke, the more she risked being pegged for an American. Caution was tantamount. The past week's stories may have rekindled the frenzied attention that once surrounded any news of her. She had been on the run plenty of times and knew the drill: eyes open and mouth shut—unless asleep.

Trish fished out a rumpled paper from one of the vest's many pockets. "It's the number for the Domestic Line. Call it. They'll send someone for you so you don't have to risk yourself in a place like this."

Jessica took the paper and unfolded it. The top read "Women Helping Women" and listed services addressing domestic abuse, shelters and counseling centers, and dates for gay pride marches. Addresses were a network of church basements across Northern Ireland. Cities included Strabane, Londonderry, Belfast, Lisburn, and Armagh. Seeing the foreign names made her realize she had no idea where she was. She refolded the paper and put it in her back pocket. "Um, what city am I closest to?"

Trish narrowed her eyes. "You're on the east coast in Larne now. Belfast is thirty-seven kilometers south." She continued when she saw the confused look on Jessica's face. "That would be about a half an hour's drive. Like I said, I'm heading north to Antrim if you want to change your mind."

Jessica opened her mouth as if to say something, then quickly shut it with a firm shake of her head. "I appreciate your help. I don't know what I'm going to do next."

"Give the gals on the help line a call. Sometimes it's good to have someone who'll give a listen. Don't stay here too long," she said as she hoisted her body up into the lorry's cab. "All right, then. I'm off." She pulled the door shut, adjusted her mirrors, and started the engine.

The white van creaked its way out of the station, and Jessica suddenly felt very, very alone. The same black despair from earlier threatened again. Some basic instinct kept her from throwing herself out of a moving car or off a bridge. Not understanding why or how, she was able to find the strength to continue to place one foot in front of the other. At least figuratively. Hungry and exhausted, she sat down on a bench littered with wrappers, cups, and old newspapers. The tea had time to steep, infusing the water with a slight rose-like flavor. It might have passed as palatable if it did not threaten a diabetic coma.

The last of the food consumed, she wadded up the wrappers and shoved them into the white, grease-stained bag, and gathered up the other trash to put in the bin. Sections of the newspaper had fluttered to the ground, pages haphazard and weakened by landing in the wet of a spilled drink. On the front page was a picture of a face that was vaguely familiar to her. The photo showed a recent event. The bishop was dressed in the vestments of a regular mass, the long narrow white stole adorned with an intricate embroidered cross at both ends. His face was open in a wide smile. Others around him looked up at him with obvious respect and affection. More lines creased the sides of his eyes and mouth, but the smile was the same. No straw hat was needed for her to recognize the face as the man photographed with Gus and Bridget. The caption stated that Bishop Kavan Hughes was to say mass at Saint Peter's Cathedral in honor of the retirement of the beloved Father Ignatius Storm and would be attending the dinner on Saturday and a reception after the services on Sunday.

Jessica carefully tore the times and places from the paper. As an afterthought, she decided to take the Bishop's picture, too. Before she folded it up, she looked long and hard at his face, searching for the truth of Tim's words. She expected to feel a connection, in the same way she expected to feel the soles of her feet take root when walking around the shores of Lough Neagh. Feeling nothing did not mean there was nothing to feel. Only that she didn't have a way to decipher it. She shoved the clippings into her pocket and produced the "Women Helping Women" sheet of phone numbers.

She walked inside and stood at the counter with its assortment of candy bars and gum, shuffled her feet and cleared her throat to gain attention. She bit her lip and gathered nerve.

The oily-faced clerk shifted his heft. "Yeah?"

Lifting her chin slightly, she looked him in the eye and asked, "Mind if I make a call?"

BELFAST, NORTHERN IRELAND

"YOU'D BEST PUT yourself in the emergency shelter for the night, and we can find a better solution for you in the morning." A woman dominated by a mass of wild red hair spoke the words in a soft voice made forever hoarse by a broken larynx. Her diminutive frame made her look more like a child than a woman in her mid-thirties. She wore a faded yellow t-shirt, green skirt, and oversized hoop earrings and a nametag proclaiming her as "Thea." "I'm glad you called when you did. The A8 by Newtownabbey gets awful jammed. We were lucky to make it back into the city before the thick of the traffic started."

Jessica stared at the walls of the room, wondering how many women had sought its shelter. A poster of a woman with a heart-shaped bruise around her eye proclaimed, "Love should not hurt." Another admonished, "Stand up. Stand out. End abuse." She shifted the ice pack off her cheek and ran a finger along the crusted bruise. A television was on in the corner, tuned to a local news show. A radio could be heard playing soft music in another room. Tables and chairs held scattered magazines and newspapers.

She felt self-conscious and horrible sitting in that office, having a flock of women with worried and understanding expressions tend to her. They had provided her with the ride she needed, and that was all she wanted from them. They asked her a barrage of questions, and she gave only a mute stare in response, respecting them more than to give a phony name and address. The rules of running and staying hidden in a foreign country were different, and there were few safe moves. Hiding her American accent was one. They took her silence as trauma, but the mention of spending a night in a shelter brought her to attention.

"Shelter? What kind? Where?"

The staff women exchanged glances, happy that she was finally talking. "It's the Central Shelter. You'll only be there long enough for them to find you a place in a women's home. Might be a night. But being a weekend, I'm thinking it'd be two. Most places have a room freed up on Mondays."

She gave a huge smile, trying to exude reassurance and making spending the night in a homeless shelter sound like a class trip. The other women milled around, anxious and expectant, wordlessly begging Jessica to fold into their waiting arms.

"No."

"You're safe," she pressed. "The facilities are very clean and very secure. There's nothing to concern yourself with. You'll go, have a meal, and a room to yourself. Someone will help you with the process of finding aid. Men and women are strictly separated. You'll be quite safe."

"I'm not going." The women had no way to know that what Jessica feared was not an abusive husband or a boyfriend. Her memories were still fresh of being found in a shelter in Boston where the Charity was a presence, where its network thrived on greased palms and satiated addictions. Michael would remember what tricks she used in the past to evade detection and would no doubt have the shelters covered. Discovery was only a matter of time before one of his people walked through the front door of "Women Helping Women" and saw her sitting there.

Thea pulled her chair up beside Jessica. "You can't go back to him. You both need time to sort things out." She pursed her lips and hesitated, groping for the right words. "He's done this before, and he'll do it again unless he gets help." She gently touched her own chest in the same area where Jessica's open shirt exposed the fading bruise. "I've been there," she rasped. "You've taken the first step. You're stronger than you think you are."

Before she could stop herself, Jessica scoffed and squinted her eyes shut before she rolled them. Thea had no idea who Jessica was and her words sounded more like platitudes rather than inspiration. Jessica could not say yes or be enveloped in their care because to do so put them at risk as well. They provided a safe ride to Belfast. She'll repay them with a hefty donation. Anonymously. But she would not stay.

"You called us, no one else. That's tellin' me you want things to change."

Jessica responded, infusing her words with a brogue, careful to sound less American, not fake Irish. "I'm sorry. I cannot. Too many people there. Too much in and out."

Thea nodded slowly as she received silent urging from the other women. "We have another bed available. The facility is very safe, but doesn't have all the amenities you might like. The setup is more dormitory style. Bath is shared. No kitchen to speak of. The woman who's there now is one of our aid volunteers. You'd only need to lay you head. The room's not grand, but comfortable."

Jessica looked around the offices of mismatched furniture and worn rugs occupied by women who could only heal if she allowed them to help. "Any television or radio?"

Thea grimaced and shook her head. "No. 'Fraid not. We'll give you a couple of books to keep you happy 'til Monday morning, though."

"I like that better."

"And we come 'round to fetch you bright and early before anyone else arrives."

"Arrives?"

"Yes. The shelter is in a church. The first service is at nine. We'll get you at eight if you don't wish to attend mass and bring you back here while we sort things out. We don't usually place people there, but if it's between that and going back to him, I'd like to see you take the bed."

"I'm sorry. I'm very nervous around people. Do you have another place?"

"I'm afraid not on such short notice. The sleeping quarters are quite separate from the sanctuary where the services are held. That section of the cathedral's not open to the public."

She stared at a spot on the floor. "Cathedral? Which one?"

"The basement of Saint Peter's Cathedral on the edge of the Catholic district."

Jessica raised her head and searched their faces for any guile. All she saw were wringing hands and worried brows. "Okay. Sounds perfect."

Saint Peter's Cathedral

THE RECEPTION IN the community hall at the cathedral was exactly what one would expect for the retirement of a beloved priest. Parishioners of all shapes and sizes wandered about the large room while the usual battalion of volunteers—ample bosoms behind flowered aprons—replenished and prepped the trays of food brought in by willing hands. Women moved about with familiarity and ease while most of the men stood stiffly to the side, uncertain of how to behave so close to God's house and wishing they had a nip before leaving their flats. Other men, elbows of jackets shiny with wear, counted the chairs set at tables and determined if tonight's party needed more.

A steady stream of generations lined up at the buffet tables, steaming with potluck favorites. Grandmothers clucked and cooed over children dressed in their Sunday bests. Great-grandfathers pecked their way through the buffet, judiciously filling plates for themselves, still amazed at their fortune, saucers filled for the impatient toddlers at their knees. Mothers and fathers sat in tight circles, happy for the brief respite of diligence, knowing that helping hands were all about.

Father Storm shuffled his way into the room and was barely over the threshold before well-wishers surrounded him. Memories and stories flowed.

A man with brilliant red hair stepped up. "My gran-mum was christened in this church and you christened her children and grandchildren. Thirty-seven O'Learys at last count, Father! Two more on the way! We make it easy on you with all the twins we got. One baptism, two souls saved. Can you stay a few more months?"

"No one has the Word like you do, Father. You'll be sorely missed."

"You'll come visit us at Christmastime, won't you, Father?"

"You married my sister, and she never forgave you!" Peals of laughter and a face reddened. "I mean you performed my sister's ceremony to a drunken idiot. She thought all the marriages you did were blessed with luck. But he upped and died when he fell on 'is head and left 'er a house, so I guess she was right."

"My brother lives up the coast. We'll come for a visit once you settle into your new home. I heard Father Casey was a bit frail these days but still seeing visitors. You'd like a visit, wouldn't you, Father?"

"I was shakin' in my boots when you found me behind the rectory, Father. But you took me in, cleaned me up with a few kind words and a meal. I never forgot your kindness."

"The Sisters of the Holy Cross have always relied on your kindness. We'll be certain to maintain our monthly solicitations for them. The Reverend Mother sends her love tonight. She and a few of the sisters will be at your service tomorrow."

"I was crazy with grief when the RUC shot him, Father, and your words gave me solace."

"The little ones don't understand what a sad day this is for us, Father. Don't be bothered with them running about. Kids are different nowadays."

The well-wishers formed an impromptu receiving line, each waiting patiently to say their carefully chosen words, knowing they may not get another chance to tell him how loved and respected he was. Each sentiment received a nod of his head, their own hands clasped between his misshapen knuckles. Some were lucky enough to have the sign of the cross made with his thumb across their forehead.

Eventually, someone brought him a chair and a plate of food. The stresses of the night became apparent as the height of the chair and the stoop of his back forced him to twist his head upward. The sensitive among them saw his discomfort and motioned for the congregants to kneel or sit beside him to give their wishes and blessings, and shooed them on to keep things moving.

The celebration was all a blur to Father Storm. He hid his confusion and fear behind the habits and manners forged in years of public ceremony. The *craic* of the night was high and only love was felt. He looked into the faces and the eyes of the people who had become his family and did not see the expected worry and loss. They were losing their shield and seemed not to notice that evil stood ready to enter their homes. The warning he gave last week didn't energize them to action. Tomorrow would be different. Tomorrow he would tell the world of the lies they had been told.

The activity shifted from serving steaming food, to gathering up plates and empty casseroles, to stacking tables and folding chairs. Father Storm looked into the ruddy faces and milky eyes of the remaining volunteers and nodded to himself that it was always the same white heads and the same hands that did the lion's share of the work. His parishioners had aged with him, and he wondered who would take their places as decisions were made as to who would take his. He wondered who was more irreplaceable.

He was lost in fatigue and memories when he felt a strong hand at his elbow. "Father? Father Storm? Are you all right?"

Father Storm craned his neck upward and was surprised to see a figure dressed in black clerics with a formal white tabbed collar standing over him. He blinked several times, wondering how much time had passed. "Yes. Yes. Quite. Just enjoying the moment." This had become his standard response when someone questioned his daze, learning that fragility is forgiven if it sounded intended. He let himself be pulled to his feet, steadied, and wondered how long he had been sitting.

"Half of Belfast was here today. We expect tomorrow's service will be packed to the rafters. You should get some rest."

He grasped his colleague's hands. "You've come. You needn't have." He looked around at the empty buffet tables, wiped down by two women with spray bottles and rags. "You must be hungry. I'll have a plate made for you." He shuffled his feet toward the kitchen.

Kavan kept hold of Father Storm's hands, looked at the faces in their group, and cleared his throat with a nervous cough. "Thank you for your kindness, Father. I've been quite well tended tonight. The food was as brilliant as the stories shared. It's been a most memorable evening to be here with you. But it's time to walk back."

Father Storm blinked as he tried to make sense of it all. "You're not hungry?"

"No, Father," he said and gave a sad smile. "These good people have put in a long day and are looking forward to returning to their homes. We'll see them again at mass in the morning." Kavan accepted their nodded good-byes as he supported Father Storm's shuffling steps to the door. "I thought we could say our evening prayer in the sanctuary."

The old priest squinted, head cocked in confusion as he let himself be led through the hallway connecting the community center to the side door of the cathedral. The polished floors made for easy passage, but he hesitated several times and looked at Kavan with widened eyes.

An ancient iron stand of votive candles flickered in the corner of the nave. It was close to ten o'clock at night and the sun was setting. Enough of its rays lit the interior, allowing the men to make their way to the front pew and kneel, the creak of the kneelers loud in the empty cathedral. Centered behind the large expanse of the altar sat the empty Bishop's Chair. It was tall. Almost throne-like. Its mahogany wood dark with age and its red velvet cushion faded, but not worn. Flanked by two chairs similar in design but smaller in scale, the wood freshly oiled for Sunday's celebration. Bouquets of white flowers graced each alcove; color symbolizing new beginnings.

Father Storm shifted himself so that he half sat, half knelt as he blessed himself and began to move his lips in silent prayer. Kavan intoned a blessing, seeking union in a shared prayer. At first, the words did not flow for the elderly priest, but habit overcame age and the words that drifted from his mouth were the same as when he was a young ordinand, starting out and examining each word for meaning.

Tonight, the words flowed, but he didn't turn them over and over in analysis, content that by their very utterance, blessings and protections were his. They lapsed into silence, and he glanced over at the bishop. Kavan's eyes were shut in deep concentration, mouth sucked in as he focused on his private conversation. At times, he nodded his head, as if agreeing to some truth, and other times he murmured, sinking his head to his chest, the very image of a man in torment. He waited until the concentration lifted before he spoke.

"I no longer have the strength to fight off the demons, Your Grace. The willpower needed to honor the sacramental seal between priest and penitent is weakening."

"Please. It's just us. Call me Kavan."

"Kavan." He spoke the name as if finally recalling it, with half relief and half frustration. Father Storm labored to sit up in the pew and drew Kavan's hands into his. His eyes grew unfocused as distant memories eclipsed the present.

"You're troubled, Father?" Kavan spoke gently, trying to reroute the flow of thoughts.

"I have heard confessions of liars and thieves and given the Last Rites to murderers. I've absolved the sins of all. But what you have asked of me is the heaviest load I have ever carried."

"Father," Kavan began, voice low and measured, "you've had a busy day after a very long week. You're tired. What I have asked of you is no different from any who have sat in your confessional. You have been the sole person I have trusted, and I have given all I could thanks to you. You have helped me become a better priest."

"Priest! You confessed to me your sins and continued to live your lie. I have seen fathers and husbands writhe in their guilt and shed the skin of sin, but not you." Father Storm grew agitated. "You confessed your burdens to me and continued to live in your deceit, hiding in the open and deceiving us all. Where could I have gone to relieve mine? To keep your secret was to live my own lie as you ascended to bishop. What you have done is a violation of the very core of our vows. For those who have looked to you as a pillar of strength you have cheated them by not admitting your weakness. The weight of it is too much for me." His voice, high-pitched and thready, echoed. He struggled to his feet, and shuffled to the vestry, hands tapping at his head as if to jar loose a memory.

Kavan followed. "I'm sorry. I didn't know."

Didn't *know?* Father Storm, winded and reddened from the sudden exertion, stood in front of the huge rosewood armoire and pointed a gnarled finger at the top. "There. There is where your lies are held. Take it out of here. I can no longer bear the weight of its existence."

Kavan stood in the center of the sparsely furnished room and looked around. He opened the door of the armoire, searched inside. The smell of lemon oil mixed with roses. He found only the freshly starched vestments for the next day's services. He did not have to ask what to look for. He needed only to know where.

The old priest's breathing labored. Beads of sweat bubbled up on his forehead as his fingers continued their frantic tapping. "No! No! To the left! The center!"

Kavan felt along the oiled surface. His fingers found the block of wood, moved it slightly. The center medallion eked forward, then he slowly eased it out. With each motion, Father Storm's breathing slowed and his color normalized. He finally shuffled to the wooden chair and collapsed onto it.

The entire armoire was free of dust and clutter, evidence of its recent care. The small drawer pulled out soundlessly. Kavan did not need a chair to reach its contents but pulled one up anyway to see with his eyes what his fingers already told him. It was empty.

He turned to face the father. His expression formed the question that his mouth could not.

Father Storm's eyes bulged in disbelief and fear. "I've told no one, Your Grace. I swear to you. I've not told a soul."

After a light dinner, shower, and a change of clothes, Jessica followed Thea through a side entrance to Saint Peter's. Thea cleaved onto her to ensure that her skittish guest would not run in terror at seeing the community center in use. They descended two flights of stairs and snaked through long corridors of cinderblock walls and linoleum floors. Thea theatrically produced keys and unlocked doors, dramatizing how removed they were from public areas. Once inside the room and introductions made, Thea left with assurances to meet after services in the morning.

Jessica stood with her shoulder to the wall, arms crossed as she looked through the window to the street above. Few passed through this section of Belfast on a Saturday night. Destinations for food and spirits held more allure. Two beds flanked the functional space. A curtain pulled up between them attempted privacy. Beside each bed sat a chair, table, and lamp. Books were neatly stacked in one corner of the floor next to a well-worn pile of *Tattler* and *Gossip Girl* magazines.

The odds and ends of a life salvaged were stacked under the window. A few dresses and a coat hung from hangers hooked on the water pipes that ran across the ceiling. Neatly folded piles of sweaters and pants sat along the floor. A few milk crates held a variety of figurines and kitchenware. A faint smell of soot clung to them. An assortment of brooms, buckets, and mops filled a makeshift cubby by the door.

"Can I fetch you a cup of tea?"

Jessica turned to her keeper for the night. "No thanks." She looked at the hot plate and kettle and the assortment of dried and packaged food. "Thea told me about your flat burning in the riots. I'm sorry." Thea spoke of the riots as if they were a bout of excessive heat or a flood-swollen river; more of a God-given nuisance that a person grows accustomed to because fighting against it would be futile. Jessica looked into Aoife's eyes, trying to gauge her anger. Only a resigned acceptance huddled beneath the surface.

Aoife gave a non-committal shrug. "Thank you. I've been assigned a flat and will be moving as soon as it's ready. If I wasn't here, I don't know where they would have put you up for the night. The shelters are good enough, but I guess if you've never been to one they can seem a bit frightening."

The same trigger of events put them together, and Jessica was not ready to examine it. This was the cathedral of her mother's youth, where Bridget taught the Catechism and pilfered coins from the coffers. If what Tim said was true, this was also where she would meet her father. She ran her hand along the cinderblock walls, hoping for the fire of connection to ignite. Like on the beach at Aghalee, she felt nothing, only the familiar numbness. She focused her attention on her host.

Aoife could not have been more than a few years older and moved with planned and determined actions. She had a slightly convex appearance; thin not by choice but worn down by stress and hard work. The knees of her pants showed faint patches as if bearing silent witness to hours spent scrubbing. Her faded strawberry hair was swept back and secured with a plastic clamp. A faint scattering of freckles graced her nose and cheeks. Aoife's hands, strong with knotted blue veins, were not noteworthy except for being red and chapped. Only when Aoife looked at Jessica did her impression change from downtrodden to veiled. Aoife's eyes bore into her as if nothing could keep her from seeing the truth.

"Ah. This is the best place for reflection, I'll give you that." Aoife pressed her hands to her hips and stretched her back. "On the nights I can't sleep, I go up to the nave and sit. Sometimes I pray, but most times I let my mind wander."

"It's not locked? You can just go in there?" She struggled to keep the burr in her words.

Aoife gave her a look that made Jessica feel stupid. "No worries. The doors are locked at sunset and automatically latch behind so there's no re-entry. I almost had to spend my first night in the sanctuary. I block the door with this." She waved a tattered book in the air. "Would you like to see the inside?"

Jessica shrugged, unsure of how to answer.

"C'mon. It'll do us both good. Take our mind off things for a while."

She shrugged. "Okay, sure. Why not?"

When Aoife smiled, the stresses fell from her face, making her almost pretty. Suddenly energized, she placed her steaming mug down and motioned with her head for Jessica to follow.

Aoife carefully steered Jessica through the labyrinth of halls. They walked down a long corridor and up two flights of stairs, their way lit by dim overhead lights. The first flight was modern, built twenty or thirty years before, and was part of the building referred to as the community center. The second flight was more ancient, maybe a century old and part of the cathedral itself.

They passed through a series of doors. Some they chocked open with rubber wedges, others they propped with chairs. When they reached the first large carved door, Aoife turned and waved the book with a smile, placing it down between the jamb and the door. Her demeanor was that of a teenager accustomed to being out past curfew. Her eyes and mouth were set with determination as she showed the ropes to a newcomer. They entered near the front of the cathedral and stood in a small foyer behind the altar. A huge oak cabinet stood to their right with the vestry and ancillary rooms beyond it.

The air held a combination of faded incense, fresh linens, and lemon oil. The floor was stone, polished smooth from centuries of footsteps, and scrubbed so clean the tiny flecks of mica shone like diamonds. A carved cross graced each thick wooden door. The carvings on the altar door were the most ornate, with a trellis and interweaving vines. Iron sconces held dimmed flame-shaped lights.

Aoife started to walk forward and stopped, head cocked and hand raised. Men's voices came from inside the vestry. She reached behind her, grabbed Jessica's arm and pulled her into the shadow of the cabinet. Jessica's heart pounded and she tried to leave, but Aoife held her back with an iron grasp.

The stone walls did not muffle the conversation. One voice was old and wavered. "I . . . I simply don't remember. It was there and hadn't been touched."

Another voice was younger, more patient, and restrained. "With all the bother leading up to tomorrow's services, perhaps you moved it for safe-keeping?" The next minutes filled with sounds of door hinges squeaking and of drawers sliding open and shut.

"Och! Perhaps you're right. There's been so much these past weeks. I've j-just gone all soft."

After a pause, the sound of a chair scraped against the floor. The younger voice said, "Take your time, Father. It will come to you when you least expect it. Tell me about the preparations you've overseen. You always were the best at organizing the celebrations. I remember all you did when I was ordained."

A thick chortle. "That was a fine day, Kavan. One of the best in my life to see you take your oath before God. I can barely believe so many years have passed and soon you'll be Archbishop."

Jessica stopped listening. Kavan. Bishop Kavan Hughes was a few feet away. A deep trembling shifted inside of her as if a fault line finally broke free from its tension. He was her living link to past and present. She only heard his voice, but the desperation to speak to him grew. She wanted to see his face and the smile her mother had seen, and to hear the laughter her mother had heard. Most of all, she wanted to watch the expression in his eyes when she told him who her mother was, to see for herself the truth of Tim's words.

The men continued their conversation, relaxed in the presence of one another, words punctuated with short bursts of the knowing laughter of close friends. The sound of his voice, the cadence of his conversation, woke something inside of her. She fought the feeling, thinking she was imagining a connection where logic had dictated none existed. Her head felt detached again, tethered by a gossamer thread. It was irrational, insane really, but she began to believe she heard her father's voice. She tried to shake off the ludicrous thought, no doubt fed and fostered by the isolation and fear she felt. From what she read in the journals, he never knew of Bridget's pregnancy. Still, a doubt nagged.

She pressed her face into the gap between the cabinet and the back wall, trying to see all she could. The door to the vestry opened. A gnome of a man, stooped and gnarled with age and arthritis scuffed out, supported by a man dressed in the all black suit and white collar of the clergy. The light from the sconce showed his profile, face lean, cleanly shaven, and weathered, belying the image that a cleric's life was one of endless days of indoor prayer. His movements spoke of the athletic ease of someone who comfortably inhabits his physical world. Small lines creased from his eyes to show a smile always reached them, and his light brown hair was shortly cropped and amply flecked with gray. His manner to the older priest was respectful and patient. The men turned and walked out toward the rectory, door swinging silently shut behind them.

She must have taken a step forward, for Aoife jabbed an elbow into her side and gripped her collar, holding it for several minutes after the last of their voices faded.

Aoife slowly relaxed and let a faint smile creep to her lips. "Jaysus! That was a close one! I thought I was going to piss in my panties. I've never seen Father Storm up here so late and to have the bishop, too!" She cracked open the door to the altar and peered out. "It's clear now. C'mon, let's have you a tour." She walked toward the door and, not followed, stopped. "What's on? You're shaking like a leaf."

"It's, um, it's just that . . . That was too close. I thought you said no one would be here."

"My mistake. Sorry. Here I thought we had a bit of fun, and you're about to shake apart. Let's give you a quick look 'round, and we'll go back to our room."

"They won't find the doors propped open and suspect we were here?"

"No. They were off to Father Storm's living quarters at the rectory over on the other side. The bishop has his own flat near Stormont and won't be walking through here on his way."

Jessica stood up straight, surprised her legs would hold her. "They were pretty distracted. What were they looking for?" She waited for an answer and received nothing, not even an acknowledgement of her question. She followed Aoife through the door and hesitated when she realized she was at the very front of the cathedral near the altar. Seeing the expanse of the whole nave from her vantage point was a shock. The sanctity of the space made her want to move with great care, concentrating on being silent. Their footfalls echoed in the cavernous space.

The sanctuary could seat close to one thousand people. Like all cathedrals, Saint Peter's floor plan formed the footprint of a cross. The nave's main aisle flowed from the cathedral's entrance to the altar. A second aisle intersected it to shape the outstretched arms of the cross. Two smaller chapels, named Reconciliation and Resurrection, were at either end of the transept. These areas of prayer provided additional seating when the main nave was full.

The altar sat in the center of the chancel surrounded by an area large enough to allow priests and altar server's room to perform their rituals during the service. The ambulatory was higher than the main floor of the nave where the pews sat. To reach it, parishioners had to step up a series of three steps along its perimeter—carpeted to provide a cushioned surface for people to kneel in prayer and receive Holy Communion. From her vantage point, she could see the large stained glass window on the west side. Multi-colored bits of light reflected off the organ's pipes at the far end of the nave.

Aoife, tiring in her role as tour guide, was careful to keep her voice at a respectful level. Jessica made an effort to pay attention and gave minimal responses as her mind was busy tracing over every aspect of her encounter with the men. Aoife rattled on about the cathedral's history. The long line of women who ensured the cathedral's enduring dominance as the center of the Belfast community was especially significant. Her comments were as much about the carved symbolism on the walls as they were for the women who restored and cared for them. Aoife herself was the fifth generation of her family woven into the fabric of the cathedral's history, and her pride and sense of belonging was obvious.

Jessica only half listened as they walked down one corridor and stopped near a chest-high brass and cut-glass stand. A red cord secured the ornate display case's perfectly polished doors. White satin lined the interior that contained several vessels. Jessica had never seen anything like it before. Making an effort to be engaged, she asked about its importance.

"That's what they call the Aumbry. They keep the sacraments and Holy Oil in there. The parishioners had it made in memory of two priests who were shot while anointing the wounded during a riot in the early '70s."

"Who killed them?"

Aoife looked at Jessica with fresh eyes and spit out, "Just who do you think would kill a priest in Belfast?"

Jessica stopped, unsure of how to respond. She had forgotten herself somewhere between the drama of near discovery and her silent dialog of whether or not to approach the bishop. If the disappearance of the fake brogue wasn't enough to show she was not from Northern Ireland, then an ignorant question was.

When Aoife straightened her shoulders and lifted her chin, Jessica could see the stainless steel of her inner core. Aoife's methodical and cordial demeanor evaporated, replaced by menace. What Jessica first saw as a stressed and weakened body transformed to bristling muscle as fear and suspicion surfaced. "You don't have that haunted look in your eyes I've seen with other women who escape their violent men." She paused, carefully watching Jessica's reactions. "You lied to get here, and you're not an Irishman."

Jessica could see the rapid churning of Aoife's mind. "Please don't be afraid. I'm an American, but I didn't lie about needing help."

Aoife stood up straight. "Why are you here?"

Her stomach sank. Instinctively, her eyes scanned for escape routes and doors. Not paying attention as they wandered inside the massive structure, she lost her bearings. She played for time. "I'll answer your questions, but I want to learn more about the bishop and tomorrow's service."

"No. No questions from you. Why are you here? Tomorrow's mass will be jammed for Father Storm's retirement. No self-respecting Catholic within fifty miles would miss the chance to pay their respects to the man. Bishop Hughes always brings a crowd in from Stormont. It wouldn't be the first time a service has been a target." The words laced with edge and suspicion. "Then again, you already know that."

"Look, I'm not here for—"

"And it wouldn't be the first time an American did their dirty work." Aoife cut Jessica off, her manner becoming increasingly hostile.

Jessica didn't know how to respond. She started to back up, hands up to show that no harm was intended. "You saw me arrive. I have nothing on me. I'm not here for any other reason but to get a few answers and to sort a few things out."

"You don't need anything but your eyes and your mouth to be a tool. You're here the night before one of the biggest events this cathedral has seen in years. You're a feckin' liar."

Jessica watched as Aoife moved toward her. Aoife's eyes scanned the space as she gathered the crucial information needed to determine if an attack was winnable. It was as if Jessica was watching herself measuring an opponent, sensing the space, looking for a tool or an escape route. Jessica looked for anything that would hint at a hidden weapon when Aoife gave a slight stretch to her right leg, as if feeling for something. Aoife was right-handed. Any weapon would be strapped to her the outside of it. Jessica's heart pounded in her chest. She didn't want this.

All of her attention was on Aoife. She could see that Aoife was preparing for a fight, opening and closing her reddened hands, ready, but not certain.

Aoife continued to move forward, and Jessica felt the odds against her mount. Aoife's eyes had stopped scanning and focused only on Jessica. Their movements, slow and deliberate, gave time to look for weakness and the best angle. Strength gathered. She knew the telltale signs. When Aoife moved her shoulders slightly back and lowered her chin, Jessica countered the actions by taking a few steps back and keeping the distance between them neutral.

What was Aoife expecting from her? Where was the hole, the weakness, the blind spot? Jessica's mind raced through the details of what she learned. Aoife was there, living in the same cathedral she had been integrally involved with for years. She was loyal. And she was protective.

A realization hit Jessica. "You have what Bishop Hughes wants."

Aoife hesitated, mid-stride. Blinking. "You don't know what you're talking about."

"Father Storm gave it to you and told the bishop he forgot what he did with it. You have it." Jessica continued to back up slowly, feeling her way to the nave.

The only sound was the spit and sputter of the lines of votive candles lit with prayers for peace. "I don't have anything of the bishop's."

"N-no. You've taken it, hidden it somewhere. I have to see it. It might have something to do with me." She heard the words spill out of her mouth but didn't connect with their meaning. Something was beginning to build in her, gnawing and demanding to understand.

"What has to do with you? An American?"

She was confused. How much could she say? Whom was she protecting with her silence? "B-because there are people out there who believe he's my father."

Aoife closed the space between them and slapped Jessica's cheek with an open palm. The threat had changed. Her eyes darkened with desperation. "Don't toy with me."

Jessica had no time to manipulate or craft a response. Just giving voice to the possibility was overwhelming. "I'm n-not." Her cheek burned.

"Bishop Hughes is a good man. I won't let you go about spreadin' filth about him."

"I . . . I swear to you, that's not what I'm here for."

Aoife took a few steps back. "I'm askin' you again, and I want a truthful answer. Why are you here?"

It was all too confusing. Too complicated. In a child's wish, she thought she could stop the inevitable or the past simply by willing them to be different. She hesitated, knowing she was out of options. "Because I'm afraid. Because I don't know what the truth is. But, maybe it has something to do with what he was looking for. Aoife, where is it?"

"I'm not sayin.'"

"Please, Aoife. It's important. The bishop wants it. If this thing has nothing to do with me, then put it back or hide it somewhere else or give it back to that older priest or the bishop. I don't care. But, but please just—" Her tumble of words stopped as she stifled a sob. "Help me. I need to know."

Aoife started to say something, then stopped. Conflict stitched her brows. "You said there are others who think this? Who?"

How much could or should she say? Jessica pulled open her shirt. The fading bruise and the crisscross of red scars were distinct against her white skin. Her voice and hands shook. "They've tried to kill me before. I'm not the threat they think I am. I need to learn the truth to figure out how I can be safe."

"Jay-sus," she uttered, barely a breath. She cleared her throat. "I asked you, who?"

Jessica wiped the tears from her cheeks. "I'm not . . . I don't . . .," she stumbled over the words, afraid of their truth. "The Charity."

Aoife reached down and slowly brought the dagger out of its sheath. She pointed the tip at Jessica's throat. "What makes you so sure?"

"They had tattoos. Here." She described them and pointed to her forearm.

Aoife made a choice. "Let's go." She motioned Jessica forward with a flick of the knife.

The modern hallways changed to cramped passageways as they wove their way down through the building. Aoife brought them through a barely visible door and down a darkened stairwell. Jessica steadied herself with a hand gripped to an iron railing and brushed cobwebs from her face as she felt her way along. They entered a room, not much more than a forgotten storage closet. Cardboard boxes, slightly pink in color, were marked with scrawled, handwritten labels. Hymnals, catechisms, and decorations from past pageants filled them. A broken chair leaned against a tall lamp. Folding tables gathered dust in a corner. Aoife pushed aside a stack of boxes, revealing a darkened passage. She motioned for Jessica to stay put and disappeared inside.

Few would bother to enter this room and even fewer would look behind the assortment of items lining the walls. The opening was irregular and looked as if someone forgot to place the last few stones in the wall. Jessica ran her hand along and felt its irregular surface made by hammers and chisels centuries before. A cascade of crystallized lime mixed with sandy and crumbled grit fell. She could hear Aoife's movements and knew she was not far away. A pool of light formed and seemed to hover above where the floor should have been.

For a brief moment, Jessica thought she saw the face of a young woman rush toward her, smiling to reveal a broken tooth. The image faded before it truly registered, leaving her unsure that she saw anything at all. Startled, she turned to leave when she saw something vaguely familiar. At first she thought the scratchings were graffiti. Among several indecipherable symbols was one she recognized; a circle inside the open-ended square topped by a cross. The door, the room—all of it had a familiarity that she couldn't quite place. She rubbed her upper arms to ward away a sudden chill.

Aoife emerged, wiping cobwebs from her face and clothes. In her hand was a dark box. Jessica examined it, running her palm over the intricate designs made of inlaid woods. As it warmed to her touch, a faint scent of roses grew, slightly powdery, triggering a memory of her childhood home and of Bridget. Her mother's presence was strong and real. She grounded herself by tracing her finger over the lock and hinges. "It's been opened."

Aoife rounded her eyes. "Has it now?" She leaned over, looked at the nick in the brass surrounding the keyhole, and shrugged.

Jessica continued to examine the box. "It wouldn't take much. There are only two tumblers inside the lock. It's pretty crude." She patted down her pockets, looking for anything to use as a pick and was frustrated at not finding anything.

Aoife put her hand over hers. "What's your mother's name?"

The question came out of the blue. Jessica shuddered.

"Bridget Heinchon. Some people may have known her as Bridget Harvey."

For a brief moment, Aoife stiffened as if hit, and a puff of air escaped her chest. Gripped with conflict, she looked long and hard into Jessica's eyes and winced, pained by something unknowable. She reached into her pocket to produce a thick copper wire, the kind used for electrical work. With a few quick prods, the lid opened. After hesitating slightly, she sat down on the far side of the room.

Jessica positioned herself under a light and began to sift through its contents. A slight smell of vinegar mingled with the scent of dust and roses. Photographs, curled and yellowed with age, and items once treasured, were joined by letters and different papers. The photographs were of her mother in the full bloom of youth taken at the cottages in Aghalee and along the shores of Lough Neagh. Nestled within them she found another picture of Gus, Bridget, and Kavan together. Bridget was wearing the same straw hat, tilted at a jaunty angle that shaded her eyes, but didn't hide her smile. The photo was not a duplicate, snapped moments after the similar picture Jessica had of them. In this one, Gus looked at Kavan with a guarded expression. The expression on Kavan's face as he looked at Bridget was one of pure love.

She picked up a stack of letters tied with a string, Bridget's handwriting easily recognizable with its perfectly formed letters and slight flourish at the end of each word. Her name carefully scripted over a Belfast return address. A silken pouch, barely more than three inches square, contained a remnant of a document rolled and secured with a ribbon. As she unfurled the scroll, a wrap of cool air embraced her, caressing across her neck, over her shoulder, and along her cheek.

Unscrolled, the paper was eight inches wide and roughly three inches high. Three sides of the paper had a sharp, defined edge, but the top edge had frayed, as if hastily torn or cut. Printed on it were lines of a formal form. The words were simple and would have no meaning to anyone, but obviously held a place of honor in the box owner's heart. Over the typeset word, "Father," was the neatly printed name, "Kavan Hughes." The simple words hovered over the lines, drifting upward as each letter progressed, as if hastily typed on an old typewriter.

Jessica drew in a shaky breath as she rolled up the paper, secured it with the ribbon, and replaced it in the pouch. When reunited with her birth certificate, the paper would fit perfectly along the frayed bottom edge, lines and typed words the final puzzle piece. She looked over at Aoife and started to talk, but her words choked into silence by a sudden release of emotion. Tears welled in her eyes and overflowed down her cheeks.

Aoife sat in silence and waited until Jessica pulled herself together. They looked at each other in mute agreement, circumstance dictating mistrust and fear, intuition guiding them to somewhere else.

"It's true then. You're the bishop's daughter."

Jessica simply nodded. "I have to speak to him and warn him that people have uncovered our connection." A trembling hand wiped her cheeks dry, and she closed the box.

"Think about what you just said. Father Storm gave this to me for a reason. He kept it away from the bishop on purpose."

"What did he say when he gave it to you?"

"He was spoutin' something crazy. I'm not even sure he was in his right mind. But one thing is certain, there are a great many people who rely upon Bishop Hughes. If something were to happen to him, I'm afraid of what that would mean to the community." Aoife cringed.

"Are you sure Father Storm wanted to keep the box away from the bishop? Maybe Father Storm knew with all of the people milling about that the box was safer away from the public spaces—just as you did. Maybe Bishop Hughes wasn't who he was keeping the box from."

Aoife narrowed her eyes. "What are you saying?"

"Maybe Father Storm was trying to protect him. Maybe he figured out that someone might try to use this information against the Bishop to discredit or blackmail him." Her voice grew urgent. "It's possible."

"But why not give the damned thing to the Bishop directly? Why hide it here at all?"

"Consider his situation. The bishop's schedule is public, every action known. If someone wanted to search his flat, they would have more than enough opportunity. Hiding it here was smart, but with Father Storm leaving, the hiding place would not be as secure. He gave it to you because he trusted you."

Aoife thought for a moment and nodded her head. "Fair enough. But what about you? What are you going to do with this information?"

It was a question Jessica had been dreading. Every aspect of her life she thought she knew was pulled away from her like the child's game of pick-up-sticks. One by one, the sticks of her identity vanished, leaving an ever more precarious pile. She was too afraid to examine the fragile heap.

"I don't know. Everything changed a few months ago when I found out that the people who raised me weren't my parents."

"Do you know who your mother was?"

"I just told you," she said, hiding her irritation. "Bridget Heinchon."

Aoife's expression softened. "I'm not askin' you what her name was. I'm askin' if you knew *who* she was."

Her lower lip started to tremble and she steadied it with a firm bite. She cleared her throat, straightened her back, and braced herself to say the words she dreaded. "No. I don't. She pretended to be my aunt for ten years, living alone with me. She knew she was dying, but never told me the truth. There were many opportunities to talk to me, and she didn't."

"Jaysus, Mary, and Joseph." Aoife made the sign of the cross and put her head down in silent pause. All traces of animosity vanished as she gently took the box out of Jessica's hands. In the few minutes it took to return the box to its hiding place, Jessica sat in silent contemplation, realizing the questions that had alternately burned and hollowed her were about to be replaced with answers. She did not know if she was strong enough to hold them all.

The women returned to their shared room, emotionally spent from revelations and questions to come. Habit and duty made them cautious—systematically securing and locking doors, deliberately soundless in their retreat. The nave settled into timeless silence.

From the back corner came the tiniest groan of a metal hinge. The disturbance marked only by a sudden sputtering of candles. A shadow thickened into the shape of a man. He was tall, slender, and moved with feline efficiency. A hoodie covered his head and he carried something under it, hugging it closely to his chest. He walked along the aisle closest to the wall, stopping at points to look upward at the balcony, then turning toward the altar. He was almost directly under the overhang of the gallery when he slipped off his hood to get a better look at what interested him. His red hair pulled back in a stringy ponytail.

Paddy walked freely onto the chancel and to the altar, his motions surprisingly quiet. He stood in front of the altar, then behind it—all the while looking up at the organ gallery and the balcony, turning his head one way and then the other. The service was to be a Pontifical Mass and

Bishop Kavan Hughes would celebrate from the Bishop's Chair, the symbolic center of the Down and Connor diocese.

He walked a slow circle around the chancel, then sat in the imposing chair made of black wood, hands holding onto its two arms in a position meant to look regal, his attention sharply focused at a point in the back of the nave. The numbers expected to receive communion rites at the formal mass dictated that the communicants would stand to accept the wafered body of Christ. He walked the semicircular edge of the altar area, pausing at every step, looking at the balcony and cocking his head to different angles.

He stopped at the center and brought his hand up as if to give Holy Communion to an imaginary figure. Then his hand drifted upward as if touching their nose, to estimate their height. He continued to the end of the perimeter and worked his way back, checking his calculations. Nodding in satisfaction, he walked to the back of the nave, passed the confessionals, and pulled on the door to the balcony—tugging at the handle when he found it locked. Within a few seconds, he had picked the lock and opened the door. The ancient stairs creaked as he ascended.

He performed the same ritual, walking the perimeter of the balcony and the organ gallery. The area spanned the width of the church. One side held the choir and the other side the organ. The choir's pews stepped up in height, allowing the voices in the back to carry when they stood to sing. He paused at the center of the railing and leaned over as far as he could. Straightening, he held his arms up as if holding a long-barreled rifle, pointing it to the center of the altar, then at various points at the pews in the nave. He reversed the process, ending at a carved throne of the Bishop's Chair.

He sat himself on the velvet cushion of the organ's seat and lit a cigarette, looking at the assortment of keys and knobs. He pushed a few with a child's curiosity, testing the limits and seeing what would happen. Then his feet toyed with the long foot pedals. The organ's bellows were mute and unresponsive. Without power to push air through the pipes, only an impotent click sounded. He pushed a few of the long pedals with the toes of his boot and heard the mechanisms shifting behind him. A narrow passageway provided access to the area reserved for the multiple racks of pipes.

He slowly opened the door and looked around. The room hid the unsightly aspects of the bellows while allowing the top portion of the organ pipes to be seen from the nave. All notes sounded through a vent at the top of each pipe. As the notes got higher, the pipes got smaller, some the size of a child's finger. The organ's huge bass rank held the largest and deepest toned pipes as big around as a man's thigh. To balance acoustics, the bass' sonorous sound escaped through narrow window-like gaps placed at intervals along the narrow room. The front-most section of the bass rank left enough room for him to wiggle between it and the wall and to raise the rifle. A narrow vent provided enough space to position the rifle at a perfect angle to the altar. He reached into his pocket, rolled two orange nubs of foam between his fingers, and lit a cigarette.

Alone, he did not bother to cover the sounds of assembling his rifle or wave his smoke away.

STORMONT

THE DIM YELLOW circle of light made by Bragdon's desk lamp was the only illumination in the wood paneled room. He liked working at this hour of night when he didn't have to contend with prying eyes or cocked ears. The wing where his office was located at Stormont was deserted. Any activity occurred on the opposite side of the complex where a never-ending cycle of review of Telexes from Interpol or faxes from MI5 hummed. The quiet and lack of interruption helped him think.

Connecting the dots between Magnus Connaught's MMC Enterprises and support for the blood sucking IRA was challenging. Bragdon's calls to his friends at the corporate offices of 2100 Ltd. were promptly and politely answered, illusions of warmth and respect carefully given. Yes, the peace line would be rebuilt. Thank you for your support. No, the city council would not be a problem. The new members were pleased with the election results. Connaught? Yes, know the man but not sure of the connections you refer to. Regardless of his guile, no new information flowed. The invisible network once again closed off circuitry and shorted connections before he had a chance to confirm their existence. He needed another way in.

What enticed him was that Kavan Hughes might be more connected to either Connaught or Wyeth than Hughes admitted to. Gus Adams was a boyhood friend and the other connections were merely six degrees of coincidence. Bragdon could smell a man's weakness and should have realized it earlier. Of course. The girl.

The reports he had in front of him gave him tools—if he decided to use them. Jessica Wyeth traveled to the Republic of Ireland via Gibraltar. Routine processes flagged her travels upon her entry into Ireland as a foreign national traveling from a known hotspot of IRA activity. Less than ten years before, three members of the IRA were shot by British Special Forces due to suspicion they were planning to bomb a British military installation. The dead had no weapons, witnesses perceived no threat, but the two men and one woman were gunned down nonetheless. A brouhaha ensued and ever since then, all travelers from "The Rock," as Gibraltar was fondly referred to, received a second look. They earned a third look if they were not a citizen of either Ireland. And when they traveled on a passport that was issued less than six months in advance of their travels, the agents nearly hyperventilated with excitement.

Bragdon noted with great interest that Miss Wyeth not only fit all of those criteria but one more.

Her passport had been issued without proper original documentation.

No sooner were the dweebs in due diligence asking their U.S. counterparts to comb through her records did another alert pop up on her travels. Via private jet, she traveled to Manchester, England then to Northern Ireland. Ah, yes, and the dates for her trip surrounded the Arndale bombing, but he already knew that.

Bragdon was inclined to be sympathetic to the woman who lost her identity and her home when hiding in panic from that scourge, Connaught-the-Elder. Such sympathies were obviously enough for the blokes in the States to re-issue her expired passport when she emerged from hiding and was rid of the Murdering Heiress label. With the recent pressure from Northern Ireland's Security Branch, efforts to verify her birth renewed. Authorities contacted the U.S. hospitals surrounding the area where she alleged to have been born, but no independent records existed.

Quite clearly, no child was born to Margaret and Jim Wyeth in 1967.

That brought Bragdon to inquire about the parents. James Kent Wyeth was as much of a blueblood as one person could be. Tracing his lineage through generations of Boston Brahmins uncovered no surprises. Margaret Wyeth was another matter.

Margaret Wyeth received her U.S. citizenship upon her marriage. Once that was established, it took no time to determine that she was Margaret Heinchon, sister to Daniel and Patrick Heinchon—lauded martyrs and talismans of Northern Ireland's troubles—and the infamous Bridget Heinchon Harvey.

Deep in thought, Bragdon picked and fiddled with an ingrown hair on the side of his neck.

Saint Peter's Cathedral

FOR ANYONE LUCKY enough to find a seat in the cathedral, the view of the occasion's pomp and circumstance promised to be staggering. Such masses were rare, and the faithful believed that special blessings bestowed upon those who attended. The parishioners packed themselves into the back of the nave and down the aisles, trying not to stand behind a column, hat, or broad shoulder.

Overflow pushed the crowd into the side chapels, settling at least to hear the service through the speakers wedged up against the ceiling. Mothers smoothed their hair and dresses with white-gloved hands. Children fussed in uncomfortable finery. Men sat ramrod straight in freshly starched shirts, desperate not to make a move that could bring the wrath of God or wife to bear because such simultaneous dunning would go beyond sober tolerance. All ages crammed together to witness the end of the era of Father Storm's ministry and to cater to rumors that the dashing Bishop Hughes was ascending to Archbishop and would soon be leaving for Rome, making his visits less frequent.

The approach of the start of mass was signaled by the procession of the choir dressed for the occasion in red robes with gold liturgical collars. Members carried leather folders of the day's music selection—rousing hymns for soaring voices and powerful music. The organ announced the chords—its centuries-old, hand-forged pipes produced a depth of sound that men claimed vibrated their very souls. Once settled, high soprano voices began to sing ancient Christian hymns. Notes intertwined to form a chorus of alleluia harmonies, perfectly chosen to reverberate and echo against the masonry walls.

The day's Caeremoniale Episcoporum would include nine acolytes, traditionally considered guards of the bishop but evolved to be recognition of status for recently ordained clergy and no longer required to carry the heavy mace once used for defense. In a break with tradition, Bishop Hughes requested Father Storm be the tenth, a position of unusual honor. All the men wore a white dalmatic, a long richly embroidered tunic. A matching band of embroidery graced the opening of the wing-like sleeves. In another nod to Father Storm, the chasuble worn by the bishop and the priest were of equal embellishment. Gold and silver threads created a tapestry of faith. The maniple the bishop wore was a gift from the retiring priest for his ordination and was the only item of clothing he wore that was less ornate than Father Storm's. Two acolytes stepped up, placed the tall pointed mitre on top of Bishop Hughes head, and handed him the gold, crooked crosier. Once fully attired, they bowed their heads in silent prayer and waited for the time to begin the service.

The deep traditions of the Catholic faith evidenced even in the tiniest details. The order of their march down the main aisle was predetermined centuries before. The organ and choir began to sing the processional hymn of "Holy! Holy! Holy!" The congregation stood as altar servers entered first, followed by four acolytes. Father Storm shuffled his way in, barely daring to look to either side. Bishop Hughes was next, and a collective sough of awe rippled through the congregation.

The remaining five acolytes followed, heads bowed over clasped hands, the need to look over their shoulders erased with time. The last of the altar servers entered, studiously looking only at the feet of the person in front of them, terrified of any misstep. They barely flinched as another ripple could be heard when the congregation saw the braided red ponytails of a set of O'Leary twins bobbing down the aisle. There were more O'Leary's around, and those who became bored with the ceremonies would surely begin to scan the congregation for them.

The members of the processional assumed their positions in the chancel, Bishop Hughes and Father Storm standing at the center, directly in front of the altar. Working in teams of two, the acolytes took the mitre and crosier, backing up several steps before they pivoted and exited, careful not to turn their backs on those of higher status. The bishop received a thurible, contents smoldering and smoking, and he began the ritualistic cleansing of the altar, smoke rising to the heavens as the visual representation of the prayers of the parishioners.

Jessica sat in the sixth row in a borrowed dress and hat. She had walked down the center aisle, found a single vacant seat, genuflected with a quick sign of the cross—all actions were familiar to her from years of Sundays. She had done the familiar motions in strange churches and recalled how the ceremony and traditions of the church brought her comfort as she struggled to meld into a new identity. The church had been a constant touchstone, a baseline of familiarity even as her life spun wildly out of control. But today she looked at the scene through the warped glass of a funhouse mirror.

A filament of memory emerged of Margaret and Bridget saying the first time you attended mass in any church, the Lord would grant three wishes if sincerely prayed for. She remembered sitting in the church in Perc, Kentucky, with Father Steeves at the altar, praying so hard her eyes watered. The wishes never varied. She wanted to live her life as Jessica Wyeth, openly and without fear.

All of the blessings, prayers, and readings took on a different meaning. Instead of a two dimensional figure of a man in priest's clothes intoning the mass, the man in resplendent robes was her father. She feared somehow telegraphing the connection and exposing her secret and scarcely breathed as the thought crystallized in her mind. She sat as close to the altar as she dared, yet far enough away that whatever invisible tractor-beam of blood would not engage and pull them together before they were both good and ready.

She freely explored the unspoken ties of kinship from her anonymous distance. His hands smoothed the altar's cloth in a manner that was not rote, but intended and determined. He bent to kiss an open bible in a way that was genuine and not rehearsed even though done hundreds of times over his life. He opened his arms and looked up at a point near the arched apse—or somewhere just beyond it—and praised the Lord God Jesus Christ. At times, his eyes closed in deep concentration, but when they were open, Jessica could see an expression that she could only describe as pure love. He was truly a man of faith and was as much a part of the mass today as it was of him.

Seeing his total absorption in his world and in the world of Christ, the first shadows of doubt crept in. She had wanted to meet him and ask him questions about her mother, to see his face and hear his voice as he described the vibrant and living woman Jessica had only glimpsed at through the journals. She hoped a living and breathing memory would reanimate her mother in a way she yearned for.

Tiny holes in the fabric of her conviction opened. She could not compare her faith with his. Where Bridget's silence was a powerful example of will, his was a silence that came from confidence and inner strength. Where Bridget had moved with self-conscious effort, the bishop moved with ease and grace. Jessica recognized the essence of her core. The insatiable drive that had delivered her to the cathedral on this day faltered.

If what Tim said was true, that the bishop had found and followed her throughout her life, then he had chosen not to meet her, preferring distance to relationship. She naïvely assumed she could waltz up to him, announce his paternity, and expect to be welcomed. With a hidden and sidelong glance, she looked into the faces of the congregation. Their expressions were those of trust and comfort found in the words of the man they revered.

Her need for answers paled when measured against them. Waving the flag of her parentage was pointless. Rupturing their faith by thrusting her truth on them was a selfish act she simply could not do. She had the power inside of her to keep her truth to herself. In that moment, a realization dawned that she could stay hidden from a solitary strength and not in fear. Forever eliminated from her was the assumption that she was born to Jim and Margaret Wyeth. The foundation of her existence as Bridget's and Kavan's daughter firmed. Living the life she was born into laid out before her in a way she had never seen.

She could move forward.

The mass was unlike any she had ever been to before. The event drew more participants than the typical solitary priest and altar servers. For every action the bishop performed, a small ballet of activity accompanied it. An acolyte was always in front of or beside him, presenting a book, adjusting a vestment, or standing in symbolic guard. The organ played, and the choir sang at moments to encourage prayer and reflection. The incense helped ascend the prayers, blue smoke curled upward.

She was beginning to feel the familiar lull of tradition and ceremony when a movement took her attention. The mass had progressed up to the Liturgy of the Eucharist, and Bishop Hughes spread the linen corporal over the altar in preparation for communion. Aoife, being a familiar member of the church and known to be a close friend of Father Storm's, had been asked to help present the gifts of bread and wine used as the Eucharist. Joined by another parishioner, she walked up to the altar and genuflected, presenting the gifts with a slight curtsey and bow of her head, a departure from the bristled warrior of only hours before.

Aoife looked at Jessica and reflexively gave the habitual half-smile of greeting and recognition. As quickly as the expression manifested, she flinched it away, squinting her eyes shut as if she could erase her action.

The action was simple and innocent. On its own merits, the glancing smile was barely noteworthy. But the flicker of recognition was not an action that happened inside a vacuum. In the way of either fate or coincidence, it was enough to draw attention to the young and attractive woman in the sixth row.

Unlike others who tried in vain to find a seat with an unobstructed view, Michael had positioned himself behind a pillar, giving himself a clear view of the corners of the cathedral and its balcony. By moving his body slightly left or right, he could see the entire chancel if he needed to, but his attention was elsewhere. He had walked the entire outside perimeter of the cathedral and then inside, including searching in and behind the confessionals. He was jostled and elbowed by those fighting to keep their view and was grateful their focus was not on him.

Finding nothing and no one of interest did not settle him. Instead, his heart thrummed a steady beat and the hairs on the back of his neck stood up in a feeling made familiar through his academy training. If all of the pieces and people were in place, then he had no doubt something was going to happen. Today. Within any moment.

He inhaled and felt the holster tighten. The gun gave him little comfort.

The public held no interest to him. Michael was interested in only three people today. Jessica and Kavan Hughes were two. The other he had never seen or even heard described, but he knew he would recognize without hesitation. Something about the energy that coursed through the body of a man in the moments before he took a life marked the unmistakable sign of a predator. Michael searched the sea of faces around him.

The rays of late morning light filtered in through the top windows, its shafts colored by the hues of the stained glass and made visible by the smoke of the incense. The effect was beautiful, but Michael did not allow himself the luxury of appreciating it. He kept his eyes moving, clearing his head of anything except what mattered. Any shift in attention or unexpected swell through the congregation sent another shot of adrenaline through his system. When Bishop Hughes and Father Storm moved around the altar, he watched them as he would watch prey. Every motion gauged and measured for exposure and weakness. Every angle of attack assessed.

Within this veil of hypervigilance, Michael saw the thin red line of light, its presence betrayed by the rising wisps of incense. The glowing beam appeared for less than a second before it disappeared. Neither flashing nor bright enough to gain attention on its own, he knew immediately what it was.

The razor-width thread of light from a high-powered rifle equipped with a laser scope was unmistakable. The fact that the light was red and steady and not green or pulsating meant his adversary was highly skilled, well equipped, and calm. A pulsating light is easier to pick up during the chaotic moments of a battle, aiding in accurate aim, but was as easily seen by the mark as the marksman. A green light is more visible to an untrained human eye, exposing its lethal intent as a warning. The steady pin of red was the light of an assassin, and one he knew well. The laser was a top-of-the-line product offered by 2100, Ltd.

He raised his eyes immediately to find the source, which he determined had come from a higher angle. Possible locations sifted through his mind.

An outside angle from an abutting building was not possible. Inside, the only area he could eliminate was the main floor of the nave.

His position behind the pillar blocked his view, and he began to move to a better location. The jammed cathedral made speed impossible. He paused only long enough for two people to bring something up to the altar. A portly man and a woman walked up the center aisle. The man was unremarkable, but the woman grabbed his attention in a way he couldn't articulate, and he studied her for clues. As she turned to return to her seat, an expression flickered over her face. She flinched and looked away as if suddenly exposed in a sin. Michael looked at the backs of the heads of the people in the front rows. No one stood out, except for a tall, athletic woman wearing a hat, her blonde hair tucked away in a neat bun.

Jessica.

Even if his eyes did not recognize her, his whole being did. The gravitational pull increased its force as profound relief that she was there, alive, and unharmed, fed it. No disguise would ever keep her from him again. He quickly reassessed the facts. She was a discrete distance from the chancel meaning she had not yet approached the bishop. No doubt she was figuring out exactly how to make her next move. She seemed to be alone and unwatched, although the woman who recognized her was a mystery. Another flash grabbed his attention.

The serpentine wisps of blue incense accentuated by the light pouring through colored glass served to camouflage the laser from the congregation, but Michael saw enough to track its origin to the organ gallery. The laser tracked the bishop's movements as he bent to prepare the offering and lifted his arms in salutation to the Lord. An acolyte stepped forward and stopped the beam from making a clean line to the bishop's heart, unwittingly serving his purpose as a human shield. The light flicked on the stooped figure of Father Storm, tracing a circle around his heart, then blinked off again.

Missed opportunities raised questions, and Michael knew the assassin was waiting for some signal that would determine when to shoot or to aim at another target. His answer came when the light blinked on and settled on the back of Jessica's head. She could not have felt the light, but he watched as she put her hand behind her neck and shrugged her shoulders with a shiver. This time the tiny dot of light stayed steady, no doubt waiting to confirm that the mark was indeed on the head of his prey.

Communion began and the music grew louder no longer at risk of drowning out a sermon. Starting at the outside front aisles, the deacons stood at the end of the rows and worked their way through the cathedral. The front and center pews would be the last served. The aisles filled with communicants effectively locking in anyone who remained sitting.

Acolytes fanned out along the chancel's perimeter, serving the Eucharist in an efficient assembly line. Bishop Hughes gave Father Storm the position of honor in the center of the chancel as he stood slightly to his right, placing him even closer to Jessica and within the same line of fire. Michael watched the slow progression and used the movements to hide his own.

If Michael called out in warning, the assassin would calmly squeeze the trigger as all hell broke loose in the nave below. Then he would slip out in the pandemonium that was sure to follow. Michael would do everything possible not to let that happen. He walked into the back of the cathedral and up the stairs. The organist was too deeply engaged in the intricacies of a German hymn to notice a shadow cross her keyboard as Michael made his way to the pipe chamber. He waited until a brief crescendo in the music hid his movement before he slipped through the narrow door. It closed behind him, and the music continued. His head was inches away from the huge pipes.

The blast of sound that threatened to rupture his eardrums caught him off guard. The cramped area contained every vibration, a contrivance in design meant to deepen and enrich the tones of the organ. The highest scales rang through the top of his brain, making his scalp shimmer. The deep notes penetrated inside his chest, altering the beat of his heart. He had never experienced anything like it before, and wondered if it would affect his ability to think and react. The disadvantage could be turned into an advantage. His target would not be able to hear his approach.

With the Glock in one hand and the other salvaging an eardrum, he methodically assessed the interior in a way any good assassin would. The Glock would be used only if stealth failed him. The suffocating grip recently practiced would be much more efficient this time. He could feel the subtle shift of energy inside of him as the minutes of a life counted down.

The music was some of the most beautiful that Kavan had ever heard. Voices soared and intertwined. The organ complimented each note and harmony with an array of melody meant to trigger the souls of man. Kavan stood in deep prayer as Father Storm performed the rites for Holy Communion, the older priest's movements slowed by age and emotion. This would be his last service in his beloved cathedral and Kavan wanted him to experience every moment of it to the fullest.

Many dictates were in place to prescribe everything about the ceremony—from the scriptures read, to who was in attendance, to what he wore—but Kavan determined to pick and choose what he would follow.

Creating a service that honored his longtime friend, mentor, and confidant was important to him, but he railed against the strict confines of history and sensed there was more he could do.

As much as he wanted to infuse the service with new life and vitality, he was duty bound to honor its traditions. Soon, the mass would conclude, and the time would come to make the announcement Bragdon provided him. As much as Kavan wanted to share the news that all voices would be welcome, at last, around the negotiation table, he knew, with every fiber in his being, the timing of making such an announcement was wrong. The outcome was what the parties wanted, but legitimacy and a voice were intoxicating brews when received as rewards for violence. The exact opposite message needed to be given as a response to Arndale. He felt locked in and manipulated into making an announcement he knew would lead to more violence. Waiting until after the concluding prayers would not tarnish the formal service. But how could he not make the announcement at all and still be considered worthy of Bragdon's and the government's trust? He gathered himself to stay focused.

He placed himself in the deeply prayerful state that enabled him to remain fully immersed in the love and the presence of the Lord. His celebration channeled from a higher source. He felt himself to be the conduit of God's will as he read the gospel and listened to Father Storm's sermon. The priests and acolytes moved about the chancel with choreographed grace, and the understanding and familiarity of the movements allowed him to detach from this world to commune with the next.

When the parishioners lined up for communion, Kavan stood beside his friend and asked the Holy Spirit to guide his actions. No mishap could occur. No words stumbled over. In the perfection of the moment was extreme peace. He placed the blessed wafer either to cupped and outstretched hands, or to an open mouth in a face turned upward. In this consummate moment for believers, one face above all woke him from his prayerful stupor and reminded him not only of the frailties of the human spirit but of his failure as a man.

Bridget was there.

She stood not more than fifteen feet from him, pausing in the center aisle, hesitating with indecision of whether to come forward or to take her seat again, not willing to disrupt his prayerful state. True to herself and to him, she was instinctively aware of the discretion in which she needed to conduct herself in his presence. She looked so different from the last time he had seen her, when she was weak with injury and hunger.

She was vibrant and alive and exuded a life force that nearly buckled his knees with the strength of it. The plain dress and demure hat were of a style that accentuated her beauty with their simple lines. Her eyes shone with the same keen intelligence he fell so hopelessly in love with. Her manner was confident and tentative, aware of the power of her presence, but not knowing quite how to harness it. She was cautious and judicious and did not allow even the hint of acknowledgment that would have derailed them both. At first her eyes were downcast, unsure of where or how to look up, but when she did, she was the firebrand that sliced through him. Well over two decades had passed since the last time he looked into those eyes, and he vowed then and there never to look away from them again.

Paralyzed, he watched as she lifted her chin and pulled her shoulders back as if to dare anyone from ever taking from her again. Her expression never changed. She did not smile or wince, but coolly stared at him, declaring her right to be there—declaring her right to *be*.

The line for communion waited patiently behind her. His chest tightened as he watched her take a half step forward, suddenly unsure of what to do. She raised her foot as if to re-enter the pew, then put it down again, half turning back to the aisle. Her eyes flicked from his face to Father Storm's hands as he raised a wafer. Even, white teeth bit her lower lip, and she tipped her head back, mad at herself for her indecisiveness. It was so like Bridget to push herself into action when logic told her no. Bridget's daughter—no, *his* daughter—was alive and breathtaking and here!

The swell of harmonized voices and a crescendo from the organ masked the guttural moan that dredged upward from deep inside of him. He tried to hide his gaff by coughing, but Father Storm noticed his change in attention. The old priest had been steadfastly offering the Eucharist on an outstretched hand, stopped from reaching higher by his humped back. Communicants were forced to bend down to his hand's level, giving the priest a clear view of what had caused the bishop's sudden alertness.

Kavan watched in horror as Father Storm reddened and trembled as he began to speak. "By the power of God save us! The devil is among us and flaunting the full power of his deceit."

Only the acolytes closest could hear him and exchanged confused and nervous glances.

Father Storm continued, voice barely above a whisper. "Proof of his power over man and God is here. You," he pointed his finger at Kavan, "you broke your vow to Him."

Two acolytes moved beside the priest and placed their hands gently on his elbows. He recoiled from their touch.

"Wasn't it bad enough that you used me as your confessor? So stooped from the weight of your truth that I can no longer walk upright, yet you bring her here! You're an arrogant and prideful beast." He turned and raised a shaking hand to the congregation, slightly tottering off balance.

"Do not listen to the words of this *man*. He cannot be trusted. He is a father. A *father*! The woman who bore his child is *there*!" He had raised his voice as much as he could over the music, but it was not enough to carry past the front pews. The acolytes gently edged their way in front of him. Three continued serving communion and two began to escort him to the chairs in the back of the ambulatory. Father Storm struggled against them as he pointed his finger at Jessica. "She is the mother of a child who should never have been. She is the whore."

Kavan watched as Jessica's head fell backward as if struck and her knees buckled with the weight of Father Storm's words. He thought she would turn and run from the cathedral and wondered why she hesitated. She moved as if in a daze and looked up into the balcony, then turned to him. She sank to her knees and hunched herself into a ball of prayer—head bowed and hands laced behind her head. As sudden as her crouch, she then started toward him, one arm outstretched, saying something that was lost in the rush of movement.

The music from the organ grew louder and discordant, threatening chaos from disorderly tones. The choir voices rose to meet the organ's reach. The shock of knowing the burden carried by his dear friend split him open. Never did Father Storm shrink away from his confessions, but the weight of Kavan's sin was too great to be carried by the old man. This load and the shock of seeing his beloved Bridget's eyes in the face of his daughter grew. His heart suddenly ripped in two. His only rational thought was that it must have been the vision of a woman he could never acknowledge that tore a hole in his heart. Puffs of plaster rained from the ceiling. He brought his hands to his chest and stumbled back.

Paddy's hands sweated in the thin kidskin gloves he preferred over latex, and the muscles in his legs and back screamed in pain from not moving for hours. This was part of his job—getting into position early and staying hidden until it was time. His exit was to his left, behind the pipe that played the note C-1. Then he would easily slip away with the tidal surge of bodies rushing to get out. The rifle, scope, and silencer were not important to him. He could get others. He had wiped the equipment clean of prints and serial numbers knowing they would be left behind. Simple. Except today it was not.

The foam plugs in his ears were not nearly enough protection. The sound was deafening. His skull vibrated, and he kept checking his ability to dead reckon his aim against the laser. The habit was his own nod to quality assurance that also served to keep him alert even though he felt his stamina lag from the onslaught of sound. He would aim, then briefly flick on the laser to verify his accuracy.

Suffering from the sound so close to his head, he understood why the RUC had once used unbearably loud music to drive the occupants of a suspected hideout insane. They had propped up enormous speakers and blasted bagpipe music at a tiny farmhouse south of Derry. In a few hours, the blokes crawled out of the front door, waving a white flag as they vomited. Paddy initially thought them soft, but after having his bowels bounced around on sound waves for the past hour, he had an ounce of sympathy for them.

Before the service started, he had wondered if the girl was actually going to show, but Nan was sure of it. He had learned to trust her instincts, especially if Liam verified them. They were both uncanny in sniffing people out. Nan told him to look in the front center, not too close as to risk being spotted by the bishop, but not so far back that she wouldn't get a good look at him.

He scoped out angles on the Bishop's Chair to cover his bases in case she went up the receiving line to greet him as many parishioners did after the mass. He did not see Jessica. He was looking for her jeans or a blonde head, but when the folks presented the gifts to the priests, the woman reacted to someone in the crowd. Once he picked her out, he had no question. The simple dress and hat couldn't hide what was underneath.

He raised the scope and checked his angles. Then it was just a matter of waiting until other activity hid the victim's reactions and added to the pandemonium. Communion was the perfect time. Heads bowed in prayer, people walking up and down the aisles. Lots of loud music.

He did not have a clear shot until she had gotten up out of her pew to take her place in the communion line. He aimed, she moved. The beam fell on the back of another's head. Some kind of commotion started at the altar. The old priest was waving his hand at the bishop then pointing a shaking hand at Jessica. He aimed again. The laser landed on the back of another's head. She moved in a way that showed no confusion about what she was seeing. No hesitation at all. She'd been prey before, and her reflexes were tightly coiled springs. He saw her as she turned her head to follow the path of the beam and immediately understood she was the target. She curled up into a tight ball. Paddy's aim was true.

No sound left him as his windpipe collapsed.

His vision narrowed to a tiny tunnel.

Trained, he kept one hand on his rifle as the other flailed behind him, groping for his assailant.

His chest burned with spasms searching for air as his mouth opened and shut, trying in vain to open his airway.

The rifle's *thwip thwip* as it fired was lost against a resonant bass note.
His head jerked upward and twisted, muscles convulsing.
Tiny pricks of light dulled to darkness.
Paddy never knew who killed him.

Michael sank to the floor of the gallery and pressed himself up into the shadows. His breathing came in heavy gasps, and he swallowed the bile that inched up his throat. The feeling of the tiny bones of the larynx breaking under his fingers sickened him and filled him with fear. What he saw below eclipsed anything he felt for himself. Bishop Hughes' face was ashen, and his eyes were open but unseeing as he lay on his back before the altar. He imagined Jessica's scream and watched as she clawed her way forward through the rush of people. Two acolytes led the older priest to a chair. Other men in white robes tended the bishop.

A collective gasp emanated from the crowd. Congregants in the first rows stumbled into one another in the confusion. Voice by voice the choir stopped singing, and the organ playing stumbled a few more chords before ceasing. He could see the bishop's chest rise and fall in great heaves, sucking in as much as he could. The gold and silver embroidery caught the light and made his vestments shine like metal. An acolyte propped his head up on a rolled cloth.

Michael watched all of this in a state of suspended desperation as he waited for the inevitable when someone would come crashing through the pipe room door. His world collapsed to that moment. His eyes never left the altar as he waited.

Jessica tried to push her way to the bishop's side but other people held her back. The woman who had walked to the altar earlier in the service first stood next to the old priest, gesturing with her hands and shaking her head. Then, she guided the priest to his feet and motioned for others to assist him off the altar. She turned to see Jessica and walked to her side, giving her shoulders a quick, one-armed embrace. Jessica brought her mouth close to the woman's ear and spoke, pointing to her head and the bishop. In unison, they turned and looked up at the gallery.

Another murmur rippled through the crowd, accompanied by applause. Bishop Hughes, red-faced and shaking, was helped to his feet. He nodded and smiled to his acolytes and others who brushed him off and offered assistance. Jessica reached her hand out to him. Before he could grasp it, she was shuttled off the altar. She stood in the center aisle confused. She took a step to return to her seat, then half turned as if to leave through a side door, her eyes never stopped searching the balcony. The other woman guided her out of the sanctuary.

The organ started playing again and the choir began to sing. Michael clasped his hands over his ears and squeezed his eyes shut. In death, the body released its fluids. The fetid stink of piss and shit enveloped him.

He had no idea how long he stayed there. He listened as the service concluded and congregation slowly sifted out. The choir and the organ master thumped and milled about for too long, filling him with dread of discovery. Eventually, he heard no more voices or footsteps.

His knees resisted movement as he slowly got to his feet. His head ached, and his ears rang from the onslaught of sound. He peered through the narrow gap and craned his neck to see if anyone remained. Half deaf, he kept his gun raised as he pressed his other hand against the wooden walls for any vibration of sound. Feeling nothing, he turned to leave when the room filled with light.

The woman who had been speaking with Jessica at the altar peered inside. She crouched down and entered, not hesitating when she saw the body. She was fully inside before she saw Michael. She reached for something on her leg.

Michael waited the split second long enough to see she had grabbed a knife instead of a gun. He kept his gun pointed at her head.

She raised her hands, dagger dangling by its handle. "You stopped something terrible from happening today." She cocked her head to the side and stared at him. "You Michael?"

He didn't answer as he looked beyond her. "The woman you left with. Where is she?"

"Not here. She's safe." She wrinkled her nose in disgust. Keeping her hands raised, she motioned to the body. No fear or surprised showed. "We've time enough for chit chat. The cathedral is locked up tight. Help me get this bloke out of here."

Jessica paced back and forth in the cellar room. Aoife had left hours ago, and she was beginning to panic. Even though they agreed that she was to wait a full twenty-four hours before leaving the cathedral, being patient was excruciating.

Events happened so quickly, but when Aoife didn't question what Jessica had seen or the theory she had as to what happened, Jessica didn't hesitate to follow her precise instructions. Aoife's movements were preordained and executed with precision. All Jessica had to do was stay put and wait.

She boiled a pot of water and had her hands wrapped around a Styrofoam cup of Chinese noodles when she heard footsteps descend the stairs. Jessica remained motionless as she heard the door to the women's loo open, and water run. More minutes passed before Aoife strode into the room and sat heavily on her bed, fresh from a shower with a towel wrapped around her wet hair.

Aoife rubbed her arms and legs dry. "You were right."

"Michael?"

Aoife nodded. "Seems you knew the other gent, too," she said, motioning to the bruise on Jessica's chest.

A precision shot could only have been executed by Paddy. Her memories of him were fuzzy, but one detail was clear. "Red ponytail?" She received a nod in response and knew not to ask more. The thought sickened her, but Aoife seemed unaffected.

"Newspapers won't waste ink on a body found near an abandoned warehouse. There were no witnesses."

She looked at Aoife's chapped hands and shuddered at the kinds of filth she cleaned. "Did you and Michael talk at all?"

"Enough for me to be sure your man knows what he's doin'." She vigorously rubbed her hair dry, working her way around her head. "I told him he's not to see you until you're good and ready. Not a minute before. He got the message." She reached over, grabbed the cup out of Jessica hands, and poured the noodles into her mouth. "Thanks," she uttered between mouthfuls.

"The bishop's fine, too. He had a spell or something. From what I heard from one of acolytes, Father Storm started croaking worse than a box of frogs. Hoppin' crazy, and talkin' in circles. From where I stood, the bishop had seen you and was about to crap his britches, then Father Storm started spoutin'. I guess it was too much for the bishop and he fainted." She stifled a titter and feigned a serious manner.

Jessica breathed in relief, not seeing the humor. "Just fainted? He's okay?"

Aoife slurped down more noodles, using her fingers to corral them into her mouth. "There's people who were expecting some kind of announcement. Rumors were that the bishop was to break some kind of news about the talks. If you ask me, if the man had something he wanted us to hear, he would've yelled it at the top of his lungs and kicked off anyone trying to stop him." She wiped her mouth and hands with an end of the towel. "Using the commotion was as good excuse as any not to do something he didn't want to do."

Jessica made another cup of noodles and offered it to Aoife who waved it off and rummaged for clothes instead. Jessica spooned the salty broth into her mouth, wondering what would happen next and if she was the one who needed to make it happen. Aoife's ability to take it all in without concern or worry hinted at a dark life filled with harsh acts done in the name of good. As she pulled on chinos and a shirt, Jessica noted Aoife's muscles were lithe and strong, like her own, and her arms and legs were scarred from untold struggles. She wondered what their lives would have been like without the need to fight for survival. The unspoken bond between them grew stronger.

"The ruckus was good for somethin' else, too. The light finally dawned with Father Storm that it was me he'd given the bishop's box to and told the bishop so." She pulled on socks and hunted in the back of her closet for a pair of shoes. "Bishop Hughes found me afterwards when I was closin' up the cathedral, before I . . . before your man and I . . ."

Jessica stopped her from saying more. She didn't want to hear it. "Oh. The bishop. Does he know I'm here? With you?"

"He saw us together during the service. He knows who you are and who you're connected with. You have fewer secrets than you think. Walk with me. There's much to talk about."

Aoife wound their way through the corridors and up to the nave. She stood at the center of the transept and pointed up. "I'm to have a dickens of a time explaining those." Barely visible in the dim light, two fresh holes, each less than an inch in diameter, pocked the plaster ceiling. Gray dust, ground to powder by many footsteps, tracked around the altar and into the vestry. She brought a carpet sweeper from the vestry and pushed it along the floor until the footprints disappeared. "The bishop gave me a message. He's arranging a meeting with you. I know the place and will get you there."

Aoife put the sweeper away and folded her arms across her chest, tilting her head to the side. "He also said I'm to give you the box. I've done my thinking on you. I'm not certain if I'm the person who should be tellin' you your mother's tale, but it seems that fate's appointed me."

They walked toward the passage and retrieved the box from its hiding place. Jessica held the box in her hands, no longer feeling like it was pilfered loot. It belonged to her. Legitimacy unquestioned.

"You must begin to understand. Your mother lives on for us. She's a part of our history and from what we knew, she died in prison all those many years ago." Aoife unfolded Bridget's life, year by year. The details of her adult years knit together with the pieces of her childhood Jessica already knew. She listened, suspended between worlds. She heard about Bridget Harvey, the secret meetings held somewhere outside of Belfast, the supplies and money she arranged for, and the bombing of Nelson's Pillar.

While Aoife spoke, she picked through the box connecting images with stories. Many pictures were preserved of Kavan and Bridget together, but few betrayed a deeper relationship. She was shocked to see pictures of herself, most were clippings from papers, but a few were faded Polaroids of her childhood. The most intriguing were the letters from parishes across the U.S., responses to his casual request if the monsignor had the pleasure of meeting a young woman, good with horses, a wayward daughter of a dear friend. Those from Father Schroth in Saddle String, Wyoming, Father Steeves in Perc, Kentucky and Father Archdall in Raphoe were clipped together, acknowledging their special significance. Saved were even letters from Bridget, postmarked from her years in Hamilton, addressed to names Jessica didn't recognize but knew she would always be connected to.

He was aware of every facet of her life. The hollow space inside her began to fill.

Aoife continued talking. "She had formed a network around her that was very strong and very loyal. The organization was comprised of community and civic influencers ... not the leaders directly, because they would have been too easily targeted, but those who wielded the power behind the scenes."

"Influencers? The leaders then were mostly men. Are you saying she worked with their women?"

"Yes. Your mother became the very heart and soul of the fight for civil rights and reunification here. Because of that, she was the most hated person in Britain." She cleared her throat as she told the story of Patrick's death that sparked more riots and Daniel's dying wish. "When she heard her brother was dying, nothing could stop her from being at his side. Back then, informants linin' their pockets with bribes infested the hospitals. My bet is they locked her up in hopes the elusive Mr. Harvey would visit or at a minimum figure out who was in her network. She was jailed as a criminal in Mourn House, the woman's unit at Maghaberry Prison. No one ever dreamed she had a child."

A gasp escaped Jessica's lips. "The secrecy," she sputtered. "She never wanted anyone to know. You ... you can't ... I don't want ..." She yearned to learn her mother's story, but the very act of doing so felt like a betrayal of the one thing Bridget craved.

Aoife sat quietly while Jessica sifted through pictures. "Part of her myth is that she simply disappeared, like mists in morning light. I see how it could have been with *Sagart* Hughes helpin' her. This is not my story to tell. When she's spoken of, it's with respect and awe. There's no need for anyone to know anything more about her. If people are to hear, it will be from your lips, not mine."

"She never wanted me to know all this." Over the next hour, Jessica told her story and shared memories of growing up. Tears of grief for the loss of her family that had streamed down her cheeks at the beginning of her telling eventually dried, leaving her eyes red and swollen. She was emotionally spent after telling Aoife everything. Rather than feeling empty, she felt that a hard outer layer had been scraped off, leaving room for something new to grow in its place.

"You listen to me," Aoife said, nearly growling the words. "Your mother had more heartache than you could ever imagine makin' the choice she did. She did everything in her power to give you a better life and you have to live it as best you can."

"But it's more than just my mother who would be impacted."

"'Tis at that. You've not been in the Irelands long enough to hear the whispers. You're not the first child born to a man of the cloth, and I dare-say you'd not be the last. *Sagart* Hughes had the heart of many a woman, and it'd surprise none to learn the man beneath the robes experienced all of life's offerings." She shrugged her shoulders to indicate such indiscretions were not her concern.

Jessica let herself be led back through the maze of hallways and stairs, hugging the rosewood box to her chest.

SISTERS OF THE
HOLY CROSS CONVENT

THE SUMMER SKY was a flawless blue, and the winds that usually blew off the Irish Sea finally took their day of rest. The unaccustomed warmth coaxed even the most conservative nun to slip off her footwear to dab a pale toe into the chilly waters. Seagulls swooped and cawed. The gentle swells trickled against rocky shores sounding earth's applause for God's creation. The sister's silence was a perfect tribute. To speak would have marred the perfection.

Reverend Mother Flanagan allowed herself a brief stroll on the sloping lawn before she continued her duties for the day. At eighty-five, the task of clamoring over rocks to dangle her feet in the North Channel was relegated to memory. Her mind may have retained its quick and nimble nature, but her knees had not. A blackthorn walking stick, ebony in color with knobby protrusions, helped balance her as she made her way around the manicured grounds. She paused in silent reflection to give thanks for the peace that came with simple pleasures.

A whiff of sweet tea rose mingled with the salty air brought a smile to her lips. Although her life had its heartaches, her chosen path protected her from the greater pains that plagued human existence. She shielded her eyes as she looked up at the towering rectangular walls of the convent. The circular window on the central portico reflected the sun with its multicolored leaded panes. Today, the white crosses on the peaked roofs almost glowed, giving credence to the stories of local fishermen who used them as a way to steer safely home to the harbor around the bend.

She chose the pause between afternoon vespers and the evening meal, when the activity in the convent slowed, as the safest time for the meeting. Habit dictated the sisters' spare moments be spent away from the main rooms and public gathering spaces. Today, Reverend Mother provided an additional command for privacy. The simply stated, "I'm meeting a young woman," was code enough for the other sisters to stay hidden, knowing they would be introduced soon enough if the young woman and her family agreed to spending her pregnancy in the convent. Such was the pattern of their lives.

The thick interior stone walls were determined to hold the opposite of what transpired outside. On frigid wintry days, the stones held the warmth of the fires that perpetually burned in the monstrous hearth. On this day, the summer heat did not penetrate inside, so the air stayed fresh and cool despite the brilliant sun streaming in through open windows. Reverend Mother liked to receive her guests there, feeling that the very walls of the convent helped to hold secrets.

The blackthorn cane tapped out her arrival. Very few changes had occurred in the convent. The rituals were the same, but the nuns were physically more comfortable than in years past. Central heating was installed, and windows in the public spaces were changed from narrow slivers to wide sashes that could be thrown open on glorious days as this.

Her guest waited on the wooden bench, the only furniture in the bare foyer, placed in front of the huge twin windows overlooking the lawn and sea. Her aging eyes took a moment to adjust from the glare of the sunlight to the dim interior, so the only point she could focus on was the silhouette of a young woman framed by the open windows.

The sight took her back to a day years ago when the spitting image of her sat there. Past and present merged for only long enough to see that the weight of fate and unanswerable questions pulled as heavily on her as they did her mother. Sunlight framed her. Sadness shadowed her.

Bridget's daughter sat with the rosewood box on her lap, enveloped in its fragrance that the warmth of the sun and her constant stroking released. Her back was to the window, facing away from the view. She barely looked up when Reverend Mother approached.

"It's good of you to come, Jessica." She extended her hand and watched as Bridget's expressions of uncertainty gave way to resilient confidence. The invisible ties between mother and child always amazed her.

The young woman scrambled to her feet and took her hand in a gentle grasp. The skin on her cheek was scuffed and pink from a bruise. "I was told you knew my mother."

"I did. I remember her well." Reverend Mother looked out over the water and gave a silent prayer for strength and wisdom. The daughter had the same height as her mother. "Shall we sit?"

Flustered, Jessica helped to settle her on the bench. The unadorned foyer had the same effect on all visitors. Devoid of art or tapestry, the focus was on the human. No artifices to hide behind, nothing to focus on if the conversation became awkward, no easy way to change the subject if her self-control slipped. Tears had often flowed unchecked and without judgment here. The convent was where truths were exposed. Today was no different.

Seated, Reverend Mother leaned the walking stick against her leg. She gathered up Jessica's hands. They were tanned and strong, with calloused pads under each finger. Her skin was freshly scrubbed, free from the oily dirt of horses that Reverend Mother imagined typically creased Jessica's knuckles. The nails were short from use, not manicured nor bitten to the quick as so many young women's were who had sat on that bench before her, forced to face their mistakes. They were the hands of a strong woman. They were also the hands of her mother.

Reverend Mother looked into Jessica's face and saw her wide, apprehensive eyes. The time for secrets had passed. "It's not often we have the honor of seeing one of our children again. Your mother is well remembered. Most of the expectant mothers are not more than children themselves when they arrive." She paused for a moment, reflecting on how most girls came to her before their bellies could no longer be hidden. They began their confinements with strict commands to use their time to become fluent in French or Italian to help explain away their absence. They may have arrived as frightened girls, but they left as women carrying their heavy secret forever locked inside.

"We care for the mothers and find homes for their babies. For my sisters, it is a pure joy when a husband and wife come to claim a child they feared was forever denied them. Their thankful families support us, and our actions never questioned or judged because often those who would have judged the harshest are the most humbled when in need. The circle never varies, and God's divine plan has given tremendous meaning to our simple lives."

Jessica turned her head away, sunlight filling the tear that welled. "But for my mother it was different."

"Yes," she said heavily. "She was not much older than you, so different from our other mothers. She was neither afraid nor angry at her fate. Too often, a young child became churlish at being hidden away and lashed out at us in fear and frustration. Instead, she embraced her fate, living each day in a state of contented bliss. We remember your mother because her joy of motherhood so filled her that it overflowed into us. She loved you more than life itself even before you were born."

Jessica drew in a breath and blinked her eyes. "She didn't have to give me away."

"Oh, no," Reverend Mother automatically reached for her rosary beads, deep in a pocket of her habit. Without conscious thought, she worried them between her fingers, praying to ease the confusion and hurt of a child trying to make sense of a mother's decision. "There are reasons you must understand, but the explanations cannot come from me. I can only tell you about her from what we saw within our walls. I can see your anguish at thinking you were a child discarded and disrespected, but that is far from the truth." She reached over and hugged Jessica. "Any child born inside these walls is our child, forever remembered each day in our prayers. You have never been alone."

"But I've seen the records. My mother was locked up in prison the day I was born."

"Your mother was a woman of strong convictions. At great risk and against our counsel, she left here to visit her dying brother knowing labor could begin at any moment. In those days, tremendous unrest consumed the streets of Belfast. When she came back to us, she had been severely injured and was close to death. Our infirmary could handle the needs of her birth, but they could not address the demands of her injuries. We brought her to a local hospital, but the staff there remanded her into custody."

"She was hurt? Who brought her here?"

"On that day? A man named Gilchrist Adams." Reverend Mother shifted uncomfortably on the bench, mouth working to form the right words. Her raised hand stopped the inevitable questions before they started. "Jessica, the sisters of our order take vows of poverty, obedience, and silence. As the head of the convent, I am able to speak to people outside of our order. Your mother made me take an additional vow of silence that day. She was mad with pain and feared death was certain. I vowed never to speak to anyone about her time here or your birth. I have kept my promise, but you came to me with knowledge of who your mother was, and she never made me promise to be silent to *you*, the object of that vow.

"With what she thought was her final wish, she made Mr. Adams promise to care for you forever and for you to never learn who your mother was. What she did was the most courageous and selfless act I've ever seen a woman do. The reasons for her custody I cannot say, but Mr. Adams said she begged him to bring her here, not to hospital, so she could give you life as a free child, and not risk you becoming lost in the foster care service."

"Did you know of a plan to get me to her sister?"

The Reverend Mother clasped her hands in front of her mouth and closed her eyes for a moment of silent prayer. "We did not question Mr. Adams' right to take you."

"But you knew he wasn't my father."

"Your mother quite clearly stated he was kin. We were, of course, shocked to learn you were taken to the States. He must have had all the documents and transportation waiting."

Jessica sputtered. "How easy would it have been for Gus to bundle up a baby and take her to another country? He couldn't have worked alone. He must have had help for the process run smoothly, right?"

Reverend Mother looked off at a point somewhere in the distance and did not answer.

Jessica lifted the top of the rosewood box and produced the scroll of paper. The parchment, though aged, was easily recognized. Reverend Mother placed her hands over it, preventing it from being unfurled. Instead, she indicated her interest in other items. Happy minutes were spent sifting through the pictures. Bridget's smile, alive with youth and free of cares, coaxed a smile to her own lips, and she nodded at the memories. She lingered the longest over one of Bridget with Gus and Kavan. Her mood changed from contented nostalgia to one mixed with pain. She reached up the wide sleeves of her habit and produced a packet of letters tightly bound with a coarse string.

"These are your mother's letters to me. I have read them and wept and prayed over them. They tell of a mother's love and conviction in a difficult decision made. They belong to you now." She stopped Jessica from opening them immediately, placing them with the others in the box. "Don't judge her. She lived the best life she knew how. Hers was a life of service, like ours, but her calling was different." The walking stick was again pressed into service as she brought herself to her feet. "You are your mother's child and therefore a part of us. You never need to feel alone or afraid again. Our door and hearts are always open to you."

Reverend Mother waited until Jessica stood, then she hugged her gently and kissed both of her cheeks. Her words were simply spoken, the sentiment completely unadorned, but their meaning had an impact on Jessica in a way she was unprepared for. Jessica embraced her with a sudden ferocity. She could feel the young woman's body shake with a wave of sorrow. No wails filled the hall, only one long, uneven breath. When the girl was steady, she pulled back.

Jessica, eyes rimmed and red, only gave a simple, "Thank you."

Their time was done, and her messages of love and acceptance delivered. She held Jessica's hands, faced her, and looked into the eyes of a fractured soul. No more comfort could be offered. The next meeting was far more important than any stories she could tell. She touched Jessica's elbow lightly and escorted her into a room off the main foyer.

Reverend Mother did not enter, but backed away slowly, closing the door as she left.

The room was untouched by modern conveniences. An electric bulb hung in the middle of the room on a long chain, its brown cord interlaced through the links. Windows, barely more than long slits in the stone walls, allowed enough light to reach the center of the room, leaving corners shadowed. With nothing to distract, the space was perfectly designed for mediation and quiet contemplation.

The air inside cooled, creating its own world in a way that defied all time. Bridget had also stood on the same floor. Jessica closed her eyes and willed whatever memories the room had to become hers. What were Bridget's thoughts then? Past and present teetered with the realization she had been in this room before, too, when she and her mother were still one.

Cautiously, she let herself feel, aware that she could withstand the pain. Only a few days ago she wondered if she had it in her to continue. Finding her place in the world as a whole person seemed too huge, too high a mountain to climb. The thought that she could be accepted, welcomed, loved, and safe all at once was foreign. Yet, the Reverend Mother made her feel that all she had to do was simply exist and this would be true.

Feet braced and back straight, she fingered the satin pouch and a faded parchment document. She took a deep breath and waited.

Jessica felt his presence even before he stood up from the prie dieu, blessing himself and kissing his rosary with fluid motions. She remained standing and waited until he walked over to her. For a moment, she was self-conscious in her simple blouse and skirt as she looked at her father dressed in a cassock with a purple cincture around his trim waist. But his eyes flinched away, and he nervously smoothed his hand down the placket of buttons. The thought that the confident and charismatic bishop might feel equally awkward relaxed her.

They absorbed the presence of the other without speaking. She looked up from the cassock to the caplet surrounding his shoulders. His hands and head were uncovered and very tanned, facts that caught her off guard. Why would she be surprised that he enjoyed the outdoors? Even without asking, she knew his love for the water and for hiking and that he felt most connected to God when surrounded by nature, not packaged in stained glass and incense. His smile was easy and warm and he looked at her with unquestioning love.

With no more feints or blinds, Kavan closed the space between them, hugged her, and kissed her forehead, saying her name under his breath as if committing the moment to memory. He held her at arm's length, unsure about what was proper or wanted or needed. "The very image of your mother," he said, remarking more to himself than addressing her.

Did he wonder if it was his eyes or Bridget's that looked at him, so much a part of him that he could not tell where he ended and she began? An awkward moment passed as they sorted through features and emotions. Like a schoolboy remembering his manners at his first dance, he motioned to a low bench and waited for her to sit before he sat beside her. She managed a whispered "Hi," stumbling over what to call him.

He sensed her unease. "Let's start with you calling me Kavan and go from there."

"Kavan," she said softly. Any preconceived ideas of what this day could be vanished, but there was one thing she needed before she could move on. She smoothed her birth certificate out on the bench beside her. From the pouch, she placed the curled fragment and pressed the papers together. She needed to hear his voice and to see his eyes. "Is this true?"

He didn't rush to speak, using the quiet to mark their history. "You are my daughter." He smoothed the two parchments together. "I did not dream I'd ever see you with my own eyes. Once I did, I had to meet my Bridget's girl. You never would've left Norn Iron without us speaking." He released their tension with a smile that touched only half of his mouth. "I would've found you quickly. Rest assured at that."

His words flowed into every crevasse and hollow, filling her. A catch in her throat made her speechless. Without effort, he was too imposing, too controlled for her to question him, even when he was trying to put her at ease. She resisted an urge to stub her toe into the ground and twiddle her hair in her fingers. Along with the pull of her own emotions, Kavan struggled to overcome his own.

"How does one start to sum up the parts of a life?" He surprised her by drawing her hands around the box and placing his over hers, pausing to reflect as the warmth between their hands increased. He marveled. "This is the first time I have ever touched you. You have your mother's hands and your mother's will, and I am sorry you have been so sorely tested. All that your mother and I tried to protect you from has come to be. I hope, in time, you'll find it in your heart to forgive us."

Learning of his ache was not something she expected, but understood. Her rages and anguish faded as her new life unfolded. "There's nothing for me to forgive." She shrugged. "It just is."

She started to say more, but Kavan stopped her. He pressed the box into her lap as if he feared it would slip away. "For me, this box is the sum total of my life. Not one day has gone by that I've not thought of you. There were times I sat alone in the cathedral, reading and re-reading Bridget's letters. In between the joy and awe of being so loved by a woman as remarkable as your mother, I've been withered by shame and guilt for the same. But I have also felt God's grace, and with Him I have rehearsed a thousand things to say to you. The moment has come, and I am at a loss." He looked into the distance, shaking or nodding his head in silent deliberation. After a few moments of contemplation, he began again. "Sharing a love with your mother helped me understand the power of my faith. Even as children, we found a world in each other that nothing could touch."

"I understand her diary better knowing who you are. I always sensed an acceptance in her writings. She never betrayed anything about you. Her love for you didn't end at the love for others. It was all the same thing. She loved you forever."

"Aye, and I her. She never wanted of me, she only gave. Perhaps because we had been lovers before I became a priest, I fooled myself to thinking our love was acceptable. I had a crisis of faith. I was torn between my love for her and my vows, but our relationship helped me see that even the strong can be weak and even the pious can falter. Our love also helped me understand humility, for I cheated God from my singular devotion." He looked into her eyes with an intensity that made her want to shrink. "I cannot escape the knowledge that you were in God's plan. Your very existence changed us by making us fearless. Since the day you were born, I have striven to live in perfect devotion. Please understand, her demand of me was to be a priest. She needed to go into hiding and asked me to arrange for her to be here. Her plan was never to tell me the child was mine."

"But didn't you suspect?"

Kavan's mouth firmed a split second before he caught himself. A relaxed smile graced his face. "These sisters are known for their help to women. I knew enough about them not to assume anything about Bridget—including when her child would be born. Those were horrible times and seeking shelter here for many months made sense." He wept freely when he told all he knew about the attack that maimed Bridget, her imprisonment, and how hard he tried to free her.

She blinked back tears. "Did Gus know?"

His manner changed from one of open sorrow to struggle. He picked dust off his immaculate cassock. When he looked at her again, something inside him had chilled. "Gus and I shared the heart of a remarkable and modern woman. I wasn't alone in being kept in the dark by Bridget. For anyone who guessed, Bridget let them believe you were Gus' child. He was my best friend and the most loyal man and soldier I have ever known . . . and the most discrete. He saved her life, and yours. Gus knew the day you were born you were not his child, but mine, and never spoke to me again."

Listening to her mother's story and hearing Gus' name stirred a slurry of emotions. There would be time enough to decipher them, but she wanted to focus on her father.

"You were her *Gean Cánach.*"

His face opened in a huge grin as he laughed, a reaction so effortless and pure Jessica found herself smiling along with him. "And she was my *Cliodhna*, queen of the Banshees and goddess of love and beauty."

They made for an odd family sitting there, having lifetimes to catch up on and not knowing where to begin. Their conversation started with a stiff back and forth that proved that they knew very little of each other or, rather, that Jessica knew next to nothing about him, and he seemed to know every milestone in her life. But chronological events only give a skeleton's clue and do not expose the core of the person's feelings or essence.

The learned reticence Jessica had for openly answering slowly thawed. What had been the habit of mulling over a question before responding—double-checking which narrative to use and making sure to cause no gaps or slips—loosened. When Kavan asked her a question he *listened*, his remarkable eyes not flinching in judgment.

Soon, their conversation flowed as if they had been together all their lives. No more stilted interview, the conversation rolled around them and through them, expressions exchanged in lieu of words and nods given in silent acknowledgement. The worlds that kept them apart became revealed and understood. The pain she had once felt about being a child unloved and unwanted no longer glowed with the white-hot heat of rejection and bewilderment but cooled with the understanding of impossible times and the reality that Bridget made the decisions she did to protect her. If Bridget's plan had worked, Jessica would never have known any abandonment, fear, or want. But Bridget lived a life carved by more than protecting her daughter. Long before Jessica, there was Kavan. As she looked into the same eyes her mother had loved, she began to understand Bridget's deep devotion to him.

"What about you?"

Kavan's face creased, revealing the strain of a secret long carried. "Long ago, I made peace with my sin and will accept whatever consequence I must. A few inside the Church know of my paternity. I yield to them the decision of what should be done. Anyone outside will still be led to Gus." His voice cracked as he spoke Gus' name. "Even in death I still receive the benefits of his friendship."

"Me, too," she whispered. A tear slid down her cheek.

He wiped it dry using a corner of his sleeve. They sat in solemn contemplation of their friend.

The sun was still high, but its angle had shifted so that the shadow cast by the convent was long enough to eclipse the rocky shore. The shade of the cross on the main peak touched the water. The sisters who had spent the afternoon enjoying the fine weather walked back up the lawn. The slight breeze brought with it smells of the evening's meal. A darker expression crossed over his face.

"The hardest part of today is coming. We must say our good-byes."

Animosity edged her words. "You've heard I'm being deported."

"I know. I fear it's because of me. I am in close contact with a Deputy Minister in the Security Branch. He knows of my friendship with Gus Adams and sussed a connection with you." Straight lines of anger planed his face. "The government of Northern Ireland does not have the luxury of deciding who its enemies are. The word came from Britain. Your U.S. passport was issued on documents that claimed Margaret and Jim Wyeth as your parents, but a search of hospital records proved it false. They were very thorough." His brow furrowed. "They, er, they traced your mother's identity through your Aunt Margaret's lineage. Knowing Gus was a link helped them uncover . . . uncover . . ." His voice trailed off as he searched for the right words.

"They uncovered another document that shows Gus is my father." She had no compulsion to discuss this version of the story. Jessica would not be the one to expose the Reverend Mother for something done so many years ago.

Kavan was unable to look her in the eye. She could see his despair in the lie, but understood his silence for it. She wouldn't question him.

He continued. "I helped your mother get out of prison based upon her promise to leave Northern Ireland and never return. The fact that her daughter returned with falsified documents was too great a threat for the government to ignore." He pressed his clasped hands against his forehead. "I am so sorry."

A stab of empathy went through her. "It's time anyway. I want to get back. I belong in the States more than I belong here."

A barely perceptible groan escaped Kavan as he acknowledged her wish. "I need to hear about this young man. Michael Connaught."

The use of Michael's family name put her on edge. She pressed her lips together and looked at a point on the floor. "What about him?"

"What kind of man is he?"

She stammered, unable to respond. The question threw her. She had been asking herself the same thing and didn't have the answer. After a few moments, she blurted out, "I'm not sure if I can trust him."

"But you love him."

She nodded, eyes closed.

Kavan remained silent, deep in thought. "Trust is a funny thing." He took the box from her hands, reached around his neck, and pulled out the key on a woolen cord. Without a word, he looked at the burred lock, placed the key inside it, and opened the lid. The familiar assortment of letters and pictures secured with rubber bands or string was now joined with the addition of the Reverend Mother's neatly tied package. He placed the furled parchments on top. "I only ever trusted one person with this, and I consider it the sum total of my life. Then Father Storm entrusted it to someone else. A breach of my trust, yet he was doing the best he could. Fate had that it was the right thing to do." He replaced the box in her hands and kissed her forehead. "I trust you to do what's right. Go to your young man. You've been denied happiness. Go to him. Allow yourself to be happy with him."

"His father was, um, he inherited . . ." She hunted for the right words.

"I knew his father and I know of what he's trying to do. Be happy, my daughter." He bowed his head in prayer.

They said their goodbyes but the promises to keep in touch were complicated. Kavan left, separating his departure from hers in the ritual of discretion.

Reverend Mother retrieved Jessica from the reception room and escorted her through the enormous front doors. Approaching midnight, stars filled the night sky and the moon rose over the ocean.

Empathy softened the lines of her face as she looked at Jessica. "Your young man is here. He sat with me as I gave my evening prayers."

Jessica's shoulders were slumped with emotional and physical exhaustion. Every detail of her meeting her father stayed with her. She forced herself into the present. "I'm sorry. I don't understand."

Reverend Mother spoke in a hushed voice. "At times such as this I understand our vows of silence. What words could be found to uplift a soul so broken? Solace and comfort are energies that help heal from within." Her fingertips gently touched Jessica's cheek. "A mere presence is more powerful than any word. The vow of silence taught me that listening with my whole self gives me a greater perception of a person's being than any spoken answer might. Being silent allows the other to be heard. Your young man is here," she repeated. "For you."

Jessica looked into eyes filled with total acceptance and love. It was up to her to accept them or not. "I have to leave."

"I know. Take the time you need to be still. You'll find your answers."

Reverend Mother was right. Jessica needed her own silence and solitude. She needed a home to go to where she could make sense of the new shape of her life. What other journeys were ahead of her, her time in the Irelands had come to an end. Good-byes were said. Hugs and blessings given. Jessica's emotional control was challenged, but did not fail her, as she kissed Reverend Mother. There would be miles between them, but the bond that had been created would never weaken.

The sleek BMW was parked in the sweeping drive of the convent. The car door opened and Michael stood up, stiff and uncertain. His smile was genuine but restrained. Aoife had told her many tormented men had stood on the same spot knowing they were on the brink of losing the woman they loved. This was a world of sisterhood, where men faced their consequences and prayed for second chances. Meeting Michael at the convent after all they had gone through would be a test of his metal. Aoife said the men wore a look of desperation unlike anything else.

Michael wore that expression. The muscles around his mouth and eyes struggled to maintain a neutral position, but the entire gravitational pull was down. His pain was different from the other men. His was not a simple pain of hindsight in seeing all the things he could have done differently. The past was not the only thing he yearned to change.

Jessica walked down the steps and over to his car. They stood silently in front of one another, searching for any hint of a future together. His eyes smoothed over her skin, pausing at her bruised cheek and flinching at what had happened since he last held her. He put the box in the car and gently placed his hand on the small of her back to guide her to her seat. His touch was questioning and unsure but clear in saying he was at her side and always would be. She turned to him and embraced him, and he responded by tangling his fingers in her hair and searching for her mouth with his. The kiss lasted bare seconds, and it answered questions that had burned for days.

Michael drove to a spot overlooking the Irish Sea. The stars shone in the blue-black sky like pinpoints of white lights, and the full moon rose high enough to cast shadows almost directly underfoot as they walked along a rocky point. The air was cool, and she shivered in her light silk blouse. Michael wrapped her in his arms, taking every opportunity to hold her and touch her, as if doing so would alter fate.

He was different. He squared his shoulders and scanned the area as if he walked a course strewn with obstacles only he could see. Sudden movements snapped him to attention. When he thought she wasn't looking, he would open his jaw and move it side to side while jiggling a finger into his ear. He was so physically attentive—holding out his hand to steady her, brushing the backs of his fingers across her cheek, looking at her intently directly in the face—that she wondered if his hearing was worse than he let on. The same tortured look haunted his eyes that she had seen after his rescue of her on the mountain. He had killed. In cold blood. For her. Again. She feared the weight of that knowledge would only grow greater with time.

He pressed his forehead against hers. "I would do anything to get you to stay."

"You can't leave, and I can't stay. It's just the way our lives are right now."

"I know."

"You've made choices I'm not sure I can live with. You need time, and I won't put my life on hold while you figure out yours. We both have things to sort out."

He nodded. "I know that, too."

"I've spoken with Electra. I'm going back to my farm. She's going to put in a good word for me with syndicates that send horses to the Rolex events in Kentucky. With Aintree behind me, I'm in a stronger position as a trainer. The folks in Perc aren't thrilled about me coming back, but they'll leave me alone. At least this time they'll have no questions who they're neighbors with."

"And your horses?"

She sighed. "When we left, Electra found them new owners. I'll have to start from scratch."

Michael reached into his pocket and produced a sheaf of papers. "Not so much," and handed them to her.

The papers were the complete documentation for three horses. Proof of pedigree, ownership registration, bills of sale, vet certificates, and shipping instructions were in order.

"Planxty and Kilkea!" She almost screamed in surprise. Another document froze her. "And Bealltainn!"

His furrowed eyebrows told her he had no problems hearing her exclamations. A smile grew at the corners of his mouth. "Electra and I formed a partnership and bought them from Doherty after Aintree. They were supposed to be the first animals at Ballyronan's stable. They still can be," he paused, giving her a hopeful look, "whenever you're ready."

"Maybe in time. No promises."

"Please don't say no, but I've also made arrangements for some employees at your farm."

She tensed, fidgeting with the hem of her skirt. He brought his finger under her chin, guiding her to look at him. "I've arranged for Tim to get the help he needs. I owe him that much." He stopped her before she could say more. "I've hired others who are good with horses, and they'll keep an eye on you." He kissed her forehead as he repeated her words. "It's just the way our lives are right now."

She graced her thumb over his lips. "I need time. My mountain farm is the only place I can think of to go to."

He pressed her hand to his mouth and kissed her palm, folding her fingers over and squeezing tightly. "I love you, Jessica. This mess has been all my fault. It's all over. The Charity no longer exists. I'm creating a new enterprise. It won't be as it was."

"No? Well, neither will you."

The words were meant to sting, and they did, stunning him to silence. He looked at his watch. "It's almost time for your flight. I've provided one of my jets to get you into Louisville before the horses are loaded up for the final leg of the trip to Perc via Pullman. They'll have had all vet examinations and required stops. You'll be able to check them out before they go up to the farm." He picked up a stone and threw it over the rocky cliff. It clattered down and plunked into the ocean. The motion masked his feelings. It took several more stones before he was able to talk again. "Murray made sure your house was prepared for you, too."

She warmed at his thoughtfulness. "Please give him my thanks. He knows I don't hold him responsible for what happened, right?"

"Yes. It was a rough night for him, but he's okay. He sends his love."

She faltered, not willing to admit the strong tie she felt, too. She rubbed her arms. "It's time for me to go."

They drove to the airport in silence. The Belfast International Airport was nearly empty in the early morning hour as they entered through side gates closest to the private and charter flight departures. The private terminal was a large metal building with an ornate awning and some plants in front the door. The interior lighting was dim, and the furniture was marginally better than found in the commercial flight area. A lone janitor buffed the floors to a shine and a uniformed concierge leaned wearily on his desk.

A man wearing an ill-fitting suit and thick-soled shoes stepped forward, straightening his lapels and rubbing the sleep from his face. He reached into his jacket's breast pocket. Michael instinctively moved his body in between the man and Jessica and reached for something in the small of his back. The man produced an envelope of papers and a wallet-sized leather case. He opened the case to show a badge and photograph ID that proclaimed him a Special Agent of the Security Branch. Michael remained tense.

"Miss Jessica Wyeth?"

She nodded.

"You are determined to be inadmissible for entry into Northern Ireland, having entered under false and fraudulent means. You are hereby ordered to leave immediately. This is the decree for your deportation." He gave her the papers and put his hands on his hips. The motion pulled back his jacket enough for her to see a gun secured in shoulder holster.

She huffed and shook her head. "I get it. I'm leaving."

Michael put his arm around her waist and walked forward, close enough that the agent had to step back to get out of their way. He walked her to the waiting Gulfstream, MMC emblazoned on its tail. A door opened in the fuselage, and the pilot and crew descended via the unfolded airstairs. Each of the three people were dressed in neatly tailored navy blue uniforms. The pilot stepped forward. Her salt and pepper hair secured in a neat bun at the nape of her neck.

"Greetings Mr. Connaught, Miss Wyeth," she said with a curt nod to each. "I'm Captain Laramie. This is our co-pilot, First Officer Andrews, and cabin steward, Mr. Devins. They'll be assisting us during the flight." They shook hands and exchanged greetings. She continued, "We're cleared for departure when you're ready."

"Thank you." Michael cleared his throat, voice thick. He didn't say more.

The pilot stood for a moment waiting, then she signaled the crew to return to the jet.

The pain of separation etched into Michael's face. "Soon," he said, bringing his mouth over Jessica's. He didn't rush their final kiss.

She felt his emotions better through his kiss than if he shared them with words. She responded and let her body yield into his. Together they breathed, savoring their embrace.

"Soon," she said, and walked up the airstairs. She paused at the top step but didn't turn around.

The cabin was huge for one person. The polished wood and soft lighting accented the living room-like space. The only hints she was aboard a jet rather than in a plush hotel were the curved walls, and each richly padded leather seat had its own seatbelt. A separate area was configured as a bedroom, covers turned down on the full-sized bed.

Mr. Devins acclimated her to the cabin. "Mr. Connaught's butler had all your items delivered," he said, opening a closet and showing her suitcases and boxes. "He also sent you these."

The basket of home-baked scones almost made Jessica cry. Murray's sweet and loving thought touched her.

Uncomfortable with the attention, she quickly chose a seat by the window. Mr. Devins settled her in, reciting the standard safety procedures. He made sure she had everything she needed for the takeoff before he left her alone. As the jet started to taxi, she looked out the window toward the terminal and saw Michael, hands jammed into his pockets and shoulders hunched, watching. He waved when he saw her looking. She pressed her face to the pane to see him as long as she could.

Once airborne, she gathered the packets of letters from her mother, father, and Reverend Mother. She opened them and used the length of the table to organize them by date. She read each in the chronological order they were written. Pictures progressed in time by showing the open and innocent faces of youth to expressions worn and wise. Over the next nine hours, she read as much as she could, digesting all she learned and knowing sleep would not come before she did. The most important lesson learned was she was wanted, loved, and protected in ways she never could have imagined. A letter kept in her father's rosewood box had the worn look of being opened and read many times over. It was the last letter Bridget wrote. The handwritten date read March 1, 1988, a short time before she died and merely weeks before Gus was killed, triggering all that came after. Bridget was fifty-five years old.

Jessica curled herself up on the bed and allowed herself to enjoy the novelty of sleeping in such style while flying. Hugging a pillow to her chest, she read the letter again and again until she fell asleep.

To my beloved Gean Cánach,

Your daughter is a wonder of this world. She's soon to graduate college and you would be proud of her accomplishments. She is beautiful and strong, and I cannot imagine a young woman more poised and ready to begin her life in the world.

You must understand that my body is losing the fight with injuries of long ago. The doctors in the States are keen to offer medicines and surgeries, but none promise cure and all promise pain. I'll have no more of either in my life.

I have no dying wish to see you. I have been content knowing your prayers include me and your daughter. If I'm able to write another letter after this, I will fill it with news of J and G, but for this one, I must speak of us.

Your last letter again spoke of your doubt of faith and of you questioning decisions made in your life as if you could redo them. As I look at our lives, I do not question for a moment that God has had His hand in each question formed and every answer found. He has held us in His hands every second of every day. We did the best we could do and changed many lives for the better. Your efforts in getting people to sit and listen to opinions they hate is crucial work.

You can only do what you do as a Sagart. As a common man, you would be cheated from your voice. You say it is people who willingly give you power, as if it is some form of trickery you use to get them to trust you. I disagree. It is through God's grace you heal. Go ahead and doubt God, but do not doubt in you. Ours is a faith we must leap to, it is not a fact of life. We are kept apart so our country can mend together. The simple fact that our daughter is free of the burden of our sins and our history is proof enough that our choices were right and good. So, leap with the joy of her freedom, then maybe your faith will strengthen. Do not talk again of leaving the priesthood. It is where you are able to be your strongest.

I dreamed of our times at the lough and your visits to me at MP. As with the trick of sleep, I could smell the incense in your clothes and feel our fingertips touch. The memory made me young again.

Oh, my Gean Cánach. I feel your love every day with the gift you gave me of seeing our daughter grow. Words cannot thank you enough.

Forever,
Cliodhna

Acknowledgements

MOST PEOPLE THINK writing is a solitary event, but it takes a community to breathe life into a book. I have many to thank.

The Troubles would not have come into existence if it were not for the readers of *The Charity* and their persistent asking, "What happens next?" I hope I've created an answer that will keep them up nights . . . again. My beta readers, too, have my undying devotion for their unvarnished opinions and keeping true to their pinky swears. Naming each would take pages and I'd inevitably forget someone important (as each one is), piss him or her off, and feel guilty and horrible the rest of my life.

Special nod goes to my editor, Karen Aroian, who guided me with a gentle hand, slapped me upside the head when necessary, and helped make this book shine.

The Sisters in Crime of New England has a singular hold on my heart. Your members have uplifted, supported, corrected, carried, dunned, connected, inspired, and flogged me. Thanks for being an incredible resource and community.

The Bishop's Cathedral and the Beltany stone circle in Raphoe, Ireland, St. Peter's Cathedral in Belfast, Northern Ireland, and Aintree Racecourse in Liverpool, England exist. The peace line in Belfast (called peace wall by some) is taller today than in years past. I have taken liberal license to describe physical features, locations, and histories.

This book allowed me to delve into the crannies of my family's history. My grandmother was born in the Republic of Ireland, yet her birth certificate states her nationality as English. The story of the Irelands is not finished.

ABOUT THE AUTHOR

CONNIE JOHNSON HAMBLEY grew up on a small dairy farm north of New York City. When she was five years old, an arsonist burned her family's barn to the ground. Memories formed that day grew into the stories that have become *The Charity* and *The Troubles.*

Hambley uses every bit of personal experience to create a story that is as believable as it is suspenseful. Leveraging her law and investment background in ways unique, creative, but not altogether logical, she has enjoyed robust professional pursuits that include writing for *Bloomberg BusinessWeek, Massachusetts High Tech,* and *Nature Biotechnology.*

Hambley writes about strong women from their perspective in situations that demand the most from them. No special powers, no gadgets, no super human abilities. Just a woman caught up or embroiled in something that she has to get out of, hopefully alive.

Find her at:
Twitter: @conniehambley
www.conniejohnsonhambley.com

CPSIA information can be obtained
at www.ICGtesting.com
Printed in the USA
LVHW09s1710071018
592735LV00004B/607/P

9 780692 417928